TEMPTING MIDNIGHT

Psychic Justice Book 5

ERIN RICHARDS

www.ErinRichards.com

TEMPTING MIDNIGHT
Erin Richards

Print ISBN: 978-1943800148
Digital ISBN: 978-1943800131

Cover Designer: Robin Harper @ Wicked by Design

Editor: Hot Tree Editing

PRAISE FOR
CHASING SHADOWS
Psychic Justice Book 1

"I loved this book and it never faltered from its action and suspense. The story line not only kept my attention but each chapter was suspenseful trying to find out what the kidnapper was going to do and how Juliana would deal with it." ~*Night Owl Reviews* (NOR 5-Star Top Pick)

"This story was masterfully written and illustrates just what a frightfully good imagination the author has to work with." ~*Fallen Angel Reviews* (5-Star Recommended Read)

"A whirlwind of emotions, twists, turns and rediscovered love will keep you breathless!" ~*Fresh Fiction*

"The suspense will keep you turning the pages... The characters are complex and well-developed and there is never a dull moment in the story. If you love your romance with suspense, this is one book you need to read! 5 stars all the way!" ~*The Romance Reviews*

Books by
Erin Richards

Psychic Justice Series
Chasing Shadows, Book 1
Twilight Rising, Book 2
Stealing Twilight, Book 3
Seducing Darkness, Book 4
Tempting Midnight, Book 5

Forbidden Legacy Series
Forbidden Thirteen, Book 1

Wicked Paradise

Young Adult
Vigilante Nights
Dragonfly Nightmare
Bittersweet Wreckage

TEMPTING MIDNIGHT

CHAPTER ONE

The property and evidence warehouse door clicked shut behind her, a soul-crushing sound. Eva Midnight slid flat against the wall, assessing her silent surroundings. Hidden from view, she'd waited outside the door for the last person to leave the warehouse. Half the police department knew the surveillance cameras at the door entrance hadn't worked all day. Faulty wiring or convenient sabotage? The frigid, climate-controlled warehouse doused the warmth of her self-loathing. Eva pocketed the lost key card that belonged to an evidence tech. She'd scored it when it appeared in her mailbox in an unidentified envelope. Identification not needed.

She was dead meat if anyone ID'd *her*.

Flipping Neal and his lunatic mafia family. How in hell will I ever slither out from under their thumb? Once upon a time, Eva and Neal had a happy marriage in Florida, separate from the Estenson clan who ruined lives. Black sheep, Neal, was now the crowned prince in San Jose, California. *He'll ruin me, and I'll be unable to stop the mafia prince of darkness.*

After staring directly into the dead camera aimed at her for a few seconds, Eva rushed to the property section. May as well look like she belonged there, just in case. She had no plans to steal or tamper with evidence, only to retrieve an item confiscated in a raid at an Estenson nightclub last week. Some dumbass family member had hidden a flash drive of Estenson family business regarding a drug cartel in a decorative table statue. The police had no clue what they held in its coffers. *Like who'd put that crap on a computer or a thumb drive anyway?*

Would the evidence be enough to take the family down? She contemplated the idea, flung it off. If she tried using it, it promised to bring the wrath of Khan down upon her. Neal would take her son away forever as he'd threatened multiple times, his way of keeping her in line and doing his dirty work. No one in their right mind fought a powerful lawyer, especially not one in the Estenson family. Definitely, no fighting the mafia.

Luck tailed her when Neal had reluctantly granted her a divorce. But they'd forever be linked by her son and she forever connected to a mafia family. How would they wreck her son? Tears sprang to her eyes, and she swiped them off.

"Why did I ever think he was a good man once upon a flipping time?" *Because I was an idiot, blinded by his confidence and power as an up-and-coming lawyer.* Who knew it would all turn out so bad? Who knew *she'd* become a cop *and* a thief for an organized crime family?

Following the shelf numbers, Eva located the bin containing the nightclub evidence. Gloves still on, she sorted through the seized evidence until she found the small Buddha piggy bank, already tagged, logged, and barcoded. She pulled the rubber stopper from the statue's bottom and used her penknife to slice through the tape securing the bubble-wrapped flash drive inside. She crammed the flash drive in her pocket, stuffed the stopper back in, and shoved the statue and bin into place.

The second she spun around, the door opened, a definite squeak foretelling the end of her life as a homicide detective. Heart pulsing in her ears, she dove between aisles and tiptoed toward the rear of the warehouse. Sweat popped onto the nape of her neck. She had a difficult time stabilizing her breathing and feared the intruder heard her sucking in air.

"Eva Midnight," a familiar man called out in a singsong voice. "I know you're here."

Oh, son of a boss.

"Come on, Eva. It's just you and me."

Footsteps approached her behind a rack of stolen bicycles. Footsteps she'd grown used to in the six months she'd worked for the senior homicide detective. Hosed ten ways to Sunday, she complied and met him in the center aisle.

The handsome detective hit all her awareness buttons, causing a frisson of embers to explode in her middle. But she didn't date cops, especially not engaged cops. Especially not *anyone* or her ex-husband, Neal, would go apeshit. Divorce or not, his hold was ironclad, to her utter dismay. Again, mafia bondage.

"Alex."

"What are you up to?" Detective Alex MacKenzie's smooth, deep voice skittered down her spine and set off a new round of fire in places that had no right to flare up. "How'd you get in?"

Geez, did she need to get laid or what? "Rico's badge. How did you know I was here?"

"Saw your car and got nervous. You have no business here." Alex quirked an eyebrow. "Hit the road." He turned to lead the way out.

"Nothing will come up missing, if you're worried." She walked the green mile behind him in quick steps, trying to keep up with his long-legged stride. "How did *you* get in here?"

"You don't need to know. Your actions today jeopardized both of us."

He held the door open for her, scanned the hallway, and they slipped through in single file. The door shut, and a few pebbles slid off Eva's shoulders, but not the whole mountain. It may never fully crumble.

"Meet me in my office," he ordered.

"Oh. I thought maybe you wanted to fire and strip me bare right here." Her sarcasm refused to be caged. It covered up her fear and mortification, mostly her bewilderment. Could she trust her superior with the story of a lifetime? Maybe he could help. *No way, no how. Best not to involve him. Connor stayed safer.*

He held out his hand. "Give me the badge." She dug it out of her jacket pocket and handed it to him. "You better be in my office, ready to download the goods." He leaned close and spoke low. "I won't entertain this BS on my team."

"Am I still on your team?" *Or should I just report to Internal Affairs?*

He sauntered toward the exit doors. "Remains to be seen." He disappeared around the bend.

Eva returned to the precinct a few blocks from the evidence warehouse. Not passing a soul from the back entrance, she slipped into Alex's office and plopped down on one of his rickety guest chairs. Massaging her forehead, she fought the untimely nuisance tears. A thick folder slipped off the stack of cold cases atop his file cabinet, scattering its contents across the floor. She'd vowed to attack that stack in her spare time. Now ice threatened the cases.

The door opened and closed behind her. Alex swept up the file and tossed it onto the precarious stack.

Surreal didn't begin to describe her day from hell. Eva lifted her eyes to Alex, met his vivid blue orbs, dreading his anger and loathing. Instead, she met concern and compassion, and she dissolved. A small amount of dignity was the last thing she had left to lose besides her son. Why stop the rampant flow now?

Sitting in his squeaky he-man leather chair, Alex tossed her a box of tissues.

"Thank you." She grabbed a handful and blew her nose. "I'm sorry. Guess I'm not myself. Some homicide detective I make."

"You're the best recruit I've ever had the honor to train."

"Alex." She sniffed. "I... thank you. What happens now?" Jittery, she internally prepared her ass for the boot. Par for her life's course of late.

"I'll bury this, Eva. I can help you if you're in trouble."

Surprised, her eyes bugged out. "Seriously?"

"Be honest with me." He steepled his hands under his chin the way her father did when in deep thought. "I'll accept no less than full honesty."

"Even if it can get you in deep too?"

His back tensed against his chair. "What are we talking about here?"

She trusted her young superior with her life. It had only taken a few days after her assignment to his team for her to figure him out. Her gut had only steered her wrong once, to a man named Neal Estenson, the man who'd replaced the love of her life, in a blind, stupid time in her life. *Big fat mistake.*

"Estensons," she blurted out before she rethought herself into a fiery gateway to hell.

His eyebrows quirked again. "*The* Estensons of organized crime?"

She nodded. "You know I'm divorced and went through a rough time. I was married to Neal Estenson, Daniel Estenson's last living son."

A muscle ticked in Alex's jaw. "Are they threatening you?" He tapped his smudged cell phone screen.

"Neal's a powerful attorney. He's threatening to take our son from me if I don't do his dirty work."

"Like what?"

"The raid on the Lucky Shamrock nightclub." She slipped the flash drive out of her pocket. "This was inside a seized item. It's not logged. I suggest you make a copy."

"Leave the takedown to the FBI or you'll find yourself in a six-foot hole. Then what happens to your son?" He said nothing she hadn't already concluded. "What else have you done for him?"

Ragged cuticles around her blunt-tipped fingernails earned her avoidance. "I fixed a couple traffic tickets, did database sleuthing on one of their employees." She waved her fingers. "He knows my limitations and doesn't want to jeopardize my job." She gave Alex a wonky smile. "I'm sure he sent me Rico's badge. It just showed up in my mailbox in an unmarked envelope."

"Is your son safe with him?"

"Neal loves Connor, but he knows Connor's my Achilles heel."

"As any child is to their parents." Alex snagged the flash drive off the desk, stuck it into the slot on his laptop, and downloaded the contents. He tossed the stick back to Eva. "Give him what he wants. We play this slow and easy. Don't tip your hand."

"What if he gives me another job?" She did air quotes.

"Bring it to me. I'll tread carefully, snoop around, check if there're ongoing investigations." Alex rose to his full considerable height. "I'm sorry he put you in this position."

Eva stood as well, feeling insignificant next to him. "I'm sorry too. I never thought my life would turn out like this. I barely make it through each day." Her bottom lip quavered. "The bright spot in my daily darkness is my son. Neal hasn't taken my sun from me."

"Yet."

"Don't say that." She squeezed her eyes shut a moment.

"I'm being realistic. This may not end well."

"You're just a rain cloud blotting my sunshine." She summoned a smile. "You haven't said anything I haven't already guessed. I love my job. But Neal will kill it for me. He's a master soul-sucking leech."

"Would you have come to me if I hadn't caught you?"

She thought long and hard. "Sometimes, I just want to take my son and go where he can't find me. I contemplated running if he asked me to do anything gnarly. My morals can only take so many hits."

"You can't hide from the mob."

Not unless you possess enough evidence to nail them for good. "Exactly." She hid a smile that Alex caught.

"You have evidence?" he demanded.

"Let's just say I'm working on it." She patted her pocket. "This will help gild the lily."

"It's encrypted."

"I know a guy."

"Yeah." He snickered. "Me too."

She turned to leave, halted. "Thanks, Alex. I owe you big-time."

"Just don't let me down. Don't get yourself killed either. You're off duty the rest of the day. Go enjoy your sunlight."

ఴఌఴ

Eva rolled her crossover to a stop in the pickup zone at Connor's elementary. At six years old, he attended first grade at a primo Montessori school. Neal wanted him to attend a private Catholic school, but they'd compromised on Montessori at Neal's expense. Connor loved it and Neal capitulated.

The bell rang, and Connor's classmates ran out the door, laughing and shrieking into the autumn sunshine.

She couldn't contain her own joy as she scanned the crowd for him. Benny and Jeremy, his best friends, zoomed out the door at the rear of the crowd, no Connor in sight.

A niggling doubt threaded around her rib cage, and she morphed into helicopter mom mode. "Come on, where are you, buddy?" She searched for the familiar towhead among the gaggle of kids and parents.

The crowd thinned, and that thread weaved acid in her gut. She exited her vehicle and jogged toward the wrought iron fence surrounding the school grounds.

"Mrs. Estenson," the principal called.

She ignored the principal's naming blunder. "Where's Connor? Did the teacher hold him back?"

Mrs. Wentworth's eyes squinted into deep crow's feet. "Mr. Estenson said you traded pickup days since he was taking Connor on a trip. He took him out at lunch."

Eva's knees gelled, and she clung to the gate, a wrought iron spike biting into her palm.

The principal handed Eva a note. "He asked me to give this to you."

Eva snatched the envelope with her name scrawled in Neal's tidy handwriting across the front and tore the note out.

"Leave the flash drive in the safe deposit box. I'll let you speak to Connor for five minutes tonight. Don't bother looking for him. I gave you one last chance to come to your senses, and you didn't take it. I warned you of the consequences. No need to call the police or lawyer up. You'll never win that battle."

The word punch to Eva buckled her knees onto the grass. The call to war crushed her heart, her soul, everything inside her.

CHAPTER TWO

Voices elevated and faded, and Eva's right knee landed on a piercing rock. Her fear eclipsed the stinging pain, eclipsed her entire world. A chilly breeze blew around her ears, and the waning autumn sun slanted across her face. A few stragglers and their mothers or nannies whooshed by in a blur, heads averted as she stared at them, searched among them for her son. Locks of her long blonde hair had escaped her ponytail and tickled her cheek.

"Mrs. Estenson, are you all right?" The principal's hand trembled on Eva's left shoulder. The spindly grip gave her the impetus to rise.

Back rigid and legs on terra firma, she inclined toward the woman, punched a finger in her gaunt shoulder. "It's *Midnight. Detective* Midnight. Not Estenson. Don't ever call me that again."

Blanching, Wentworth staggered back a step. "I'm so sorry. I forgot."

"You seemed to have forgotten a helluva lot." The stoic cop took over her erupting motherly emotions. No choice existed but to lock them in a box or turn into a basket case. "*I* pick up my son on Fridays. Always. You had no right to hand him over to my hus—to Neal." Her voice grew ominous, and she didn't care if she scared the pee out of the woman. She swished her jacket open to flash her badge hanging on a lanyard around her neck. "I'll bring this rathole school down for the mistake you made today."

"Detective Midnight, he had a note, signed by you." Mrs. Wentworth fished a notecard out of her pocket and handed it to Eva, her hand trembling.

Eva studied the note on fancy Estenson paper stock, seethed at Neal's slanted handwriting, and her fake signature. "He did *not* have a note signed by me! It's forged." Eva spat the words at the woman. "You just signed this school's death warrant." A tremor climbed up Eva's middle, surrounded her rib cage, almost splintered her heart into a million pieces. Squeezing her phone in her hand, she strode away. Somehow, she made it inside her SUV and punched in Neal's speed dial number.

Don't crumble into dust. Connor needs you. The phone rang on the other end, quieted and clicked. Eva prepared to go batshit on Neal. Instead, she willed tranquility into her veins. Batshit wouldn't solve the problem.

"The number you have reached is no longer in service," an automated female voice intoned.

"What?" Eva's mouth hung open. Again, she dialed Neal's number. Received the same recording, fell back against the seat, and died a little more inside. "I'll kill him. I'll fucking take his family down. Screw the FBI. They're mine."

She dialed Crystal Estenson, Neal's younger sister, the only other Estenson number she knew offhand. Again, the same stupid recording dashed her hopes to pieces. A frustrated scream escaped, and she threw her phone onto the dash.

Without wasting another moment, she sped the few miles to Neal's ritzy house in the Los Gatos foothills. A festering peace overcame her, and cop mode took over again. Her SUV screeched to a halt in the circular driveway. She darted to the front door, and the doorknob clicked open. Screw cop mode. Breaking and entering sat too low on her list of morals to kill.

Quiet as a fat Los Gatos church mouse, she opened the door wide enough to slip her slender frame through. A quick glimpse in the gilt mirror hanging in the entryway checked her. Tear tracks streaked her right cheek, and her hair hung in blonde ribbons in the wake of her ponytail's failure. She patted powder over her tear streaks, and redid her ponytail, smoothing down the flyaways. No sense in Connor freaking out over a deranged lunatic for a mother. As she composed herself, she listened for sounds in the mansion, but silence reigned supreme. No squeals or laughter of Connor playing, no maids scurrying to do Neal's grunt work, no Neal engaged in his twenty-four-seven business calls. The eerie stillness oozed into her bones, propelled her farther into the house of mafia horrors.

In stealth mode, she moved from one empty room to the next, her dread increasing with every step. By the time she scoured the second floor and ended in the massive master bedroom, she knew without a shadow of a doubt Neal had planned this well-oiled coup. He'd wiped his bedroom clean of personal belongings. A large manila envelope, her name scrawled across the front, sat on his black dresser.

A typed note attached to a folder inside the envelope read, "You played your cards, Eva. You told me you'd consider reconciling. You lied. *Our* son deserves steady and devoted parents, and that's not you, not with your new job and your new life without me." The last few lines blurred as her heart tried to leap out of her chest. She opened the folder, glommed onto photos of her in bars drinking, photos date-stamped on nights she had Connor, snorting coke, sprawled on her bed in a drugged stupor, a puddle of vomit on the floor next to empty tequila bottles. The last photo depicted Connor crying and patting her cheek to wake her up.

The court order granting Neal sole custody broke her.

She slid to the hardwood floor, barely cognizant of plucking her phone out and dialing her number three.

Her boss answered on the first ring. "Alex," she croaked. "Neal's taken Connor. Curse you for saying it out loud."

"Eva? Son of a bitch. Where—"

"I'm at his house. He's cleaned it out and canceled his phone." She ogled the folder of doctored photos. "He got some fucking judge to grant him an *ex parte* custody order on parental endangerment grounds against me."

"Meet me in my office."

"Can we meet at your house instead?" she asked.

"Guess so," Alex said tentatively.

"I'll be there soon. I need to run a last errand for him."

"Why, Eva?"

"The flash drive. He's expecting it at our drop-off."

"Why do you care now?"

"The note he left at the school said he'd let me talk to Connor for five minutes."

Alex huffed out a heavy breath. "Do it, and then I'll meet you at my house. Juliana will be there."

"I'm counting on it." Eva counted to five and understood she had to face facts. "Alex, I need to tell you something. Because of Juliana, I figured you'll understand."

"I'm listening." Alex's slow voice dropped a notch.

"Connor is... special. You know, like Juliana."

"Okay. Not sure what that has to do with anything."

"Trust me. It does. I'll see you soon." Eva clicked off.

Neal and Eva had opened the joint safe deposit box before their divorce became final. It worked in Neal's favor as he used her more and more doing his family's grunt work. *Turned out in my favor too to avoid Neal as much as possible.* She usually suffered a rash of guilt and trepidation accessing the box. She hoped he'd left a clue of his whereabouts behind. Yet, emptiness met her starving gaze, and she tossed the flash drive inside the small container, rested her forehead on the cool steel.

"Where are you, Connor?" she asked the static air of the vault's client portal, as stagnant as her heart.

She scribbled a note torn from her police notebook. "Bring my son back to me. You know this isn't right. I've done everything you've asked and then some."

Not everything. She'd refused his constant offers of remarriage. He didn't need her, not with his stable of girlfriends, not with bimbo Rachel, his latest conquest. Neal needed the control, needed to control the mother of his son, and she no longer fit his mold.

She added to the note. "We don't work together as a married couple. We're two strong people who just don't mesh anymore. You know it. You're better off with the gorgeous Rachel who worships the ground you walk on. It's better this way. We can each give our love to Connor without the antagonism that'll develop between us marring his perception of us. Please, Neal, give me my son back. I'm begging you."

Bitter seeds of revulsion blossomed in her stomach. Groveling didn't feel good on her, but groveling to Neal might gain points. Remarrying him might even get her son back.

Numb, mind spinning, Eva headed to Alex and Juliana's house in the southern foothills of San Jose. Twilight descended, and the sun plunged into coral and pink clouds, too light and fluffy for her mood. Beautiful new Mediterranean houses populated the neighborhood. Juliana had bought the house when she'd relocated from New York earlier in the year. She'd reunited with Alex, her high school sweetheart during Alex's investigation in the abduction of his young niece. It didn't take long for Alex to propose to the love of his life and shack up with her in the gorgeous house. If anyone could help her find Connor, it was Alex and Juliana. Without Juliana's telepathic link to the kidnapper, they never would have found his niece alive. Eva counted on Juliana's psychic ability to help her find Connor.

Alex's hulking SUV sat on the right side of the three-car driveway. Before she'd even turned her ignition off, he stood in the driveway, hands in his pants pockets. He'd slipped off his tie and unbuttoned the top buttons of his dress shirt. His short hair stood in chaotic spikes, and Eva wanted to tease him over his ruffled appearance. Another time, when her darkness evaporated into light.

"Thank you, Alex." He closed her car door, and she brushed her fingers over his hand. Juliana approached from behind Alex and without a word took Eva into her embrace.

Eva crumpled into Juliana's arms and gripped the woman as if she were the last being on the planet. Alex and Juliana guided her incoherent and babbling into their family room. He thrust a bottle of her favorite brew into her hand, but she set the untouched bottle on a coaster on the coffee table.

"I'm so sorry to barge in."

"You have nothing to be sorry about." Juliana handed her a glass of sparkling water. "Maybe beer isn't such a grand idea." She shot a death glare at Alex. "You need to keep your head clear."

He held up his hands in capitulation. "Thought one might help smooth the rough edges."

"The only thing that'll smooth my rough edges is my son in my arms." Eva took a sip of the lime-infused water, bubbles popping through the thick discord in her throat. "Can we issue an APB?"

"With the court order, my hands are tied. It's not technically a parental abduction. We can unofficially stake out Estenson's home and office."

Eva sagged into the cushions, the stuffing taking the weight of her world.

"Why did you want to meet with Juliana?" Alex rested his hand on Juliana's shoulder as she sat on the sofa arm across from Eva. An uncomfortable silence descended. The love in his eyes for his fiancée evoked a wistfulness Eva wondered if she'd ever banish. Neal not only killed her love for him, he'd killed her hope that there might be a good man in her future who'd love her the way Alex loved Juliana, a soul-deep forever kind of love.

Eva slipped her fingers up and down the frosty glass. Finally, she fractured the tension. "Neal's sister is telepathic, a mind reader."

"Runs in the family?" Juliana slipped down onto the sofa seat and curled her legs into a defensive position.

A black furball on the rug over the travertine stone floor caught Eva's attention. She peered out the French doors and spied Juliana's fluffy black cat sprawled on the patio. "Something like that."

"What are you not telling us?" Alex demanded. "Remember our talk earlier today, Eva?"

She beseeched Juliana with her watering eyes. "Connor has the trifecta of psychic abilities. He has touch telepathy, he's an empath, senses the emotions of others, and he's clairvoyant, sees past *and* future."

Juliana made a breathless clicking sound, and Alex grumbled a slew of four-letter words. He withdrew his phone from his shirt pocket, stared at it as if it held all the answers.

"His psychic abilities are strong and emerging. And Neal's training Connor to be a mafia spy."

CHAPTER THREE

Bored stiff, Liam McAllister grumbled his way into the kitchen, dumped his tepid beer and leftover pizza into the sink. Barney, his brother Ric's black lab, loped over to his empty dog dish and slurped scattered kibble off the floor. Ric had taken off for a date with the love of his life, leaving Liam alone with the dog on a Friday night.

"What'd ya think, pal?" Barney wagged his tail and sniffed at his dish.

Ever since Ric and Marisa Meadows, the Psychic Guild attorney, had hooked up, Liam's nights had become too quiet. At least he didn't have to worry about the loyal dog turning tail on him. The still house didn't bother him much, and he wasn't into dating for the sake of companionship. Not in the wake of a high-ranking psychic he had guarded a few months ago who'd lured him into her web. She'd turned Benedict Arnold and nearly got him kicked out of the Psychic Guild. He was still serving his sentence from his Guild tribunal hearing, his Guardian job on hiatus until his sentence ended. The worst crap of all, his trust in women had flown the way of the dodo birds.

The lab barked and sniffed his bowl. "No more or Ric will kill me." He ruffled the fur on Barney's head, tossed a tennis ball down the hall. The dog scrambled after it, his toenails clicking and scraping the ceramic tiles.

Rubbing his forehead, he sat at his desk in their shared office and booted up his laptop. The Psychic Guild had handed him a special undercover assignment while he waited out his sentence. Once he served his time, he'd return to the Guardian rolls to guard whatever psychic needed protection. Damned if he'd ever fall for one again, though. That ship sailed with those extinct dodo birds.

He typed his credentials into the search database and tripped into another witch hunt for anyone related to Kenneth Delaney, the man who'd almost trashed Marisa a few weeks ago. The dead man had held a top-level position in the Cabal, the sinister group recruiting, using, and abusing Guild psychics and more lately non-Guild psychics. The Guild remained the preeminent organization sanctifying and organizing psychics. They'd recently learned the Cabal strived to decimate the Guild, if not merge with them, and usurp power. Delaney had been the Guild's first unearthed link to the über elusive and mysterious Cabal organization. The Guild had been working to dismantle the Cabal for years without the evidence to ID its principals, unable to strike at those in charge. Liam punched words in the search bar, and a long list of search results popped up. He leaned back in his chair, hands clasped behind his head, and examined the list.

The blaring of his cell phone shook him out of his analysis. He grabbed it so fast off his desk, whiplash taunted his neck. "Boredom kills," he muttered, massaging his neck.

Niles Nevins's name flashed on the screen—the leader of the Guild Protectorate who oversaw the Guardians.

"Dude, what's up?" Liam grinned at the welcome intrusion.

"Did you just *dude* me? Who are you and what have you done with Liam McAllister?" Niles joked in his typical gruff fashion. "For a moment, I mistook you for Ric."

"Feeling especially jaded tonight." Liam shut down his laptop, set his tablet on top. "Any new Cabal leads?"

"No. You up for a little Friday night excitement?"

"You're putting me on a case?" Liam slam-dunked a ball of paper into the trash can and cracked the knuckles of his left hand to divert his surging excitement. He leaped up, and Barney trotted circles around him, tail wagging and ready to play. "I still have a couple more months on the beach."

"We'll see. This may fly under the radar. I'll pick you up in a few."

Liam's pulse sped up. "I like the sound of that." Niles had already hung up.

Guild Guardians were usually transparent in who they guarded. Lately, they'd had to investigate and guard psychics in peril, like Marisa, under the radar for more secure protection. The belt-tightening stemmed from increased Cabal threats and even murders. Niles had declared a public bulletin indicating the Guild had kicked Liam out, pending reinstatement of his Guardian status, if ever. The ruse became a necessity to prevent the Cabal from looking in Liam's direction as he investigated on the sly.

At the honk of a horn, he gathered his leather jacket, gun, and tablet. He locked the door behind him and joined Niles in his shiny, new electric car.

Before the tires hit the street, Niles said, "I received a call from Alex MacKenzie."

Liam groaned. "Not another dead psychic." Why else would a homicide detective call Niles?

"Not yet, and I want to keep it that way. That's where you come in."

"Whoa, you're going against Guild laws and giving me a Guardian assignment?" Liam reached over the center console and tried to lay the back of his hand on Niles's forehead.

Niles whipped his head away. "Funny. This needs to stay covert. Alex is overly concerned."

Liam sobered. "What's the danger?"

"He didn't go into details." Detective MacKenzie had taken the lead as the Guild's official liaison to the San Jose police in the Guild's fight against the Cabal. The Guild trusted him implicitly.

"Why me, then?"

Niles braked at a red light and turned to Liam, shadows obscuring his face but not his portentous words. "I have a weird feeling. This case might need to remain off the Guild grid, especially if the police are involved."

"And I'm off the Guild grid." The dam on Liam's excitement burst into a river of adrenaline through his veins. Too many long, dry months had left him working his regular job at McAllister Security & Investigations and little else while his brothers saved beautiful psychics and fell crazy in love.

"Bingo."

"I'm game." Liam scrubbed his hands together.

"No doubt."

Niles knew the lack of Guardian work was slowly eating Liam alive. The pending job also gave Liam not a small amount of relief that Niles still trusted him. Even though his older mentor had stood by his side at his Guild tribunal, likened to a court trial, Liam needed the affirmation like candy to a child. Soon the three McAllister musketeers would ride in the rodeo together, kicking ass and taking names.

Niles parked in front of a two-story house in Alex and Juliana's southern neighborhood. The street boasted new homes in a neighborhood of substantially priced real estate, costing far more than Liam and Ric's place. Newly planted trees cast feeble shadows along the sidewalks.

"Sure you can stand your new ride unprotected on the street?" Liam unfurled his long legs from the sardine can and snagged his tablet off the floorboard.

"Ric's rubbing off on you." Niles slapped his shoulder hard enough to feel the jolt through his torso.

"The cost of living with him and saving a buck."

The left garage door rolled up, and Alex loomed in the deepening night, a tall shadow near the corner of the garage. "Hey," he said.

"Alex." Niles shook Alex's hand.

Alex nodded at Liam. "Hey, Liam. Didn't know you were coming."

"Didn't know either," Liam replied. "What's the scoop?"

Niles and Liam followed Alex into the empty space in the garage next to Juliana's car.

Alex checked the closed access door. "I have a situation with one of my detectives. She's a good one, and I want to keep this under wraps for a few reasons." Niles tipped up his chin for him to continue. Alex hit the remote on the garage door, and it rolled to the ground, a barely discernable sound in the tense silence. "She was married to Neal Estenson, divorced now."

"Mafia Estensons?" Niles asked.

"Yep. They're a small offshoot of a larger mafia family in Italy. Significant enough to tread on eggshells."

Liam wasn't sure which was worse, the mafia or the Cabal. Regardless, his night looked brighter. Strengthening his mental walls to keep empathic emotions from interfering with his head, his heart skipped a beat and he waited for a shoe to drop.

"He took their son today, dropped off the radar. Doctored a bunch of photos and affidavits painting her an unfit mother, drughead. Found a judge to sign an *ex parte* order granting him full custody. No visitation rights for at least three months, and then supervised."

"She Guild?" Liam waited for the other shoe to hit the ground.

"No. The boy's psychic. Runs in the Estenson blood, although his father's not psychic. Apparently, his sister, Crystal Estenson, earned the psychic genes."

"Are the Estensons Guild?" Liam asked.

"No," Niles replied, his spine steel-rod straight. "How old is the boy? Is Estenson planning to use him?"

"He's six." Alex popped an antacid into his mouth.

A sigh of relief escaped Liam. "A child that young is just coming into his abilities. They can't reliably use him."

"That's exactly what they're planning. The boy is remarkable according to his mother. The Estensons know it."

"What's his talent?" Niles asked.

"*Talents,*" Alex replied. "He's a freak of psychic nature. Touch telepath, empath, and past and future clairvoyant. Even Juliana's awed."

"*Dayam,* that's more talent than Juliana has, and we thought her a freak of nature," Liam blurted out, tugging at his short hair. A strange dread trickled into him, washing away his adrenaline. The dread increased as he absorbed tiny amounts from both Niles and Alex, leaving him jittery. "So why am I here?" He strengthened his mental walls to block the emotions the two men emitted.

"I want Guardian protection on the mother," Niles replied. "Off the books."

"I want the Guild's help to find and protect the boy," Alex added. "Niles and I agreed to fly under the radar on this one. We'll investigate as a parental abduction. However, since Neal has full custody, the investigation won't be ruled a full-blown abduction. Legally, he has every right to take his son."

"By illegal means." Liam fingered the gun in his

shoulder holster. An intense need to find the boy and reunite him with his mother infused him. A sudden craving to take down the Estenson family drove off his chill. He was crazy to contemplate it since he had enough on his plate investigating the Cabal. He itched to type in the Estenson name in a web search.

"Does this bear any resemblance to your niece's abduction?" Niles asked Alex.

"No, but Juliana's concerned his psychic talents might be exploited into connecting with bad elements."

"Of the mafia kind." Liam's gun became a lonely lodestone. His own empathic abilities had been strong by the time he turned six. With consistent and proper training, his abilities could've escalated fast into the power he enjoyed at twenty-nine. If Neal Estenson's sister was the only psychic in the family with a single talent, who was training the boy in his other talents? A million questions for the boy's mother revolved in his mind, and his eagerness to immerse himself in the case grew palpable. He stepped toward the door.

"Let's meet the mother." Alex led the way into the house. "Her name's Eva."

"Eva Estenson?" Niles asked.

"Midnight, maiden name."

Liam's shoes stuck to the glossy, unblemished cement floor. Sweat popped on his hairline. "Eva Midnight?" His words came out on a croak, sinking into a groove in the cement. A place he wanted to sink his entire body.

"Liam?" Niles clinched Liam's arm.

As Liam shifted his eyes, *she* stood in the doorway, her slim figure silhouetted by the interior lights. Her long hair lay like a mantle of gold around her shoulders, covering her breasts and her shoulder harness housing a handgun. Her beautifully familiar face, her pert nose, and high cheekbones created a storm of memories. He nearly fell into her vivid blue eyes that sparkled even in the single light bulb adjacent to the door. Once again. A dangerous woman now, a dangerous attraction that'd destroyed him once.

"Liam?" She clutched her neck, seemed to absorb him from hair to shoes for a long moment, turned, and sprinted into the house. The door automatically shut behind her, leaving the three men in a muddled darkness. Emotions hit Liam from Niles and Alex, and he staggered, the mystical glue on the floor releasing his feet.

"I take it you know one another?" Alex asked. "I sure hope that's a good thing for both your sakes."

"Didn't look good," Niles piped up, forcing Liam to rebuild his mental walls before the overwhelming emotions drained him. "Liam? Care to explain?"

The sheer temptation of Eva set him in motion. By rote he stomped into the house to confront a mixed emotional past he never believed he'd revisit. Confronting the mafia might be far easier than Eva Midnight and the dumbest mistake of his life.

CHAPTER FOUR

Shock arrested her voice as Eva rushed through the kitchen. Liam McAllister? *What the ever-loving hell?* Awareness shivered over her in cold and hot waves.

"What's wrong?" Juliana chased after her into the cozy family room. "Did you run into a cemetery full of ghosts?"

"One ghost." Eva tried to digest her shock, but it refused to cave. "Liam McAllister."

"You know him? Alex didn't say he was calling the Guild." Juliana clapped her hands once, smacking sense into Eva. "Perfect. I'm not sure how much help *I'll* be since I've never met Connor."

"Not perfect. Far from perfect." Eva picked at the cuticles on her left hand, needing to distract herself from the implications of *him* in her life again.

Liam entered the room with Alex and an older man Eva didn't know following behind. Liam's gaze drank her in, in the way he used to whenever he hadn't seen her in, hell, practically every time she walked into a room. *Man, he looks good.* Tall, built, long and strong legs. He had a powerful body, carrying himself with confidence without leaning toward arrogance. Holy hell, she'd missed that handsome McAllister face, the lake-blue eyes that rivaled her own, the McAllister blade nose and well-defined, high cheekbones. Of the three brothers, Liam in the middle, always sported an unruly head of chestnut hair, not too short and not too long. Nothing had changed. Everything had changed. Of course, his guarded face showed a few more years of age. A somberness had etched tiny crow's feet at the corners of his eyes. Almost invisible laugh lines bracketed his pinched mouth. His somberness altered the fun-loving young man she'd known. Had her departure done a number on him? Had *she* killed something inside him?

"Eva." Liam's eyes tapered into a hostile squint. "It's good to see you. When did you return to San Jose?" He modulated his voice. Or maybe he held no emotion where she was concerned. Maybe he'd written her off. Yet nothing hid the sexy Southern inflection still in his tone from his early childhood years in New Orleans. After his parents had died, the McAllister brothers had moved in with their aunt, uncle, and cousins in San Jose, and the ensuing years had wiped out most of his accent.

"Eight months ago." Being born and raised in San Jose, Eva much preferred drier California to soggy Florida. But there was a time in Florida she wasn't sure she'd ever return home. At least not alive. She'd first met Liam in San Jose during college. After returning, random fond memories of their one intense year together had resurfaced. Staring him in the face shoved *all* the memories to the forefront. "It's good to see you too. You're looking well." More questions and inanities crowded her brain. Three other animated faces latched on to the train wreck she hurtled toward. "Why are you here?"

The older gentleman behind Liam slid between hulking Alex and Liam, and she focused on his distinguished face, the fatherly vibe he exuded. For the life of her, she couldn't recall how to shut down her brain the way Liam had taught her when encountering psychics. Juliana might even be picking every word out of her brain like birdseed to a starving raven. *"Hey, Juliana, throw me a life raft, will ya?"* she grumbled in her head.

Juliana sidled to Alex's side, and he grasped her hand. Not one facial muscle ticked to indicate she'd read Eva's mind.

"I'm Niles Nevin." The stranger introduced himself. His cultured voice attempted to calm her storming emotions. "I'm the Psychic Guild Director of the Protectorate, which is a fancy way of saying I manage the Guild Guardians."

"The Guild?" A slow build of anger burned down a layer of shock icing her insides. "Liam knows my view regarding the Guild. I'd appreciate no involvement from them. Sorry to have troubled you." She spun toward Alex. "A word, please." Bristling, she strode stiff-legged into the kitchen devoid of prying psychic eyes, ears, and tactile touch. Thank her employment status for small favors that Alex possessed little psychic ability.

The moment he entered the kitchen, she rounded on her boss, not caring if he gave her the boot off the force. "How dare you call *them* in without my permission? This isn't a Guild matter."

"How do you know Liam?" He crossed his arms over his not-insubstantial sculpted chest, his shirt stretching tight over his muscles.

"Does it matter? You know I'm not a fan of psychics."

"Yet, Connor—"

"He's my son!" She jabbed his right shoulder. "Doesn't mean I have to like—" She tossed her arms up, counted to five. "Alex, Connor is my heart, the breath of my body. He is what he is, and I love him even more for his peculiarities. I want him to be normal and not enmeshed in psychic mumbo jumbo."

"He's not normal," Liam said from the doorway. "And you can't hide who he is from him."

"Butt out, Liam. This isn't about you and your psychic family." Eva clenched her fists to her thighs, forcing herself not to flee, not to hide in a deep dark cave. Forcing shut the door to her memories and the crappy choices she'd regretted making over the years. "This isn't about us. There's no room in the picture for history right now."

"It's about getting your son back. When all is said and done, you take your son and try to live as normal a life as you can." Liam's low rumble churned up memories she had buried for so long. "You might not have a choice." Truth rolled off the menace in his words.

Connor may very well need psychic tutoring. He may decide to join the Guild when old enough to make a choice. For now, she wanted him any way she could get him. If it meant working with the Guild, then she'd suck it up. If it meant working with Liam McAllister, she'd suck that up too, somehow, someway.

"Fine. Whatever." She flounced past the two men and rejoined Juliana and Niles seated in the family room, enjoying friendly chitchat, speculating about her and Liam. Their murmuring voices quieted. Alex brought in wine and bottles of beer on a tray behind her, and Liam flopped down into a plush recliner. She stood in the center of the room, on display, as they all appeared to wait for a bomb to detonate.

Alex handed her a glass of white wine, and she took a fortifying sip. "I've sent everything I know about Neal and his family to Alex already. He's an über secretive man. I don't know much about his family. He never told me they were mafia until his brother died. I'd never even met them until eight months ago."

"You moved to San Jose and then divorced him?" Juliana asked.

"We were already enmeshed in the family from Orlando. It didn't go well and Neal became mean." Abusive was more like it, but she wasn't ready to confess the sins of her marriage or her stupidity. "I promised Neal I'd move to San Jose, regardless. It's my hometown."

"Do you think Neal returned to Orlando with Connor?" Alex asked.

"No. Since his older brother died two years ago, he's become the Estenson crown prince. Earlier, he was the black sheep, living in Orlando far from under the domineering thumb of his father. His father hated his choices to go to college and join a law firm in Florida. Neal didn't give a crap. He disliked his brother, and it was easier to stay away from his family. That's why we got on so well. He was free, fun, caring. Once his father dragged him back into the family fold, he changed."

"Is Neal in financial difficulties?" Alex asked.

"Not that I'm aware. We had a comfortable life in Florida. But the endless money and the kingly Estenson lifestyle have created a monster in him."

"The change seems awfully sudden," Niles pondered aloud.

Eva shrugged. "He never outright said it, but he always resented his brother. I think he's wanted this forever but was too proud to admit it." *Or too calculating.*

"Will he hurt Connor?" Juliana swirled the wine in her glass, her flawless cheeks paling.

Eva shook her head. "Connor is the sun that orbit's Neal's life."

"I don't mean to upset you further, but this is no time to skirt the truth. Neal may unwittingly hurt him if he tries to leverage Connor's psychic abilities or pushes him too hard before Connor's ready," Liam explained, his familiar voice pacifying and charismatic, as if he wanted to lure her back to him. *As if.* "Neal's psychic sister should know this can't happen, if she's any good."

Eva gripped her gun in her harness and her knees

crumpled. Alex guided her to the sofa and made her sit next to his fiancée, a comforting presence, even though Juliana was a powerful mind reader and touch telepath. She put distance between herself and Juliana to avoid an accidental touch. "What... what do you mean?" She downed her wine and set the fine crystal on the coffee table before it shattered in her grip.

"Don't worry about the crystal," Juliana whispered in Eva's ear.

"Please don't do that, Juliana. I can't shut my head down right now."

"I'm not reading your mind, hon."

Despite Juliana's touch telepathy, Eva squeezed her hand and refused to let go. Only a few months ago, Alex and Juliana had confronted their own abduction case. A lunatic psychic had kidnapped Alex's niece and almost killed Juliana when their minds connected. If anyone knew an inkling of what Eva was suffering, Alex and Juliana did. She wanted them on her side, even if forced to work with the Guild, and even if she had to confront Liam earlier than she'd planned.

A burst of vibrating excitement hit Eva, and she zeroed in on her reason for meeting with Juliana. "Juliana, do you think you can connect to Connor through your mind reading? You've done it before. Could you do it again?"

"That was a fluke with a strong telepath I'd met beforehand. If Connor was near me and he projected extreme emotions, I might."

"How strong is he?" Niles asked. "When did he gain his first ability?"

"If he has three abilities, they're weak at this age," Liam said.

Eva studied her black sneakers, willing the floor to open up and slurp her through a portal leading straight to Connor and away from Liam McAllister, the man most likely to decimate the remainder of her heart.

"Eva?" Alex prompted.

She lifted her head, avoided Liam's frank stare. "I think he's strong in all three. He's been reading my mind since before he could speak. As a baby, he could touch me and understand what I was feeling. The moment he spoke full sentences, he told me things that'd happened in my past." She disregarded the gasps riding the air. "He knows of Liam and asked to see a photo of him. I told him one day I'd show him, tell him all about you. He needed to know the man I loved before his daddy." *The man she loved more than Neal.* Connor never said that, but she always suspected he knew. After he asked the questions about Liam, she'd begun to use the mind-cloaking techniques Liam and his older brother, Jake, also a telepath, had taught her. The techniques eluded her in her current frazzled state.

Silence descended as everyone contemplated her admissions.

"He knows me?" Liam sank to the rug and sat with his back against the couch leg. "If he hates me, I may be the wrong man for this job."

"He's curious, but he doesn't hate you." Eva swished her hand in the air. "Can we get back to this mind-connection business?" If she didn't change the subject, her intestines would explode. And she was far from ready to confront the long-buried entrails of her past. "This investigation shouldn't include Guild involvement. The Estensons aren't Guild members."

Niles consulted his phone. "Because the Guild swayed them not to join when Lucretia Estenson, Neal's grandmother, wanted to join. According to Guild archives, they didn't want organized crime members in the Guild. Lucretia understood. No one in the family has tried to join since."

"I don't know about cousins, aunts, or uncles, but Crystal Estenson is the only one in Neal's immediate family with mind-reading talents."

"She may be able to train Connor to some extent. Let's hope she doesn't screw with his head," Liam, the town crier, offered.

"Thanks for that little tidbit. It makes me feel *so* much better." Sarcasm laced Eva's tone.

Alex moved between them, blocking Liam from her view. "Did you two have a bad breakup? Niles, should you call in another Guardian?"

"A mutual parting of ways." Disdain tightened the skin of her face. With no effort, her mind summoned the way Liam's hands caressed her skin and the taste and texture of his lips.

"Mutual between you and yourself," Liam muttered. "Whatever. Call in another Guardian."

"No. I want Liam on this case," Niles said. "He's already off the Guild books publicly. We can make him appear like a disgruntled Guardian who wants nil to do with the Guild."

"I don't understand," Juliana piped up. "What difference does it make if it's public knowledge the Guild is involved or not?"

"We're under too much pressure with the Cabal on our backs. We don't want the mafia nailing us to the wall as well. Best to keep this clean from Guild involvement. Liam has tons of investigation experience. And his ability to coerce from his empathic touch ability may come in useful."

Eva snorted. "Yeah, I know how useful that can be."

"Apparently, it wasn't useful enough in a certain matter seven years ago." Liam pushed off the floor and stalked to the French doors, his movements stiff and jerky, his fists balled at his sides.

A cement-heavy silence smothered the room. The

jarring sound of Eva's foghorn cell ring nearly made her pee her pants. She snatched it off the coffee table and punched the *on* button to the unidentified number.

"Neal?"

"Eva. How are you faring?"

Back rigid, she thrust off the couch. "Where's my son?"

"Right here." Neal fumbled the phone, giving her an opportunity to turn her recorder on and click on her speakerphone.

"Hi, Mommy!"

"Baby, I'm so glad to hear your voice. What are you and Daddy doing?"

"We're on an adventure. It's secret, so I can't tell. Daddy said you'll join us later when we're ready for the surprise."

Fuming, Eva stomped into the kitchen, flicked the lights on in the pristine space of earth tone granite and travertine. *Son of an Estenson bitch.* "Oh, okay, baby. I miss you and love you. Wish you were here with me."

"Me too. Don't be sad. Don't be angry at Daddy."

A bitter laugh escaped her. "Are you reading me again?"

He giggled. "I can't read you over the phone. Oh, I gotta go. Daddy wants—"

"Nice try, Eva." Neal's voice grated on her last nerve.

"Give me back my son. You doctored those photos, and you need to get the custody order rescinded."

Neal clucked his tongue in his cheek, an irritating tell of his cunning. "Ah, Eva. You wear your delusions so well."

"I've done everything you've asked. I risked my job today snatching that flash drive. Why are you doing this?" Then it dawned on her. Maybe he wanted her to get caught and fired, because then she'd have no excuse not to come back to him in his warped notion of a happy family life.

"You refused to do what I asked. I wanted my son to

have a stable family with *both* his parents in the same home. I wanted you back. Despite everything, I still love you."

The argument had gotten stale. "Why? You think everyone's beneath the Estensons. I'm middle America and not mafia echelon." *Because I'm a cop who can take down your entire organization?*

"That's my father talking. It's one reason I shielded you from my family all those years. True, you're not one of us, but I never cared, and you know it."

"So now you're marrying one of your bimbos? Do you think they're better mother material? Better Estenson material? Does your father approve?"

"You're not loyal and supportive. You're not home enough. Your career means more to you than I do."

Eva rolled her threadbare eyes. "Jeez, Neal, are you hammered? You're going round in circles contradicting yourself."

"Why are you in Almaden?"

Eva lurched in the arched doorway between the kitchen and family room. "Are you pinging my phone?" she yelled. She's a cop for hell's sake. Why hadn't she already guessed Neal was tailing her all over the city?

"What do you think?"

"If you must know, I'm at my boss's house."

"The detective engaged to a well-known psychic? It's funny how you hate psychics, yet you'll kowtow to one for help. It's why you don't deserve Connor. You can't help him develop his talents. You've inhibited and forced him to hide his abilities."

Truth quieted the storm brewing inside her, and flames clawed her chest. "I just want him to be normal, to keep others from treating him like a freak."

"Doesn't matter now. He's among his kind. He'll be three times the psychic that blonde beauty is."

"I'm coming for you, Neal. Count on it."

"I *am*. The whole Estenson clan is counting on it." The phone clicked off on his ominous final words.

She might have just signed her death warrant, but she'd die trying to get her son back where he belonged.

CHAPTER FIVE

Liam sat in the passenger seat of Eva's crossover vehicle as she steered down the Almaden streets toward downtown. An empty juice box and a scruffy baseball rolled around his feet on the floor, evidence of a boy in Eva's life. They headed to the police station to get the tracker removed off Eva's phone, her only conduit to Neal and Connor.

Begrudgingly, she'd allowed the Guardian assignment and even agreed to drive him home. However, she refused to allow him to stay at her house after Niles and Alex begged her to accept his guard. Multiple times, she'd reminded them she was a cop, capable of protecting herself. A cop with the mafia on her back like an eight-ton gorilla. And it sure as hell didn't help her son much. But don't tell her that.

After the phone call between Eva and Neal, the team had discussed options to tackle the case. Alex sent copies of the photos to Liam's cell, and Eva's towhead boy looked so much like her, it made him wistful. To avoid opening his memory crypt too far, he didn't study the photos for long.

Cutting himself off from Eva emotionally was probably a lousy idea, but he had to do it or deal with the damage of their breakup. Damn, she tortured him regardless. Her haunting jasmine scent seduced him, dampened his annoyance, and ratcheted up his curiosity. Her agitation detonated the fragrance in the stuffy vehicle, overriding the dried-up pine scent tree clipped on the passenger visor. He inhaled another whiff of the heady fragrance to distract his empathic mind from wallowing in her trepidation and a curious excitement.

An Ireland mountain landscape surrounded by lush fields of green and a far-off castle vaulted into his mind unhindered by the walls he erected. The landscape of a place he'd wanted to visit helped him focus his empathic abilities or helped him erect and strengthen his mental walls. Even so, he'd always had a hard time blocking Eva's emotions. She was always too intensely passionate, and he too in love. One big reason for their split.

Like moths to a flame, they flitted around each other in the pervasive silence.

"How's your family, your brothers?" Eva broke the silence on a less-nuanced topic.

He tapped his dark tablet screen, dying to investigate the Estensons. "Family's well. Jake and Ric both recently met the loves of their lives, psychics they guarded. They're in new-relationship heaven."

Eva coughed and her peachy, flawless cheeks reddened. He remembered stroking her silky skin with his fingers, his lips, remembered causing a million blushes just from a touch, a look, a word.

"Well, we know how that works." She laughed to defray the salty tension of avoidance.

Refusing to play her games, a thread of ire roasted his blood. "We'd gone beyond new, and you know it."

"You want to hash this out now, Liam? We've already done this number a dozen times. There's nothing left to hash, but I'll hit the high points one last time. We met in college, dated a year, mutually agreed to split when I got a scholarship for my master's in criminal justice at the U of

Central Florida in Orlando. I left. You stayed. We *both* moved on. I came back. We meet again out of the flipping blue. There, we're done."

"Jeez, Eva. When did you become so brash? Cop school screw you over?" Liam paused for a moment, glanced in the rearview mirror at a dark-colored sedan several car lengths behind. "Did homicide work harden all your softness?"

"Screw you and the Psychic Guild you rode in on." She slammed her left palm on the steering wheel, and overcompensating, wrenched the vehicle to the right. "My son was just kidnapped by the mafia. *The mafia.* Do you get it? I think I have a right to be a bitch."

The chasm was too great between them. Their pride, or stupidity, had widened it irreparably long ago. Regardless of that insurmountable valley, Liam nearly gloved her right hand in his on the steering wheel, but he fought the disaster-inducing impulse. He couldn't handle touching her, especially if she remembered he still had the random ability to coerce with a touch. "I'm sorry you're going through this. You don't deserve it."

She white-knuckled the steering wheel, and he wanted to peel her fingers off and smooth them out one by one. "How do you know I don't deserve it? You don't know what I've done for the last seven years."

"You didn't do those things in the photos, I know that."

"How do you know that? Just because I said so?" She groaned. "Oh, right. You can read emotions."

"Eva, why are you itching for a fight? We had a good run, it ended. I was an ass, and I've apologized a hundred times. Now I just want to help you recover your son and get the mafia off your back."

Another pea soup silence bogged down the air in the car. He cracked his window, and cool autumn air swirled the jasmine out of his nostrils. Eva sniffed, and her grip on the steering wheel relaxed. The sedan remained at a discreet distance, turning when Eva turned, slowing when she did.

"We've got a tail," he announced.

"I know. I've made a few turns, and he's stuck on me like shit on my shoe."

Liam rubbed the back of his neck, adjusted his shoulder holster. "Were you planning on telling me?"

"Why? You figured it out on your own." She held up a hand in defeat. "Okay. Okay. I'll be a good team player. But remember, I'm the cop here. Not you."

"I have a gun," he teased to lighten the mood.

"And I bet you know how to use it too." Her voice lilted up.

"Damn straight."

"Well, cowboy, just follow my lead, okay? And we'll both stay safe."

"Whatever you say, Detective Midnight." In spite of the threat behind them, Liam sensed a slight turn in their rekindled relationship—for what it was worth—in their few bantering words. Maybe they'd eventually come to terms with the real reasons Eva stayed away from him all those years. Or why he didn't try harder. Probably after hell froze into a desolate tundra. He sure couldn't get her to change her tune the two times he'd flown out to Orlando after she'd left San Jose. The message hit him loud and clear the second time she'd snubbed him, and her mother refused to let him in her apartment.

Eva made a few more turns, sticking to the main streets, still heading in the direction of downtown police headquarters. The sedan followed, the distance between them narrowing.

"They're gaining on us." Liam drew his gun, checked the chambers.

"Hold your fire."

"Just prepping."

She scrutinized him for a moment, her gaze fluttering the grass on his mountainside until he strengthened his granite walls to shut out her emotions. "You look good with a gun."

"I had a gun when you left."

"You weren't a full-fledged Guardian and didn't have a carry permit. Plus, you McAllister bros were just getting your business off the ground. If I recall, Jake was the only PI with credentials."

"Yeah. Didn't take long for Ric and me to immerse ourselves in the business. Once I quit hunting stolen artifacts full time, I got serious about the biz."

"Jake ever take the bar exam?" Eva squinted in the mirror. "They're on our tail now."

"I see them. Nope. He's a partner in his girlfriend's law firm, though."

"Sounds like a story."

"Long one. Maybe I'll tell you sometime." The chitchat routine centered him on the tailgating car, quelled his nerves. Reminded him of the intense year they'd spent together. A time he believed would culminate in a marriage proposal once they'd both finished college and established their careers. *Why am I focusing on dead and done crap again? Why did Eva return to my life? Is it a sign? No. No suffering through that heartache again. Stick to business. Stick to the memories, easier to deal than reality.*

The sedan killed the distance, its headlights buried in Eva's bumper. "Speed up about five miles." He straightened in the seat, rolled down his window.

The tailgater kept a steady pace behind Eva. "They're Estenson goons."

"You sure?"

She scowled. "I've been around enough of this clan to know."

"Why would Neal threaten you if he wants you back?

Or was he conning you?"

"Not Neal. His father's minions."

A glacial sweat broke out across the back of Liam's neck. Mafia shit just got real. From what Eva had told them earlier, Neal's father took no prisoners. "Are they wanting you to take a hike?"

"Daniel Estenson wants me... dead."

Liam swung on her so fast, his head almost bounced off his neck. "What the hell? What *aren't* you telling me?"

"It's about more than my son." Unfazed, she continued driving toward the police station.

"What did you do?"

"Wow, you go straight to me doing something. Thanks for the vote." She yanked the car into a hard right, and Liam's head bonked the headrest.

"Sorry." She rolled up his window. "This stays between us. Not even Alex knows."

Before she could utter another word, the sedan rammed into her rear bumper, jolting them forward. Seatbelts locked, cutting across his torso. Eva gunned the gas and shot forward. The sedan lost no ground.

"Don't say another word," Liam ordered. "Your car may be bugged."

"No shit. *Mafia*, man. Nothing they do is aboveboard. I was only going to tell you that Neal's father hates my guts. As long as I'm alive"—she elevated her voice for listening devices—"I'll be a pain in his ass. A big-ass pain in his old flabby ass."

Liam hadn't signed up for a mafia death hit. Bad enough dealing with Cabal death threats, but this. *Screw me to hell and back.* Another bumper-to-bumper hit from behind jolted Liam's shoulders and knocked his spine against the seat.

The SUV sputtered and limped forward. Eva gunned it, and it died on the spot. She hit the ignition button, the car caught, then died again. "Oh, come on!" She slammed the dash. "Don't fail me now."

"Get out your gun." No one had exited the darkened sedan parked behind them. "Should you call for police backup?"

Eva released her weapon from her shoulder harness. "No police. The more we keep this undercover, the better our chances."

Two muffled pop-pops preceded the left rear tire blowout, then the right, leaving them dead in the water. The vehicle stuttered to life and held, but running on flats ended their trip to Nowhere.

"Make a run for it?" Liam whispered, studying the multi-storied buildings on his right. "We can hit the police station from here."

"My thoughts exactly," she whispered back. "But you need to keep a low profile." She scrambled in the back seat, tossed a baseball cap at him and an old baggy hoodie. "Put these on." She stuck a pair of aviator sunglasses on his face.

Liam stowed his leather jacket on the floor of the back seat, weaseled into the tight hoodie, and shoved his tablet into his waistband. "This isn't Connor's jacket unless he's a giant?"

"It's mine. I like my running clothes baggy."

The familiar jasmine and Eva's distinctive scent suffused him. "I remember." Man, did he ever remember. An untimely rush of blood stirred in his groin.

"On the count of three, run for the three-story, then to the rear. I know a shortcut to the block behind it. Straight shot from there to the station. You up for a run?"

The first genuine warmth he'd felt since the moment Eva reentered his life caused him to smile. "I still run daily."

"Well then, let's hit it. Take the back alley to the right, then make a right and a straight shot to Mission." Eva took one last glance out the rearview mirrors and cut the engine. "One, two, three."

Liam opened his door, ensured Eva was in the clear and jetted to the front of the vehicle, hunched over to hide his height. Eva shot across the front landscaping of the three-story office building, Liam on her tail. Gunshots trailed them, muffled by silencers. Footsteps pounded behind them. She was quick as lightning, and they zigzagged to avoid flying bullets, dodging behind pillars, trees, and a tinkling water fountain.

"Don't stop." She ground to a halt behind a column close to the doors and popped off three quick rounds.

"Eva," he yelled from the shadows of the building. "Hit it. We have the lead."

"Eva, doll. Give it up," one of Estenson's goons yelled. "You won't get out of this intact."

"Wanna bet, Jordie? You just threatened an officer of the law," she shouted, held up her badge and aimed again. "Police! Drop your weapons!"

Lush evergreen bushes along the side of the building hid Liam as he crept closer to Eva's position behind the front pillars.

"You know his minions by name?" Her hatred enveloped him, and a stab of jealous irritation pierced his chest.

"I have a special place in hell for Jordie."

"Ah, Eva, your credentials don't mean crap. We all know you're not calling this in," the man replied, looming closer.

Liam jumped out from the relative safety of the bushes to hide behind a six-foot-tall plinth balancing a decorative urn on top. It was almost wide enough to hide his breadth. "Eva," he whisper-shouted.

"Dammit, go! I got this," she replied over her shoulder. "You never did listen."

He wasn't about to leave her to the pair of thugs out for blood. Midnight blood. And she was wrong about him not listening. He listened. It was the understanding that did him in. In this case, she was making an insane stand against the mafia. He wished she'd called for assistance. No one ever called him a coward, but battling the mafia had never made it on his bucket list. The hoodie and cap disguise didn't evoke a sense of security, even with the gun in his hand.

"Big D just wants to talk," the man next to Jordie said.

"Not what Jordie just said, dumbass," Eva replied. Grumbling between the two men escalated, died down. "Drop your weapons. You really want to do this in public?"

"Public, private, don't matter." Jordie waved his gun. "Ends the same either way."

Sirens pierced the night, growing louder. A knot unwound in Liam's gut. At least Eva couldn't complain he'd called in the sound of gunfire. *And you care, why?*

The sirens goaded the men into action. Jordie fired at the pillar; Eva yelped and jumped back behind it. Bitter acid scorched Liam's throat.

"I said, drop your weapons," she shouted. Liam understood she was stalling, using police protocol to solidify the arrest.

The screech of tires, brakes, and flashing red lights broke the tableau, slashing blood across the building's facade and bouncing off the windows in red sparkles. The night exploded in a wild cyclone of gunshots, police yelling commands, and thumping footsteps. Someone knocked Liam from behind the plinth and kept on running. A final gunshot blasted the night, slashed Liam's upper left arm. Red-hot pain creased his arm, and the hit jostled him against the plinth.

"Li—" Eva cut off his name, and she caught him in her embrace, holding him upright against the pedestal.

Nausea blossomed, and he propped his forehead against the cool stone. "You just got me shot." He stumbled and tried to veer out of her arms and her dangerous touch. Stars overhead burst into tiny fragments and dove toward him. The starlets grew brighter until they absorbed his sight completely. Eva shouldered him to the cement, combing his hair off his face, whispering words he desperately wanted to hear. But her touch propelled his brain on another path toward reality.

CHAPTER SIX

Liam tried to escape Eva's arms, but she refused to let him face-plant onto the cement steps leading to the building's lobby. Her emotions hit him strong and convoluted, doubling him over. He couldn't curb his empathic psychic abilities. Sucking down the rising acid, he tilted against the pillar, letting it hold him upright. Eva's anxiety washed over him, toting a giddy joy about being in his presence after so many years. *Go figure.* Liam latched on to her joy and rode the wave to another swell of alarm directed at him. Something unfathomable, something she'd held inside for too long. He almost gripped her wrist to try to coerce her to divulge her dark secret.

"Liam, are you still here? Focus on me." Eva cupped his chin, her touch electrifying, encouraging his craving to coerce her to fess up. "Ambulance is on the way."

He needed to get a grip and fast. Unable to focus on his mountain landscape, he flipped his internal switch up to visualize himself embedded in his body, a coping mechanism for his empathic deluges. He visualized the bullet hole and the boiling river of lava streaming down his arm. It took a few tries to flick the intangible switch off Eva's emotions. He still couldn't shake her weird contradictory feelings about him and her distinctive fear of the Estenson clan.

"Hands off," he croaked out. "I can't turn you off."

Eva jerked away as though he carried the plague and wrung out her hands. "I forgot."

Sirens and screeching brakes swarmed the vicinity. Police surrounded them. Eva ID'd herself and briefed the officer in charge. Fighting her disorder hovering inside his mental periphery, Liam wrapped his good arm around the pillar. Part of him wanted her touching him, wanted to find out what secret she'd hidden deep. The longer she touched him, the more he'd glean from her. The bane of his existence. His empathic abilities had driven her across the country and closed the book on their relationship.

Paramedics groped him, peeled off the tacky, rust-stained hoodie. He concentrated on maintaining his off switch by watching Eva shoot him apprehensive feathers and fearful daggers as she downloaded the night's events to another officer.

"I had engine trouble," she explained. "A dark sedan stopped behind me. I think they planned to jack the car. They shot out my tires, and my vehicle stalled. They got out, threatened us, and I pulled my weapon and badge. They refused to back down."

"Explain how you ended up near the building," the male officer intoned as if bored.

"They pulled guns. My friend got skittish and bolted. I ordered them to drop their weapons several times. They refused. They chased. I chased. They shot my friend. Here we are."

The sedan behind Eva's SUV had disappeared before the cops arrived on the scene. Liam noticed his gun was gone too. Eva covered up a shit ton to protect her son.

"Sir, what's your name?" a muscular female paramedic asked him. She alone shouldered him over to a gurney and eased him onto the padded top, protecting his gunshot arm.

"Liam McAllister," he said in a low voice to hide his

identity to the gathering bystanders.

"What city are you in?"

"San Jose."

He aced her other questions to establish he remained in his head, or at least part of him. The other part remained with Eva and her increasing insane life and lies.

He hadn't experienced such a thrill in a year, well, not counting the night his brother Ric had gotten shot. Getting shot in *his* arm may have been worth it, even if he had to confront the tempestuous love of his life who'd gutted him when she'd driven across the continent. A bullet hole in the arm sure as heck helped Ric's personal romance game. *Romance? Why the hell am I thinking about romance? Had the gunshot brained me too?*

The paramedics raised the gurney into the ambulance. The police refused to release Eva for a ride along. Disheveled and grim, Detective MacKenzie materialized on the scene.

"Alex," Liam called, peeking around the paramedic.

"McAllister?" Shock riddled Alex's voice. He gave the paramedic a one-minute finger. "You get hurt?"

"Shot in the arm."

"Sorry, man. Should I call your brothers? Niles?" Alex winced, no doubt thinking about Liam's overprotective brothers learning he'd been shot on a secret undercover case. He may as well kill himself before they did the deed.

"Detective, please step aside," the female paramedic ordered.

"Call Niles." The ambulance doors sealed out the world. Liam groaned, focused on the needle the paramedic stuck in his arm.

By the time he arrived at the emergency room, his left arm had evaporated under the drip of pain meds. They wheeled him into a bright cubicle and stripped off his long-sleeved shirt, bloodstained and torn.

"Detective Eva Midnight," the lilting voice of an angel announced outside the cloth cubicle walls. "Mr. McAllister's under my protection."

"Wait out here, Detective," a nurse replied, not at all scared off by the badge. Liam gave her props while snickering at the "protection" bit. Eva might think about quitting the police force if all her victims suffered gunshots while under her protection.

Medical personnel worked on him, and Liam had to flip on another focusing switch to avoid the emotions of everyone touching him. Pain meds made it easier to plant himself on top of his serene emerald mountaintop, not a soul in sight until he spied the familiar curvy blonde standing in a crenellation high atop the castle walls, her back to him as usual. For the first time, she turned, and his breath hitched. The woman beckoned to him, and Eva's delicately boned face featuring her vivid blue eyes, button nose, and full bow lips made up his fantasy woman. He choked on his spit. Had it always been Eva?

"How bad, doc?" he risked asking, his voice husky.

"Graze and a nasty scrape. No surgery for you, son."

Tension flowed off his shoulders, and he unclenched his hand.

"Didn't we patch another McAllister who also suffered a bullet wound in his arm recently? You McAllister boys might want to rethink your career options."

Liam sniggered. "Yeah, doc, my little bro, Ric, got shot. He's recovering quite well. Thanks for asking."

The doctor chuckled. "I take it that means you have no intention of getting a safe office job anytime soon?"

"Bullets don't discriminate."

"Then try not to get yourself killed. One bullet graze is enough. You own your war scar now."

The nurse elbowed the doctor aside with her tray of bandages. "I'll take it from here." She winked at Liam.

"We'll get you patched up and back on the streets."

The grateful comedy routine kept him focused off Eva and the hands touching him. He couldn't afford to slip under a tsunami of emotions. As the nurse bandaged his arm, he shut his eyes for a few winks. When he opened them, Eva filled his vision. Her bedraggled blonde hair cloaked her breasts, encouraging him to touch the golden strands, wrap her hair around his finger the way he used to, and tug her into the haven of his body.

Good arm glued to his side, he flung off his crazed thoughts. Hell would have to freeze over before he allowed her into his heart again. Too late for allowing her into his life. That sunken ship had been hauled into port for repairs.

"McAllister," Eva said. "How you doing?"

"Did they get away?"

"Yes. We'll talk in private once you're released."

"Does that talk include the truth?" A sharp pain impaled his arm, and he winced as the nurse tightened the gauze.

"Truth? Eva Midnight doesn't know the meaning of truth," Jake's voice boomed in the room.

"Well, I'll be damned. Eva Midnight." Ric's awed voice chased their older brother's gruff snark. "Back from the Florida dead zone."

Liam flinched again. Damn Niles for doing the right thing and calling his brothers. He wasn't ready to confront them about his arm, let alone Eva, the sole source of driving Liam to a destructive anger and hate binge fest for a month after she'd parked it in Florida. Many a night they'd carried him home from various bars or had to pick up the pieces after he'd suffered one too many empathic torrents. So many times, during those dark days, he'd lost his ability to erect his walls or flip his mental switch. He almost didn't make it out alive.

"What's with all the McAllister brothers getting shot lately?" Ric hammered the last nail in his shitstorm coffin.

"Only grazed. At least she's not a psychic or fellow Guild member," Liam retorted to force the issue elsewhere.

The nurse fled the he-man crowded cubicle, the tray of medical paraphernalia rattling in her wake.

"Ric, Jake." Eva nodded. "Nice to see the McAllister brothers as brute as ever."

"What's shakin', Eva?" Ric asked. "Long see, no time."

She scrunched up her forehead, trying to make heads or tails of Ric's screwed-up metaphors. "Well, I'm living in San Jose, working as a detective under Alex MacKenzie. He likes me, so maybe you might one day." A sly smile toyed with her dry but still luscious pink lips.

"What are we waiting for? Doctor release?" Jake asked.

"Guess so," Liam responded, recognizing his oldest brother's need to escape the hospital, or Eva. Neither brother held any love toward her, not after they'd picked up the broken pieces of him. "Can you go check?" Jake couldn't escape the room fast enough, and the cubicle door rattled in its frame.

"What did Niles tell you?" Liam allowed Ric to help put on his bloodied shirt. Eva tossed the hoodie in the trash, picked up Connor's baseball cap from the floor, and stuffed it on his head. "Am I still incognito? Are we leaving together?"

"Over my dead body." Ric leaned a hip against a rolling cart and crossed his arms over his chest, cringing at his own gunshot arm. At least Eva hadn't tried to *kill* Liam. "Niles gave us a nutshell version of your new assignment, the abduction and the family in question. Doesn't matter, you're done for the night."

"Sorry, nope." Eva leaned against the wall and folded her arms over her delectable breasts, mimicking Ric's stance. The memory of the perfect globes created a stirring in his groin he hadn't felt in a long time.

Ric bared his teeth. "Think again, Detective Midnight-*Estenson*. Did Liam commit a crime? You arresting him?"

Grinning, Liam lay back and willed a bucket of buttered popcorn to appear in his hands.

Eva paled, and she seemed to cave in on herself. "He's not under arrest. The Guild knows the scoop, as does Alex. After what happened tonight, I'm terrified to go home alone. I'll take care of him."

Shock riddled Liam. He sat up straight, brushed off her attempt to help him, not wanting her touch on him again. Truth smacked him in the face from her trembling hands and pallid exhaustion. She was beautiful to him in so many ways. All he wanted was to give her son back to her and end the misery the Estensons had caused in her life.

Jake stormed into the room, a nurse behind him. "You're free to go," he said. "Lily and Marisa are waiting for us at Lily's house." Jake lived with his girlfriend, Lily, in a loft apartment her lawyer father had leased him in their family home before he'd met Lily. Now, the two were inseparable in what had become the family gathering spot.

"I think our bro has other ideas." Ric held out a hand, and Liam seized it with his right hand. His legs supported him without swaying. *A good sign, right?* The wound on his arm barely stung.

The nurse handed him a paper bag of pills. "Take the antibiotics per directions until gone, and pain pills as directed, only as needed. Nice seeing you three. Try not to make it a habit."

Silent, the three hulking McAllisters surrounded Eva and trudged to the sliding doors in the emergency exit, Liam foregoing the exit wheelchair.

Hugging his arm in his sling, he stopped outside the doors and turned to Ric and Jake. "You know how long I've waited to return to Guild work. I'm stoked to have an assignment."

"Even if your assignment"—Jake slashed his hand in the air—"got you shot in your first minute?"

"She's holding back, man," Ric said. "You really want to go through that bullshit again? She messed you up once. Don't let it happen a second time. The Guild need not be involved in a mafia abduction."

"I can hear you, you know," Eva said through gritted teeth. "Take him home then." She spun around and speed walked toward the parking lot.

"Look, man, it's her son. He's six years old, just a baby. He needs Guild protection." Liam turned to follow Eva. "I'll catch you up tomorrow. After the ambush tonight, I don't want her going home alone. I don't give a rat's ass who she is." His gaze never left Eva's form as she made her way in the lamp-lit parking lot to an unmarked police cruiser.

"You mean who she *isn't*." Jake stomped toward his black Corvette parked in the first spot beyond the entrance.

"I get it, bro." Ric came abreast of him. "People change. Maybe it's your turn now."

Liam squinted at his brother. "Turn for what?"

"A new life, a new love."

Another round of shock blasted through Liam's fatigued muscles. Did he want another shot at Eva? Would she contemplate it now, especially with a powerful psychic son who needed psychic guidance and who belonged to the Guild?

"Eva, wait up," he shouted, slapped his brother on the shoulder and jogged toward the enigma kindling all his senses.

CHAPTER SEVEN

Eva parked her unmarked police car in her covered spot at her condo complex. The two-story buildings were old but well-maintained with newer drought-resistant landscaping of small patches of lawn, rocks, and evergreen plants. Her interim living quarters suited her busy lifestyle.

"You live here?" Liam asked, sounding disdainful to Eva.

"Why?" Her defenses mushroomed. *Big deal if I rent a suckass two-bedroom condominium. Not everyone can afford the Estenson lifestyle.*

"Ric and I own a house a half mile away."

"Oh." Her disdain withered. "Surprised we haven't run into each other."

"I'm not home much. Our company and Guild biz keep me busy."

"Lucky you can afford a house in the Bay Area. Sticker shock hit me when I returned. I'll never afford to buy a place."

The inane chatter helped assuage her edginess about Liam sitting in her car, in her presence, about allowing him inside her inner sanctum. Her home represented her safe harbor where she and Connor relaxed, played games, and mapped out trips around the world they wanted to take someday. An African safari topped Connor's list, and she'd promised him they'd at least go to the San Francisco zoo soon.

Tears welled and her head fell back against the headrest. "I miss him so much, Liam. I just want my son back."

Liam reached to touch her arm, hesitated, and retracted his hand. "Sorry, my defenses are shot. I can't touch you right now."

The rich, earthy aroma of patchouli cut with citrus delighted her nose, and she inhaled Liam's signature cologne. "Appreciate it. I'd rather you not read my emotions. It's bad enough I just squeezed out a tear. Tough cop, right?"

"You're human first, a mother second."

"Your brothers hate me. Do you?" Part of her needed Liam not to hate her. It shouldn't matter, yet she thought it might placate her angst being around him, the fear she might fall into a well of bad choices again.

"They're just wary. I was involved in a bad Guild case earlier this year, got screwed over by a high-ranking psychic who played me and used my abilities for her gain. She set me up for a fall, major Guild infractions, earned me months of suspension, which recently got extended three months due to helping Ric on a case. I'm *persona non grata* at the Guild."

Eva knuckled her runny nose. "Did that long, rambling answer mean you don't hate me?"

"Hate's a strong word." Liam opened the passenger door. "We going in?"

"Yeah." She touched the door handle. "Hey, Liam. Thanks. I'm sorry I dragged you into my mess."

"You didn't. The Guild did."

"You *chose* to accept the assignment." Her eyes met his in the dark interior, inky pools of blue to mirror her own.

"Why didn't you walk?"

"I haven't changed. I'm still a good guy."

She skimmed her fingertips over the back of his hand. "I'm glad." Glad on too many fronts to single out of her twisted emotions.

Eva led the way to her lower unit. The end unit gave her a bigger fenced patio yard, perfect for Connor to play in a safe environment. Someday, she'd move into a house to give him a real yard and room for the dog he'd weasel out of her.

The second she spied her front door, heebie-jeebies assaulted her in a prickly creep across her shoulders. "Hold up," she whispered, drawing her gun. Liam bumped into her back and winced when his wounded arm made contact. The heat of his body warmed her sudden chill.

"Ah, man. Now what?" Liam's mouth landed so close to her ear his breath teased her neck.

"Stand to the other side of the door. I don't want you to get hurt again." She waved her gun toward the shadowy bushes hiding the backyard fence. The porch light didn't penetrate the side yard and left it in deep shadows, a good place to hide.

"What's going on?"

"I left a sliver of paper in the doorjamb. It's on the stoop now. My interior light's out too."

"Dammit, Eva. How long have the Estensons been bullying you?"

"Long story. Hit it. The perp may still be inside."

Mumbling, Liam backstepped into the shadows, cradling his bad arm. "Call for backup this time."

His words drifted away as she entered the dark condo, left the door ajar behind her. A security light always burned in her living room, chasing away the dark. Once her vision adjusted to the darkness, she cringed. Someone had turned upside down or tossed everything movable around the small room.

A rustling rose from the master bedroom down the short hallway on the left, and she tiptoed toward the half-closed door. Connor's door stood open on the right, his floor blanketed with everything he owned in a haphazard mess, his twin mattress standing on end, stuffing littering the floor like little clouds. A deadly tempest of fury vibrated down her spine, kicking her into remedial action.

She bypassed her bedroom door to the hinge side, kicked it open. "Police!" she yelled.

A short, wiry perp hurtled toward the master bathroom. Eva lunged for him. "Police! Drop your weapon," she shouted, trained her gun on him. The man stopped, raised his arms along with the nine-millimeter he wielded. "Set your weapon on the floor, slide it to me slow and easy."

He swiveled to face her. Slowly, he set the gun on the floor, rose, and kicked the gun toward her feet across the ceramic tiles. A balaclava hid his features, but she recognized his body shape as another one of Daniel Estenson's men who'd been tailing her for weeks. He wasn't one of the assholes in the sedan earlier, which meant Estenson had all his dogs in a full-court press.

"Sweetheart, nice to meet you face to masked face." His wicked grin showed a hint of black beard and mustache through the holes in the ski mask.

"What do you want with me?"

"Read me my rights."

"Better yet"—a gun barrel tapped the back of her skull—"let's not and say you did," another Estenson caveman chimed in behind her, his voice smoker raspy.

Before her next blink, a muffled whack split the tense tableau, and the man behind her thumped to the floor. The wiry minion lunged for his gun, and she whacked him in the sweet spot on the back of his head, knocking him out. She hauled his arms behind his butt, secured a zip tie around his wrists, and stuck his gun in her waistband. The takedown took only seconds but felt like eons.

Legs stiff and unsure, she stood and met Liam's shocked expression, pain wrinkling his forehead.

"Now will you tell me what's going on?" he demanded, deliberately gripping her hand in his strong, warm clasp to gauge her emotions. She felt the power of his mesmerism ability, the triggers in her brain trying to force her to own up.

Fighting his coercion, and under the weight of the night's events, her emotions collapsed. An emotional wave hit Liam, evidenced by the jolt to his chest and his stagger toward her.

"I can't block myself," she whispered to avoid any potential listening devices.

"I know." His voice was strained. "Sorry. I slipped. I'm doing my best to block you."

"You're ready to crash." She cupped his cheek, dropped her hand as if he was cursed. As far as it concerned her, he was cursed. A few seconds longer and she might have gutted herself in front of him. "Let me call this in."

"You sure you want to?" he challenged, reversing his earlier request to call for backup.

She ran her fingers down her tangled hair. "No. I need to send Estenson a message."

"You're sure it's his men?"

"Positive." She kicked at the small, burly guy. "This is hitman Eric Estenson. A distant cousin."

"What hellhole have you fallen into?"

Ignoring him, she said, "My only concern is Connor. If I call this in, what will *they* do to Connor?"

"What will they do to you?" Liam squeezed her hand, then let it go. She wanted to weave her fingers with his and pretend she'd never left San Jose seven years ago. It wasn't the first time she'd wished for a do-over. Except for Connor.

He'd made all the crap years in Florida worth living.

"Keep using me for target practice." She rested her forehead against his good shoulder, a whiff of fear and antiseptic cleanser checking her reality.

"Let's dump the bodies and go." He leaned in, said in her ear, "You're coming home with me. Or we'll go to the Guild compound."

"I'm jeopardizing my entire career."

"What's more important, your career or your son? Or your life?"

"Good point."

Groaning, the burly man flopped on the floor behind Liam. Liam wheeled around and whacked him again.

"Don't kill him!" Eva whispered harshly. "I don't want you implicated in my shitshow."

"I've got him under control." Liam spoke in a distinctive Southern twang in his efforts to disguise his voice. "Give me a zip tie."

Eva handed him a couple large plastic ties, and he secured the man's wrists. She retrieved a roll of duct tape, and then taped both men's ankles, covered their mouths, and turned their beanies backward. After a herculean effort and longer minutes than Eva wanted, they finagled the two Estenson minions into the trunk of the standard Estenson black sedan. She chucked their phones and a couple bottles of water into the trunk. Last thing she needed was a mafia kill on her resume.

Midnight came too soon, and the neighborhood quieted. Interior lights and TVs shut down, and once Liam followed her into her trashed home, Eva bolted the outside world out. Exhausted and sore, she slumped onto the hardwood floor and propped her back against the slashed arm of her sofa.

"Have a seat." Her gaze zinged around the room. "Somewhere. Sorry I'm such a sloppy housekeeper."

Liam shot her a quick grin. "You always were a stickler for everything in its place." He carried a wooden dining chair into the living room and plopped down onto it. "Do you want to tackle cleanup now or later?"

"You don't need to help."

"I'm here."

She tossed a slashed pillow onto the sofa, stuffing spilling out. "Later. I'm beat."

"What were they hunting?" He rubbed his wounded shoulder, his gaze penetrating her psyche, warming the wintry tundra of her dead heart.

"Me, I guess."

"Don't play me, Eva. Do you think they left listening devices? I can do a bug sweep tomorrow."

"Doubtful. They aren't too sophisticated. They prefer more tangible methods as you saw tonight. Let's hit it." Liam had a slow, searing way of gazing at her, as if he wanted to devour her. It always turned her on. Cheeks flaming, she gained her feet and held her hand out to him, withdrew upon realizing her mistake.

Liam seized her hand anyway. "Will you tell me everything when we get to... our destination? Your son's life may depend on it."

She tightened her fingers in his and stepped closer until her chest brushed his. Tingles zinged across her breasts and spread a swathe of heat up her neck. "I'll tell you what I can."

Liam growled, shifted closer, his breath fanning the hair covering her ear. "It's all or nothing." He breathed in deep, as if to memorize her.

God, she'd missed him. Missed everything about him, well, except his psychic ability and the fact he surrounded himself with psychics twenty-four seven. "I get it. I can't do this alone," she said. "I've tried to reason with Neal, tried to do everything he's wanted, to my detriment. But I cannot abide him taking our son and using him against me."

"Connor needs the Guild." Lips to her ear, Liam mashed his solid chest against her breasts, his thigh pressed to her leg. He kissed her forehead, released her hand, his lips warm, enticing, and so sensuous, she wanted to melt in his embrace. They'd always had such an intense relationship every minute of every day, always fresh and exhilarating. Until she'd ruined them.

Reality whapped her upside the head, and she jerked away from him. "I know nothing of the kind." The lie rolled off her tongue, steeled her softening heart.

CHAPTER EIGHT

By the time Liam and Eva arrived at the Guild compound in the western foothills of San Jose, the day had tapped Liam out mentally and physically. Dull pain radiated the length of his arm, draining the last of his energy.

Liam set Eva up in a guest suite with two bedrooms, every light blazing at her request. He crashed hours later suffering from swirling emotions with only a bathroom and narrow sitting room between them. Not the safe three thousand miles from the west coast to the east coast.

A torture fest set up shop in his wounded arm and forced Liam awake at seven in the morning. He downed his antibiotics and pain pills with half a bottle of tepid water. Not a sound emerged from Eva's room, and he fought the urge to gaze upon her, to take her into all his senses. He didn't know how he'd trudge through this case unscathed. He'd so easily lost himself in her when they'd dated in college, the only woman he ever envisioned marrying. Until she wasn't. And no one ever came close to replacing her.

A year post breakup, he'd half-assed played the field for a couple years, then after his Guardian suspension and the wench who'd betrayed him, he'd become a self-imposed monk. He wanted no complications, no emotional demands slurping the juice out of his soul tank. But his sixth sense warned him Eva would break through his barriers and refill the tank. Eva sparked new life in him, and she never left his mind. Not then, not now.

The door to his room pushed open. The woman in question stood on the threshold, tousled blonde hair framing her beautiful pale face. Last night, she'd packed an overnight bag and now wore an oversized T-shirt that hung to midthigh. Her shapely legs screamed for the sun. Exactly the way he remembered her back in their day.

"Hi." She ducked her head. "Thought I heard you awake."

"Sleep okay?" He leaned his back against the wood headboard.

"So-so." She tugged at the sleeves of her T-shirt. "Can I come in?"

He patted the edge of the bed, but she sat in the corner armchair. "Do you want me to check your bandage?"

He shook his head. "I'll hit the Guild infirmary later."

"I feel bad I got you shot."

Her blue eyes tried to suck him into her wicked ways, and he lowered his gaze. To her boobs. Eye bleach might help end his rising lust. Her petite feet, toenails painted blue, became a reluctant truce for his sight. Okay, he fabricated the wicked ways thing, but *dayam*, looking at her served up a plate of reluctant desire in his groin.

"My Guardian job's no different from being a cop. Same hazards."

"I know. I remember how stoked you were to join the Guardian ranks. We discussed the risks."

"You were on board with them." But she hadn't been on board with the Guild, nor okay with his ability to read her every emotion, or her inability to block him out at times. In the end, she just hadn't been okay with a psychic mind period. It terrified her. He terrified her.

"I still am okay with the risks. I'm a cop, and I'd be a fool to say otherwise."

"Thought you were studying forensics psychology. Wasn't that your master's scholarship?"

"I finished my master's." She shrugged. "My prospects changed after I had Connor, met Neal."

Her face shuttered and her body stiffened. That line of questioning dead-ended.

"Clean up and I'll get breakfast." He shoved aside the covers and swung his legs over the side of the bed.

"Breakfast works. I promised to tell you all. Then we need to work on our plan." She stood, stretched her legs, thrust out her breasts, stretching her spine. Her nipples peaked beneath her thin T-shirt. Liam licked his lips, fought the heat spiraling toward his groin, glad for the baggy sweatpants he'd found in his locker downstairs.

"Milk and sugar for your coffee."

"Yes." She smiled. "Muffins if you have any."

"Cranberry."

"You remembered." She plucked the band off her bedraggled ponytail and shook out her hair, and he wanted to twine his fingers in her golden locks. "Just like old times."

"Not exactly," he groused.

Eva stopped in the doorway, turned to him. "We've grown up. But the Liam and Eva we used to be are still here."

"It's not *Liam and Eva* any longer." Annoyance blackened his mood. Why did she have to kill the moment?

"I didn't mean that. You're so freaking literal." She flounced away, her hair spilling down her back in a golden wave, killing his resolve to maintain his emotional distance.

Grumbling a streak of curses, he padded barefoot down to the kitchen to scrounge up breakfast. The Guild compound's part-time chef was already preparing breakfast for the Guild's random overnight guests and residents.

Loaded tray in one hand, he erected his mental walls and reentered the suite. A fruity shampoo wafted off Eva's wet hair as she combed it in front of the bathroom vanity. Without a word, she excused herself and gave him privacy to take a quick bath to prevent his wound from getting wet. A very cold bath.

Coffee in hand, she waited for him to rejoin her in the sitting room before digging into breakfast.

"You didn't have to wait." He toweled off his hair, hating that he'd had to wear yesterday's pants again. At least he had a clean T-shirt and briefs in his locker. At least the Guild hadn't confiscated his locker.

"Gives us an opportunity to uncomfortably play with our food and avoid each other's gazes while I tell you my life's deep, dark secrets." She buttered her muffin, a smile flirting with the corners of her lush, pink-tinted lips. Lips he remembered pressed to his, pressed to every inch of his body. *Son of a bitch.*

"You haven't lost your brutal frankness." He tossed the towel into the bathtub and joined her at the small dinette to doctor up a strong cup of java.

Once they'd taken a few bites of fortifying breakfast, Eva eyed him critically. "I loved Neal once. He wasn't always an Estenson." She fingered air quotes. "Four years older than me, he was a young lawyer in a top Orlando law firm when I met him during grad school. He had nothing to do with his family until his brother died."

"Bro died and daddy called?" Liam chewed a piece of overcooked bacon, the crunch obliterating the sound of his voice.

"Unbeknownst to me, Neal lived in his brother's shadow. Daddy gave everything to Daniel Junior and the baby of the family, Crystal. He left Neal out of the family business, let him go off to do his own thing. Neal hid the truth from me and everyone else. I had no clue his family was a mafia family. They're small fry, so they hadn't hit my radar, not in Florida where they don't have a presence. He just faked his way through my life, biding his time to take over for his father. He won the lottery when Junior died. I swear the man has two personalities. I never saw the Estenson personality until Junior died."

"That's when you returned to San Jose?"

"Not immediately. He had cases to finalize. But he made a lot of trips here. After the first couple trips, he'd come home and harass me about what I'd been doing, where I'd gone, who I was with. It was weird. He'd never been a jealous man, but something snapped in him or his father got to him. He told me I had to act the Estenson wife from now on, demanded I quit my new job in the police department and be a stay-at-home mom like a good Estenson Stepford Wife."

Liam's spine arrowed straight against his chair, and he braced his frozen insides for something he wasn't sure he wanted to hear.

Eva fidgeted with the muffin wrapper on her plate, her short, blunt fingernails ragged and gnawed. "His personality became night and day. He'd known since we met that my career meant a lot to me, that I could never be a stay-at-home mom forever. Connor was in preschool, and I already had shorter work hours to be home for him after school. Neal just got worse and worse and demanded more and more." She flicked crumbs across her plate. "I won't go into the details."

Liam's heart skipped a beat. "Did he abuse you?" Searching for intangible answers, he hit a knot of her emotions, unable to ferret out a single thread.

Eva swirled her finger in muffin crumbs, shifted her eyes anywhere but on Liam. Her actions were answer enough.

A fiery rage, colored with empathy, forced him to pace around the table. He recoiled as his bad arm jostled in his sling. Stopping across the table from her, he asked, "How bad, Eva? Tell me."

"First mental manipulation, then verbal abuse. When I told him I wanted a divorce, that I couldn't be the Estenson wife he wanted, he hit me for the first time... choked me." Her hand fluttered up off her plate. "The rest doesn't matter." She scoured her hands over her face, as if to scrub away the past.

Liam gulped. He had to know where the train wrecked. "What else did he do to you?"

"Doesn't matter. It's water under the bridge."

He stomped over to her. "It matters. *You* matter."

"I shouldn't matter to you after all these years. Let's lay that tidbit on the table for the housekeepers to wipe up."

A growl climbed Liam's throat. He refused to goad her further and sever the tightrope they both balanced on. "Fine. Whatever. We concentrate on Connor and clearing you." He didn't know what he wanted from her. They'd said everything there was to say *ad nauseam* when they'd split. So why did he want to hash it out? *It's not like we're hooking up ever again. That ship sailed and sank.* The flotsam had also started a long chain of lousy relationships. Because no one ever compared to Eva, he admitted lamely to himself. *I'm doomed six ways to Sunday.*

"Anyway, we moved to San Jose. Neal had already bought his McMansion in the foothills. I stayed with him for a month in a guest room to ease Connor into our new life until I rented my place. The divorce proceeded and here we are."

"Why did he give in?"

"To show he cared for me, willing to give me what I wanted. He'll never stop trying to win me over." Her shoulders sagged in defeat.

"Do you have shared custody?"

"*Had.* Shared custody with me as primary custodian. We split weekends, and on Neal's weekends he kept Connor until Wednesdays. I picked Connor up from school on Wednesdays those weeks and kept him until Neal's next Friday."

"Would he hurt Connor?"

"No way. Neal loves Connor to pieces. But he may use Connor to hurt me. Since Connor's psychic talents are emerging fast, Neal wants to leverage them in his family's business."

Liam stood still. "Did he tell you his specific plans?"

Eva tidied up the table, using a napkin to dust crumbs onto her plate. "Not outright. He hinted, 'Connor could be useful and always have a job in the Estenson organization.'"

"He wants his boy to be a criminal?"

"Not necessarily." Eva kinked her neck left to right to stretch her shoulder muscles. Nothing had changed about her, and he wanted to lay his hands on her slender shoulders and massage away the emotional roller coaster creating havoc on her muscles. "They own legit businesses."

Liam scowled. "When someone wants to use a psychic, it's usually for illegitimate means. For instance, there's an underground, nasty bitch of a group called the Cabal recruiting Guild members and using them for illegal purposes to elevate their status with power, money, and everything in between."

Winding her damp hair into a ponytail, Eva strode into the bathroom. "I think our best chance is to infiltrate the family somehow."

Liam hovered behind her, and her narrowed, smoldering gaze raked over him in the mirror.

"You're not getting off the hook that easy. Why are they gunning for you?"

She braced her hands on the vanity. "Neal invited me to his house one night for a family dinner. He wanted to show Connor we still got along as a family. His father was there, as well as Crystal and a few other Estenson relatives including his father's half brother, Davide Estenson. He's high up, a big Italian guy."

"Did you know Davide or anyone else in the family?"

"Never met them until that night, except Crystal. Wished I never had."

She slid out from between him and the vanity. Liam followed her into the living room, the faithful puppy, the need to know everything about her smothering his good senses. He didn't want a stake in her or her son. It screwed with him. He'd been there, done that on a case that bit him in the ass. On the flip side, anything and everything she knew may help get Connor back. He just had to suck up the fact that her presence had blown the dust off the painful and mostly pleasurable memories he'd locked in a sealed coffin.

Eva perched on the loveseat, propped her elbows on her knees. "After dinner, the men skedaddled to Neal's mancave while the little ladies cleaned up." She smirked. "Daniel Estenson is old school. It's why he'd never leave his business to Crystal, and why he was gunning for Neal to return to the family after Junior bit it."

"But Crystal has a place in the family business?"

"When she's not screwing every hunk who crosses her path, she's the VP of HR, such as human resources exist in a mafia family and their dozens of business ventures, legit or not." Eva's eyes lit up as though a light bulb flicked on in her brain. "Oh my God." She snapped her fingers. "That's it." She vaulted up and paced the small room in quick, stilted steps, a big grin stretching to laugh lines fringing her sloe eyes. "Since the Guild has ousted you, and the Estensons don't know you from Adam, we'll plunk you on a path that crosses Crystal. She'd go gaga over you. You're totally her type." She wanded her hand in the air up and down his body. "Psychics draw her every time."

"Are you saying I should wine and dine her?" He rolled his shoulders and cracked his knuckles to sidetrack Eva's enthusiasm slipping under his mental wall.

"And whatever else she'll want."

"Hooking up?" Being a paid gigolo never hit his playbook.

Eva blushed. "It's a way in. You play her right, and she'll be on you like a vulture to roadkill."

"How do I fake it? She'll see right through me."

"Fake identity. Apply for a job."

"I refuse to do anything illegal." Liam knocked his fist into the wall. "There's got to be a better way."

Eva emitted a tiny, frustrated scream. "She's the ticket. She loves dating psychics and even wants to marry one."

"I'm not *marrying* her." He sneered.

"It won't get that far. But once you're in, you're family."

"That's what scares me. I might never get out." He banged his forehead against the wall, faced her again. "You don't even know where she is."

"I know where she hangs. I can almost guarantee Neal isn't constricting her from her daily fun times, her girlie routines."

"Are you going to tell me why they're after you, aside from Neal wanting back into your pants?"

She grimaced, and he suppressed a laugh at her comical expression. She never wore a grimace well. "At that dinner party, I was walking down the hallway, and the men had left the door of the mancave open. They were planning a major money-laundering and counterfeit scheme. They had diagrams, maps, notes spread all over the table. Later, the room was empty, and I snapped shots of everything they'd left exposed on the table, including notes about using psychics for mind reading and coercion purposes. I'd pocketed my phone and was scrutinizing the paperwork when Daniel Estenson came up behind me, threatened me. He said if his plan failed, I was dead."

"You still have the photos?"

"What do you think?"

The door thrust open and hit the interior wall with a bang, the knob denting the drywall. Liam lunged for his gun on the sideboard and pivoted around.

"Dude, I need to talk to you." Red-faced, his brother Ric filled the doorway, his eyes shooting flames at Eva. He clenched a file folder in his hand.

Relief skated down Liam's spine. "Can it wait?"

"Does it look like it can wait?" He waved the folder at Liam. "Hallway. Now. She stays here." Ric shot more death rays at Eva while she hung her gun holster over her shoulder.

Liam set his gun down and followed his seething brother into the hallway. Ric led Liam to the end of the wide corridor in front of a window. Morning sunlight painted white and gray stripes on the hardwood floor. The verdant Santa Cruz woods surrounding the compound's rear landscape appeared friendlier than Ric.

"What crawled up your ass overnight?" Liam rounded on his brother.

Ric opened the folder and showed him a blown-up photo of Connor Estenson's face. "Did you get a good gander at this photo?"

"Yeah, I got a copy on my phone."

"How 'bout this one?" Ric showed him another close-up of Connor. "Recognize those eyes? The set, the color, the eyebrows, the bridge of his nose?" Connor smiled up from a

Star Wars cake, six flickering candles stuck in the middle.

Every muscle and tendon in Liam's body froze, and a red shroud of angry heat encapsulated him. Why hadn't he noticed? "McAllister eyes," he croaked out.

"Remember, *Connor* is Mom's maiden name. Check the calendar on the wall behind Connor. The timing sync's up to the end of your time with her."

Liam gripped the photos so tight his fingers creased the heavy stock. "Connor's my son?"

CHAPTER NINE

The gate locked behind him, leaving his key card, wallet, phone, and tablet in the room. And his gun. *Bonehead moves.* He never left the compound without his arsenal. But the shock to his system refused to abate, and the only thing on his mind was Connor Estenson. *Screw that.* Connor McAllister. And his lying mother. Damn his stupid trust meter resetting him to square one with her. Liam stomped into the woods behind the compound, following the gravel path to a reflection spot. He held the photos in his hand, unable to stop gaping at the towheaded boy. Why hadn't he noticed the resemblance? *Because you were too lambasted at seeing Eva to allow anything else to sink into your lame brain.*

"Because he looks too much like Eva," he barked at a chittering squirrel before it scurried into the underbrush surrounding the trio of boulders he leaned against. The woods cocooned him and propelled his wild emotions back onto him in the stagnant trees. "You were too focused on Eva flipping your life upside down."

Rubbing at the creases denting his forehead, he continued hiking deeper into the woods blanketed in shades of amber, orange, and the red of autumn leaves among the evergreens.

He had a son. A six-year-old son. Every emotion he'd

ever experienced ebbed and flowed inside him.

He reached the *T* at the end of the path and sat on the stone bench surrounded by the cool, peaceful woods. Eyes misting, he studied the photo of Connor. For the longest time he sat, until a scuffling set of footsteps kicking the gravel approached. Eva's exotic spicy perfume assaulted his senses, stirred up his wrath before she hiked into view.

He waggled the photos at her. "Why didn't you tell me Connor's my son? Why the fuck did you keep him from me all these years?" He hurdled up and towered over her, hands clenched to keep them from shaking answers out of her. "He's my son. Admit it!"

Face closed off, Eva folded her arms over her chest and backed up a step as if to protect herself from his anguished rage. Sorrow washed off her, admitting her guilt, and he almost forced answers out of her. But he feared losing her trust, feared hearing too much.

"You remember the second to last time you came to Florida after we broke up, tried to talk me into a long-distance relationship, even though we already agreed to split? We hooked up; it was hot, intense, unexpected. Our last hurrah."

Cords twanged in his neck. "I remember."

"I was on antibiotics for a sinus infection, and they screw up birth control effectiveness. Nothing but *us* entered my mind. I simply forgot."

"Still doesn't explain shit." He clutched the photos to his chest, wishing to hold his son for the first time.

"We broke up because we had different lives to lead. You were starting your career with the Guild and opening your family business. I got accepted to grad school across the country. We agreed to go our separate ways." She paused, scrutinized his expression, but he kept his face neutral, his emotions in check. It took everything in him not to touch her and feel her lies, or truths. To feel her period.

"Go on," he said between gritted teeth.

"You would've ditched your family, your career, your entire life if I had told you I was pregnant."

"Damn straight. You know I reluctantly agreed to break up."

"I know this sounds clichéd, but I couldn't allow you to throw away your life because of my mistake. I couldn't hold you back from your dreams. You belonged here with your family, the Guild."

"That wasn't for *you* to decide." He waved the photos in front of her again, his arms flailing to redirect his toxic energy.

"You told me several times you didn't want kids," she blasted back. "At least not until you were settled and in your thirties."

He asked for it, and she bashed him with the truth. "Now you're just throwing my words into my face to make your excuses look better. Screw you, Eva. You just couldn't handle me being psychic, or my family or the Guild. We scared you."

"Damn straight you did!" She stamped her foot in the gravel, a few stones crashing into the woods. "Do you know how horrible it is to walk into a room where everyone reads my every thought, my every emotion? Even you! You couldn't stop reading me. Every time you touched me, every time we had sex, you dropped your walls. My body was a freaking fishbowl. I couldn't deal. Nothing scared me more. You know how much I loved you touching me, how intense we were together. Well, part of me hated it. It tore me up inside. Surely, I wasn't the only woman you dated who felt different. You knew all this. I never hid my feelings. You finally, *finally* agreed splitting up was the right thing for us on your last trip to Florida. You agreed you needed to handle your abilities better."

Liam hung his head and kicked a pinecone after the pebbles into the woods. Everything she said was true. Nothing had scared her more than exposing her vulnerabilities, and she couldn't hide them from him.

Her hand alighted on his arm, and he flinched. "Don't touch me if you can't handle it."

She curled her slender fingers around his forearm. "Liam. I did none of this to deliberately hurt you. My parents moved to Florida to help me with the baby. They agreed I was doing the right thing, even though they both liked you. I was too hormonal to see any different. Then I met Neal after Connor was born. My life just snowballed into a new reality. It became easier when you weren't there every day. I could lock and unlock our time together whenever I needed. It sounds like a bunch of excuses, but I don't know what else to say. It's the truth. I didn't want to lock you down into a life you didn't want. I wouldn't be that woman and have you resent me for it later."

"You deprived me of my son. I don't know if I can forgive you for that."

"I don't expect you to. For what it's worth, I tried to reach out to you a million times during my pregnancy and the first year after he was born. I wrote you emails I never sent. I still have them all. Remember I even called you a dozen times. You wouldn't take my calls, and I couldn't leave that newsflash in a voicemail. Time flew by, and it became harder to reach out to you. My mother convinced me to let it go, that no good would come of you relocating to Florida and living through your massive resentment. She convinced me your avoidance was telling. I never thought I'd return to San Jose, not since they came to be my support system."

"But you left them." Scorn dripped from his sneer.

"They're buying a house here for me and Connor where they can spend half the year."

"Do they know about Neal and his abuse, the mafia ties?"

She swished dried leaves and pine needles with the toes of her sneakers. Birds chirped and squirrels chittered in their bright and perfect world. "They know about his mafia ties. I had to tell them something about the divorce. But you're the only one I've told about the abuse. My father would kill him."

"Let him," Liam grumbled and turned away from her, the indiscriminate woods a more palpable sight. He recalled the phone calls he'd wanted to take from her and forced himself to reject. Just the sound of her voice set him back ten steps for every step he took forward in recovery.

Liam fought her touch on his arm, strengthened his internal doors on her surging emotions. He couldn't afford another hit to his system. "Did you ever plan to tell me, especially now since you're living in San Jose?"

She squeezed his arm. "Look at me, Liam. I don't want to talk to your back."

Face stoic, he turned to her, shook off her hand, but she gloved his fist in her hand.

"It's okay. You can read my emotions."

"Bad idea." He flexed his fingers in her grip, knocking her hand off his. "Answer my question."

"Yes. I encouraged Neal to return to the family homestead so I could get back here. Connor has only known Neal as his father, and I never wanted to confuse him. I know I'm in over my head with Connor and his psychic gifts. I've known for a couple of years he needs his father. He needs *you*. But I've had to tread on eggshells. Neal doesn't know you're Connor's father. He never saw the birth certificate."

"You named me his father?"

"I used your old nickname and your mother's maiden name."

Lee Connor. "Why didn't you come to me the minute you hit California?"

"Because Neal was putting me through the wringer. I feared for you."

"All the more reason." He marched down the trail toward the back gate, the frolicking squirrels scattering in his wake. Birds took flight as if he'd shot at them. "And why didn't you tell me last night? What were you waiting for?"

"I couldn't get the words out from my shock at seeing you." She rushed after him. "Where are you going?"

"I'm making plans to get *my* son"—he beat his chest— "back from that asshole." At the gate, he signaled to a perimeter guard to let them in the compound yard. "I'm going after my son. Not for you, but for me."

"I expect no less. I'm sorry, Liam. I never meant to keep him from you. The guilt has eaten me alive every day. I hate myself for it, and I'll never forgive myself." Eva sniffed. "Can we agree to get Connor back, then we'll deal with the rest later? I swear I'll never keep him from you again."

"Whatever, Eva," Liam grumbled. A numbness had taken over his body and brain. It wasn't even noon, and he was as fried as if he'd spent the day drowning in other people's emotions.

Jake and Ric met him inside the main building lobby, commiseration written across their expressions. When they spied Eva, fury and loathing wiped the commiseration away and the three McAllister brothers became an epic storm circling her.

"Is it true?" Jake growled out. Liam mashed his lips together and wobbled his head.

Eva gave them the hand. "I don't need your 'tude right now. I just need to get my son—our son—back. Then we can deal with the consequences. This is between me and

Liam."

"*Your son*"—Jake inclined toward her—"will need all three of us for training. He has my mental telepathy, Ric's clairvoyance, and Liam's empathic abilities. Did it ever occur to you that he inherited a psychic talent from each of us?" Jake swished his finger in a circle to encompass his brothers. "A psychic prodigy we haven't seen in generations."

Groaning, Liam sank his fingers in his hair and dragged them across his scalp. It was all too much to bear. It hadn't sunk in that he was a father. He wasn't sure it ever would, at least until he laid eyes on his boy. Until then, they had to tread on feathers on the most crucial case of his life.

"Right now, Eva needs to tell me where I can get on Crystal Estenson's radar," Liam said. "I'm infiltrating the Estenson family." He slipped his phone out of his pocket and studied Connor's photo until he etched his son's face on his brain.

CHAPTER TEN

Liam dressed casually for an evening at Crystal Estenson's favorite weekend haunt, the Lucky Shamrock, an Estenson-owned bar.

After the confrontation with Eva that morning, they'd spent their research time in a stilted, icy investigative mode. Keeping his and Eva's emotions in check exhausted Liam. So many times, he'd wanted to touch her, to force her to speak words he swore he didn't want to hear. They'd scoured and examined every stick of information Eva knew about Crystal Estenson. The Estensons kept a low public profile, which resulted in sparse internet information. But he had enough for his "date."

He tugged on a pair of slim jeans and a gray striped pullover sweater he found in the rear of his closet. At least his guardian aunt had decent taste and he didn't have to wear a red Rudolph the Reindeer sweater. Crystal was into men who wore sweaters and liked her men casual. *Just kill me now.*

Crystal also loved her men psychic with all their walls down, the worst part of the plan. Liam needed to keep his mind as clean as a hospital operating room, his blocks impenetrable, and hope her telepathy didn't include sneaking through mental walls. Until he met her, he wasn't sure how to play it. He sure as hell didn't want her reading his every thought. His mind portrayed a treacherous place in his current state.

A son. He had a son.

With the one woman he'd once believed he'd have a family with someday. The woman who had set the bar for every other woman in his life.

Not like this, though. Not after he'd given that dream up years ago. She'd rocked his foundation to the core and changed his entire life that day.

He spritzed on Crystal's favorite men's cologne, woodsy and musky, mixed with a hint of black pepper. He hacked out the clogging gag in his throat. That Eva knew Crystal so well hurt his gag reflex. Apparently, Crystal had downloaded a book upon Eva during a girls' night out Neal had forced Eva to attend.

After delivering the detestable cologne, Ric had taken Eva to pick up her vehicle and to sweep it and her home for GPS, audio, and video bugs. They owned an investigations and securities company and used the latest technology on the market. Why not put their expertise to use? Ric planned to install surveillance for her protection and to change her locks. She'd also picked up a new cell in order to use her old one just for Neal. Liam wanted to do it all, but the less time he spent with Eva in public, the better for their infiltration into the Estenson family. It also minimized the reeling hit to his heart.

Man, he wanted to hear his son's voice for the first time, to know he was okay. He'd already missed the first six years of Connor's life, and he didn't want to miss another second. *Freaking Eva Midnight, a beautiful curse on his life.* At least she'd done one thing right in giving their boy a family name.

He dry scrubbed his hands over his face for the umpteenth time. His cell blaring Ric's drum solo tore his mind off the unimaginable.

"Yo, dude, you ready?" Ric asked.

"As I'll ever be."

"Good thing you don't have a Guild tattoo."

"You think I'd rip off my clothes on the first date with a mob daughter?" Not all the Guardians and Guild members felt the need to deface their bodies with the Celtic logo tattoo. "You secure Eva's place?"

"Yeah. She's kosher. Man, it sucks to be you right now."

"No shit, Sherlock."

"Do you think this Crystal chick is your ticket in?"

"We'll find out tonight, if she shows."

"Don't forget your Riley phone and ID."

Liam patted his pockets to ensure he had his backup phone and wallet, feeling naked without his perpetual tablet. Guardians always had a fake ID for their cases. He hadn't needed one in a long time. "Did you give Niles and MacKenzie the 411 about the new sitch?"

"Yeah. Commiserations and congrats all around."

"Did they suggest any changes in the plan?"

"None. They agree if this works, it's your best shot into the Estenson family. According to Eva, Crystal always brings her serious boy toys to family functions."

"No way Neal would expose Connor to strangers if he's trying to hide the boy."

"They're a tight-knit family. Eva believes Neal's at the secure family compound in the ritzy Los Altos hills. She's never been there. Crystal's only brought one or two serious boyfriends to the estate. An Estenson man killed the last one after he betrayed her in a bad deal."

"Thanks for the vote."

"Don't betray the wench."

"Sherlock, you're so full of stupid-ass wisdom today."

"I'm worried." Ric's chipper voice sobered.

"And I'm agonizing over my son's safety."

"That's a total get. Be safe, bro. Call for backup if you need. I'll be hanging in a sports bar across the street from the Lucky Shamrock."

Liam plugged his phone on the charger to leave behind. One last scowl at himself in the mirror above his dresser and he slogged out to the sedate sedan he'd borrowed from the Guardian fleet set up through their dummy corporation. Nothing was traceable to Liam or the Guild.

By the time he arrived at the bustling Irish pub and parked after circling the wagons a few minutes, his mood hadn't brightened. Maybe he'd hook up with Crystal Estenson. Shake up his normal routine, his morals against one-night stands. Gigolo didn't sound too bad in his current frame of mind. Eva warned him to go slow, be a gentleman, and hard to get, let Crystal do the pursuing. The scratchy sweater was already driving him nuts and leaving him wanting to soak in the ocean to ease the itch across his back. A striptease for Crystal might kill two birds.

A live band played in a corner of the bar. Screeching bagpipes chased the drums and guitar riffs. The soulful highland music cut across his dire thoughts and settled him down. He just might like his assignment tonight. The Irish pub evoked a blast to the past of Irish and Scottish pubs. Dark, cozy, and energetic.

Forcing a smile, he drilled into the atmosphere one footstep at a time. He took a perch on a stool at the long, scarred bar, ordered an ale, and perused the crowded room for a tall woman with dark chestnut, board-straight hair. From the picture Eva had shown him of Crystal, she was hot in a prowling, panther way. He hoped she didn't eat him alive. Been there, done that.

Moving around the floor of the bar searching for her made it too obvious, and he waited on his padded stool. According to Eva, Crystal *always* found her prey. An hour later, he nursed his second beer, his thoughts buried in the band. A touch alighted on his shoulder, a skim of fingernails across his neck. Goosebumps followed her nail tips.

"You're new here," the sultry, low voice said in his ear.

He swiveled his chair, and his eyes landed on one of the most beautiful women he'd ever had the privilege of meeting. The eagle had landed. The photo of Crystal hadn't done her half a justice. He gave her his best puppy-dog eyes as he slurped up her dark mantle flowing over her shoulders. Her glistening hair flanked her voluptuous breasts, which overflowed the top of her revealing, midriff-bare blouse. She wore second-skin black leggings, leaving nothing to the imagination, and her best fuck-me spike heels shot her five-ten height close to his six-three.

"You look like you could use a tall drink... of me. Play your cards right, and I might let you take a sip."

He said in her ear, "You're playing with fire. Sure you want to get burned?"

She jiggled against his bad arm, arcing pain down to his wrist. If he didn't play *his* cards right, he'd be in a world of hurt. The deafening music dissipated, and the band declared an intermission. Crowd noise increased as people began to talk.

"I love a challenge," she said. "I'm Crystal Estenson."

He held out his hand, which she ignored to his mental relief. Bad enough she'd plastered her sinful body against him. "Liam Riley." She double-air kissed his cheeks, and her hands landed on his shoulders.

"Well, Liam Riley, buy a girl a drink, will ya?" She signaled to the man sitting on the barstool next to Liam. He vacated the stool, and she tugged it closer and sat, back straight and boobs on display.

Liam's gaze followed her movements. Deliberate and focused, he radiated his thoughts outward, shuttering everything else but Crystal Estenson in his mind.

"I've never seen you here before." Crystal moved close, their shoulders touching, her long silky hair teasing the back of his hand resting on his thigh. Her exotic floral scent gloved him in a cocoon, seeped into his senses, and flirted with his lust.

"First time. Recent Bay Area transplant."

"Well, I'm betting it won't be your last." Her sultry voice skated down his spine, and he suppressed a shiver.

In his best sexy drawl, he said, "If *you* hang here, I can guarantee it won't be my last."

She giggled like a schoolgirl. Liam fought down a thread of disgust, smothered it with a phony hum of pleasure.

Crystal's hand lay on her thigh, her long, pointy fingernails painted black. Liam gloved his hand over hers. The connection was instant, electrifying, and intense. Her excitement and desire barreled into him, butted against his disgust. He'd hooked her.

"I was hoping to find more of my kind to hang with," he said for her ears only. "Am I wrong about you?"

Confusion furled her brow for a moment. He smoothed his hand up her toned, bare upper arm. Intense yearning accompanied his touch, and her chocolate eyes widened, turned darker, then hooded. Her nipples pebbled her thin blouse, and he grazed his thumb across her left one, feeling it harden into a bullet.

"What are you?" She exhaled a tiny gasp. Her breasts heaved in and out.

"You haven't figured it out yet?" He chuckled.

"Empath?" She clamped his hand between hers and placed their sandwiched hands on her thigh again. "I've wanted to meet a true empath forever and a day. Haven't seen one with dual powers like yours."

"How do you know I have dual powers?" Liam beamed,

shutting his mind down to her mental intrusion and barrel of emotions.

Crystal pouted. "Oh, love, don't do that. Don't close me out. I feel your mind touch mine, the push and pull."

"Because you're a mind reader." Liam's eyebrows peaked in a questioning slant.

Crystal glanced down the hallway leading to the restrooms. "Let's talk in the owner's lounge. It's quieter, more private."

"Are you the owner?"

"Family-owned." She released his hand and hopped off the barstool. "No one'll bother us."

Game, set, matched. "Maybe it's not such a good idea. Let's save it for another time. I just want to enjoy the ambience."

"I just want to talk. You said you wanted to find others like you. Well, your search is over."

A slow squeal of bagpipes built into a crescendo, and the drummer kicked his bass drums into a staccato of sound that eclipsed the voices in the bar.

Crystal signaled to a barman. He set a bottle of champagne and two flutes on a tray. She turned to Liam still sitting on the barstool, and before he knew what was happening, her mouth met his. She kissed him, her tongue darting past his lips, teasing his tongue with pulsating flickers. Not one other part of her touched him, but her passion speared a path to his groin. She tangoed her tongue around his and deepened the kiss. As abrupt as she'd attacked him—for he could think of no other word to describe her jabbing tongue—she broke the kiss. She skimmed the crotch of his jeans, applied light pressure on his erection. "We'll just talk. If you want more, I can arrange it."

"Do you make a habit of hitting on strange men right out the gate?" He shouted in her ear to be heard over the spiraling music. He opened his mind to her emotional response.

"No." She shook her head.

The truth of her response streamed inside him, toting with it a ration of fear and more excitement than the moment warranted. What did she fear?

Liam hopped off the barstool and let her lead him to the rear of the bar. Two overstuffed sofas, chairs, a large flat screen, and mini bar filled the cozy lounge. Flickering fake candles in wall sconces provided an atmosphere for seduction.

Crystal locked the door and gestured for him to sit on a sofa. He took the bottle and glasses from her and poured the champagne.

She accepted the bubbly liquid and held up her glass. "Let's toast our awakening."

Liam clinked his glass to hers, the dull click of cheap bar glassware, and said, "To the first of many nights to unravel."

"Amen to that." She downed half her champagne. The pink tip of her tongue snaked out and licked a drop of liquid off her bottom lip. "Now tell me who you really are, *Liam Riley*."

CHAPTER ELEVEN

Body numb, Eva sagged into a chair in her living room. A couple of springs drove through the lumpy padding on the garage-sale chair, making it a soon-to-be dumpster chair. After cleaning up the mess the Estenson minions created in their scare tactics, she'd spent her time into dawn engaged in online research. Every light still blazed inside her small home as the sky lightened and slanted slits of gloom through the blinds.

Ric McAllister had scanned every room for audio and video bugs the night before, found nothing, then planted his own surveillance equipment inside and outside her condo. Not for the first time did she wonder how Liam made out with Crystal, if Crystal even showed up at her weekend wheelhouse. Had they literally "made out?" Spent the night together? Or maybe Neal convinced her to remain scarce during his nefarious scheme. A thread of unnamed emotions tied her intestines into knots.

Dying for a stronger kicker in her coffee, she sipped the cooling liquid fuel. Yet, she refused stronger, not that she drank alcohol in the mornings. She needed to keep her wits about her, especially after several hours scouring the secure police databases and internet on Estenson business and the judge who'd signed the custody order. Nothing popped out to implicate Judge Alfred Martinelli on an under-the-table Estenson payroll. She'd reviewed a dozen past cases for any hint he'd rendered the wrong decision by duress or a payoff. So far nothing. Yet. Her witch hunt still had unopened doors.

Her old cell phone rang, and she seized it off the coffee table, clinking her half-empty mug on the glass top. Unknown caller.

"Hello," she said warily.

"Mommy! It's me."

She bolted upright. "Oh, baby. How are you?"

"I miss you. When are you coming to the new house?"

A sprinkle of snowflakes seemed to drift down upon her scalp. "I miss you too. Honey, why are you whispering? Is Daddy there?"

"Daddy doesn't know I'm calling you." He spoke so low she had a tough time hearing him.

Ideas and thoughts revolved in her mind. Playing it cool, she asked, "Give me a hint about the new house. Are there lots of trees? Are you near water?"

"I can't tell you. Daddy will catch me on the phone. I'm not s'pposed to go into his office."

"Okay." The snowflakes turned stinging. "Don't get caught. I'll be with you soon, and then you can tell me about your adventures."

"Mommy." His voice dropped so low again, she knew something was wrong. "My head hurts, and Daddy won't give me medicine to make it feel better."

Eva shoved off the sofa, clenching the phone so tight it creaked. With extreme effort, she modulated a serene pitch. "Why does your head hurt?"

"We've been playing games, you know, those special tricks I can do with my mind."

She sank to her knees, fighting a slew of tangled emotions. "Are you doing a lot of them?"

"Yes."

"All day long?"

"Uh-huh."

"When did your head start hurting?"

Connor took a moment to process her question. "After lunch yesterday."

"Connor, you need to tell me where you are if you know. I can bring you medicine, but you can't tell Daddy we talked, okay?"

"I won't because he'll get mad at me for going into his office." He paused, and Eva pictured him chewing on his bottom lip. "I don't know where we are."

"Where is your father now?"

"He's in a meeting with some other men in the outside office. Granddad is there. They think I'm still in bed."

"What does it look like outside?"

"It's a big house on a hill. We had a fire in the firepit, and we lit big candles all around the yard."

The Estenson Los Altos compound? "Is there a swimming pool?"

"No, but Auntie Crystal took me to the beach yesterday before she went home. It quieted my head and made my headache go away. She let me go into the waves up to my ankles. We saw a seal! And dolphins!"

"How long did it take you to drive to the beach?"

"We hopped down the stairs. A lot of stairs." He tittered. "Aunt Crystal got tired halfway, and we had to sit and rest."

"Okay. Don't tell Daddy you told me. I'll keep it a secret."

"Mommy, I gotta go. I hear footsteps."

"Be careful and hide if you need to. I love you, baby."

A sob strangled his voice. "I don't wanna play Daddy's games. My head really hurts."

A scuffle ensued in Connor's background, and the phone clicked off.

Sobs rolled up her chest. For a moment, she thought she'd die right there on the floor. Her phone rang again, and she blearily eyed the display. Ric McAllister. She clicked speakerphone on.

"I heard every word," he said.

"What's he doing to my son?" she croaked out.

"I'm not sugarcoating this, girl," Ric said. "Neal is forcing Connor to use his psychic powers too fast and too often without giving him a break. He could be forcing him to use all three of his powers at once. Any psychic who uses his powers repeatedly without rest pays the price. Headaches are one form of currency, depletion another."

Eva bolted for the bathroom and barely made it to the porcelain throne. Suffering a final dry heave, she sat on the tile floor, her back against the tub. She wiped the back of her hand across her mouth. "Sorry," she blubbered into the phone, wishing for the millionth time that Ric hadn't filled her condo and phone with bugs. At least her bathroom was a safe zone.

"No need to apologize." Commiseration lay heavy in Ric's usual upbeat tone.

"What will happen to Connor if Neal keeps up this pace?" The implications of Neal's torture of her son wrecked another piece of her soul.

"I'm coming over there."

"No. Just tell me." She combed loose strands of hair off her face, fighting the craving to bury her fingers in Neal's eye sockets.

"We don't know Connor's capabilities, not since he has all three McAllister abilities. But it's too soon, too much even with one psychic talent, and at his age. It'll get worse if they continue at this pace."

Eva gritted her teeth and pushed off the floor, wobbled a moment on unsteady legs. "How bad?"

"A young psychic's mind can fracture under too much

duress. He can get lost in his own mind."

I will end Neal. Eva doubled over again, hugged the doorframe. "Permanently?"

"Yes." Ric's voice came out on a huff. "Let's focus on getting him back. Did you find anything on your search? Anything about Martinelli?"

"Nothing concrete." Eva couldn't fault Ric for trying to sidetrack her. "Connor has your future clairvoyance ability. He's not as good as you."

"He's young still."

"When did you have your first clairvoyant event? What did you see?"

Ric laughed. "Connor's age. I saw a man who resembled my father attack my mother in her bed."

Eva giggled. "Did you rush into the room to save her?"

"I gathered my brothers. Bats in hand, we stormed the bedroom, caught them in the act. My dad was attacking her all right. I can't ever unsee that."

"I bet they freaked." The icemaker groaned and a load of ice clunked into the freezer bin, reminding Eva of time not spinning backward.

"They did. Told us again never to come into the bedroom without knocking first." Ric paused. "When and what was Connor's first episode?"

"He was four."

Ric gasped. "That's young."

"He saw me dressed in my street uniform arresting a drug dealer who tried to kill me."

"Did it happen as he described?"

"To the *T*." She sat on her heels to pacify her nausea. "Thanks for distracting me. I'm fine now." Nothing inside her believed her words. "Can you send the phone recording to my cell? I'm going for a run to clear my head before I return to my research." Something about her research niggled in her brain. She'd barely made a dent in the judge's case files, but certain similarities tied some together, and she wanted to explore further. She patted her shoulder harness. "Have my gun."

"Sure thing. Stay safe. I'll keep monitoring the equipment." Ric hung up.

Eva returned to her computer, rethought her next step, and shut it down. Time to pay Judge Martinelli a visit. From a concerned mother. If the PD fired her, so be it. At least she'd get answers, whether good or bad.

The drive along Highway 280 and into the foothills shot her nerves to the moon and back. A long hot summer had browned the grass on the hillsides between well-watered estates of forest-green lawns and trees of every kind, some evergreen, some yellowing for the fall. An ebb and flow of desolation and hope.

Martinelli lived too close to the Estenson estate in the Los Altos hills. Those few case files she'd skimmed coalesced into one big fat paid-off judge. Wispy, white clouds danced around the dawning yellow orb breaking across the eastern sky, adding to the flickering shadows of the tree-lined streets. She turned left onto the long cul-de-sac leading to the Martinelli house, the largest house on an acre-sized lot. The behemoth mansions evoked what you'd expect for a California judge's home. The bonus of a decorative iron fence with a controlled gate surrounded the estate.

Eva swore under her breath. She made the curved turn in the cul-de-sac and parked a few hundred yards down the street. Hightailing it back to the Martinelli property on foot, she skirted the perimeter fence and ran its length in the neighbor's front yard, hiding behind boulders, bushes, and a jungle of privacy evergreens. A small escape gate between the yards caught her attention. Unnamed bushes and flowering mandevilla vines on both sides of the fence obscured the old, unused gate from the casual eye.

Crunching on dried yellow leaves and spent rusty mandevilla blooms, she thrust vines aside to locate the lock. She used her multipurpose pocketknife to cut through the vines securing the gate to the fence and picked the decrepit lock. Slipping through the creaking, rusty gate, she realized how the Sunday hills were eerily quiet compared to the 'burbs. Not a dog barked, not a bird chirped in the early morning hour, no lawnmowers or blowers or neighbors bickering, or kids playing. How nice it must be to live in such quiet seclusion at times, if you were into the country lifestyle. Nope. Eva belonged to the hustle and bustle of the noisy, engulfing city.

The burgeoning sun lit up the red-tiled roof, a bloodred wash evoking an eerie sense of doom. She skirted the front of the Spanish-style mansion. Mindful of surveillance cameras, she remained visible, without flashing her badge. No need to add additional charges to her breaking and entering rap sheet. Dark wood double doors marked the front of the house centered at the curve of the circular driveway, flanked by expansive lawns and flower gardens to the right. A mini orchard of fruit trees surrounded by large oleander bushes hemmed in the other side of the house. Amber and crimson leaves still clung to life on the tree branches, resembling the spindly hope clinging to Eva.

When she reached for the doorbell, she noticed the door ajar. She toed it open farther. Ceramic shards speckled the gleaming Mexican tile entryway. A console table lay on its side, mail and magazines strewn onto the large foyer's floor. The sensation of snakes slithering across her shoulders almost sent her retreating. She fought the impulse and drew her gun, pulled her badge from under her shirt, and located it front and center on the lanyard around her neck.

"Police!" she shouted. "Is everything all right here?"

No response. No sound, nothing.

"If anyone's here, show yourself. If you're hurt or in trouble, call out." The stillness sent that insidious snake wiggling down her spine.

Taking cautious footsteps, she followed a trail of broken ceramic, scattered silk flowers parading autumn colors, and strewn pieces of small furniture down a wide hallway to the back of the house. The comfortable couch, chairs, a bar and large flat screen had been left undisturbed in the family room.

"Police. Is anyone home?" Shifting through the expansive, polished marble kitchen and untouched dining nook, she entered another narrower hallway leading to a bathroom, pantry, laundry room, and a guest bedroom suite. All empty. The final door on the right was closed, and the snake zigzagged across her back.

Ear to the door, she listened for sounds inside. Not even a whisper. She turned the handle, gun in strike position, and toed the door open.

An eerier silence enveloped the judge's home office. The burgundy, tall-backed desk chair faced a large picture window overlooking the lush gardens. The last roses of the season flourished in reds, corals, and pinks, and a fall array of chrysanthemums dotted the garden landscape, surrounding a small waterfall and gazebo. A garden worthy of losing oneself within. For the last time.

Ice cubes joined the snake, and Eva shivered as she slunk to the chair, pivoting around to clear the corners of the room. She skirted the massive hardwood desk, aiming her gun at the chair, and kicked it to swivel it around.

Judge Martinelli slumped forward, clothed in a pair of faded jeans and a gray polo shirt. A small, ragged bullet hole, dead center in his pale forehead, dripped dried blood down his nose, splotches of rusty red staining his shirt, matching the lethal wash of red on the roof.

CHAPTER TWELVE

Eva called in the homicide to the Los Altos police and waited, wracking her brain for a legit excuse to visit the distinguished judge on a Sunday morning. Only chaos came to mind, and she called her boss, fighting the urge to dial Liam. Liam might still be with Crystal. The idea turned Eva's stomach green and slushy.

Birdsong in the front gardens accompanied her punch to the security unit in the entryway to open the iron gates for the cops. The chirps and trills mollified her as she gave Alex the 411. His growling reprimand flew in one ear and off into the blue yonder with the birds, flapping madly to escape her travesty.

"Neal is hurting my boy. Ask your fiancée how badly he can hurt Connor if he goes overboard. Ric McAllister didn't hold back," Eva almost shouted into the phone. Sirens killed the Sunday morning hush, and first responder vehicles streamed up the driveway. Since Los Altos was a small community, they worked with the county sheriff's office, and both agencies converged on the estate.

"Visiting a judge's house, on your own, is career suicide," Alex scolded.

"My entire life is in suicide mode. Just tell me what to do."

"You can't hide from this. The investigators will pull

your name from Martinelli's case log and know why you're there."

"But he's a criminal judge handing out custody orders."

"He was the judge on call for the emergency order."

"So, I go with the truth."

"Don't tip your hand. Say only that you wanted to plead your case because your ex got the order behind your back and it's all fabricated."

"That's the truth."

"I know."

"They'll want to question Neal."

"Good. It might lure him out of hiding." Smug satisfaction edged Alex's voice.

"Or drive him deeper."

"No choice here, Eva. You screwed up."

"It's not like I offed the man," she said between gritted teeth. She held up her badge for the first responders rushing the porch. "Anything else? I need to go."

"Have them call me if they need a background check."

Eva kept her badge visible and headed into the lion's den. She was screwed ten ways to next Sunday. How much worse could her life get?

After a grueling hour of questions, the detectives reached the end. She admitted she'd crept in through the old gate because she didn't think the judge would let her through the main gate. Fortunately, the bullet hole in Martinelli's head didn't match her firearm.

"Detective Midnight, do you have any idea who killed Judge Martinelli?" the lead detective asked her almost as an afterthought.

"I don't know. I'm new to San Jose, and I've never met the man."

"Your ex-husband is from a known crime family. Do you think he or his family may have done this?"

Why sure, officer. Kudos to you for the obvious. "My ex-husband got what he wanted. Why kill the judge now?" Scoring points might help her... or not.

"Why did you divorce Mr. Estenson?"

"I found out who he was," she replied. "The Estensons are nothing in Florida. Neal had no ties to his family there, and I didn't know who they were. Plus, cops and mafia don't mix."

"At least you're on the right side of the law. You're free to go. Don't leave town anytime soon."

"Am I a suspect?" She accepted her badge from him, noting the absence of her gun.

Ignoring her rhetorical question, he replied, "We need to run tests on your weapon."

She'd already given the detective Neal's old phone number, the only number she had for him, and his last known address. Let them figure out how to locate the asshole. Maybe Alex hit the nail on the head, and they might unwittingly help Eva find her son.

Before her wheels exited the cul-de-sac, she received her expected text from Liam to meet him at a Guild safe house. He texted her the address not too far from her place. They'd already agreed to steer clear of her condo, his house, or the Guild compound to keep his anonymity and a degree of separation between their lives.

After a gut-wrenching drive back to San Jose, something unwound in her chest when Liam opened the door. He stepped aside to let her in the small, updated older home. Thick forearms, sculpted abdomen, and cut shoulders set off internal bells she didn't remember she possessed. His familiar face spread embers through her anxiety, loosening knots in her shoulder muscles.

"Glad to see your morning's shitstorm didn't harm you." Liam led her into the cozy kitchen where he had spread linguica sausage, hash browns, English muffins, and a scrumptious-looking smoothie concoction on the bar counter. All her favorites. She noticed his tablet turned on to a recipe site and hid a smile.

"I'm starving." She bestowed a radiant smile on him. "Thank you." She loaded up a plain white restaurant plate. "You always knew how to make breakfast for me. All you McAllister boys were into big breakfasts."

"My mother always said no sense in starting your day without breakfast to roll you through the clock."

"I wished I'd known your mother." Eva took a gulp of the mixed fruit and yogurt smoothie and her taste buds exploded. Liam's parents had died back East in a car accident when he and his brothers were in their early teens. The boys had transferred to California to live with his father's brother, aunt, and cousins.

"She would've liked the old you."

"Not the new me?" She needed Liam on her side, needed to avoid his antagonism. Bad enough she hated herself for everything that'd happened.

"I don't even know the new you." He clanged his coffee mug onto the counter, sloshing hot coffee onto the quartz.

Ignoring his justified attitude, she asked, "Did Alex happen to call?"

Liam sat on a barstool next to her, spinning his half-empty mug in the puddle of coffee. As he watched her inhale a few bites of food, the severity of his expression faded. "He called."

"I need to talk to that boss man of mine." She swallowed roughly, unclear where the lines separated her work and personal life. *Hell, what lines?* Everything had blurred.

"He's only looking out for you."

"By feeding you a blow-by-blow of an active criminal investigation?" She snorted. "He's compromising his own job."

"Because he cares. He's a good man, one of the Guild's

own by his association to a powerful psychic. He's the Guild liaison to the police."

"I know who Juliana is. You don't have to keep reminding me of all the psychic and Guild players in my life." She washed a bite of muffin down with her coffee.

"You're connected to us for life." Liam wiped a skosh of apricot jam off the side of her mouth. He licked his finger and wiped it on his jeans.

The tingles he left behind had nothing to do with his empathic skills, and everything to do with his touch. A touch she had craved too many times and for so long. No denying she had missed him. She would've married him if their paths hadn't led them in such disparate directions. Both had been too stubborn to give up their dreams for love. How young and stupid they'd been. No, not stupid. Practical. It's what her father always said, "You can't build a career on love. Once you get settled, love will come."

"Again, no need for the schooling." Eva took a last sip of her cooled coffee and pushed her mug and plate aside. "Get anywhere with Crystal?" *Did you hook up? Do the nasty?* She thumped her palm on her head to quiet the voices.

"I want to know about the judge first. Why did you go over there?"

They'd always played this, "you first, no, *you* first" game. Not trying to best each other on who had the better story or news, but they legit always wanted to hear what the other had to share out of respect.

Eva picked at her ragged cuticles. "It's not good. I'm surprised I'm even able to hold down that massive breakfast."

Liam paled. "When was the last time you ate?"

"I don't know." She twisted her ponytail around her fingers. "Breakfast yesterday?"

Liam slid the plate of linguica closer to her, and she shook her head.

She took out her phone. "Do you want to hear your son's voice?"

Liam's eyes lit up like the national Christmas tree. He clamped his hand on her wrist, then wrung out his hand as if flames erupted from their touch.

"This is why I risked everything to talk to Martinelli."

By the time the recording finished, Liam's eyes misted, and he slammed his fist into the wall.

"I spoke to Ric." She stifled a sob. "Got the scoop on the headaches. I'll kill that bastard if he keeps this up." Eva approached him, cupped his chin, and let him read whatever he wanted from her open-book emotional thoroughfare. "How bad is Neal hurting our son?"

He jerked his chin out of her grip. "Sorry, I can't have you touching me right now. It's not you, it's me."

"I know," she replied. "Even if it was me, I know. You don't have to pretend how much you hate me."

No response. She'd hit his sore spot. Acid churned her breakfast in her belly.

"If he keeps training Connor on all three gifts, even on one ability, all day long, he'll break Connor."

A sob rolled up, and she clapped her hand over her mouth. "Break him, how?"

Liam banged his forehead against the glass patio door. Evergreen trees and tall shrubs hid the neighbor's houses on all three sides of the small backyard, giving the house the necessary privacy for a safe haven. "Stunt or block his abilities, break his mind, plant him in a coma, he may even connect to another psychic who could control him. I don't fucking know. It could be one or all."

Clutching her middle, Eva sank to her knees onto the hardwood floor.

"How much does Neal know about psychic abilities or training?"

"Next to nothing, other than what he knows of Crystal.

She's the one with the abilities and connections." Eva didn't know how she even sounded coherent. The only thought keeping her lucid was the fact that Connor was still alive, and that she had Liam McAllister on her side.

Liam touched her shoulder, a bare brush before his fingers sifted through her unraveling ponytail.

"How much do you hate me?" she asked.

"Hate's a strong word," he mumbled. "Can we put *us* on a back burner?"

"Are you saying there is an *us*?" She picked at the wood grain between floor slats, dismantling her budding hope. Did she want him mixed up in her tempestuous connection to a crime family? Could she have a life with him without losing herself again? Did she still trust him?

"Don't push it, Eva." Liam stomped into the kitchen. Dishes and pans clattered as he cleaned up breakfast using only one hand, keeping his bad arm pinned to his chest.

Eva handed him half-empty plates. "Get anywhere with Crystal?" Palm damp, she bounced on her heels, ready to dissemble at his response.

"I have her hooked." He scraped leftovers down the garbage disposal.

"Did you sleep with her?" The whirling of the disposal chomped at her jealousy.

"I told her I was a gentleman and didn't do hit and runs."

A tight smile twitched her lips. "You are a gentleman. Always have been."

"Glad you still recognize that," he groused.

"What else? Did it make her angry not to get her way?"

"Nope. Thrilled her. Said 'I could marry a man like you.'"

A streak of jealousy so green ran through Eva, she slammed a plate into the dishwasher, clanking it against another. "Wow. You did hook her."

"She did everything you guessed. She's definitely the

dominant one. I played her boy toy, exerted my dominance at the right moments so she didn't think I'd wussed out. She bought it. *She* insisted we go on a real date tomorrow night."

The green thread expanded in Eva's rib cage. "Did you expose your empathic abilities?"

"Yes." Liam wiped down the counters, slung the sponge in the sink, and shut the dishwasher door. "We traded psychic war stories. Said she might have a job for me."

Eva drummed her fingers on the counter. "Legit job?"

"She didn't elaborate. I'll know more tomorrow."

She traced the veins in the counter, each one leading to nowhere, like the dead ends in her mind. "Did you kiss her or make out?"

"Does it matter?"

"Just wondering." *Liar, liar, pants on fire.* "If she didn't at least kiss you, she may only be interested in you as an employee."

"There's no doubt I'm in."

His evasive response tightened the green thread around her heart. "Okay," she muttered. "Glad the plan's working."

"Eva." Liam sighed. "I'm not getting involved with the mafia family for real. I'm sacrificing myself to get our son back."

Sidetracking her zooming mind, Eva set her cell phone on the counter and set the burner phone next to it. "Is it a sacrifice?"

"Why do you even have to ask? She's so far from my type."

"She's beautiful, alluring, coercive."

"Give it a rest." He cast a pointed glance at her phone. "Did Ric trash the tracking app?"

"Yes, including a tracking device Neal stuck inside. He's good."

"Yeah. Ric handles the technical aspects of our business. I do security design and client management."

As if on cue, her phone rang and vibrated against the counter.

When Eva flipped it over, an unknown number flashed on the display.

"If it's Connor, put him on speaker. I want to hear my son real time from now on."

Eva punched the speaker. "Neal?"

"Good guess," Neal said.

"Can I talk to Connor?"

"Not after today's stunts."

A frisson of alarm danced up Eva's back. "What are you talking about?"

"One, you discarded your tracker from your phone. Two, why are you cozying up to a judge? Think you can get him to reverse his order? Better think again."

"What do you know about Martinelli?"

"I know you were at his house. I know you found him dead. Oh, wait. Maybe you killed him."

"Maybe you killed him. Why, Neal? You got what you wanted. What are you afraid of?" She vowed to finish her research on the judge and dig into his court orders.

"I didn't kill the judge," Neal said as if talking to a child. "No one will pin the crime on me."

"On an Estenson minion then. Speaking of minions, why is your father gunning for me?"

"Don't know what you're talking about."

"Don't fuck with me. Estenson men shot at me, ransacked my condo. It's enough to bring the lot of you up on charges." Not enough to do any good, though.

"You're smart enough not to get the police involved."

"I am the police, dumbass. What's your father's deal?"

Liam sliced his finger across his throat and threw her death ray looks.

"Maybe you have something he wants. Doesn't matter. I want *you* back. Plain and simple."

Eva balled her fist on the counter. "You can't have it both ways. Dead or me. What's it gonna be?"

"You know what you have to do." The line clicked off, and Eva slammed her phone on the counter.

"Why antagonize him?" Liam demanded. "You want him taking his revenge out on Connor?"

Her conviction wavered, but she said, "He won't hurt Connor."

"Bullshit. He's already hurting him."

Eva massaged her scalp, unable to stop the sudden burn of tears. Sobs shook her shoulders. Liam skirted the counter and hooked his good arm around her. Face buried in his chest, she breathed in his familiar citrus and spice, the cologne she'd bought him a million years ago. She allowed her mental blocks to dissolve. Liam vibrated against her as her unchecked emotions hit him in a tsunami.

"You're still wearing the cologne." She took fistfuls of his shirt, her fingers pressed against his solid, muscular chest, blazing a path to her frosty southern tundra. His arms, his chest, his entire being was so familiar, so warm, and safe. Why had she ever left him? Why hadn't she listened to her intuition when she first discovered she was pregnant?

"I still love the scent." His voice was throaty.

"I'll never forgive myself if something happens to him. If I had told you from the beginning, none of this would've happened. All I wanted was to go to school, get my degree, and start my career. Then I found out I was pregnant and it rocked my world. My parents helped take care of the baby so I could finish school, making it too easy."

"If your parents are such a big part of Connor's life, why aren't they here?"

"They plan to come at Thanksgiving to hunt for a house for all of us to live in. They knew Neal wouldn't let me keep Connor out of state. My dad's ready to kill him." Another bone-creaking sob bowled through her rib cage. "Will you ever forgive me?" She sniffed hard before she turned Liam's shirt into a snot rag.

"Someday. I know you had your reasons. I just don't get them."

"Oh. Okay. Is there anything more you want to know?"

"About Connor? Everything."

"About my reasoning? About my life?"

"Later." Liam's arm dropped away, and he handed her a fistful of napkins. "I want to finish digging into the judge's case files. If we can find a connection pinning him to the Estensons, it might help the murder investigation, get them investigating the Estensons, blow Neal out of hiding."

Eva mopped her face and blew her nose. "I've bookmarked his case files from our database." She waved at her laptop in her backpack on the table.

Liam retrieved her backpack while she cleaned up the mess she'd made of her face. She pulled her hairband off and finger-combed her unruly waves. Liam had always loved her long blonde hair, and she'd never changed it. Silly, she knew, even when friends tried to coerce her into an updated style. She arranged her hair in front, softened it around her face. *Stupid, stupid, stupid. Like you even have a chance with Liam now. Whoa. What chance? Mental forehead smack.*

When she rejoined him at the dining room table, he was ogling her screensaver, a picture of Connor taken last summer playing in the waves at their local beach in Florida.

"With his towhead and his other facial features, his bow lips, he looks just like you." Liam traced her screen, outlining Connor's face.

"His eyes are all yours."

"The color's yours too." Liam's eyes darkened, a stormy sea of emotions Eva couldn't identify. "Show me the case files. Let's see how the Estensons bought the judge off."

He moved into the second chair, and Eva sat, the seat warm from his body, his scent infusing her. The chairs were so close, their thighs touched, sending liquid warmth between her legs.

"Stop it." Liam's order came out on a gruff growl.

She blinked rapidly. "Stop what?" she demanded.

"The hair, the emotions, the allure, the what-ifs. I'm not doing this with you."

"Then stop reading my emotions." She slapped the table between their devices. "This! This is the reason we broke up, and why I stayed across the country."

"And I told you it would backfire." He grumbled a few muffled four-letter words.

"I got it, Liam. 'I told you so,'" she mimicked. "And now I'm suffering the consequences. Thanks for telling me my life has been a shithole since I walked out of *your* life." *And lost myself in a deceptive monster.* "As if I didn't know it already." She scooted her chair away, placing three feet between them. "Can we just do our research?"

"Yeah. Whatever." He tugged her chair closer with one hand and settled her laptop between them. Heads bent together, they examined Martinelli's court decisions starting from the most recent ones. He stopped her hand on the mouse and quickly withdrew as if scalded. "Go slow, I don't read as fast as you."

Not that he tried to drill into her mind, she hid her emotions the way he'd taught her long ago.

"I know this robbery defendant, Gerry Trenton," she said. "Alex questioned him on a homicide investigation last week."

"Gerry Trenton? He was a Guardian. The Guild booted him out for that robbery. He broke into a warehouse and filched a truckload of cell phones and tablets."

"Nothing unusual about the case. Acquitted."

"Except he committed the robbery. The Guild's telepathic witnesses read it in his mind. It's why they booted him out. We don't harbor criminals."

"Can't enter telepathic responses as evidence, though."

Liam typed in Trenton's name on his note app. "Next one." As Eva scrolled to the next case file, Liam's body tensed up. "Hold on. I know Miguel Santorini. He left the Guild two years ago. He has touch telepathy, married a mind reader who never joined the Guild."

"Why did they leave?"

"Something about the Guild being too intrusive."

"Were they intrusive?" She'd always suspected them of such.

Liam's shoulders moved in a tiny shrug. "Not that I'm aware. Maybe it was an excuse to go on a crime spree. Check out the charges. Three robbery counts, resisting arrest, assaulting an officer."

"Martinelli let him off. Do you think he's guilty?"

"Didn't know him well enough." Liam tapped his name beneath Trenton's. "Next."

As Eva scrolled from one case to the next, every few cases involved a former Guild member who'd left the Guild on their own volition or the Guild had kicked out. Liam paced around the table, slowed, and emailed the list of names to Niles.

"What do you think?" Eva chewed on the tip of a pen. "Holy shit. I missed it. The last two cases involving Guild members also involved an Estenson minion by the name of Nicolai Abramo, Little Nikky they call him. One of the guys who shot at us on Friday."

Air in the room thickened as the connection solidified.

CHAPTER THIRTEEN

Eva hadn't seen Liam so animated since Friday as he dialed the Guardian director.

"Niles, Eva and I found case info implicating former Guild members with the Estensons *and* Judge Martinelli. I emailed you a list of names." Liam explained what they'd unearthed. "I don't just mean the Estensons may be connected to the Cabal. What if the Estensons *are* the Cabal?" He listened a moment, then clicked off.

"What exactly is the Cabal?" Eva basked in the familiarity of Liam and leaned closer, as if to surrender to her regrets.

"An underground group recruiting and building a network of psychics. They kill off psychics who don't toe the line. They use their recruits for any legal and nonlegal purposes for the Cabal's gain."

"Like a crime family."

He nodded. "Last month, the Guild discovered the identity of one of their leaders. Police killed him in a takedown before he divulged information about the Cabal. We prevented him from destroying one of our high-ranking members and a shit-ton of others through an AI-manipulation software he'd developed." Liam displayed a photo of an attractive man in his mid-thirties on his phone. "Recognize him?"

Eva held his phone steady. "No. But Neal went postal when that case hit the news. He was picking Connor up from my place when he received a call about the same time. He contracted with a software-gaming company, and he was pissed that his managing engineer quit. Someone raided their offices, source code stolen, and backup files destroyed. They've been trying to recreate the source code from older backup copies."

"It was a Guild-triggered raid. The managing principal, Delaney, tried to kill several Guild members. He didn't quit, cops killed him." Liam's thumb flew on his text screen. "We take down the Estensons, and I bet the Cabal tumbles. This may be the major break the Guild's been hunting." His eyes twinkled and seemed to scoop her up whole with simmering desire. "If I'm right, you have no idea what this will do for the Guild."

"What will this do to our son?" Eva's chin quivered.

"He's top priority. We ensure Connor's safety factors first in every step." His thumbs flew on his phone. "I just set up a war meeting with Niles, Alex, and my brothers. I want you at hand."

"I'll do whatever it takes. Where?"

"Everyone meets here. It's off the Guild grid."

"If Crystal Estenson urges you to join her or to do... other things, you may need to compromise your morals."

"Whatever it takes."

"It could get ugly."

"We have the police on our side, right?" He winked at her in an uncharacteristic buoyant expression.

"Alex and I can only shield so much criminal activity."

"We'll try to do this without breaking laws. A top Guardian rule." Liam propped his elbows on the counter.

"I'm scared for Connor." Eva leaned on the counter across from him, battling within to not touch him. "I don't want him embroiled in a psychic war."

Liam ran his fingers down her arm, gripped her wrist, and absorbed her fear. Her legs gelled on the spot as he drew her into his safe mental harbor for the first time since they'd reunited. She allowed his coercion, his ability to calm her even if for a momentary respite from her turmoil.

"I've always loved how you can coerce my bad emotions out and replace them with your happy, healing vibes." She flipped her hand around. He twined their fingers together, and she let him soothe her jagged edges until he wrenched his hand to his side, killing the moment.

"Sorry. I can only do that for a few minutes before it hurts my brain."

Eva's phone blared, ending the tense moment. She lunged for it on the table. "Neal?"

"Mommy, it's me, Connor."

Eva's insides lit up like the sun after a long winter storm. "Hi, sweetheart." She punched on the speakerphone, and Liam lunged around the counter to be closer to his son's voice. "Does Daddy know you're calling me?"

"No," he whispered. "I snuck into his office again. Don't tell him I called."

Clouds of panic dimmed her sunlight. "I won't tell. It's our secret. Is he home?"

"No. He left to go to a meeting. Aunt Crystal just got here, and she's taking a nap."

The clouds floated off, taking her cold panic with them. "That's too bad he's working on a weekend. How are you today?"

"Is your case over? When are you coming?" Connor's voice broke, and Eva jabbed the phone into her forehead.

"Soon, baby, soon. Did Daddy make you practice your special gifts today?"

"Yes. All morning." Connor sniffed. "He wouldn't let me watch *SpongeBob SquarePants* until I told him what I dreamed last night."

"Does your head hurt?"

"Only a little. He gave me some medicine."

"Okay. Good. I'm so sorry Daddy's being a big meanie."

"It's okay. He lets me stay up late and have ice cream. Aunt Crystal plays games with me."

Liam clinched the phone to keep her from gouging herself with it. Eva wanted to make up for all the years of Connor's absence in Liam's life. She wished she had the ability to twist time, and to shut down the demons steering her away from him and the flames of long-buried phobias.

"What did you dream about?" she asked Connor. "Was it a waking dream?"

"Yes."

"Tell me about it," she said. Liam scratched his chin and scrunched up his eyes. "A clairvoyant vision," she mouthed, and he nodded in understanding.

"I saw you with a gun pointed at Daddy. You were being a police officer."

Eva's heart thudded in her rib cage, prepping to launch itself outward. "It's just a dream." Her voice quavered. "I would never hurt Daddy." Not all Connor's visions became reality, but this one hit too close to home.

"But it's one of my true dreams," he insisted. "You were mad at Daddy, and he was mad at you. You said he stole me from you, and he wouldn't let you see me. Is it true, Mommy? When are you coming here?"

"Oh, baby. Daddy's just being overprotective from the bad guys on a police case I'm working. I have lots of strong policemen to keep me safe." *Or at least one strong Guardian who may or may not want me dead. Sometimes you had to lie a little to live a little.*

"But Daddy was hurt," he insisted. "I felt you mad at him. Then something hit my head. It hurt so bad I fell asleep. The birds in the cage were there. I don't remember waking up. Did I die?"

Eva stifled a sob, cupped her mouth. Liam looked ready to kill, all dark and tense and diffusing a strong waft of his cologne and pungent fear. "No! It's all just a bad dream, baby. I'll see you and your father soon. We'll be together again as a family, the three of us." She shot daggers at Liam, waving her arm, trying to improvise. "Keep this our secret, okay? You know I love you so much, right?"

"It's our secret. I know you love me." He paused. "I know the other man wants to meet me too. I want to meet him."

Eva scratched her temple. "What other man?"

"The one you're with. The man you used to know before Daddy."

Liam stood stock-still, frozen in limbo and time.

"Maybe we'll see him someday, and you'll meet him."

"But, Mommy—"

She had to redirect him off Liam before he blew their cover. "Connor, can you look on top of Daddy's desk or in his drawers to see if there's mail for me?" Something *must* have an address on it.

"There's nothing on the desk. I already tried to open the drawers to look for a pencil. They're all locked."

Faintly, she heard Crystal calling Connor's name. "Baby, hang up and hide from Aunt Crystal. Don't let her know you were talking to me. Okay? I miss you so much. Love you to the space stations."

"And back to Earth," he replied in a rush. Connor clicked off, and Liam stomped away, a safe distance between them. She gave him a few moments to gather his bearings. Before either uttered a word, her phone rang again. Another unknown caller.

"Nice try, Eva." Crystal Estenson's deep, husky voice crackled her speakerphone, triggering Liam's dash back to

Eva's side. His heat cloaked her, and she had the strongest longing to wrap her arms around him to roll him into her too.

"Tell me where my son is, Crystal."

She barked out a cackle. "Don't go stupid on me, girl. Neal won't like you talking to Connor."

"Don't get him in trouble. You two are already hurting him. You need to stop whatever you're doing to his head. He told me he's in pain."

"Don't you fret none. I'm the psychic here, not you. You always wanted to smother his talents. That's just as damaging to a psychic. Of course, you wouldn't know. You're a normal. Poor boy, he needs real psychics to train him. In fact... I know a man who can help him learn how to use his empathic skills. Between the two of us we'll turn Connor into a psychic machine. Have no fear, Eva Midnight. We'll take care of your son. He's loving it and can't wait to join—" Crystal abruptly put a stopper in it. Had she tipped her hand? Did she mean join the *Cabal?*

Eva traded wide-eyed glares with Liam. He wound his finger in a circle to get her to keep Crystal talking.

"Talk some sense into Neal, Crystal. You know what he's doing isn't right. He doctored those photos and reports for the court case."

"I have no clue what you're talking about. All Neal wants is you to come back home to him. I have no clue why. You're too much trouble. I guess you must be a wildcat in bed because he only wants you. I tried to set him up with some girlfriends, but he's only interested in fucking them, nothing more."

Crystal's glee turned Eva's stomach and not because Neal was hooking up with Crystal's bimbo friends.

"Cat got your tongue, little Eva?"

"Connor's not even Neal's son. Did you know that?"

"For all intents, he is. Why I can probably get my

hands on a termination of bio-daddy's parental rights and the adoption papers you signed for Neal to adopt." Eva suffered through a pregnant pause. "You really are too stupid to live. Watch your back, girl. See you never."

The phone clicked off.

Liam's eyes shot switchblades at her. "Tell me you didn't allow that bastard to adopt *my* son."

Eva shook her head so hard her brain cells packed their bags. "No. I told you I planned to out you as his father. When it was safe."

"Do you think she's bluffing?"

"Leave it to Neal to doctor those papers too, especially if he had a judge in his back pocket. One of their illegal enterprises is fake passports and ID's."

"Then why kill the judge? I don't get it."

"The Estensons probably have a slew of judges on under-the-table retainers. As for Martinelli, maybe he was threatening to expose them, or cut ties? Or maybe it wasn't the Estensons at all. Maybe another scumbag blackmailed the judge. It's not cheap to live in Los Altos or to send his three kids to Ivy League universities." Eva wilted onto a dining room chair.

The front door opened, startling Eva into reaching for her missing gun. Ric and Jake McAllister, Alex MacKenzie, and Niles Nevin crammed the cozy living room. They absorbed every molecule in the small space, smothered it with their testosterone.

She scurried to the backyard patio to escape the testosterone brigade and all things psychic. The only psychic she wanted in her life was her son.

And Liam? Oh, hell to the no. She couldn't deal with his psychic abilities seven years ago. What made her think things had changed? *What makes you think you can even deal with Connor?*

Shitstorm, welcome to my world.

CHAPTER FOURTEEN

The patio door slid open and closed in a whoosh, disturbing Eva's peace. "Care to join us?" Alex penetrated her brain fog.

"Sorry." One by one, she smoothed out the mess she'd made of her cuticles. "I needed a moment from all things psychic."

Alex chuckled. "Gets overwhelming."

"At least, *you're* not Guild." Sitting in a lawn chair, soaking up the autumn sun, she stretched out her legs, crossed her ankles.

"I am by association." Alex sat in a chair opposite her. She'd never seen her boss so dressed down in faded blue jeans, sneakers, and a T-shirt. Then she remembered it was Sunday. Again, Juliana Westwood was one lucky woman. *No, I do not have a thing for my boss. No way, no how. That'd get me kicked off his team, drop-kicked to the bowels of Hades for even thinking about him in that way. Bad enough Liam now absorbs my every waking moment not centered on Connor.*

"Does Juliana overwhelm you? What does she have?"

"Mind reading and touch telepathy."

"How do you deal?"

"How do you deal with Connor?"

She flushed and glowered at his nonanswer. "Not so

well. He can read me as well as his favorite picture books."

"You need training. Juliana can help. She has patience the McAllisters lack."

"Did she help you block her out?"

"Yeah, in high school. It was easy because of my twin telepathy. I slip, but she's also learned not to dip into my head. The touch telepathy deal is weird and new. We're still working on conquering it." He winked.

"It's one thing I worry about with—" She clamped her mouth shut.

"With Liam?"

"Connor," she blurted out too late to retract what her mouth almost fessed up to.

Alex chuckled and drizzled her in warmth. It reminded her too much of Liam's blissful laughter... when he laughed. "Juliana's touch telepathy is similar to Liam's empathic abilities. She sometimes reads my internal emotions, the way Liam does, but more often suffers visions of what I've done."

"Ouch. Bet that gets you in trouble with a capital *T*."

"A little. Makes us accountable to one another in a good way. Although her seeing the things I do on my job isn't good for her stress levels. How does Connor's clairvoyance and empathic skills work?"

"I'd also like to know." Liam hogged the patio doorway, his hulking brothers hovering behind him.

"Hello, Eva Midnight." Jake McAllister rammed through the trio of McAllister hunks. "Nice to see you again."

"Is it really, Jake?" She rose from the cushioned patio chair and confronted her firing squad. Jake approached her, all buff and tough in black head to toe, his long dark hair hanging loose around his shoulders. Rocker long, rocker thick and lush.

In a sudden shocked move, Jake enveloped her in his

steely arms and crushed her to him. Air whooshed out of her in a cry for help. "It is. You know I always liked you and wanted nothing but the best for you. You were good for Liam... until you weren't." He rubbed her back. "I always applauded your convictions and knowing what you wanted out of life with your schooling and your career."

Tears sprang to her eyes. "I'm sure you don't applaud my stupidity in hiding Connor from his father or his uncles."

He loosened his arms. "We all do stupid. You have time to rectify it now. Liam will come around."

"Who are you and what have you done with the fierce Jake McAllister?" Stunned, she wiped her tears on her sleeve and stepped out of his uncomfortable embrace.

"Love does strange and wonderful things to people." He winked and rejoined a smirking Ric and a scowling Liam. Niles Nevin stepped into the crowd of hotties, and it was much more palpable in the free-flowing patio air, a smoky chill clearing the tension. "We have a lot of love to give our nephew. First, we need to get him back."

"Get him period." Liam shot more daggers at Eva, strange daggers, tentative and soft, not so frosty and dark.

"Let's brainstorm before we lose more time." Niles waved the he-man crew into the house, and they circled the round table. "The names from Martinelli's cases are all psychics, either Guild members or had interviewed to join."

Eva white-knuckled the table edge. "What does that mean?"

"That the good ole judge was eating out of the Cabal's pocket," Ric replied.

"That the Estensons may be Cabal, period," Liam said. "I plan to pick Crystal's brain on our date tomorrow."

Alex joined the fray. "We need this squeaky clean if we're going after them for the judge's murder *and* Cabal crimes."

Liam turned his tablet screen toward Niles and Jake. "Check these cases involving psychics. Petty criminal misdemeanors, a few felonies. All walked scot-free. Who paid the judge off? The Cabal? The Estensons?"

"Why kill the judge if he's doing such a stellar job?" Jake scrolled down the screen, scanning the case log. "Whoa, wait a minute. Check this out."

Eva stood on her toes to see past Jake's left shoulder and Liam peered over his right, three heads glued together. Eva pointed at the defendant's name on the screen. "He's one of Daniel Estenson's guards at Estenson Software."

Liam whistled. "Not who he's talking about."

Ric crowded in close. "Oh, man. The man who almost killed my girlfriend."

"Who are you talking about?" Eva squinted.

"Kenneth Delaney. He was a witness in this case for the defense," Jake replied. "Owned a Cabal software company we just took down."

"That's why the Estensons are scrambling to piece their company together after it was raided and their source code copped." A strange sparkle of excitement spanned Liam's face. She boiled under his scrutiny and the body heat of the hunks encircling her.

"We just stumbled upon a gold mine, boys." Gleeful, Niles fist-bumped the air.

"Except for a couple important factors. The man linked to both sides is dead." Alex interjected the obvious status of Judge Martinelli. "The Cabal knows the Guild took down Delaney and his company."

"Which means the Estensons know." Pain paling his face, Liam clutched his wounded arm to his chest. "We need to keep an even lower profile. I'm not allowing our Cabal takedown to interfere with getting my son back."

A round of assurances hovered cautiously in the air, and Eva sank into a chair next to Jake. The heat had fled her body, chased by a chill so deep, she didn't think she'd ever feel normal again. "If they link me to the Guild or to any of you, we're all dead. From intel I've gathered on the Estensons since I've been in San Jose, they shoot first and ask questions later." Eva kicked the chair, and it tumbled and clanged to the hardwood floor. "Neal knows I was at the judge's house. What else does he know?" Her intestines gurgled, and she fled the room, again to the relative haven of the cool and comforting backyard.

After a few moments coming to grip with her new and ill-omened reality, Alex rejoined her, his hand reassuring on her shoulder. "Liam wanted to ream you a new one for subjecting your son to a crime family."

"I'm doing enough reaming myself to satisfy the devil." She lowered her head between her knees while she tried to temper the acid in her gut. "I can't confront him or his brothers. If Connor didn't need me, I might just sink into a black hole and never resurface." Neighbors rustling about their yards and a lawn mower permeated their silent lull.

"If you don't mind me asking," Alex began, "once you discovered Neal was part of a crime family, why did you stay with him?"

"At first, his allegiance to the family was unclear. Once I found out he still belonged to the family and our marriage went south, it didn't take long for me to make plans."

"Neal didn't want the divorce, right?"

Shudders shook Eva's shoulders. Alex wrapped his arm around her and tugged her close. She fisted the soft cotton of his sleeve. "The only way to get my son back and end this is to go back to Neal. As his wife."

"Will Neal even take you back?"

"Probably." Cupping her mouth, she scurried to a planter on her right. Her breakfast made an unceremonious return to a lush green camellia bush waiting for cooler weather to bloom. Eva sank to her knees on the grass, rested her head against the travertine planter top. Shivers commandeered her body, bone-jarring, soul-shattering.

The patio door slid open. Liam and Alex spoke in low tones. Alex approached with a bottle of lemon-lime soda and a cool, wet washcloth.

"Thank you." Leaning on the planter for support, she sipped the soda, rinsed her mouth, and spit it into the planter, garnish to her breakfast.

"Did he hurt you?" Alex's hand alighted on her shoulder, imbuing her with a skosh of strength.

Silence. Did the world need to know her story?

As though he read her mind, he said, "Anything can help. I'll be blunt. You've never backed down from the worst criminal in the short time you've worked for me. Not even that serial killer who chopped up the pieces and buried them in his backyard. Nothing phases your cold detachment when you're on a case. This time it's personal, your life, your blood and soul. But you've expressed convincing evidence of abuse."

When she glanced up from tracing the striations in the travertine, Liam stood behind Alex, listening to every word. She owed him. For the sake of her son, for his sake, for their sake. If *they* existed in the end. But damned if she'd give them the details she had buried. Not even her mother knew, and her father would kill Neal if he knew.

"I'll go back to him, for my son, for the purpose of you obliterating the Cabal or to expose the Estenson family crimes. I can do it." She patted the secret flash drive sewn into the lining of her jacket, assured she still had possession.

"Not if he'll hurt you." Anguish created gullies in Liam's forehead. "Dammit, Eva. Why didn't you tell anyone?"

Eva pushed to her feet, balanced the soda on her palm,

balancing the words surfacing and begging to spill out. "I told my therapist. She helped me extricate myself from my marriage without Neal or his father gunning me down. Do I have to tell the whole fucking world what he did to me? About how stupid I was to let him? How a cop became a victim when I'm supposed to help others?" *Let him?* Not like she could stop him without jeopardizing everything she held dear. He'd threatened her, her son, and her parents if she uttered one word. She hated to admit that her life had become a cliché of abused women everywhere. "Well, it's out now."

One reason she'd pursued a job as a police officer rather than her original goal as a forensic psychologist was to help people in both law enforcement and psychology. How had the tables turned on her? Or had she hit the dead end of her destiny? And then right back into the life of Liam McAllister and the Guild, after having fled them from ignorance and panic, from the man she had loved to the ends of the earth. The man who now offered her compassion in the softening of his face and the sympathy in his eyes.

Niles cleared his throat and crushed the uncomfortable truths floating above their heads. "Let's figure out our next move." Eva flashed him a commiserate look, glad to table a conversation she'd return to later.

"I have a list of every beach accessible near a long staircase along the Pacific coast," Alex said as the small party returned to the cluttered dining room table.

Liam stood close to Eva, waiting to catch her if she fell, or to commit treason or something worse. His comforting presence killed the erratic bees buzzing in her empty stomach.

The group spent the next several hours poring over evidence of the Guild and not-so-Guild kind that made Eva want to hit a kill switch on her brain. All the while, she continued to freak out knowing she'd have to infiltrate the Estensons by giving Neal a second chance. If Liam infiltrated them via Crystal, how could Eva or Liam restrain Connor from telepathically or empathically discovering the truth about them and blurting it out?

"Eva, you look ready to crash." Yawning, Alex stood. "Go home and rest. You're off work for a few days."

Her eyes smarted and bugged out. "I'm on forced leave?"

He held up his hand. "Your son needs you free and clearheaded. You can't focus at work with this hanging over you. Plus, Los Altos PD needs to clear you of murder charges."

"Didn't know I was a suspect," she grumbled. "Fine. I'll use the time to keep investigating. Send me your intel on the beaches. Maybe a location will ring a bell."

"I'll contact you in the morning." Liam feathered his fingers over the back of her hand. When her desire hit him, he staggered, and she mentally whacked herself up the side of her head. Exhaustion prevailed over her ability to block Liam's intrusions.

Scrambling from the testosterone brigade, she hurried to the door, stopped, and addressed the room. "I know this isn't a real police case, but I appreciate everything you've all done."

"It's a Guild case and good enough for me," Niles replied, packing his briefcase. "Connor's one of us."

"He's a McAllister, and it's a family case." Jake slung his arm around Liam's shoulders. "No matter the circumstances."

Eva jogged to her car to avoid more talk of psychics and Guilds. She bumped her forehead on her steering wheel, knocking sense into her addled brain. Like it or not, she was Guild by association. Fear and stupidity had kept her from reaching out to them sooner. Regret became an anchor weighing her down in a quagmire of confusion.

By the time she parked in her covered spot at her condo complex, exhaustion bogged down her every limb. A large pot of strong coffee was on tap for a late-night of research. No matter how tired, she refused to stop now.

Families settling in for Sunday dinner provided normalcy in the still twilight. The sinking rays of the sun bathed the garden's western edge, painting the beige stucco walls coral. Despite her fatigue, she never let her guard down. When she stepped onto the sidewalk leading to her secluded front door, heebie-jeebies sank another anchor in her belly.

Since Ric installed video and audio surveillance at the front and rear doors, she felt somewhat secure and hadn't left her thread of paper in the doorjamb. Yet an air of malice tightened her throat. She stuck her key in the lock, prepared to punch in Liam's birthdate in the security alarm pad. *It is what it is.* The alarm chime didn't sound. She reached for her shoulder harness, realized she didn't have her gun. It took a moment for her vision to adjust to the twilight gloom of her shuttered living room.

"Hello, Eva." A cold front attacked her, and her heart stuttered the way it did every time she saw Neal. He snaked out his arm and shut the door behind her. "Nice security setup." He swept his arm at a pile of tiny audio and video bugs. "I came prepared with my best tech guy. Guess I have the better one." It was always a competition with him, against her, his brother, and now for his father's good graces.

"What do you want, Neal?" She breathed in deep, tried to slow her galloping heart to no avail, reached again for her absent shoulder harness beneath her leather jacket. *Stop the world so I can get off.*

"Where's your firearm?" His back to the door, he blocked her escape. He fingered a tendril of loose hair off her cheek, his long, slender fingers lingering proprietarily on her temples, sliding into the hair over her ears. Like a terrorized victim, she let him, knowing if she fought back, he might threaten Connor, or worse. His summer-tanned, sculpted face, blade nose, and high cheekbones always used to evoke her desire. His tall lanky body once made her heart sing. The way his intense gray-blue eyes slurped her up as if she were the only being on the planet used to weaken her knees. Now, the man conjured an unreal sense of loathing and caused her body to ice over. She almost forgot how to breathe.

"Sunday's my day off." She adopted a rigid self-defense stance. "Did you bring Connor?"

An evil bark of laughter preceded his words. "Don't be dense."

"Martinelli's dead. He's not in the Estenson pocket any longer."

"You read too much into things."

"How else did you get the custody order to *my* son?"

"Pictures are worth a thousand words."

"I hate to bring ants to your picnic, but hello, fake photos." She gritted her teeth.

He inclined forward, and she clenched her body for the storm. "He's my son too."

"How did you do it, Neal? How long have you been forging my signature?"

"I can make it all disappear." He inched closer.

Pressing her back against the wall, she squared her shoulders, held her ground, dying a slow death inside. "What's your ask?"

"Nothing's changed. You return to me. Quit your job, be a mother to our boy, have a couple more kids with my DNA streaming through their blood. Become a real Estenson family."

The same old litany still stunned her sensibilities. He

knew how much she hated him, but his arrogance and new narcissistic tendencies refused to believe it. When had he swerved to the dark side? Or had he blinded her to the truth from the beginning?

"If I quit my job, you won't have an insider at the police department."

"I can live with that."

"What about your father?"

His eyes kindled with unsated need. "I'll call my father off."

"You admit he's gunning for me?"

Again, he edged closer, less than an inch to spare before his body touched hers. The ghost of alcohol on his breath lay heavy on her neck. Another newer thing about him. He'd never drunk much until his brother died.

"Would you like a drink?" Alcohol put him to sleep. Maybe a glass or two would do the trick.

"Now you're talking. You'll join me." It wasn't a request. He unbuttoned a couple buttons on his casual dress shirt. Ever the impeccable lawyer, now mob son, even on a weekend.

Alcoholics anonymous is searching for its number one idiot. "Of course." Eva smiled, forcing her lips taut to prevent them from quivering. "Bourbon?"

"Absolutely." He sat on the sofa and rested his legs on the coffee table, crossing his ankles. "*When* you come back, you'll be rid of this dump."

She set two glasses and the half-filled bottle on the coffee table. He patted the sofa next to him. "It's not so bad."

"Consider my offer, Eva. It's the only way you'll see your son again."

She sat beside him, a foot between them, took a sip of her watered-down drink. She loathed bourbon almost as much as she loathed him. The bottle on hand served to appease him when he bullied her or to smooth over transfers on visitation days. He gulped half his tumbler and smiled at her, showing a hint of even, white teeth, the smile that used to spark her every cell, erode her every resolve. Now it wired her multifaceted disgust.

"What about all your other women?" she asked.

"What women? You're the only one that counts."

Musky cologne wafting off him irritated her nostrils, and she tweaked her nose. "You were screwing around on me before we even said the *D* word. Why do you think I divorced you?" *Play up the other divorce angle, steer him clear from the mob angle and the other reasons.*

"They meant nothing. I'm willing to devote myself to you one hundred percent. It's all I've ever wanted." Leaning closer, he rested his hand on her thigh. "I haven't slept with a woman since I've been here, not even Rachel. She's history anyway. Scouts honor." His hand slipped between her clenched legs, sliding toward her crotch. "I'm waiting for you to get this cop thing out of your blood and return to where you belong."

"I don't belong to you." *Here we go... Neal's celebration of stupidity.*

"You belong to Connor, and you both belong to the Estensons. We're your family."

Wishing she had her gun, she shrank into the tattered sofa back. The conversation had turned to the dark side, and poisoned chips dotted the cookies. She wished for a suit of armor to replace her jeans.

"Think what our blood can create. Maybe we'll have another exceptional child."

Neal had bought her story that Connor's psychic DNA came from her family. Their marriage had gone sour by the time Connor outwardly exhibited psychic abilities, and she'd lied about having a psychic genealogy to protect Liam.

"Why does it matter to you if any child we had possessed psychic talents? It's a burden as well as a gift."

His thumb dipped between her legs, pressed into her crotch, and she tried to ease away. His glass tumbled to the floor, and he twisted her hair in his fist, hauled her closer.

The sting of his grip burned like embers in her eyes. She tried to calm herself by taking deep, even breaths, but it only ratcheted up her terror. Didn't matter that she was a cop. He knew there was too much at stake to report him. That bitch karma waited for the green light to pass "go." Until then, she'd suffer at his hands. No matter what.

His mouth settled on her neck, and he tugged on her hair, scoring needles across her scalp. His other hand dug into her crotch and he lifted her onto his lap. Pain lanced her most intimate places, and a tear dripped from her right eye. Teeth latched on to her neck, the stinging pain forcing her to gasp.

"Neal. Stop it!" She shoved against him, struggling from his lethal grip. "Let me go."

"Not until I get what I want."

"I'm not fucking you."

"You'll want to. Eventually." He sucked on her neck, soothing the wound he'd made; then his lips trailed up her jaw and landed on her compressed mouth. "Come on, Eva. You know you want me. You'll always only want me."

"Screw you." He'd gone past the pale, and it didn't matter what she said at that point. Piss him off or not. Wouldn't matter in the end game.

"I want you to. But not now. Now's for making plans." He eased up on her hair and the searing pain abated. "Go to dinner with me tomorrow night. Let's start over, fresh." He shifted his hand off her and shoved her off his lap. "Tonight was only for show. I swear it will never happen again."

How many times had she heard his empty promises?

The thought of her son and the steps she'd take to get him back revolved in her mind, flinging those empty promises in circles.

"Okay." Her voice wobbled. "Dinner tomorrow," she said. "My choice."

A dazzling smile lit up his face. His smile had charmed her in the beginning, showed how he'd treat her with love, respect, and loyalty. When had his smile turned him into the devil?

"Where would you like to go?" He twirled a lock of loose hair around his finger. She waited for the painful tug on her scalp. "I love your hair so much."

She'd almost cropped her hair to her scalp to rid her memories of him touching it, to show how she'd moved on from him. Yet, she refused to stoop to such levels. She'd had her long hair before she met him. Why change what she loved to spite him?

"The Acropolis."

"Your favorite. Shall I pick you—" He released her and held up his hand. "Sorry. You'll want to meet me there. Is seven okay?" She nodded. He slipped his phone out of his front pocket.

In one swift movement, he shoved the phone in her face and whispered in her ear, "Any funny stuff, and this gun will land up at the Los Altos Police Department with your fingerprints all over it. Connor will *never* visit you in prison. You'll be dead to him."

She gasped at the photo of her first police revolver, a gun Neal said had been stolen from their Florida house before they split up.

Neal kissed her cheek. "See you tomorrow, my love." He left her sitting too stunned to budge.

He planned to frame her for Judge Martinelli's murder if she didn't bow to his demands.

Eva dug out her cell phone, texted her mother.

Send the package now.

Numb, Eva zombie-shuffled to Connor's room, flicked the lights on, and crawled onto the zoo-print bedspread on his twin bed. She clutched his favorite stuffed lion in her arms. The inescapable silence roared, and with an animal snarl, her strength grew.

CHAPTER FIFTEEN

Liam called Eva umpteen times and got her damned voicemail. He dialed her one last time before he hit the road to check on her. "Come on, Eva. Pick up."

Nothing. He grabbed his keys and his phone rang. Without checking the screen, he answered, massaged the gullies on his forehead. "Eva, you okay?"

"It's me, bro," Ric replied. "All the surveillance at Eva's condo's dead. I'm heading over."

"I'll meet you there."

"No. You need to maintain your cover."

Liam fisted his hand as if preparing to pound Estenson to a pulp. "I've been trying to get hold of her since you left."

"I'll report what I find. Stay at the safe house. She might show up."

Liam stared at his phone, willing it to ring, speak, do something. When the doorbell rang, he nearly imploded. He sprinted through the living room and opened the door without his normal security checks. Eva stood on the porch, an overnight bag looped over her shoulder, a golden stuffed animal tied to the strap. Her pale face, soft cheeks, and luminous eyes under the porch light turned him on in ways no ex-girlfriend should. A neighbor's TV murmured and an owl hooted, yet her sharp intake of breath silenced the night. Danger stood before him in the tantalizing guise of temptation.

"I need to crash here tonight."

Liam let her slide past him in the doorway, her every emotion pummeling him. One look at her pale devastation was all it took to raze his defenses against her. "What happened?"

She dropped her bag onto the floor at her feet. "Neal showed up. Found all the bugs."

"What did he do to you?" Liam clenched and unclenched his hand at his side.

"Same old bullshit." She waved off his concern, and it ticked him off even more. "He still wants me back. I agreed to go out to dinner with him tomorrow night."

"Why? We can do this without you suffering further at his hands. I'll proceed with my plan with Crystal." The idea of her in distress and getting back together with Neal, even feigned, killed a little part of him.

"An Estenson hitman killed Martinelli with my old service revolver. Supposedly stolen from our house in Florida. My prints are all over it. Neal will ensure it makes it into evidence if I don't meet his demands."

Shock immobilized Liam, and his heart vaporized for her despite willing it to play Switzerland. "What demands?"

"He's willing to start over. Let bygones be bygones." She shrugged her hands. "Dinner for now."

A strange niggling doubt weaved a rug in Liam's gut. "What aren't you telling me?"

Eva pressed her fingers into her eyelids. "Once Connor exhibited real psychic abilities, I told Neal his abilities came from my side of the family, not his father's side. Neal believes it."

"Why?"

"To protect you. Our marriage had already hit the skids, and I didn't know where we'd end up. Connor and his psychic abilities enamored him. One night, he…" She sucked in her middle, turned her back to him. "He insisted on knowing what kind of psychic abilities Connor's bio daddy possessed. I told him if we had a baby, the baby would have the best of both worlds from our psychic grandparents. My maternal grandparents are gone as you know, and my parents bought into the lie. It rerouted him off the trail of discovering Connor's real father."

"Which plunked him on the path toward having a baby with you." Liam's voice fell lethally low. Shaking, Eva remained silent, her back to him. "Eva?"

"I'm not proud of crap I did to escape our marriage, to get out alive and intact." She spun around. "The rest of it was necessary to remain on good terms for Connor."

"And to keep the mafia off your back."

"Or the Cabal." Her eyes met his, held, and he sank into her ocean storm of pain and anguish, wishing he had the ability to erase the tempest dulling their vibrancy.

"You aren't intact, and you know it," Liam said. He reached for her, withdrew his hand, not ready to take in emotions he might not be able to stem.

"My body's intact. Not much else." She bent to retrieve her bag, and he beat her to it, their hands touching until hers dropped in a spray of emotional alarm bells.

Liam ditched the bag and gripped her shoulders, bringing her closer to him, without completely touching. He didn't think he could handle such an intimate touch. He cracked his knuckles against her shoulders to expend his emotional energy.

The stuffed animal on her bag drenched him in memories. He'd won a stuffed lion for her at the county fair. Cost him fifty bucks, but she'd wanted it so bad, he refused to let her down. "Is that Lion King?"

She chuckled. "Yeah. The only toy that quieted Connor when he was teething. It's seen better days, but it's his favorite stuffed animal. I'm surprised Neal hasn't asked for it, for anything of Connor's, or that his goons didn't steal it from my condo."

"Did you ever think Connor would need me to guide him through his psychic abilities?" The loaded question kept rising in his mind.

"Every moment of every day from the first moment Connor read my mind. Since you and your brothers taught me how to block my thoughts, I helped Connor through the early years. Things snowballed, and we wound up here."

A warmth Liam had a difficult time identifying flooded his body, chased by a freeze of determination. "I won't let you go back to him."

"We don't have a choice." She sagged against him, but he separated to protect them both from the barrage of emotions.

"Next time, will you be able to escape him intact?" An empty fluttering ballooned in his gut. The pause grew so long and heavy he made a small sound in his throat. The strain of her emotions, her absolute desolation deluged him and joined his own fear until they were inseparable. "You're afraid you can't escape him once you let him back in."

"I can do this, with you and the Guild backing me up. I need to finish what I started."

Steel straightened Liam's spine. "What do you mean what you started?"

"Taking down the entire Estenson clan." She quirked her sleek blonde eyebrows. "I've already set in motion the dismantling of the Cabal for the Guild, although I didn't know it. I'm finishing it."

"Tell me everything," Liam demanded.

"Tomorrow." She cupped his cheek. "I need to crash before I pass out. I promise no more secrets. I'll do everything in my power to get your son to you even under a sole custody order. You two won't lose more time apart. Connor will love you. He's sweet, loyal, and trusting. He already knows you hold a special place in my heart."

Tender and soothing, her fingers feathered his face, and he fought her emotions. The mental war nearly did him in. He wanted to sink into her, and he wanted to bitch slap her for keeping his son from him. Most of all, he wanted her touch setting off shimmers of lightning inside him. He'd missed her so much; he'd sacrifice the hit to his ego to have her in his life, in his heart, and soul. "I would never take him from you, Eva."

"You might have him completely if I don't make it out alive."

"Don't say that. I won't let Neal snuff you out." He leaned into her touch.

"You may not be able to stop him. His father suspects I'm out to get them. That's why his goons were shooting at us Friday night. It's why they tossed my home."

Before his defenses crumbled to dust, Liam escaped from her dangerous touch, putting a safe distance between them. "What evidence do you possess?" She retrieved her bag off the floor, hugged Lion King to her, her whole body droopy with exhaustion. "Okay," he said. "Tomorrow's soon enough. Please tell me Connor's safe."

"Connor's the second coming to the Estensons. How do you think I've been able to remain so chill?" She sauntered down the hallway, steered to the left.

"Take the master bedroom on the right. I'll sleep in another room."

Slowly as if she had no energy to argue, she pivoted to witness Liam's blush before heading down the hallway to the master bedroom suite. He followed as if afraid to lose her. Not a large space, the bedroom held a king-size bed, two nightstands, an overstuffed armchair, and a dresser across from the bed. All new, including the deep green and taupe jacquard bedding. A newly remodeled bathroom in the white and gray marbles of the latest remodel craze sat next to an empty closet.

"This is too much for me. You take it." She rounded on Liam in the doorway.

"It's a Guild safe house. All I need is a bed. There are two more and a shared bathroom. I'm good."

"I don't deserve your kindness." She tossed her bag on the bed.

"I'm not an ogre."

"Far from it."

"Accept the Guild's kindness at face value. You're helping us, and we're helping you."

"What about... us?"

"Us?" Hope slammed him, and he strengthened his grip on the doorframe.

"Right. There is no us. Forgive me for losing my mind for two seconds." She perched on the bed and kicked off her black sneakers. "I'd like to sleep now."

"I'm not Neal. You don't need my approval."

A crimson tide engulfed her cheeks. "Not what I meant."

Without another retort, Liam shut the door on her. Another door slam and he sank onto the queen bed in the first guest room, the closest to Eva's room. After all, he remained her Guardian. He dragged his fingers through his hair, kicked off his sneakers, and unbuttoned his jeans. Cool autumn air kept the house at a perfect temperature, no longer requiring the air conditioner, too early for a heater. His body temperature remained high due to the slew of emotions besieging him, and he lay on top of the covers.

Muffled freeway noise filtered in, as well as a large dog barking next door, a much gruffer bark than Barney. It took a while for sleep to arrive as he got used to the different house sounds. Had nothing to do with Eva Midnight, the love of his life, sleeping two doors down, in a bed large enough for two.

After a short time, he rolled out of bed for a last security check on the doors and windows and made his final stop in Eva's room. She curled in a ball beneath the covers, lost and forlorn, and it torched his heart. He flicked off the bedside light, forced himself to shut the door and not cave to his urge to coil his body around hers.

Midnight rolled closer, and he remembered the night he'd met Eva. A New Year's Eve party at an outdoor event under a clear night, a million stars shining down upon them. They'd partied among a group of mutual college friends. The clock struck midnight, they turned to each other, and he knew he was glimpsing the face of his destiny. Midnight. He'd kissed her, kissed in the New Year that became the best year of his life as he fell in love with the woman he believed he'd one day marry. For every major event in their year, they celebrated in the same spot at midnight and graced the next day with their good luck and fortune from the previous day.

He'd known she was applying for scholarships, which might take her out of California. He'd first believed they'd suffer through a long-distance relationship while she studied for her master's degree, then return to San Jose. They'd stupidly never talked about it, and he never voiced his wishes. Only at the end had she admitted her fears, what it meant to be with a psychic. It nearly killed him when he'd agreed to break it off. The memories lambasted him.

The moment the digital clock on his nightstand displayed midnight, a scream shattered the muted sounds of the Sunday quiet and served up Monday. Liam seized his gun and jetted down the short hallway to the master bedroom. Drawing his gun into position, he waited outside the closed door, heard another scream, and kicked the door in.

Like a cornered animal, Eva crouched in the far corner between the wall and the nightstand, half hidden in the shadows cast by the furniture. She whimpered and buried her head between her knees, balled into a fetal position, Lion King smashed against her chest.

Liam flicked on the overhead light, checked the suite for intruders. Eva's terror arose from within, and her loathing and disgust slammed into his wide-open doors. The emotions buckled his knees, and he balanced against the bedframe. He sucked up the pain binding his heart and stumbled toward her.

When she lifted her head, her deep-rooted terror scuttled out of her eyes and into him. He collapsed to the floor and took her in his arms. She fought him at first, striking out with both fists, kicking him, crying while he wrenched her close. Cheek resting against his racing heart, she looped her arms around him and peace finally claimed her.

"Who turned out the lights?" her voice quavered.

"I did on my last security check."

Liam leaned his chin on her head, her silky hair tickling his face. He soaked in her sensuous scent, so familiar, so enticing, and doused with more fear than he'd ever experienced from another. The unforgettable memories of holding her close, the love he'd held for her drove out his wariness. He rocked her in his arms until her heart rhythm normalized.

"I'm sorry," she whispered.

"Shhh. You have nothing to be sorry about." In that moment, he understood how Neal had manipulated her and done unspeakable things to her, verbal, mental, and physical. Gates wide open, every emotion she felt consumed him. He'd once loved her to the depths of his being, and with every cell of his body, and all that love he'd tried to bury and resist resurfaced. Now she'd returned ready to right her wrongs. But something had broken inside her. The knowledge that she'd kept his son from him never started the engines on his hate. How could he hate the mother of his child, the woman he'd never stopped loving?

"Are you reading… feeling me?" She hiccupped.

"Do you mind? I can't block you." *I need to feel you.*

"No." She rubbed her cheek against his chest, and his heart pulsed like a moth beating against a lampshade.

"From the beginning, Neal encapsulated me into his cocoon of warmth and protection."

Liam's back tensed. "Did you need protection?"

She snorted. "Not physical protection. Life had snowed me. Connor, school, working, everything became too much. Even with my parents helping, I suffered from overload. Neal became my beacon, my shining star to lighten the load. We had a whirlwind romance. He swept me off my feet, and we married within six months. We agreed I'd quit my job while I finished school. Mom continued to babysit Connor, and things were great. I concentrated on my studies during the day and devoted my afternoons and evenings to Connor and Neal. Neal doted on Connor. Loved him from day one." Liam's arms stiffened. "It was a healthy love. Neal's kind and gentle with kids. He never got angry with Connor even when his wrath turned on me."

"Not good enough if he's causing our son pain." Liam knocked his fist on the floor.

"I know that now. I know so much more now." She swished her hand through the air, landed it on his arm, a warm weight he feared losing. "Florida ruined me. It ruined us."

The words split the fracturing chasm of his soul into two distinct pieces. He hated it, and he loved it. He hated

Eva being in his arms, and he loved her soft body cocooned within his. The protectiveness didn't even factor into it, but it hung on the periphery. He wanted to kill Neal for the pain he'd caused and continued to cause Eva.

"The nightmares come often." She clung to him. "I feel him all over me. I hear him. His charm, his seduction, his demented love. Manipulation, arrogance, obsession."

"Abuse?" Every muscle in his body hardened.

"He's textbook. I'm a textbook victim, a survivor. He may as well have shoved a stick up my ass and called me a sucker. I admit I never should've gone to Florida. It wrecked me. Except for Connor, my one bright ray of sunshine."

Liam's legs spasmed from his crouch on the floor. Eva's story engrossed him, and he didn't want to upset the moment by moving. "It wrecked me too." He nuzzled her hair, drawing in her berry-scented shampoo, a haunting fragrance.

"Losing you killed my defenses, opened me up to dangerous suggestion I never recovered from. Neal became an easy distraction until he became my tormentor." She chuckled wryly. "I dreamed of you riding in on your white horse and rescuing me. Anyway, I finished my master's early, and without Neal knowing because he was so involved with his family by that point, I attended police academy and graduated, got offered a great job. My parents paid for it, and he never knew until I came home one day with a gun, a badge, and newfound courage. He blew a fuse. I told him I wanted a divorce that day. Worst day of my life."

"What did he do to you?" Anger seared the tight muscles of Liam's legs.

"He tried to make me see reason, decided he'd let it slide that I'd gone behind his back and became a cop. He said he'd 'let me' take the job if I stayed with him, blah,

blah, blah. Even though I'd already made my decision, I told him I'd think about his offer. I slept in the guest room that night. Woke up, him on top of me, inside me. The room was pitch black; he always kept the lights off." Her voice had grown so low Liam almost missed her last two words. "It's the recurring nightmare I keep having. The lights help minimize them, drive him away."

His mind seized up and booted out her emotions before they consumed him. Cramps engulfed his leg, and he mustered his words. "God, Eva. I'm so sorry. I'll ensure he doesn't live to hurt you or anyone else again." Pain lanced his skull. Eva's pain. "My leg's going numb. Can we move to the bed? Are you okay with that?" The kid gloves came out. He'd never dealt with an abuse victim before, and he took his cues from her.

Eva loosened her hold, craned her head to look him in the face, grazed her fingers over the stubble on his jaw. "I think you're the only one I feel safe with. Even after all these years and everything, it's always been you."

Liam scooped her in his arms and set her on the bed as if she were broken in a million pieces. In a sense, she was fractured. Not in body, but in spirit. The old Eva he knew still lived within her, and he wanted her back more than anything. The years of separation vanished.

He turned the lights back on. Upon her silent invitation, he climbed onto the bed and folded her into his arms, the stuffed lion smashed between them. She embraced him close and rested her cheek on his heart.

Teeth grinding, he touched the tiny reddened wound on her neck. "He bit you?" She nodded.

Neal is so fucking dead. "Is this okay?" he asked. "Will you let me be your haven?"

"Do you want to be my haven?" She splayed her palm on his heart. "I hurt you—"

He tapped his index finger on her chin. "We're both to

blame. I knew what you wanted. I knew you freaked about my lifestyle, and I tried to force it upon you."

"You didn't force it upon me. I just couldn't live with that choice. I tried so freaking hard. Accepting the scholarship in Florida became my ultimate excuse. I was weak, Liam. I've recognized it for a long time. Then Neal swept me into his web and plied me with his charm and love." She paused. "He does love me. Now and then I experience the old Neal, the good Neal."

"But do you love him?" Liam's arms steeled around her soft curves. Every part of her touching him erased the years of separation. Her arms around his torso reanimated his soul. Her shapely legs pressed to his set off a craving so deep it floored Liam.

"I haven't loved him in years. I haven't been in love with him in over two years. That ship sailed the first time he—"

"Hit you?" Liam wrenched her closer as if to protect her from Neal's fists, his mouth, and his every glance.

"Tried to choke me after he tossed a cup of hot coffee down my chest. I refused to make him breakfast after Connor and I had eaten, and he couldn't bother to show up." Liam growled. "He'd supposedly gone to the gym. Probably to his current girlfriend's house."

A muscle ticked in Liam's jaw. "He was cheating on you too?"

"Once he became the heir apparent, he did anything he wanted. Seemed as if he'd waited for his brother to die to fling open the gates to his assholery."

"How'd his brother kick off?"

"Shot point-blank in a Vegas hotel room. Evidence is nil, Estensons have covered it up for whatever nefarious reasons they conjured up. As far as I know, they've already exacted their revenge."

Eva's reticence oozed into him. "Did he have a wife who

hated him?"

"His wife adored him. She embraces the mafia life as though born to it. They have twin boys, two years older than Connor and a three-year-old daughter. They're gold in the family."

Liam stretched out his legs, distancing them from entwining around hers, keeping the hard evidence of his desire in check. Eva's scent was enough to drive a man crazy with need. "Is Neal capable of murder?"

"He's so far from the man I fell in love with. I don't know what he's capable of." She yawned wide.

Liam scooted away, and she seized his arm. "Don't go."

"We both need sleep."

"I don't think I can sleep. Alex sent a bunch of aerial shots of houses close to the beaches with stairs. I want to study them."

Liam lay on his side, facing her. He kept his hands close to his body, cradling his bad arm, and pressed a kiss to her furrowed brow, smoothing out the wrinkles. "Can you sleep with me here? We can look at the houses in the morning with fresh eyes."

"Maybe." She scrubbed the comforter between her thumb and fingers.

Her moist lips drew him closer, courted his desire. Liam's gut clenched, and he took in the shyness on her face, stopped. Yet she tilted her head closer, skin flushed. Her full lips parted, enticed him, and his lips possessed her. Eager and soft, her mouth tempted him with the faint flavor of wintergreen. When she didn't object, he crushed her body to his, teasing her lips apart with his tongue. Eva deepened the kiss, wound her tongue around his and leisurely explored the inside of his mouth, the faint taste of her toothpaste mingling with the beer he'd downed earlier. Liam dipped his tongue in and out of her mouth, and Eva whimpered.

A feverish need consumed him, and if he didn't stop, he didn't know if he could. A tiny part of his brain, the part not concerned with her in his arms, kept demanding one of them gain their wits soon. As if he'd coerced the thought upon her, her head jerked back, eyes as dark as the ocean's surface at midnight. Tempting him. Tempting midnight.

"Liam," she whispered, her fingers covering her mouth.

"Shhh." He kissed her forehead, her emotions an echo in his body. As she turned her back to him and drew his arm across her hip, he spooned her. The chasm between them dissolved and old suspicions melted and dried up. Sleep claimed her fast and deep, while he lay dying a languorous death in her arms.

CHAPTER SIXTEEN

Eva awoke after seven, surprised to find Liam's arm draped across her middle, holding her close to his body, driving off her demons. The memory of their kiss carried a flush to her face and a swirl of lust between her legs. He kissed better than she recalled, and her memories were impeccable. When Liam had kissed her, everything flooded back, how she loved the feel of his lips on hers, loved kissing him, how he always made her feel safe and precious. Renewed hope sprouted amid her barren wasteland. But she couldn't mask her desolation, the decimated remains of guilt and betrayal littering her post-Neal wasteland.

Even in sleep next to her, he wore contentment on his face. As if he sensed her thoughts, his breathing changed, and he stirred under her scrutiny. A groove on the bridge of his nose and the stiffening of his body changed his contentment to resolve.

Yawning and ignoring the ginormous elephant in the room, she thrust off the covers. "You awake?"

Liam's eyes flitted open, and he released his arms from around her. "Getting there. Did you sleep?"

"Better than I've slept in a long time."

He smirked. "You always did in my bed."

The evidence of his morning arousal strained the front

of his jeans. "You were a hard habit to break." She pressed a kiss to his forehead. "Thank you."

He swung his legs over the side of the bed, scrubbing his tousled hair. "I'm taking a shower. House alarm's set, so don't go anywhere or you'll wake the neighborhood."

"I'll fix breakfast and study the beach photos."

"Do the Estensons own a beach house?"

"They own houses all over the world. If Neal's traveling between San Jose and a beach, it's got to be within a short drive or plane hop. The family owns private jets."

"Of course." Sarcasm dripped from Liam's tone. "Yachts and limos, I bet."

"One yacht and a car lot." Eva stared at her stockinged feet, wracking her brain for any tidbit Neal had shared. "Enemies hide in plain sight. Exactly what he'd want me to think."

CRXSO

After a fruitless morning of research, and an even tenser afternoon dancing around one another, building mental and physical walls, Eva and Liam parted in the garage. For the first time since waking in bed together, he touched the back of her hand, absorbed her jittery nerves.

His eyes softened. "Play it cool tonight, don't provoke him. Ric will monitor the tracker in your phone. Text him 911 if you need help. Don't let your pride stop you from texting or force you to handle Neal on your own."

She weaved her fingers within his strong clasp. The feel of his skin against hers drove a trail of goosebumps up her arm. "Same with you."

He grinned. "I'm not scared of Crystal."

"Don't underestimate her. She's treacherous." She untangled their hands and patted his chest. "I care for you. I hate that my mess may get you in hot water with the mafia."

"Or the Cabal." He inclined forward, kissed her forehead, and she almost tipped her head back to drag his lips onto hers. "Doesn't matter, not with Connor at stake."

A half hour later, absent her gun, Eva entered her condo. She checked the new hidden cameras, sighed in relief that no one had infiltrated her inner sanctum overnight.

A hot shower did little to settle her nerves. The sexy black, strapless dress parading a flouncy hem elevated them. The dress hugged her body, one of Neal's favorites. She spritzed on his favorite perfume and topped it all with her silk and fur-lined cape. She vowed to rid herself of anything Neal liked once she rid herself of him.

The restaurant boasted a full crowd for a Monday evening. Laughter, talk, and gaiety soared above the low hum of classical music. Dressed in a charcoal gray suit, dove dress shirt, and a deep purple tie, Neal waited at the bar. He almost stole her breath away. Neal had killer looks that attracted more women than any man had a right to attract. Classic tall, dark, and handsome. Lethally handsome. Lethally dark. A voluptuous blonde chatted him up, leaning across his arm, giving him a healthy view and feel of her boobs.

He laughed at something she said, and Eva's stomach plummeted into jittery land again. The bimbo could have him if she wanted. But the moment he saw Eva at the bar entrance, her cape over her bare arm, he excused himself and stalked over to her.

"You look amazing. I love that dress on you." In a deliberate tactic to set her at ease, he kissed her cheek rather than her mouth.

Eva knew his moves. She shifted to the side a tad and his lips landed half on her mouth. She parted her lips and kissed him back, a quick hello kiss among lovers. Although it sickened her, it served her purpose. He grasped her upper arms and towed her closer.

She splayed her hand on his shoulder to halt him and gave him a fake coy smile. "Let's see how dinner goes."

Neal only moved a fraction, triggering a clench of her belly. "Are you saying there might be more? You've certainly changed your tune."

Leaving his question to dangle enticingly in the air, she shrugged. He always loved a challenge. *Game on.*

Neal settled his hand proprietarily in the small of her back. He signaled the hostess, and she guided them toward the private rooms. The shadow of flames danced on the hallway walls from fake candle sconces, lighting their path to Neal's heaven and Eva's hell.

The hostess opened a door into an intimate room, candles lending the space romantic appeal to the unwary. Neal's personal bodyguard Gavin—since crowned king, he employed bodyguards—stood in a dark corner, his beefy hands in a loose clasp in front of his paunch in his cheap, too-tight black suit.

"Mrs. Estenson." Gavin inclined his head. "Good to see you."

She bristled at the use of her former name. Everyone and their Estenson dog knew she'd restored her maiden name. Neal had ranted in front of his entire family about her wanting to rid herself of the Estenson clan as well as the oh-so-exclusive name. *Piece-of-garbage name. He can choke on it.*

Of course, he was right. *Because he's an idiot on a power trip and thinks he owns the freaking universe.* Little had she known that act of "defiance" would goad him to ram her against a wall, unzip his pants to drive the Estenson back into her, his way. Unfortunately for him, Connor woke up and interrupted Neal's attempted rape. No need to dwell on her old hell when her new hell sat in front of her.

The waiter brought in oysters on the half shell. Eva stifled a gag. *Seriously? Transparent, much?* Even though she loved oysters, Neal ordered them for their mythical aphrodisiac properties. *Well, hello, precious.* She picked up an oyster, spritzed lemon on it, and let it slide down her gullet. Neal watched her like a hawk as she devoured two more. They never did a thing for her.

"Good, darling?" He scarfed his last one, smacking his lips in a way she loathed.

"Not as good as Florida oysters."

Waiters served the entrees Neal had preordered, all her favorite foods: smoked salmon, asparagus risotto, and sourdough bread. He opened an expensive bottle of champagne and poured the golden liquid into crystal flutes. The tang of spicy sauces assailed her nose.

"To us again." He clinked his glass against hers.

"To our family." She clinked again and gulped the champagne, bubbles popping in her nose.

Neal's eyes lit up. "Do you mean that?"

Playing him like a fiddle, she kicked off her right stiletto and stroked her foot up his ankle. "I hate the division between us. I want Connor to have his mother and father together again." She stirred the pot. No admitting that she didn't mean him. No confessing how much she wanted Liam in her life again, not just for Connor, but for herself. *Lies and deception, party of one.*

"Eva." He gloved her hand on the tabletop. "You know it's what I've wanted. I never wanted the divorce, or to step out of our marriage. I've regretted my actions every day."

"I know, Neal." She chanced a playbook of demands. "If we try again, things can't return to yesterday. You have to devote yourself to me. No more other women. No more—"

"Done and done. I won't ever touch you again in anger. Babe, you know how it was for me. Danny dying, the pressures my father unloaded on me. It dragged me under a darkness I had a tough time clawing out of."

"How is it different now?" She eased her hand out from under his and tucked an errant lock of hair behind her right ear.

A sly smile tugged at his lips. "I'm taking over the business. Dad's planning to step down in a few years. He's already handed over half the reins."

"He won't trust you if I come back."

"If?"

"When, if, whatever." She slugged down the rest of her liquid fortification. "He's gunning for my body on a cement slab."

"He agreed to call off the dogs if we remarry and you quit the police force."

She waggled her head. "I love my job. Connor's in school now, he doesn't need me at home all day." She trailed her toes up his leg. "Besides, I can help you. You know that."

"You're too honest to do our dirty work."

More lies rolled off her tongue. "What's a little more corruption? I'm learning my way around."

Head kinked to the side, a too-long silence immersed Neal. "Let's take this one step at a time."

"I agree. I might need more convincing." She licked her lips enticingly. "We were always good in bed." True that, until he fucked his way up the Florida panhandle. "I miss you in my bed." Nearly gagging on the word bed, she poured herself one last glass of champagne. Any more, and she'd find herself passed out and handcuffed to Neal's four-poster.

"Then let me convince you." He set his cloth napkin on the table.

"After we eat. We'll go to your house, see where it leads us." Hopefully, into a minefield of disclosures.

After dinner, Gavin drove them to Neal's house in the foothills. The moment she walked in and spied the candles burning and sniffed melting chocolate riding the air, she knew he had every intention of bringing her to his house one way or another. He'd never go to so much trouble for a possibility.

She kicked off her shoes and headed to the bar in the family room. "I'll fix you a drink. Why don't you take your suit and tie off?" The small pot of steaming chocolate and tray of fruit pieces, her favorite dessert, turned her stomach.

"This night just gets better and better." He headed toward the stairs, stooped to pick up his overnight bag. "I love this side of you. I miss this so much. You know, I bought this house for us. You don't need to live in crappy condos anymore."

The love she'd once felt for Neal had evaporated like a puff of smoke until nothing remained of it on the horizon. Maybe her love for him had never truly existed. Maybe all the love she had remained with Liam, and she'd misplaced it in the shell of her marriage to Neal.

"Oh, Neal, you're sweet." *Douche-canoe.* She frowned at the bar, her back to him. His footsteps receded upstairs. A full bottle of bourbon beckoned. She scooped up ice and it clinked into the bottom of a cut-crystal tumbler. Fishing into the tiny pocket inside the seam of her dress, she slipped out a capsule of white powder and tapped the contents into Neal's bourbon. She topped off the glass, stirred until the powder dissolved. The capsule contained enough Rohypnol to knock out a horse. Gave her plenty of time to punch his ticket and get out of Dodge.

CHAPTER SEVENTEEN

Liam met Crystal Estenson at the Lucky Shamrock at her request. She hadn't wanted him to pick her up, but she allowed him to drive her to the fancy, new Italian bistro where she'd finagled an eleventh-hour table.

"Does your family own this joint too?" He palmed her lower back, and they followed the hostess to their table in a corner booth. Crystal pressed her body into his hand. Tendrils of her desire swirled in his mind. He had this in the bag. If he didn't screw up.

"We don't need to own. Because we are."

"The Estensons." He chuckled. "Good to know." He felt like he was crawling out of his skin.

"Not just the Estensons—" Her lips compressed tight. They sat across from each other in the intimate booth and the hostess vanished. Candles flickered on the table, the air redolent of spices from the old world of Italy, a much more palpable scent than Crystal's floral marinade.

Liam gloved her hand beneath his. "I get it. I use my gifts in ways that skirt the sidelines." *Scout's honor. Not.*

"Exactly what I wanted to hear." The desire and excitement rolling off her sifted into Liam, softening his twisting emotions. She weaved her fingers in his for a quick squeeze, and her lust drove a stake into his groin. Easing out of her hold, he picked up his menu, dampened her lust with a coercive thought. She recoiled as if scorched, and he hid a smile behind his menu. They ordered drinks and scanned the menu.

"I feel like I know you so well," she said, setting her menu on the table. Yellow flecks glinted in her dung-brown eyes.

"Our psychic connection?"

"No. Something about you. Although I read minds, I don't make a habit of reading my dates. Hear me when I say I'm *not* reading you." He nodded, knowing his blocks were impenetrable. "I've never felt this way with another."

"Psychic?"

"Man." Slashes of red stained her cheeks. "I'm sorry if I'm coming on too strong. I have a credible sixth sense on character."

Liam stopped her hands from wringing the life out of each other. Her bold truth burst into him. "I'm reading your emotions. Do you mind?"

"You see I'm telling the truth," she said. He nodded. "Does it thrill or scare you?"

He closed the deal. "A little of both." Truth.

They spent their date talking about random facets of their lives, dancing around their families, and flirting with every word. Dinner came and crawled. Although he was starving and the excellent food hit the jackpot, he counted the minutes until their last sip of coffee.

He kept counting the minutes until he saw Eva again. *Just cut me open and stuff me with reality checks.*

Speaking of... he reached for the check, and Crystal snatched it up first.

"Dinner's on me. I know you aren't working, and this place is too expensive for you."

Not willing to argue with his new sugar mama, Liam held up his hands in surrender. "Thank you." In the real world, he'd never allow his date to pick up the tab. Call him old school.

"No 'I'm the man' argument?"

"I know my limits."

"You can repay me in other ways." Echoes of the candle flame set off tiny exploding stars in her eyes. Liam rubbed his thumb across her wrist, doused her desire with his own reluctance, and the gold stars petered out.

She settled the tab, and Liam took her hand in his. "Let's go work on payback," he said.

The valet brought her car around, and she said, "You drive. I'll direct."

"Where are we headed?" He shut the passenger door for her, then darted to the driver's side of her luxury sports car.

"You'll see. But I have to make it a short night. I'm on babysitting duty for my nephew."

A poisoned arrow numbed his heart for a few seconds. "Are his parents out of town?"

"Something like that. He's with his grandfather tonight." She paused, a mellow, thoughtful expression on her face. "You know, I think you might be able to help him."

"What do you mean?"

"He's special." She placed her hand on his thigh, creeping toward his crotch. Confronted with a bounty of riches in a woman, his dick had a mind of its own. She chuckled. "You see how much you like me." Pain lanced his groin at his restrictive pants. As if sensing his discomfort, she unbuttoned them, and the hiss of the zipper retracting pierced his resolve.

"What do you mean special?" She clamped her fingers around his iron erection, and he swerved, overcompensating and jolting them in their seats as he swung the car back into the lane. "Easy, Crystal. You want me to crash your expensive sports car?"

She purred. "I want you to come for me while driving."

As she began to pump her hand up and down on him, a ton of bricks hit his shoulders. Eva. He couldn't do this to Eva. He couldn't do this to himself. *When did you start having feelings for Eva? When did you ever stop, you moron?* Summoning an epic dose of lethargy to temper her urges, he clasped her wrist. "Not like this, Crystal." She emitted an aggravated groan, and her hand fell off him in a limp heap. "When I fuck you, I want it to be in the right place and right time. Not like sixteen-year-olds in a car."

Crystal's shoulders drooped forward. "You're too good to be true."

"Is it only about sex with you? If so, I'm not sure I'm in."

She stroked a placid hand over his knee. "Where have you been all my life?"

Contemplative silence shrouded the interior. Crystal waved directions, and he weaved in and out of traffic toward downtown and into the parking garage of a newer high-rise of luxury condominiums.

Crystal's grip on his wrist stopped him before he peeled himself out of the two-seater. "I want more than sex from you, and I'm willing to wait. I'm willing to do the whole wooing bit."

Hiding a flinch, Liam flipped his wrist and linked his fingers in hers. "You won't regret it." He might regret being a tool after he reset his moral barometer. "I get the sense no one has ever wooed you. I plan to change that." Guilt blistered a hole in his gut. He hated the lies, hated the idea of Crystal having access to his son. He hated that it wasn't Eva sitting in the car, stroking him. Curse him to eternity for his resurfaced feelings for Eva as if their time apart, her betrayal, and secrets had never crapped on his life.

She giggled like a teen girl. "I don't know why I feel such a connection to you. Damn if I can't deny it. I've never believed in fate, but I sure do now."

Connection? All he felt was her insatiable hunger. He strengthened the shield on his mind to prevent her from busting his balls. Even though he didn't feel her telepathic intrusion in the natural emotions she exuded, he had to walk the straight and narrow.

"Connections are strange between men and women." He bent over the center console to nuzzle her neck, the cloying scent of unidentified flowers clogging his nose. "Fate is even stranger. When it happens, you know it's real." Locking his hands down from touching her, he brushed a line of kisses up her jaw, ending with a brief kiss on her full, berry-stained lips. When she tried to force her tongue down his throat, he edged away, plucking at the crotch of his pants. A show of lust, an act of betrayal to his head. His dick never followed his head's lead, which benefited his game mode, not much else. In the dark confines of the parking garage, they spent the next fifteen minutes touching and kissing until they both drew apart, gasping for evaporating air. His heart wasn't in it, and he hoped she hadn't noticed. Surreptitiously, he wiped her mouth cooties off on the back of his hand.

A text message dinged her phone and she whipped it out. She groaned. "I'm sorry. I need to get my nephew earlier than planned. Drive back to the bar so you can get your car." She reapplied her lipstick, smacking her lips as if she'd eaten the canary. "My father's impatient. I don't want him getting frustrated with my nephew."

Curious and more than a little annoyed at senior Estenson, Liam drove out of the garage. "You said he's special. What did you mean? What kind of help did you have in mind?"

"He's a young empath needing guidance and training. You appear to have yours under control, something I want to explore further. Tomorrow, if you're game. If all works out, I can put you on payroll for a special new position."

"I've had years of practice. I'm good at what I do."

"No doubt." A sexy purr accompanied her words.

Play it cool, man. Don't tip your crooked Guild hat. "Does everyone in your family have psychic abilities?"

She hooted. "It skips generations. We're the only two in the family, although I have a cousin who has middling touch telepathy, not worth mentioning. He's wrong more times than right. He just likes to snow my father, trying to work his way up the ranks of my family's businesses."

"Is your nephew good?"

"The best I've ever seen."

"How old is he?"

"That's the rub. He's only six, and he has so much potential I want him to have the best training."

"Why do you think I'm the best?" A steady pulse beat in his veins.

"I've been exposed to a lot of psychics in my circles. I have an excellent sixth sense for psychic abilities."

"You're not wrong. Your concern for your nephew seems extreme, though." He hated the desperation wafting off her. He wanted to kill Estenson senior and junior. He wanted to kill Neal for daring to raise an abusive finger or tongue toward Eva.

"You didn't touch me, and you knew what I was feeling. You can read emotions without touching. Am I right?"

A crimson tide painted his neck. "In extreme cases." Easy lie. He rarely needed to touch anyone for his extrasensory perception to kick in when in proximity to his victim or willing accomplice. Touching quickened the sensation, made it deeper, more open. When in a crowded room, emotions hit him from all sides, so touch was the best way to discern emotions a particular person projected.

"Your silence is telling. How do you protect yourself in a crowded room?"

Shitballs in space. Is she reading my mind? He tested

his blocks and they remained unwavering. A knot unknitted in his shoulder, leaving a million in its wake. "I have my ways."

"Do they always work?"

"No. It's why I prefer smaller, more intimate gatherings."

"As do I. Like this."

Wincing at his sore arm that'd had its share of pain all night, he parked near his car in the restaurant lot and took her hand in his. He kissed the underside of her wrist. "Until tomorrow?"

"Meet me at the bar in the morning. Nine thirty?"

"You hold your business meetings at a bar? Surely, the Estensons have cush offices."

"The bar's closed and quiet, secure. Off the grid."

Glacial fingers galloped up his spine. Did he want to know what she had planned in the back room of a closed bar?

Liam dashed around to the passenger door, but she'd already hopped out. One thing he noticed about her was that she preferred doing the gentlemanly things on her own. Eva warned him about her power tripping. The fleeting idea of becoming her gigolo encouraged his Italian dinner to stage a comeback.

Crystal rubbed her breasts against his chest and kissed him soundly on the mouth, trailing her tongue over his lips. "Down, girl. There's more where that came from. In time."

Her glossy lips turned into an inky black pout under the perimeter lights. "Mr. Take-it-Slow-and-Easy. Let's not go too slow, shall we?" She waltzed away, shaking her bootilicious ass for all it was worth.

"Tomorrow, Crystal."

Liam watched her drive off... until he felt the barrel of a gun poke the center of his back.

CHAPTER EIGHTEEN

Neal sat close to Eva on the sofa in his sterile, black and white family room looking down into the Santa Clara valley. She suffered the stench of his new peppery-spice cologne and the bourbon wafting out of his parted mouth. Myriad lights peppered the city below, mirroring the starlit sky above, echoing her pinpricks of unease. Eva felt like a cornered ghost stuck in the darkness of the in-between. She sipped her Pinot Noir while he gulped his bourbon, leaving a bare sip to buoy up his ice cubes. It took a mere thirty seconds for Neal to list against the sofa.

She touched his hand cupping the glass. "Slow down, you may not make it to later. Or do you need the alcohol to seduce me?"

Eyelids droopy, he tilted toward her and slammed his head onto her breasts. She recoiled into the sofa. "I think you're right." His voice slurred. "Maybe I had too much at dinner." She rolled him off her, and he righted himself, propped up by the sofa arm behind him. He pinched the bridge of his nose. "Let's go up. I want you so bad." Even in his sedated, inebriated state, a hard-on tented his slacks.

He sandwiched her hand between his hand and his deflating dick. *Score one for Eva.* He groaned and pressed her hand down.

"Let's go upstairs. I can make it all better," she purred.

He'd softened and released her. "Will you spend the night?"

"Well, I don't have a car." She forced a smile.

After a slow slog up the stairs and Neal tripping twice, she leveraged him onto his bed. "Don't worry, babe. I'll wake you, and we'll have fun, sexy times," she muttered. He flashed her a wan grin and rolled onto his side, winking out like a dying star in a black hole.

Not wasting a second, she ran downstairs to his office, turned on the audio and video frequency scrambler Ric had given her, and locked the door. The aluminum briefcase sitting next to Neal's desk beckoned, nectar to a starving bee. He hadn't bothered to replace it after they'd split up, and the sticker with Connor's name remained beneath the handle. She slipped on a pair of latex gloves and punched in the code, satisfied with the quick click of dual locks opening. His laptop sat front and center. She pried the lid open to a blank screen covered in fingerprints, some were Connor's teeny prints. Wistfully tracing them with a gloved fingertip brought him closer to her.

Would the programs on her flash drive disguise her keystrokes and open up his hard drive for copying? Or would it expose her and lock the computer down tighter than Hannibal Lecter? Or did he have a self-destruct app installed? No. He wasn't that smart or diabolical. *The dumbass hadn't even replaced his laptop.*

Doubts roiled in her brain even as she poised to stick the blank flash drive in the USB slot. As she shut down the naysayers stabbing her mind, she inserted the flash drive into the computer, hit the power button as her tech geek instructed, and watched the screen flash to life.

She activated the password app. It took three of the jitteriest minutes of her life until it froze on the password: *Eva4ME4eveR. Dread clawed at her as she punched in the password to the screensaver photo of herself, Neal, and

Connor from their last Christmas together in Florida. One of the worst days of her life.

They'd spent a long day at her parents' beach house, cooking a ton of food, partying in the house and on the beach in the Florida sunshine. Other than Neal drunk off his ass all day, it had been a glorious holiday, made special for Connor. Until midnight left her bruised and battered. Neal had forced himself on her, the last time they'd had sex. He vowed never to touch her again in anger. He didn't keep his vow. She vowed to take him down one bruise at a time until he had nothing left but a broken body and soul. Her vow remained her number two priority.

She followed her instructions and began downloading the entire contents of Neal's computer onto the flash drive. Every second that crawled by, she held and released her breath waiting for the laptop to blow a gasket, to self-destruct, to set off alarm bells, to say "Hello, Eva. You're dead." But the download continued until a green light shone steady on the screen.

She set everything back the way she'd found it, grabbed the bourbon and her wine glass, and returned to Neal's bedroom. She emptied half the bottle of booze into the bathroom sink and rinsed away all traces. Neal lay in the same prone position, and she struggled to strip him down to his birthday suit. She spritzed her travel bottle of perfume on the other pillow, and slammed her fist in it, spreading it wide to make a dent the size of her skull, wishing to the almighty gods of revenge she'd punched Neal's balls instead of a defenseless pillow. Next, she slicked on her lipstick and kissed the collar of Neal's shirt, his sweaty neck, and his cheek. Let him think he'd had the best sex of his life and didn't remember a second.

One last thing, she took a photo of him sprawled on the bed, a smile of revenge easing across her face, and then flipped him the bird.

The drive share back to her car and then home took forever. By the time she entered her steaming shower to wipe Neal off her skin, exhaustion wilted her against the tile. Water sluiced down her hair and body, rinsing the salt of tears off her face. If she didn't get her son back, she'd go stark raving mad. Didn't matter if she suffered a major hit to her psyche. And body.

CRINO

Parking lot lights seemed to dim as the gun lodged against Liam's spine. He opened his mental walls, and a stream of disorder and arrogance filtered in, toting a healthy dose of jealousy.

"McAllister," Lucas Saldivar grunted out. Liam knew the voice well. A Guild Guardian who'd joined their monthly poker games a few months ago with his friendly demeanor and happy-go-lucky charm. "Hands up where I can see them." Only a slight Spanish accent fringed Lucas's voice. His parents had emigrated from Spain when Lucas was ten. His eight-year-old sister exhibited rare telekinetic abilities they had no clue how to train or control. They came to America to seek the western Guild's assistance, since the Guild had the only two known telekinetics on its rolls.

Palms forward above his shoulders, he complied, trying to trick Saldivar's brain with coercion. Instead, the gun poked his spine harder. His coercion ability didn't work every time or on every person. He had to connect empathically with a person's emotions and impel the emotions back onto the person discharging them. Saldivar had probably learned to block him.

"What the hell, man? This a joke?" Liam tried levity. "You got me. I'll pay you back on poker night. Count on it." They held monthly Guardian games to provide a fun break between duties with their fellow Guardians. Gun slinging never entered their bonding games.

"What are you doing with Crystal Estenson?"

The gun barrel jabbed between his shoulder blades, causing pain to lance down his spine and reverberate up his gunshot arm. *With friends like these, who needs enemies?* Had Saldivar figured out the Estensons were Cabal? Did he think Liam was involved with them?

"I asked you a question." Saldivar cocked the trigger on the gun.

Liam lost his thread to the man's emotions. "It a crime to date a beautiful woman?"

Saldivar snorted. "Crystal doesn't date. She *owns*."

A strange mix of dread and sorrow washed over Liam, dissipated as quick as it hit. Had Saldivar flipped on the Guild? "Does she own you, Lucas?"

"Crystal and I have an understanding." The door to the restaurant tossed out a crowd of satiated people who headed toward them. "Move into the shadows." Saldivar prodded Liam's back with the gun. "Keep your hands up."

Liam sidestepped into the shadows of the building and a few stick trees on the far side of autumn. "How do you know Crystal?" Without an empathic connection, he had a hard time deciphering Saldivar's words.

Saldivar sniggered. "You leaving the Guild? Can't blame you since they keep extending your suspension. I bet it's killing you to lose out on Guardian jobs."

"No denying that." His mind whirled at the mind bender. One of them wouldn't make it out of this conversation to blab it to the world. "You leaving the Guild too?"

"You'll never leave your brothers and the Guild. You've all fought to keep the Guild intact from the threats over the last few months." Rancid dumpster odors lodged in Liam's nostrils as he waited for the hammer to drop. "Which means," Saldivar continued, "you're up to no good. I can call Crystal right here, right now. How will my call end?"

"What do you want?" Liam needed to gain the upper hand before Saldivar blew his cover or blew a hole in his spine. "This have anything to do with your sister?"

Saldivar nudged him farther into the darkness around the corner of the building. Liam cast his gaze around until it halted on a few short two-by-fours stacked against the building.

"Carina's safe from the Guild after they left her to rot in a mental facility."

The memories of his sister's story resurfaced. The Guild had welcomed the Saldivar family, and their best telekinetic member had trained Carina Saldivar to manage and understand her abilities. But Carina was unable to shield her mind. After two years, the Guild suggested the Saldivars admit her to a paranormal institute to protect her mind from psychic intrusions and to further develop her defenses to function in the world. If she didn't get a handle on her mental defenses, her telekinetic powers had the potential to break her mind. The family complied, Lucas became a junior Guardian when he turned eighteen to protect his sister, and Liam heard nothing more about Carina. He'd always assumed she'd received the necessary aid and training. Could she be a Cabal psychic under the Estensons' dominion now?

"I'm sorry about Carina. I hope she's okay."

"Better than okay."

"Does she work with Crystal or the Estensons?"

Saldivar grunted out a laugh. "You can say that."

"Are you turning on the Guild, Lucas?"

He snickered again. "I bet the Guild will love to hear that *you're* turning on them."

"Who said I was turning on them?" Liam's gunshot arm screamed bloody murder, and he desperately wanted to drop his arms before the pain muddled his brain further. "I bumped into a beautiful woman at their family's bar. She likes psychics. Big deal."

"That's not all she likes."

"I get it. She's into you. I'm not encroaching on your thing with her. We talked shop, nothing more."

"Shop, my ass." Saldivar edged to his side and trained the weapon on Liam's temple. "You're flipping on the Guild."

"What do you mean flipping on the Guild? Who said my meeting had shit to do with Guild business? Dude, I run a securities company." Liam played dumb, trying to get Saldivar to drop a hint about the Cabal or the Estensons.

"I'm not spelling out the obvious."

Liam set Saldivar's face in his peripheral vision and released his bombshell. "Do you mean flipping on the Guild to hook up with the Cabal?"

"Ding, ding, ding. You said it, not me." Saldivar flicked the safety on and off his gun, and Liam lost focus on the acceptance pouring off the man. "Now you know. Now you die."

In the face of Liam's apprehension, an adrenaline rush bloomed in his core. Another puzzle piece fit into place. "Dude, it doesn't have to go down this way." Liam beat the bushes in his mind for a way out of his conundrum, gauging the distance to the two-by-fours. "If you're playing both sides of the fence, we can do it together. Crystal's all yours. She only wants my mind to help her business."

"Fuck you, McAllister."

"You're right about me flipping. We're on the same side. We can work the Guild from the inside and maintain our cover. Game?"

Saldivar's bewilderment swarmed Liam. A moment of silence followed the gun's barest shift off his temple. Footsteps shuffled behind him, pebbles scraping the tarmac. It was enough. Liam dropped to a crouch and lunged forward. A muffled shot rang out, the bullet flying wild. He snatched up a two-by-four, swung up, and slammed it into the side of Saldivar's head.

CHAPTER NINETEEN

Pain shot up both Liam's arms, and his wounded arm blazed a million suns of death. The blow to Saldivar's head knocked him out, exactly as Liam anticipated. He didn't kill his friends and fellow Guardians even if they had tripped into the dark side. The Guild scored points in keeping Saldivar alive. They might learn more about the Estensons and the Cabal.

Strength waning, Liam managed to drag the downed Guardian to his vehicle and leverage him into the cargo hold. He slapped duct tape over Saldivar's mouth and ankles and zip-stripped his wrists behind his back.

He called Ric. "I have good news and bad news," he said. "First, take me off speakerphone."

"I'm with Marisa."

"Take me off speakerphone."

"Dude, she's Guild. What's the big deal?"

Not that he disliked the new love of Ric's life and wasn't technically on the Guardian roll book, he still followed Guardian rules. "Jeez, Ric. It's Guardian business. Get a clue."

Ric conceded, and Liam explained what'd happened with Saldivar.

"No, man. Not Lucas." Ric groaned, and his lab woofed in the background. Liam missed the dog. Helluva lot easier to deal with lonely times with a dog than the cards dealt to him this week. "Bring him to the compound. I'll call Niles. We'll meet you there."

"I blew my cover tonight." Liam steered his vehicle toward the western foothills.

"Not if we contain Lucas."

"We can't hold him indefinitely."

"Let's see what Niles suggests. This gem landed in our laps tonight. He who hesitates doesn't get the early worm."

"Don't put all our chickens in one basket?" Liam quipped. "And don't spoil my thunder?"

"Now you're talking my language." Ric chuckled at Liam's attempt to mimic his mixed-up metaphors. "I knew I'd drag you into the Ric side."

"On second thought, bring Marisa. We'll need her."

As Liam clicked off, a low rustling grew in the cargo hold. "Ease off, Saldivar. You can spew your lies to Niles." Saldivar kicked the back seat a couple times, rocking the vehicle. The Guild had trained Saldivar to block his mind and thwart certain psychic abilities since he didn't possess his own. Although Liam's oldest brother, Jake, read minds, he couldn't pierce a blocked mind. Marisa Meadows, Guild attorney, knew how to drill through most blocked minds.

Liam's thoughts rolled to the Estensons and logically to Eva. Was she okay? He couldn't stand the idea of her with Neal, and it left a thriving pit of unease in his gut. Whatever abuse the bastard had dished out had changed her from the joyful, studious, loving, and loyal woman he'd known during college to frightened and reckless, not to mention paranoid. He hated what the bastard had done to destroy the woman he'd known and loved. *Love... still love. You've never stopped loving her.* Given what he'd seen over the last couple nights, he had no business getting angry at her past actions any longer. Yet, the real reason he couldn't get mad at her was due to how everything about her lit the first fire inside him he'd experienced in seven years. One glimpse of her had fanned the ashes into embers. One touch fanned the embers into flames. He detested the idea of dousing that fire.

Thirty minutes of weaving through San Jose's never-ending traffic, he drove into the Guild compound parking lot. Glowing lights bordered the back patio and illuminated the first floor. Pools of yellow light on the ground demarcated the backyard perimeter from the dark woods beyond.

His brothers and Niles streamed out the side door leading to the kitchen and the Protectorate's private rooms. Incognito was the name of the game. No telling who else in the Guild may be playing both hands. The pending Cabal downfall just hit Level Ten and burned to a crisp any trust among the Guardians and Guild at large.

"Get him into the war room." Niles motioned for Jake and Ric to lug the struggling Lucas Saldivar down a hallway to the Guardian's war room.

Marisa waited by a picture window in the windowless room. Her long, black hair covered her breasts in her snug black sweater tucked into skinny jeans she'd painted on. Liam's mouth watered, and Eva's image from his mind replaced the sight of Marisa. Marisa had shot Ric on the beach in Santa Cruz a few weeks ago in front of him, and the scene still haunted him. But his distrust crumbled the more he got to know her. She'd spent nearly every night at their house since the two had hooked up, and it was tricky not to respect and like the strong, independent, and loyal lawyer. Ric loved her like crazy, and that's all that mattered to Liam.

"Hey, Marisa," he said. "Sorry to interrupt your night. We need your particular expertise."

"So I've heard."

They tied Saldivar to a rolling desk chair, and his eyes

darted from one to the other, shooting switchblades at them. His gaze rested on Marisa. The most intense feeling of hatred wafted off him and jolted Liam. A ghost of a smile played on the ex-Guardian's mouth before his menacing grimace stripped it bare.

Emotions stung Liam, and he staggered against the large conference table, bracing his palms flat on the scarred laminate surface.

"Whoa, bro. You chill?" Ric asked.

"Outside." Sweat popped on the nape of his neck. "Marisa, you too."

Legs unsteady, he hobbled into the hallway, Ric and Marisa on his heels. Stopping several doors down, he confronted the disquiet in their eyes. "He won't make this easy on you, Marisa. The hatred emanating off him is excruciating."

"Can he hurt her mind?" Ric wrapped his arm around Marisa's waist, drawing her close to his body. Ric may be able to protect her body, but nothing could protect her mind from one hell-bent on wrecking it.

"He's not psychic. He can't hurt me." Confidence loaded her voice.

Ric pressed a kiss to Marisa's temple. "I don't want you to do this if you feel threatened."

"We've known Lucas for years, and he's never exhibited a psychic gene. It's not in his profile," Liam replied.

"But you feel something off?" Marisa glued herself to Ric, her hand splayed on his chest. Liam had to glance away at the love and devotion on her face.

Man, he wanted Eva devouring him with such love and adoration. *Whoa, back up the bus. She's still in the no-fly zone. But damn, his heart wanted what it wanted.*

"My typical empathic senses." He stretched out his noodle legs, wiped his hand across his damp nape. "His hatred's strong, with a side order of smug."

"Maybe we nix this." Ric rubbed Marisa's arm, his unease sailing off him in swells Liam recognized all too well.

"Karma has no deadline. Let's nail him now." Marisa gently pushed against Ric's embracing arm.

"The second you feel off, pull out of his head," Ric admonished.

Marisa shot him a withering glare. "Let me handle my own abilities, Mr. Clairvoyant-Who-Doesn't-Hold-a-Telepathy-Clue." She squeezed his hand, softening the impact of her words.

"I have a clue by the name of Jake," Ric grumbled, following Liam into the war room.

Will I ever again find the one woman who'd wrap me around her finger? With absolute pleasure and passion, he'd allowed it with Eva once. Each moment with her never left his mind, and if he dwelled on her too long, he thought he'd die without her in his life again. They continued to dance around one another, their history, and the elephant in the room every time they were together. He didn't know how to pierce the bubble and look at her the way Ric seemed to consume Marisa with all his senses.

Niles and Jake bracketed Saldivar sprawled in the chair. Silence hung so heavy it prickled into the myriad kitchen scents always hovering in the room. Marisa sat across the table sandwiched between Liam and Ric.

Niles sat at the head of the table, the chair squeaking a protest as he wheeled it forward. He tented his hands beneath his chin. Niles came from a long line of psychics, but he didn't possess a psychic bone in his body, which elevated him to the Protectorate's Director when the Guild Council voted not to appoint a psychic to lead the Guardians. They didn't want to muddy waters of discipline or trigger biased decisions.

"We'll start with the easy questions," Niles said. "When did you betray the Guild, Lucas?"

"Who said I betrayed them?" He grinned wide, but his eyes remained dark and flinty. "You've got it all wrong. Liam's the one playing with fire, risking the Guild. The mafia's not known for leniency if you betray them."

"No one said one word about me risking the Guild. Can't a man talk to a beautiful woman once in a while?" Liam shot out.

"You know Crystal Estenson's not on the prowl for a hookup."

"Does she want more from everyone she expresses an interest in?" Niles asked.

"You got it."

"For what purpose?" Niles's spine straightened against the chair, defying the fatigue paling his skin.

Saldivar shrugged, pursed his mouth. A flash of pain punctured his eyes, and he glared at Marisa.

Liam had to give her credit. She didn't blanch, gave no clue she was reading Saldivar's mind. As far as anyone was concerned, she was a fly on the wall. Liam had to block everyone in the room from his empathic senses to focus on Saldivar's disdain and hatred.

"Again, for what purpose? Mafia or Cabal?" Niles asked.

Sweat beaded Saldivar's upper lip. Liam saw his gaze latch on to Marisa's eyes. A tiny jolt rocked her, and scarlet ribbons painted her neck and jaw.

She reached under the table and grasped Liam's hand resting on his thigh. The tiny thunderbolt blasted past his blocks, showered him in a jumble of shock, fear, and pain.

"Do you want to stop?" he said out the side of his mouth.

As she shook her head sharply, Jake shot her a questioning glance from across the table. Marisa had projected her telepathic thoughts onto Jake who was also a mind reader. They were one big silent phone circle. The curse of too many psychics in one room.

"Did Crystal Estenson recruit you into the Cabal?" she asked.

"The Estensons have nothing to do with the Cabal." Saldivar betrayed nothing in his body language or in his curtailed emotions.

"I see," she replied, barely withholding a sneer. "Did you ever betray the Guild?"

"Nope."

"Are you in a relationship with Crystal Estenson?"

"Crystal doesn't do relationships."

"What's your *connection* to her?"

"We had a few good times."

"Why do you care if Liam *dates* her?"

He took a too long moment to think. "I've got my Guardian buds' backs. The Estensons are bad news. You know, *organized crime*. Liam needs to steer clear. That's all."

Marisa's squeeze on Liam's hand aimed to fracture his bones. Horror surged off her, and he knew something was terribly wrong. Saldivar never broke eye contact with her.

"Look away, Marisa," Liam demanded.

A grin spread across Saldivar's ruddy complexion.

Ric swiveled Marisa's chair around to force her to break eye contact with Saldivar. "Marisa, baby, talk to me."

She quaked until her head lolled back and she passed out. Murmuring to her, Ric gathered her into his arms.

"What did you do to her?" Scarlett suffused Ric's face as he swung on Saldivar.

The betrayer's grin widened, a look of pure arrogance. "The question you should ask is, what did she do to me?"

"I'll get Elizabeth from the infirmary." Liam hurried out of the room to find their top healer. He needed a break from the emotions coiling in the room—Ric's fear, Jake's rage, and Saldivar's smugness. He propped his side against the wall in the hallway and dialed Elizabeth. "Sorry to bother you so late. We need you in the war room. Marisa passed out during a Guardian interrogation." Elizabeth lived on the compound, one of the Guild's few full-time residents, and one of the rare few Guild members Liam trusted. The number had dwindled to extinction population that night. How many other Guardians had flipped sides?

Once Elizabeth arrived, he briefed her on the situation, leaving out references to the Estensons, Eva, and his involvement. He held the door open for her and her bulky healer's bag. Liam didn't miss the love in Niles's eyes as he took in the attractive woman, disheveled in her haste in slim yoga pants and a pullover. Even without makeup, Elizabeth's fifty-something face appeared years younger with an unlined complexion and vivid green orbs. Elizabeth and Niles had hidden their relationship for far too long. Liam hoped they didn't wait much longer and lose their chance at their eternity.

After a quick examination of Marisa, Elizabeth addressed Ric. "Her vitals are okay. I won't know more until she awakens. We can run a brain scan." She rounded on Saldivar. "What did you do to her, Lucas Saldivar?"

He flicked his right hand up in a disdainful wave. "Not a damn thing. I'm over here, she's over there." He waved his hand at the table. "She's the psychic, not me."

Elizabeth consulted her tablet. "Let's see. You had a brain scan when you joined the Guardians." She swiped through several screens, punched in passcodes. Saldivar's skin adopted an ashen pall. A psychic brain scan differed from a normal X-ray, using machines perfected for their use in identifying extrasensory perception. Not foolproof, it still provided evidence of psychic activity even if the activity didn't spit out a label.

A tense air radiated around the room, the only sound Elizabeth's blunt-tipped fingernails clicking on the screen.

"Ah. Here we are," she said, and Liam felt gooseflesh pop on the nape of his neck. "You want to tell the group, or shall I?"

"Wait a minute." In one fluid motion, Niles surged to his feet and slid over to Elizabeth. "Are you saying Lucas has psychic ability not indicated on his chart?"

She shoved her tablet in Niles's face. "It's right there on his scan."

"Why does the report say none?" Niles swiped several more screens on the tablet, his anger rising with each swipe. Liam almost compelled Niles's anger backward to force him to calm down, stopping the mental motion to protect his exhausted mind.

"What is it?" Ric demanded. "Hello, my woman here doesn't need this right now. Not after the whole Delaney debacle."

The mystical clouds parted, and reality slammed them all with clarity. Liam and Jake rounded on Saldivar. Liam lunged across the table and fisted the man's shirt. Marisa had almost died from mind coercion once before.

"What'd you do?" Liam shouted.

Saldivar maintained a steady and silent grin.

Jake slapped his large hand on Saldivar's skull and exerted downward pressure. "Answer, man, or you don't want to see what my hand will do to your skull. I might not be able to stop it."

"According to his scan, he has telepathy of a sort," Elizabeth replied. "About all I can tell from my limited experience. Doc Wildwood can interpret it better." She clutched her ubiquitous strand of pearls around her neck. "Ric, carry Marisa to the infirmary."

"No," she croaked out, eyelashes fluttering up. "I'm okay. Can you get me water? Or vodka?" Ric settled her in the chair and pushed it as far from Saldivar and his penetrating gaze as the room allowed.

"You changed the results, didn't you?" Liam hopped off the table and squashed Saldivar between him and Jake.

"Now, how would I do that?" Saldivar smirked.

Elizabeth declared Marisa on the mend, and Niles crouched down in front of her. "Care to share? Or do you need time to recuperate?"

"Now." She gulped from the bottle of water Ric handed her, swallowed the pain relievers, the currency they all had to pay for abusing or plain using their psychic abilities. "He didn't change the results. Check the lab technician, then check the results of every other person the tech monitored. I bet you'll find a correlation and a boatload of Guardians wallowing in the same boat. Time to batten down the Guild hatches. Shit's gonna hit the fan hard."

"You bitch." Saldivar growled at her.

"You believed I couldn't smash through your blocks? Think again."

"What did he do to you?" Ric raised her hand to his lips.

"He possesses a minor ability to manipulate. Not coercion *per se*, and not mind reading either. He twisted my thoughts to mystify and prevent me from breaching his blocks. Once I breached him, he attacked, which forced me to fight to maintain my mental position. I passed out from the fight."

"Your internal protection mechanism's working." Elizabeth gathered up her medical supplies. "I'm out of here, leaving you all to the secret club." Niles gave her a "call you later" hand signal and the door clicked shut behind her.

Jake whistled. "Son of a bitch. That's a new one on me."

"Me too," she replied. "And by the by, he lied to you all, if you didn't figure it out."

"You're all hitting the skids. Doesn't matter what you

read from me." Red-faced, Saldivar twisted his arms in the bindings tying him to the chair arms.

"Because the Cabal's planning to take the Guild down?" Liam asked in Marisa's direction. Her sharp nod gave the answer. "I knew it. The Estensons are Cabal, not mafia."

"They're organized crime to the outside. Their hidden world is the Cabal. Lucas works with Crystal as one of her heavies. In fact, Crystal manages the recruitment of psychics, which includes raiding the Guild."

"You read all that from him?" Ric's eyes bugged out.

"Once I slipped past his blocks, his mind spun vinyl. May as well have given him a truth serum."

"Is he feeding Crystal Guild information?" Niles paced the room, his soles squeaking on the tile floor.

"Not clear," she replied.

"You can bet your ass other Guild members are playing both sides too," Jake growled out. "It's worse than we ever imagined."

"We're onto them now. It's the best lead we've had. We can contain it," Ric replied.

"Anything else before we boot Saldivar down to the dungeons?" Liam asked. The "dungeons" was their nickname for the secure basement setup for both short- and long-term secure "guests."

"You can't detain me." Saldivar fought his restraints. "I can have you arrested for kidnapping and unlawful detention."

Jake whacked him upside the head. "Shut. Up. We trusted you. We let you in on poker night and allowed you into our lives, our families, and you go Benedict Arnold on us."

"I received a better offer. A family who cares about my family. My *whole* family."

"We care about Carina." Niles ceased pacing, and a

smidge of sympathy accompanied his scowl at Saldivar. "She needed more care than our abilities. She admitted herself to the other facility because she wanted to get better."

"They ruined her, and no one gave a damn. Well, Crystal gave a damn."

"How's she doing then?" Ric blasted back. "Where is she?"

"What's it to you?"

"Take him downstairs." Liam swished his arm at the door. "FYI, Lucas. We have every right to detain you. It's in your contract, and the police have vetted our contracts."

"Fuck you, Liam. Fuck all of you. The Guild's dying. The Cabal has what it takes to last." Saldivar inhaled and exhaled, then continued. "Try to find another who's loyal to the Guild other than you four. You may as well shut the Guild down. Who you gonna trust? You don't know what Guild secrets have been handed to the Cabal on a silver fucking platter. They know everything, and they have the resources to fund the war for the long haul. Count on it." He nodded at Liam. "You won't see it coming."

CHAPTER TWENTY

Eva scrubbed the night off her skin under a scalding shower, ridding her body of Neal's touch, his breath, his every word. All she wanted to feel was Liam, his heart in his every touch and look, his lips on hers, his body cloaked around hers. When she was in his presence, she believed in hope and a forever as if the last seven years never existed. As if her betrayal never jacked him up.

As much as she wanted to erase the past, the years without him existed. Connor existed. Her life with Neal happened. Did she have it in her to let go, give herself to Liam, if he even wanted her? Or to walk away from him when all was said and done?

Eva slathered on lotion to cool her raw skin, and then donned leggings, a snug T-shirt, and her leather jacket. Now that Neal had invaded her home, she no longer felt safe, regardless of the surveillance Ric McAllister had installed.

After scanning her car for GPS devices and finding zilch, she squealed out of the carport. Exhaustion with the added burden of frustration and grief weighed her down. Checking her mirror every few seconds for tails, she drove in circles for a few miles, and then headed toward the safe house.

Anticipation fueled her lead foot. She hit the garage

remote and parked next to Liam's SUV. Although he stayed at the safe house to maintain his distance from the Guild, he'd given her free rein to use the house. In that moment, she wanted the distance from anything Estenson related. And she wanted Liam, even if they just brainstormed, and even if they never touched one another.

Never in a million years did she think they'd ever share a house under any circumstances.

"Jeez, Midnight. It's not like you're *sharing*, sharing a house. It's not a freaking love shack." She rolled out of her seat and grabbed her weekend bag from the trunk.

Resigned to hearing about Liam's night with Crystal, she entered the kitchen through the garage access door.

Liam studied the contents of the full fridge, his wet hair slicked back, a towel tied around his waist and nothing more. Not a lick of clothing covered up his muscular torso and sinfully strong arms. Only the towel covered his end-of-summer-tan skin.

Every cell in her body tingled, calling on every ounce of discipline. She dropped her bag on her foot and danced around the pain. The sound spun Liam around, and he pulled his earbuds out of his ears.

"I didn't hear you come in."

"No doubt." She smirked to force closed her open mouth. "Guess you weren't expecting me."

"Not exactly." He angled a hip against the counter, set his earbuds on the granite. "Everything go okay with Neal?" The words tripped out slow as if he was spitting out glass shards.

Disconcerted, she wanded her hand up and down the length of his torso. "Washing Crystal off?"

Her damp hair drew his attention. "I could say the same about you washing Neal off. Did he hurt you?" Liam advanced on her, stopped an arm's length away, close enough for his fresh spring soap to infuse her senses. Drops of water glistened on the dark smattering of curly hair on his chest.

Eva wanted to run her fingers down his torso, wanted to feel the solid strength of his chest beneath her touch. He scared her, though. The last few times with Neal had tortured her brain, steamrolled her body. Killed her soul. Too many emotions rolled into one big ball of turmoil she didn't believe she'd ever crumble, even though Liam might hold the sledgehammer.

"Eva?" Liam reached out to her and dropped his arm before he connected. "What did he do to you?"

Unable to speak, she sealed her mouth against the sob beating up her throat.

"Can I touch you?" he asked softly.

Eva shuffled backward. "Not a good idea." For a slew of reasons, not the least of which were the emotions he stirred in her. "Tell me about your night."

Liam grabbed a T-shirt off the back of a chair, returned to the counter, and turned the coffeemaker on. "Happened just as you said. I've hooked her." Even though she sensed him holding back, Eva breathed easier without the extra distraction of his sinful abs. Pulling on the shirt, he kept a safe distance from her, tugged the hem over the top of his towel, as if teasing her. "She wants me to attend a meeting with her Monday morning. Plus, she thinks I can help Connor."

Worry pricked her. "What if Connor recognizes your connection to me?"

"What do you suggest? This opportunity is gold." Liam crossed his delectable arms over his chest, and Eva licked her lips. "Why do you know her so well?" He canted his head to the side, evaluating her every nuanced movement, if not her emotions. Thank the devil of her personal hell for small favors.

She plunked down onto a dining room chair and

stretched out her legs. "She's as transparent as glass." Goosebumps skated across her skin, and she drummed the table, her gold filigree ring ticking against the wood. Liam squinted at the ring, started to say something, shut his mouth. "It's a gamble to introduce you to Connor. You'll have to reassure him telepathically not to speak about you, not to give any sign he knows you or your link to me."

"He *doesn't* know me. Won't Crystal read me if I shoot him telepathic thoughts?"

"Son of a mob boss bitch. You're the psychic, you tell me." She flung up her arms, and then cradled her face in her hands. "I don't know. He may believe you if you—" A light bulb blinked on in her head. "Tell Crystal you want to meet him in a room alone first, that it's the best way of training him, to establish first trust."

Liam's eyes widened. "How did you know that?"

"The night we met, you took me to a secluded spot under the stars and told me about your psychic skills."

"The best day of my life." His countenance remained stone-cold sober.

Eva drew in a tiny breath of reality. "When, or *if* he recognizes you, tell him it's part of his training to train with other psychics. You brought medicine I gave you for his headaches because you experienced headaches."

Slitting his eyes at her, Liam scratched his head. "What if he still spills to Neal or Crystal?"

"Tell him it's a secret. He loves his secrets, and he's good at keeping them, especially when he knows I'm involved."

"I don't know, Eva." Worry dented his forehead, and he slid his fingers from his scalp to rub his unease away. "Sounds risky."

"I know my son." She met his glare. "*Our* son. Connor will keep your identity secret because knowing you from my mind was always a secret between us. Neal never knew about my 'special friend.' Connor respected that. Our son has an old soul."

"I want him to stay alive so I can know his soul," he growled out.

"There's no other solution except you not going."

"Not happening."

"Okay, then. I suggest you put some clothes on. We have other things to discuss." Corralling her nerves and chucking them in a dungeon, she snatched up her bag and headed to her assigned bedroom. No one had touched it since she'd left. The bed was half made, and Lion King took a prime position on her pillow. She stroked the stuffed animal, taking comfort from the little thing that tied Connor and Liam together.

Fortifying her emotions, she slogged into the dining room and set her laptop on the table next to his ever-present tablet. Barefoot, Liam joined her in his T-shirt and soft, worn jeans. He'd slicked back his wet hair and spritzed on the cologne she wanted to wallow in. *Psych ward, here I come.*

Eva sat at the head of the table to add distance between them. He glowered at her deliberate action and scraped his chair closer, trapping her in place before her idiot genes waved the red flags.

She popped the new flash drive out of her pocket and stuck it into the port on her burner laptop. "I downloaded the contents of Neal's laptop."

Liam ogled her. "No way. Is the man stupid or what?"

"Yes. Very." Perspiration popped on her hairline as she tapped in keystrokes.

"How'd you get access?"

"Neal's ruled by three things, in no particular order. His dick, his father, and bourbon." Eva downloaded her night, fast and succinct to avoid emotional baggage. By the time she recounted the bedroom scene, Liam stalked jerky steps around the table. One look at the torment etched across his face launched bands of fire up her chest.

"Nothing happened, Liam," Eva said.

"I know." He stopped behind her. "But it could have."

"I know him too well."

"So it appears." Avoiding touching her, Liam reached over her shoulder and studied the laptop screen. His citrus, spice cologne infused his tranquility into her, a haunting reminder of the past and his ability to coerce. In that moment, she wanted his calming vibes. "What happens when he wakes up and goes on the warpath?"

"He won't." She hadn't yet touched the flash drive, waiting to slay this conversation first.

Liam made a clicking sound in his throat. "He'll pursue you harder now."

"It's the plan you and I agreed on." A callousness framed her voice. "Don't back out now."

"He may smell your perfume on him—" Back-stepping, he coughed into his fist. "—but he won't smell *you* on him. He'll know. A man knows these things."

"He'll not suspect. I've done it before." One way to escape him on particularly bad nights in the prelude to divorce.

Liam groaned, but his gaze softened on her face. "What a dumbass."

"He's blind where it concerns me." She lifted her shoulders, let them sag in defeat.

"What happens if he believes you had sex? Won't he expect more?"

Neal loved the chase as long as he understood he'd obtain his prey. Eva planned to string him along. If it meant a few kisses and touches, she'd debase herself. A lengthy pause joined the hiss of the heater blowing warm air from the ceiling vent.

"Don't answer that. I'm not letting it get that far." Liam towed a chair closer to her and sat. "Let's do this." He waved his hand at the computer.

Relief snapped her to the here and now. She initiated her encryption app and opened the flash drive's file directory.

"You think it's safe to open files?"

"We'll give it a go. Worst it can do is fry my burner, and we're shit out of luck." Eva tapped her fingertips on the keyboard. She brushed her fingers over the other flash drive sewn in the hem of her jacket. They needed more evidence against Neal and the Estensons for the FBI to bust them. Now she dreaded mixing the FBI with the Guild if the Estensons were in fact Cabal. *The clusterfuck of all clusterfucks. With my son in the middle of a looming psychic war.*

"Start from the top and work your way down." Liam scrolled his index finger down the folder directory containing over two dozen entries. "Skip the programs and go to the files, docs, graphics."

Eva froze, smirked at him. "Do I look like an idiot?"

A flush worked up Liam's neck. "Sorry. Just voicing what I would do."

Eva flashed a weary smile to soften her admonishment. "We've always thought alike."

"FYI, you *look* like the smart, beautiful mother of my child." Liam leaned closer, inched his fingers toward her hand. "You look like the reincarnation of my past and the hope for my future with my son."

Air in the room boiled, diminished, and then encapsulated Eva's thoughts and emotions. The vent air blew the balloon away, leaving her engulfed in only thoughts of Liam McAllister. Her turn to blush, she rolled off her suffocating leather jacket and it fell to her hips on the chair seat.

"What do I represent in your present?" Mouth turned up at the corners, she arched her eyebrows.

"The present is what it is," Liam responded. "A fight to

get our son back."

"And destroy the Cabal and the Estensons." Eva shut him down, afraid to speculate further, kicking herself for asking the stupid question.

"There you have it." Liam thumped his fingers on the table, stirring new life in the course of their investigation.

Eva clicked on a folder marked "ABC," and it held a slew of additional folders, each with a last name. She clicked on "Abramo." Empty. "Adams." Empty. She scrolled down the list and every folder revealed its emptiness. Not even hidden or encrypted folders contained a thing. Zip.

"Do you recognize any names?" Liam asked. "I don't."

"No." She screen-printed the list and saved them to the hard drive for transfer later.

"We'll have Niles compare the list against the Guild roles or known Cabal defectors."

She checked all the folders on the flash drive. Empty. "I don't get it. I copied his entire hard drive. Xander assured me the transfer software would get past any anti-copy and encryption program."

"Let's get Xander over here," Liam said, his frustration evident in his hoarse command. "Or I can call my guy."

"The fewer people who know, the better."

"We can't afford not to bring in a few trustworthy techs. Do you not trust Xander?"

"Of course, I trust him. He contracts with the PD."

"Any chance he works for the Estensons too?" Liam strode into the open living room.

Eva sneered at him. "Really?"

"They have moles everywhere."

"Including me."

"You said it, not me."

Eva would have hit him if Liam's gorgeous grin hadn't accompanied his words. His grin ignited his haggardness and turned him from Grouchy McGrouchy to the fun-loving college student she used to know and love. Before life, careers, and a son whacked him upside the head.

Eva yawned wide, her fatigue hitting her fast. The night with Neal had drained her. It took a supreme effort of mind and body to thwart or anticipate his every thought or movement. Her heart had never even made an appearance. "I'll call him in the morning. I'm beat."

"What if there's a hint of Neal's hideout on there?" Liam fiddled with his tablet as if itching to turn it on and conjure up clues. "Don't you want to find it now?"

"Connor's probably at the family compound tonight. Neal's at his home. We certainly can't go in guns blazing unless we hire a military unit." As much as Eva wanted her son back, practicality won out. "Remember, Neal has full custody. I... we have no legal rights to him."

"You're giving up on our son?" Liam's voice rose with a blotchy, red tide up his neck.

Eva jumped up, thrusting her chair back so hard it clattered to the floor. "Screw you, McAllister. Why don't *you* tell me what really happened tonight?" She stomped out of the room.

Before she reached the bedroom doorway, Liam clasped her arm from behind, his grip unyielding. The heat of his body assailed her, his heady cologne chasing its tail. Eva sank back against his solid strength.

"I'm sick with worry. Fatigue can mess a person up into missing things. We can't let that happen, not with our son's life in jeopardy. We take this slow and careful, or it'll bite us in the ass," she explained.

"I know," Liam said in her ear. "I'm sorry. You're right, I'm not thinking."

Out of exhaustion, stupidity, or any number of other feelings, Eva shifted to the side and laced her fingers in his. He gripped her hand tight, and she shut down her mind to him, just in case. "I don't want to be alone tonight."

CHAPTER TWENTY-ONE

The back of Eva's legs nudged the mattress, and she stopped leading Liam, stopped thinking. With one hand entwined with his, Eva caressed Liam's injured arm. She had to feel his muscles and his taut skin. His pectorals coiled tight as if afraid she might strike him... or kiss him. *One action didn't trump the other.*

"Eva, I don't know if this is a good idea." Liam swept straggled hair off her face and hooked the strand behind her ear. His touch tingled down her body. "You flipped my world upside down. I don't know if I can—"

Mesmerized by his solid strength and firm muscles, she rested her index finger on his lips. "Shush. I just don't want to be alone. If you can't be in the same room with me, I'm okay with that."

"What about being in the same bed?" He unlaced his fingers from hers, and she missed the firm power of his touch.

Her laugh came easy for once, and she plopped backward onto the bed. "We'll see how it goes." She kicked off her sneakers and bunched up the pillows beneath her head, her legs dangling over the side. "You never told me what happened tonight."

Liam flicked his hand dismissively and perched on the bed beside her, a safe expanse between them. His feet hit the floor in a soft thump. Reticence wafted off him, and Eva didn't need to be a mind reader or empath to sense it.

"I wanted to ensure you were okay first," he finally answered. "That Neal didn't hurt you… or touch you." His black T-shirt rippled across his abdomen. Eva wanted to touch him and appease his insecurities. But she had no right. He had every right to the insecurities she'd caused him. The odd frostiness his concern gave off skittered up from her toes in a wave of snowflakes.

"He didn't touch me." Liam didn't need to know every nuance of her night. Her truth was the truth Liam sought. Anything else in between didn't matter. She turned on her side to face him, his body stiff and wary. Did an unfathomable chasm still separate them, making warring strangers look friendly by comparison? "Why are you so uncomfortable around me?"

"Eva." Liam heaved out a breath. "I can't concentrate on anything but Connor."

"We were never this way before, even during contentious moments."

"This isn't *before*. We'd never encountered life-or-death situations. We didn't have a son."

"Then maybe you should leave." No real insistence layered her tone, yet her words seemed to startle Liam in the squaring of his shoulders.

He rose from the bed. "If that's what you want." He towered over her, not budging a foot.

"It's not. Don't think I don't feel your turmoil. I've lived it for seven years. I know how devastated you are and how you may never like me in any capacity again."

"My faith, my trust has gone to shit. Not just because of you. There've been others, specifically the psychic I last guarded who put me on suspension. She used me from day one, then betrayed me, and got me in a boatload of trouble for using my coercion for illegal means. I knew better, but she suckered me. Nearly got me booted out of the Guild."

"Like I betrayed you."

"I'd say your betrayal was epically worse." He gave her a rueful smile, but his words still shot a gaping hole in her heart.

She stretched out on the bed and flung an arm across her face, hiding her pain. He'd always been brutally honest with her, and as much as the truth hurt, she preferred it. Better to hear and live the truth than to hide behind the shadows of lies and deceit eating her alive.

The bed sank again as it took Liam's weight. This time, he stretched out beside her. He didn't touch her, yet his indifference had evaporated, and she felt a skosh of undeserved empathy.

"Tell me what you left out tonight," Eva tentatively said.

He curled his fingers around hers resting on her stomach. "First off, we found the beach house. It's in Laguna Beach. Owned by a holding corporation associated with the Estensons. There're signs of recent habitation, and the long staircase Connor mentioned is a couple blocks away. We have it under surveillance."

"With Crystal and Neal here, Connor has to be close."

"He is. Crystal left early to take him off his grandfather's hands."

Relief riddled her tattered heart. "What else?"

"A Guild Guardian busted me in the restaurant parking lot after Crystal took off."

Eva jackknifed upright. "What?"

Liam drew her back down on the bed. "Relax. We diffused the situation at the Guild compound." Liam told her about Lucas Saldivar.

"So, you have him in Guild jail?" She rolled on her side toward him.

"Yeah. We can't hold him for long."

"No, *really*? That's illegal detainment, if not abduction."

"The Guild has seventy-two hours where we can hold someone before calling in the police. MacKenzie will go along with any extended hold period."

"Wow. I had no clue." She picked at bits of fuzz on the slim span of comforter between them. "The false brain scan reporting is huge, isn't it?"

"It'll wipe out the Guild from the inside out. We don't know who to trust. Niles is working with the Guild doctor to review the records of the technicians who did the scans back to the dawn of scanning machines. The Guild's now on a heavier lockdown."

"Another nail in the Cabal-Estenson connection."

"You got that right. If we discover that all the Guardians who left the Guild over the last decade are working for the Estensons..."

"Bingo." Eva caught Liam's forearm, unable to wrap her fingers around his corded muscles. A muscle flinched beneath her touch, stilled. "If those Guardians who left have psychic powers and are working for the Estensons, what is the Cabal planning?"

"Wish I knew." Liam caressed her hand still resting on his arm, ran his finger over her ring, tapped it as if he wanted to ask her something.

His warmth appeased her tightly strung muscles. Eva didn't feel his empathic intrusion and knew he blocked himself from sensory overload. His blockade benefited them both. She wanted him to keep talking and avoiding her emotions. The longer they played on neutral ground, the wider he'd open up. The more they dallied in the middle of the road, the longer he'd remain lying next to her.

"Do you know Lucas?" Liam asked.

Thinking, Eva pursed her lips. "No. I've met few Estenson minions."

"What names has Neal mentioned? Maybe we can connect some dots."

"Gavin. He's Neal's personal guard and driver. I've never seen him exhibit psychic ability, but then I haven't been around him for any length of time. Daniel's goon Jordie, the one who shot at us."

"I don't know a Gavin or Jordie. But we'll check it out."

A thought clanged in Eva's head. "Liam, with all these psychics they're stealing from the Guild and recruiting from outside, do you think the Cabal is holding them captive for a mega, psychic shitshow?"

"Possible. Where, though? It would have to be impenetrable to psychic powers, or an outsider might sense them. Or they could cause a cataclysmic mind event."

"What?" Eva shot up again. "Psychics can band together and cause destruction?"

"Ever heard of *Carrie*?" A muscle ticked in his jaw, and she wanted to temper it down, soothe all his fears and anger. "Many telekinetics together can create disaster far greater than Carrie's cataclysm."

"Holy smokes." Eva tugged her fingers through her ponytail, pulling the band off. "I thought that was just fiction."

"You need to learn this. Our son—"

Eva tossed up her arms, threw her hairband on the nightstand. "I know. I know. No need to keep reminding me." She scrubbed her face, a harsh wash of reality. "I wanted to baby him as long as possible before he succumbed to his talents." She hopped off the bed. "As long as it doesn't hurt our son, I'll let you and your brothers train him properly. I swear on his life."

"I know you get it, Eva. I'm sorry. I'll stop beating the dead horse." Liam joined her in front of the mirror above the dresser. His expression reflected the wariness on her own pale face. Again, she wanted to smooth away the tiny lines around his eyes. She longed to kiss the frown off his mouth. She wanted way more than she deserved.

Sliding past him, she edged out of his personal sphere of space. "If the Cabal or Estensons are raising a psychic army, they're hiding them in plain sight. They're too arrogant. Neal's always been vocal about how his father's shit doesn't stink and how he gets away with murder. Daniel's team of lawyers is legendary."

"Were you his only mole in the police department?"

Eva turned to Liam and rolled her eyes. "Are you kidding? I wasn't even Daniel's mole. I was Neal's peon stooge. Remember, Big D wants me six feet under. He'd never use me in a million years unless to set me up for a fall."

"Why, Eva? You never fed me that story. And *you* know more than you're letting on."

She toed her overnight bag, wanting to settle into her bedroom alone, but not bad enough to chase Liam out. "Guess we both need lessons on trust."

"Spill it."

"Because I wanted out. I hurt Neal's pride, and I know more than he wants an outsider to know. I've heard conversations, seen things. The usual stuff a wife of a mobster sees."

"What stuff?"

"Neal talks in his sleep when he's drunk." Rain tinkling on the aluminum roof gutters carried a tranquil white noise to the tense room. Eva loved the rain, the feel on her skin, a drink from the heavens to scrub everything bad for a fresh start to a new day.

Lying back on the bed, she patted the mattress, an invitation for Liam to rejoin her. Without hesitation, he stretched out on his side facing her, ankles crossed. Eva no longer felt the wariness drip off him as if the rain had sluiced it away. Not exactly all bubbly free of his emotional tangle concerning her, yet a new warmth from his presence enveloped her, and she metaphorically submerged into it.

"I don't want to dredge up difficult emotions, but can you talk about things Neal blabbed in his sleep?" Liam asked.

"Most of it's fragmented. Not enough to do damage. He holds animosity toward his father, especially his father's treatment of me. He's mentioned money laundering, but not where or when, so it's easy to say they're into money laundering. A murmur about a weapons cache in a warehouse, but the Estensons own warehouses around the world." Annoyed at her inability to piece anything together, she wound her hair in a bun, tired of it tickling her face.

"Daniel ought to wipe up the floor with his blabbermouth son."

"Neal's too important. Next best action is to off the disposable cop wife who knows too much."

Liam's fingers grazed her thigh. His heat penetrated her leggings and left jet trails on her roasting skin. "You're not disposable to Connor. Nor to me," the last words came out on a husky whisper.

She met his intense gaze. "I made myself disposable to you."

"Here we go, right back to seven years ago," Liam retorted, curls of ire trickling out. "*We* made a crappy decision. I don't hold it against you. My part has plagued me ever since."

"You've made it sound like I was to blame for everything." A sense of relief dulled the edge of her irritation.

"Only for keeping my son from me." Liam scooted closer, his leg brushing against hers. Invisible sparks sizzled between them. Eva comically tried to stifle a yawn, felt her skin pull tight into her hairline. "Am I boring you?" He laughed, so light and carefree, it melted another cube of her heart.

She grinned weakly, and the corners of her mouth pulled down. "Sorry. It's almost two. I'm beat. We'll have another long day tomorrow. Alex gave me a referral to a custody attorney for when we can move without placing Connor in peril."

"Then sleep, babe."

The familiar endearment soaked her in warm and fuzzies. "Will you stay?"

"If you want."

"I want." Eva's eyelids drooped, and she began losing her battle against sleep.

Liam tugged up the knitted afghan at the foot of the bed and covered them both. Eva had almost drifted off to a troubled sleep when she felt the lightest touch of Liam's lips across her mouth.

"Liam," she mumbled against his lips.

"Shhh. Go to sleep." With his good arm, he cocooned her into the haven of his body.

CHAPTER TWENTY-TWO

Gasping for illusive air, Eva bolted upright, a scream ready to rip from her mouth. Head fuzzy, she twisted in a pretzel, taking in her whereabouts. When her flailing hand hit a body next to her, she scrambled out of bed and stumbled against the wall. Neal? She knuckled her eyes, stared again, and recognized Liam's face. The nightmare that hurled her out of a deep sleep was so real, it could have been Neal lying beside her. Her heartbeat began to even out, leveling her breathing.

During the night, they had unknotted from one another. *Long years of him sleeping alone? Right. Wishful thinking? More like stupid-why-do-you-care thinking.* The clock on the nightstand struck six, the red glowing numbers the only light in the dark room.

Eva slipped on her sneakers and sweat jacket and headed to the back patio for a dose of cold, rainy air to wash the nightmare out of her system. Dawn hovered in the distance of time, but scattered landscape lights chased the flickering shadows away, the golden puddles dimming as the solar power wore out. She slid a chair out from under the patio cover and curled up on it, hugging her legs to her chest.

The California autumn chill cloaked Eva, a far cry from the balmier climate of Florida, the site of her recurring nightmare featuring the bane of her existence.

"What am I going to do with Neal?" she muttered to the inky clouds scuttling across the dark sky. "I have the will, but I don't have the way to nip him in the bud."

Heebie-jeebies joined the sensation of Neal's fingers caressing her naked body, testing the sting of soft ropes tying her wrists and ankles to the bedposts.

She quaked, and her teeth clattered. "Come on, get your shit together. Connor deserves better."

What if she had to go back to Neal for the sake of her son? Contemplating her limited choices and her inability to detach her emotions from reality, she propped her chin on her knee. If it came down to it, she'd bite the bullet and endure. For Connor. It was too risky for Liam to immerse himself into the Estenson family, not after the altercation with Lucas Saldivar last night. Another Guardian or psychic might recognize him, or Connor might blab in either excitement or wariness.

Tears slid down her cheeks, thawing her frigid skin.

The sky lightened toward a gray dawn, and neighborhood lights winked on, the glow of normal everyday life. Eva finally dozed, the knowledge of her next steps spinning perilously through her mind.

CXSO

Liam smoothed his hand across the top of Eva's head, her soft hair damp as he sifted his fingers through the locks. A stake pierced his heart when he'd spied her curled in a ball on the patio chair, damp and cold. When had she left the bed? Why was she sleeping in the drizzle? He touched her wet cheeks and jerked back as if scalded. "You're freezing to death."

He scooped her into his arms, a weightless bundle of emotion and sorrow bogged down by wet clothes. A bundle of immense... love swelled and slammed against his rib cage. He'd known he was falling all over for her since the moment he'd sighted her at Alex MacKenzie's house. Even after he learned she'd hidden his son from him, he knew he'd never walk away from her. Her return to San Jose triggered their fate. They were always meant for each other, to be in each other's lives. It no longer mattered that he'd lost the first six years of his son's life. They had many more years ahead to catch up. They had a chance together as a family. He only had to grasp it and convince her to accept their destiny.

Liam elbowed the patio door shut, jostling Eva in his arms.

"Liam?" She buried her head against his chest, snuggling closer. "Why is it so cold?" Her teeth chattered.

"Why were you sitting in the rain?" Liam asked not unkindly.

"Communing with nature." Her shuddering grew so intense it set off freak flags in his head. "It's purifying."

He rushed her into the master bathroom and propped her on the toilet seat.

She waggled her hands, failed in her attempt to unzip her jacket. "I can't feel my fingers."

"No kidding." Liam unzipped her jacket and tossed it onto the floor in a wet heap. "You need to get in the shower. Now."

"Not that cold," she slurred.

"Cold enough." Liam reached for the hem of her T-shirt, and she half-heartedly slapped at his hand. "I'm fine."

"No, you're not. Either we take your clothes off or you get in the shower fully clothed. Either way, won't matter. You're already wet as a drowned rat." A gorgeous, drowned rat with hair of spun gold and a body to make a grown man sink to his knees and worship at her feet.

"You're such a pest." Her shivers knocked her halfway off the toilet seat.

Liam caught her before her butt kissed the tile floor. "Damn it, Eva." He turned on the water and steam billowed up from the shower floor, clouding the glass walls. He grew hard and muttered a string of dark curses at his untimely arousal. He refused to let his feelings for Eva interfere with rescuing Connor. No dark cloud of misperception over whether Eva was coming or going would get in the way. "Nope. No way," he grumbled to himself.

Once Eva found a wobbly balance, he propped her against the glass wall of the shower stall.

"Do you need me to peel your clothes off?"

Again, she tried to work her fingers to no avail. "Sorry. I'm a mess. I don't know what I'm doing anymore, Liam." She gripped his shirt in her fists and hung on to him. "How am I helping Connor when I'm such a basket case?"

"Eva, baby." Liam tightened his arm around her, not giving a damn what her body did to his, or how her wet clothes were plastered to her body, revealing every luscious curve. To hell with his body's betrayal. He couldn't stand to see her anguish. No woman deserved the load of bull handed to her on a silver mafia platter. His mental walls vaulted up to avoid reading Eva's emotions, to keep it real. "You're doing everything you can, especially against those assholes fighting you every step. You escaped the mob when so many don't."

She bumped her fist on his chest. "You call this escaping? Not while they have my son."

"You've taken the right steps. You aren't going in guns blazing and endangering his life or your own." He braced his arm around her waist in case she toppled over again, and he managed to kick off her sneakers, and then his own. "Do you want me to strip off your clothes?" His voice sounded gravelly to his ears.

She chanced a quick peek up at him, her eyes bright and twinkling. "Only if you take yours off."

Liam groaned, the promise of the warm shower spray too enticing now that her cold, wet clothes had thoroughly chilled him. "Don't tempt me." His fingertips dug into the flesh of her hip as she shifted within his embrace. A raw, elemental attraction sprang into his awareness. Her pouty lips entranced him further.

"Fine. I won't." Her fists unclenched and she spread her palms flat on his chest. Otherwise, she didn't budge a muscle to remove her clothes, pressing closer even while her shivers continued to roll up from her toes. The steam building in the room along with his body began to warm her, and her color returned to a normal pinkish. Liam bundled her into his arms, and she yelped in surprise.

She feebly beat her fist on his shoulder. "Don't do it, Liam. I swear, I'll—"

"You'll what?" Liam shouldered the shower door open and stepped into the cascading water. He set Eva on her feet, and she wrapped her arms around his neck, plastering herself against him. They embraced under the spray for a moment, gazes hooked on one another. Liam's body tightened painfully in reaction to her lithe body glued to his. He bound his arms around her and surrendered to the water's heat... surrendered to Eva. His empathic walls slipped, and her desire barreled into him. He strained under the effort to erect his solid walls, but her memories and desire drenched him, her light scouring away his darkness.

"Feel better?"

"In so many ways." She tipped her face to the relentless shower spray and let the water sluice down her delicate skin.

Liam's flesh stung from the heat. He wanted to strip off his confining clothes, then Eva's clothes, piece by slow piece. But he feared the outcome of taking such a leap, dreaded what it threatened to do to his head and heart.

Eva's nipples hardened against his chest and created such a stirring in his groin he almost tripped over the edge.

"Take off my blouse," she said as though reading his mind. "My fingers are stinging from the heat."

Liam shook back. "Not a good idea." *It's a helluva great idea.* The devil on one shoulder stabbed pitchforks into his heart.

"It's what you want. Remember?" she teased.

"Is it what *you* want?" Liam maneuvered her to the side of the stall so the water no longer splashed their faces.

Eva unlinked her arms from around his neck and slipped her hands beneath his T-shirt, skin meeting skin. Just her touch on his bare flesh launched exploding fireworks inside him. No empathic abilities needed. He cranked off his circuits to avoid reeling from her emotions. She lifted the hem of his shirt, encouraging him to help her remove it, and he resisted, gloving her hand in his. Hunger raged through him, the implications strong and heady, too powerful and too tantalizing.

Nothing inhibited him from pressing his mouth to the hollow of her throat and breathing in the natural scent of her, the scant fragrance of her vanilla body lotion. Scents he had loved forever, locked tight in his mind's vault. The doors had blown open, and everything he'd sealed up waited in his arms, ready and willing to throw the last seven years to the wayside and sweep them back to the incredible year they'd spent together... and beyond to the future.

Eva tipped back her head and pressed her slick neck against his mouth. Her nipples pebbled beneath her thin T-shirt, and he realized then she wore no bra. He cupped her ass cheeks in both hands, and holding her up, he slid his mouth down to one enticing breast. His pulse rocketed, and his erection throbbed against the fabric of his jeans. Water beat on his back, not as hot as before, and soon he'd beg for ice water.

Her lips parted and Eva thrust out her chest. He accepted the invitation, his mouth latching on to her right nipple, sucking through the thin cotton. The small offering would never be enough. He wanted all of her.

Her hand alighted on the crotch of his jeans and cupped his painful bulge. They shared a gaze that transcended words, the way it always was between them.

"Ah, Eva. Eva."

Eva cupped the nape of his neck. "Don't stop touching me with your mouth."

"How far do you want to take this?" he asked as her fingers slipped up and down the front of his pants. A fierce growl escaped him.

Water droplets clung to her blonde tresses, sparkling like precious diamonds. Her plump, made-for-kissing lips earned his full attention until she drew a hairsbreadth away.

"I'm dead inside, Liam. You're making me feel again." She slipped her fingers inside the waistband of his jeans, and he lurched against the shower tile, towing her with him, using the wall as their support. "Now kiss me again."

The water turned cool and he turned it off. They stood in the shower stall, dripping wet and hot as hell. Her tantalizing eyes and sexy grin were all the encouragement he needed to capture her mouth with his, destroying any objections by either. Their eyes locked as he kneaded her perfect ass, hauling her close enough to feel his erection.

From the moment Liam had first laid eyes on her at a campus party when the clock struck midnight during their final year of college, she'd tempted him in ways no other woman had. They'd become inseparable, and he'd panted after her like she was a drug. Now in his arms, all those feelings rushed him, a potent joy only she had ever created in him.

The sweet, sizzling touch of her lips killed any reticence he'd experienced since she'd reappeared in his life a few days ago. Eva parted her mouth and a tiny whimper escaped. She dug her hands into his hair and held his head to hers to deepen the kiss. He slipped his tongue between her tempting lips and touched hers, kindling untamed passion, sensually moving together. Lip-locked, her breath warm against his face, Eva's knees buckled. Before they crash-landed and without breaking the kiss, Liam lifted her in his arms. He staggered into her bedroom, and dripping wet, sank onto the bed, their limbs tangling.

Incapable of checking his body's response, his erection throbbed like a wounded soldier, and the confines of his wet jeans were killing him. Breaking the kiss and sucking in air, Eva stretched out on top of him, her soft curves creating a firestorm. Her lips landed on his as if his mouth was air. She deepened the kiss, and he opened his mouth to allow her tongue to tango with his again. The hard length of his shaft ground into her thigh, and he groaned low in his throat. She rocked against him, grinding herself on him. Electric currents of arousal pulsed through his body, sending him spiraling into places unknown. He couldn't fathom Eva Midnight was touching him, let alone kissing him as though he were a drug. Her vanilla jasmine scent soaked his senses. The soft but firm touch of her lips demolished the door to his memories.

His chest rasped the bullet tips of her breasts, and she clutched his shoulders, her fingers doing a number on the skin of his neck. Liam broke the kiss, leaving her panting, and smoothly rolled her beneath him. He trailed kisses across her jaw, her neck, and kissed his way down to her breasts. As if touching her was his heaven, his hands explored her abdomen, stomach, and hips, remembering and absorbing the subtle changes in her body. Writhing beneath him, she tried to lift her shirt, but he stilled her hand.

"Not yet," he rasped out. "I want you like this."

"Wet and wild?" Her soft laughter whipped another round of lust through his veins.

"Wet, wild, beneath me in any way." He refrained from moving and spoiling the moment. He didn't want to utter another word to fetch reality back into their heads.

Her skin had warmed, his breath leaving goosebumps across her neck. Pressing his erection into her softness, he stole another searing kiss, tongues tangoing, arms gripping each other tight, allowing no air to penetrate between their bodies. Panting, Liam ended the kiss and nipped at her lips, adoring the fever in her stormy blue eyes. He dragged his lips under her jaw and just breathed in her skin, stilling her frantic thrashing before he totally lost himself.

"Are you sure you want this, want me?" His voice was gruff, demanding.

She slipped her hand farther inside his pants and fondled his erection. Painful lust barreled straight to his groin. "Is this answer enough?"

As desire zipped through every point of his system, she found the buttons of his jeans. Between them, they undid the metal buttons, and he peeled his soaked jeans to his ankles and kicked them off. A smoldering need sprang up with his erection. Impatient with a desperate lust, he worked a condom out of his wallet while she stripped off her wet clothes. Laughing, they rolled together on the bed, her naked breasts smashed against his flesh, killing his ability to think, except for one thing. He needed her to say it.

"Are you sure, Eva? I don't want this to wreck you." Or us, he wanted to add. But it wasn't about them. It was about what Eva could handle after suffering from prick Neal's hands.

"I want this... you." She straddled him, positioning herself for takeoff. "I've always—"

Hands on her hips, Liam buried himself in her, and with a cry of pleasure, she rocked back and met him thrust for thrust. He traced her velvety skin, latching on to her hips to guide her. Eva rode him, demanding everything from him, no guidance required. A storm of sensation ripped him apart until her climax quivered through her, and he shouted out his own climax. Gasping for diminishing air, Liam rolled her beneath him and kissed her tenderly, taking her breath into his lungs and savoring the feel of her once again where she belonged.

He'd come home, a place he'd denied himself for so long.

Liam elbowed up from her and rolled on his side to face her, the comforter cool against his fiery body.

"What now?" Breasts heaving, Eva doodled invisible words on his skin, her touch mesmerizing.

"I won't deny I still have feelings for you. You rocked my world then, and you've rocked it again now." He dragged his fingers through his wet hair. "I don't want to regret this later. You should know that I may not be able to walk away from you. Not ever again. But then I might." He heaved out a loaded sigh. "I don't know."

"I'm not expecting anything beyond this moment." Eva rolled onto her side and ran her fingertips across his arm. "You were my first love, my greatest love. I never got over that even when I moved on."

"What are you saying?" Liam wanted to believe in a future for them, a tenuous belief that never disappeared and carried with it a train crammed full of baggage. Too much of that baggage now tied her to the Estensons.

Face dark and shuttered, Eva pushed away from Liam.

"I don't know. This"—she waved her hand over them—"is probably a bad idea. Other than Connor, nothing has changed between us."

Everything had changed. *Didn't she see it?* "For a few moments, I thought—"

Reality blared forth from Liam's secret phone. Only one person would be calling his new burner phone.

Crystal Estenson. Saved by the mafia bell.

CHAPTER TWENTY-THREE

Unable to tear her gaze off Liam, Eva watched him leave for his assignment with Crystal Estenson. Unease tapped her chest.

After quick showers and an even quicker breakfast, they'd said their goodbyes with an arm hug in the "morning after" awkwardness. But Eva felt far from awkward inside. Her blood zinged, and the soft and firm feel of Liam's lips on hers, the way he tasted, and the feel of his amazing body refused to abate. She touched her fingertips to her lips to hold on to the feeling for as long as possible. In losing herself in Liam, Eva had returned to a safe, loving, and fulfilling place she never wanted to leave.

"Liam McAllister?" she uttered in disbelief. Hooking up with him again was a disaster in the making. How could she live with him, knowing who and what he was? On the flipside, didn't her son deserve a two-parent household?

"Whoa. Eva Marie Midnight. What makes you think there's any kind of household with Liam in your future?" She rolled her eyes and opened her laptop.

An update email from Alex flipped her mind off Liam.

> I found nothing concrete to implicate
> the judge in shady dealings, bribery,
> or blackmail with the Estensons or

anyone else. Not enough to kick the matter to the judicial committee to reverse his custody order. Not YET. We're working it from both the Cabal and Estenson angle. We'll get there. Don't worry. Keep up with your research. Keep churning ideas and memories regarding the Estenson family.

Eva knuckled her eyelids to rid her mind of the anguish resulting from the lack of evidence. There had to be something to prove Neal had paid off the judge, proving the Estensons called the hit. She touched the flash drive sewn into her jacket seam. The information didn't implicate the judge. If the info surfaced, it would only plonk her at the end of a bullet and hand the Estensons the win with their get-out-of-jail card and her son.

Her old cell phone dinged a text message, and she dug it out of her jacket slung over the chair. When she saw the anonymous sender, her palms grew moist. No one else but Neal texted from a blind phone.

Eva, meet me at your place in an hour. I want to discuss Connor, and us. I love you.

Would he ask her to shack up with him? Get remarried? *What?* Screams echoed in her head, and she stomped down the seed of acid sprouting over her breakfast.

The short drive didn't calm her stress. The seed grew into full-blown nausea. Not even thoughts of Liam and their oh-so-decadent morning quelled her runaway emotions.

All the blinds were drawn in her condo, sealing out the world. Eva punched in the new security code, stifling the annoying beeps, and flicked on the lights. She still hadn't put everything back to rights after the Estenson goons had their field day. Eva swiped a finger across the light layer of dust coating the dining room table. A chill pervaded the still atmosphere.

The cold carried memories of freezing in the rain earlier, the memories of Liam's arms around her, his hands skimming up her body, caressing, teasing, tempting. The tantalizing scent that belonged to him only. His lips pressed to her skin, latching on to her nipple. Eva fanned her face and almost took off her jacket, her nipples sensitive against the leather shell. The doorbell rang and startled her out of her delicious reverie.

With a twist of trepidation and eagerness, she opened the door to reveal a quad of full-uniformed county sheriff's officers. Questions revolved in her head, and a sinking dread leaked the answer.

"Eva Marie Midnight?" the short, balding cop in front asked.

"Yes." Her right hand clenched the collar of her jacket, stopping short of her neck. "Can I help you?"

"Step back, turn around, and place your hands behind your back." Numb, she obeyed.

The cool steel of handcuffs bit into her wrists, the click of her detainment another nail in her coffin. "What's this about?" A slow flame killed Eva's momentary bewilderment, murdered the stupid-ass idea that Neal had plans to woo her back or return her son. No one answered until after the tall, blond officer with a buzz cut, Officer Stephen Monroe, patted her down and confiscated her badge and ankle knife. Her short life as a police officer and even shorter stint as a detective flashed before her eyes and settled into a memory pocket of her brain.

"You are under arrest for the shooting death of Judge Alfred Martinelli." Monroe echoed the words already zinging through her brain.

❦

Outside the Lucky Shamrock, Liam erected his most impenetrable lock on his memories of Eva. The insane and incredible morning with her consumed his thoughts the entire drive to the bar, derailing him from dwelling on the pending day. He couldn't afford the distraction while dealing with Crystal.

Mind locked tight, Liam strode into the bar. The interior light dimmed into a gray gloom after the doorman locked the door behind him. *Prison, much?* Squaring his shoulders, Liam knocked on the door at the end of the short hallway behind the barroom. Hoping he hadn't overdressed, he straightened his suit blazer and ran his hand down nonexistent wrinkles in his dress slacks.

"Enter, love." Crystal's sultry voice greeted from behind the door.

"Do you call everyone *love?*" Liam plastered on a smile and shut the door.

"Only you." Swinging her hips, she sidled over to him. A tight leather motorcycle jacket covered up her skintight black sweater, and black leggings encased her shapely legs. Red designer spikes rounded out her ensemble at one end, and her wavy chestnut hair framed her movie-star made-up face at the other end.

"You look like a panther ready to eat its young." Liam kissed her cheek, held his breath to avoid her cloying herbal perfume reminding him of a summer day in a sheep shed.

As he tried to ease away, Crystal grabbed his hand. "Just you. Now give me a proper kiss. Or have things changed between us?" Her slim eyebrows hiked up in a questioning slant.

"Nothing's changed. Since this is business, I wanted to maintain a proper demeanor. You never know who'll barge in, right?"

Crystal brayed out a cackle. "You're too good to be true." She released his hand and stepped toward the small conference table at the left of the room. "And you're right."

"What do you want me to do?" Liam left his mental doors open and concentrated on the fresh-brewed coffee permeating the air, intangible energy to fill his veins.

"We've experienced shady business dealings with certain partners. I'll be questioning one today, reading his mind if he's receptive to my telepathy. I'd like you to gauge his emotions, see how they match his responses. Afterward we'll compare notes."

"Does he know you're telepathic?"

"It's not a secret among our business partners. I doubt he has the ability to block telepathic intrusions. He's not psychic, and as you well know, most normal people can't block diddly."

"No kidding. Menials are open books."

"Menials? Hmm… I love that." She handed him a mug of coffee. "Dash of cream and a pinch of sugar. Am I right?"

Liam slammed shut his mental doors. "You read my mind?" Without reaching his eyes, his smile stretched his mouth.

"I couldn't help myself." Her mock pout transformed her face into clown territory and curdled Liam's stomach.

"Then you won't mind if I keep my barriers up." Attempting charm, he traded his own clown-contrived grin with her, dodging his usual sober demeanor. "It's the only way I can concentrate on your supplier."

Crystal raked her claws down his sleeve. "I guessed as much. Anyway, I can only read one mind at a time."

"Most telepaths can read a room. Do you pick up random thoughts when you're in a room full of people?"

She averted her face to the side. "Believe me, my talents are incomparable." Liam recognized the lie, felt the emotional baggage attached to it: sorrow, anger that her telepathy remained subpar. Every telepath Liam knew could read a room without even trying. Though it pained them, they had to concentrate harder to separate one thread from another, the norm for a mind reader.

He gripped Crystal's shoulders. In response, she sagged against him, an uncharacteristic gesture for her take-charge personality.

"I'm trusting you more than I should," she said. "My father warned me to be careful around you. Anyone, really."

"Would you rather I left?"

She turned and craned her head back. "Absolutely not. I already ran a background check on you as we do on all our potential employees and proved to my father that you're squeaky clean."

"As I expected." Liam's fake dossier was so clean, she could lick dinner off it.

"My intuition pays off nine times out of ten."

"What happens to the tenth?"

"Depending on the day's outcome, you may see how the other ten percent live. Or not *live*." She accentuated her last word, ratcheting up worrisome spikes in Liam's blood. Rising on her stilettos, Crystal trailed kisses down his jaw and to the neckline of his dress shirt. "I'm glad you're not wearing a tie. May get in the way later."

She handed him a folder with employment papers and a nondisclosure agreement. "Sign the NDA now and read the rest later."

He scanned the NDA, hitting the salient points, before scrawling his fake signature on the dotted line. Didn't matter. Fake signature. Illegal transaction pending. Neither would hold up in court. Might get him killed in Estenson court, though.

A knock on the door juddered through Liam. *Go time.*

"You play my heavy." Crystal's arm grazed his chest as she moved to the head of the oval table, her back to a battered dark wood credenza against the wall farthest from the door.

"Sure thing, boss lady." Liam opened the door.

The doorman waited on the other side. "Marcus Redland to see Miss Estenson."

Liam and the doorman bracketed the door to allow the thirty-something man to enter the room. He carried a slender leather briefcase. The doorman pointed at it and gave Liam an all clear thumbs-up. Slim and lanky, Redland sported a shaggy haircut, a dangling skull and crossbones earring in his left ear, and a tattoo peeping out the neck of his buttoned-up dress shirt. Liam wasn't ready for illegal dealings. A bead of sweat dribbled down his spine.

Crystal made introductions, and Liam stood by her shoulder after the two sat at the small table. Close enough to get a jittery vibe off Redland. Too close to smell the man's nervous acrid sweat.

"Why so jumpy, Marcus?" Crystal didn't need to read his mind.

"You know you always make me jumpy." Redland chuckled, slicked the sweat forming at his hairline into his hair. "Beautiful women are my downfall."

"Touché." Crystal tapped her fingernails on the smudged glass tabletop. "Let's get down to business. Business never makes you nervous."

Marcus pulled a tablet out of his briefcase. "I know when I can make you a bundle of money."

Everything the man said hit the emotions pouring off

him, giving Liam no reason for doubt.

"Yourself as well?" Crystal asked.

"You know me too well."

"Goes with the territory. I've done my due diligence."

"No doubt."

Bored by the small talk, Liam shifted his feet, waited for them to discuss the weather or football. He was eager to complete his assignment and meet Connor. Careful to keep his mental barricades in place, he centered on the meeting.

Crystal and Redland bowed their heads over his tablet to scrutinize financial projections and plans. Liam caught a few words. Money. Mexico. Border. Rolls of wrapping paper. It didn't take a rocket scientist to figure out they were talking about counterfeit money. He'd seen the play in a comedy movie. Did this scam work in the real world?

Crystal's perfume burst over their heads. A skittish anxiousness drifted off Redland. Liam nudged his outer thigh close to Redland's shoulder to get a better empathic feeling. Arrogance layered Redland's trepidation and uncertain lies circled Liam's skull. Hunger for power and money killed his fear. Redland would do anything to make his mark in the world, including deceiving a mob family.

The shit for brains had balls of steal.

"Sounds too good to be true," Crystal announced to Redland. "I want to discuss this with the chief, get his approval. Okay with you?"

The man stood, gathered his tablet close. "Let me know. I'm ready to sign today. My offer won't last long."

"Yes, I know. You have others crawling up your ass for a chunk." Crystal held up a finger. "It'll only take a few. Liam, show him to a seat in the bar."

After Liam returned to the back room, he eyed Crystal. Visibly vibrating, she stood in front of a large oil painting of an Italian villa nestled among rolling fields of emerald grape vines.

"What did you read off him?" Liam asked.

Crystal faced him and deflected. "You tell me first." Her undisguised skepticism ran rampant in his mind. Did she even have a microscopic telepathic ability? Or was she deceiving everyone?

He cleared his throat with the questions popping up like weeds in a well-watered garden. "He's hiding something. Lying. I sensed his intense anxiety *and* smugness. I believe he's trying to pull one over on you. You take the deal, and I bet it goes south."

"If I don't take this deal, my father will kill me," she blurted out, red blotches bursting on her cheeks.

"Why? He should be ecstatic you dodged a bullet." Liam approached her, assimilated her growing anxiety.

"Because he cherry-picked Redland. He hates to be wrong, and he'll tell me I'm overreacting."

"Until the deal goes south. Then he'll know you were right."

She landed a scornful glare on him. "That's not exactly how my father will react. He'll blame me."

"Was there anything in his presentation that set off red flags?"

"It's brilliant, and he's a proven entity. His product and services have the potential to make a boatload of money for the company."

Liam sensed her picking her words carefully for his benefit. Nondisclosure agreement or not, she wasn't stupid. "Did you read anything from his mind that contradicted his words?"

Down flew her eyes to study the floor, giving Liam another glimpse into the lies Crystal had told him about her mind-reading abilities. He released his mental blocks. *"Hey, Crystal! Are you reading me? I'm wearing black chonies, your favorite kind. I'd love to take them off for you later and show you what you've purchased,"* he mentally shouted the words.

No change in expression, no movement, no nothing.

"Point-blank ask him what he's not disclosing. Together, we'll pick his brain."

"It's what I planned. I'm so glad we're on the same page. I knew you'd be an asset to the Estensons."

He touched her jaw. "I'm here to serve."

She pressed her cheek into his palm. "In any capacity?"

"We'll see how today goes. No rush, right?"

"If we diffuse this to my advantage, then I might need to rush." She pressed forward, her voluptuous breasts skimming his pectorals. "You've already turned me up to a million degrees. I might need to ground my heat on you."

Liam pressed his lips to hers, and her return kiss possessed him. Her kiss grew slobbery, biting, and he choked on the spit she churned up in his mouth. He couldn't force a hard-on to stand at attention if he paid his dick with a parade of blowjobs.

Saved by the bell, her phone rang. As she lunged for it on the table, Liam wiped his mouth off on the back of his hand.

"Hello, Father." She motioned for Liam to retrieve Redland.

Leaving the door ajar, Liam eavesdropped on her conversation from the hallway.

"I'll pick up Connor when I'm done. By the way, I have a psychic who can help him with his abilities." She paused for a short moment. "Yes, he's good. I've checked him out." Her voice dropped to a whisper, and Liam repositioned his ear to the crack. "I think I can get him to join our other *project,* and he'd make a great tutor for Connor. If you know what I mean."

Not one part of Liam hated eavesdropping. It came with the territory of psychics. He hadn't even met Connor, and he already knew he loved him more than life. How crazy was that?

"He's doing what to the others?" Alarm elevated her pitch. "I thought the nanny had him under control, and he was doing his homeschooling, not taunting every psychic mind in the house." Liam wished he was a fly inside her phone.

"Well, Dad, he's a powerful psychic. Remember my misadventures learning the tricks of the trade? And I don't have half the abilities he has." A short pause and she frowned. "Barrel of laughs. I'm good when I want to be." Another lengthy pause. "Then tell the nanny to give him some children's pain relievers." Her words stabbed Liam's heart. "Neal's wrong about it retarding his progress. He shouldn't let his kid suffer. Soon as my meeting's over I'll pick him up."

Liam darted toward the barroom, pretending to button his fly and tuck in his shirt to cover up his delay in case Crystal mentioned it. "Mr. Redland? Miss Estenson's ready to hammer this out."

By the time Liam and Redland returned to the conference room, Crystal sat quiet and composed at the table. Redland returned to his seat, and Liam took up his post at her shoulder, blocking Redland from her body. A tray in front of Crystal held two glasses of bourbon. She licked her bottom lip, worried it for a second. Liam knew the signs of her nervousness. Did she need alcohol to chill? Hell, he did after hearing her one-sided phone conversation. At least he didn't fret about ditching his walls. Crystal only had the capacity to read one person at a time, if that, and her sole focus remained on Redland.

Liam's phone vibrated once, twice, and then three text messages against his ass. Only his brothers and Niles had his number. Unable to interrupt the flow, he forced his attention off his phone, rubbed at the forming dents in his forehead.

"We've considered your offer. I think we can do business." She held up a finger to freeze Redland's jubilant smile. "First, the Estensons want seventy percent, not forty."

"It's my people at risk," he intoned evenly, expecting the rebuttal.

Tension escalated, and Liam squeezed Crystal's shoulder to relax her. Her emotions swamped him, and he knew she could read Redland's mind with no problem now.

"No, Redland. The Estensons are absorbing the bulk of the exposure. That's why you came to us. We have the manpower, the smarts, the network."

"I came to you because this deal will benefit both of us." He thumped his reed-thin fingers on the table. "If you don't want to work together, I can take my services and product elsewhere. There're plenty fish in the sea. But what will Daniel say? He's counting on this deal to beef up his bank accounts. You and I both know where this conversation's heading."

Crystal shifted forward as if to force her words upon him. "Don't threaten me. I have authority to reject this deal."

An evil grin gave her a Wicked Witch of the West demeanor. Liam exerted a slight force on her shoulder to settle her back in the seat. Anger dimmed, and she sported a new confidence, proving she hid another card up her sleeve.

"Show me a sample." She swiveled her chair and grabbed a counterfeit bill detector from the cabinet behind her.

Redland honed in on the contraption, and Liam suffered the sharp pain of the man's terror in his chest. When severe emotions ran rampant in a room, the pain began. Redland was lying and Crystal planned to bust him.

"Have you ever seen one of these?" Crystal caressed the small electronic device.

Crimson painted his cheeks. "Do we need to do this again? Daniel already verified three batches of the product."

"I want to see this baby in action. If your product passes the newest technology used by the feds, then we're good. We have a deal. Seventy, thirty. Don't pretend you didn't know we'd want seventy all along."

"Sixty, forty and let's call it a day."

"Seventy, thirty or try to hawk your wares elsewhere. See how well you get on. In Iceland or a locale equally lonely and wintry." Redland reached for a glass of bourbon, and Crystal snaked out a claw to stop him. "To celebrate after we strike our deal."

He withdrew his hand, held it palm forward for a second. "Fine." Liam honed in on the man as he bent over his briefcase, assured by the doorman that he'd confiscated Redland's weapon at the front door. Redland set a fat envelope on the table and slid it to Crystal. "We retrofitted our machines, tweaked a few things. Daniel was pleased with the new output." He bowed his head at Crystal. "You will be too." Sweat slid down his temples, and his nervousness joined the sharp stabbing pains. Crystal's smugness calmed, like a serial killer about to claim her twentieth victim. It didn't bode well for a good outcome. The deal had gone south, and Crystal would boot Redland out on his ass to hawk his defective counterfeit bills to a more unsuspecting target.

She drew a stack of fresh-minted hundreds from the envelope and slid the paper band off. Closing her eyes, she sniffed the bills, a pleasant smile drawing her mouth wide. "Smells like the real deal." She opened her eyes and inspected the stack, fanning it one way and then the other. "Amazing."

Redland smirked in response to her accolades. The tension simmered, and Liam's sharp pains dulled in the wake of Redland cooling down.

After fanning the stack a second time, Crystal fed the bills through the counter. A blank slate shut down her expressions, but Liam felt her glee. He tried to get a look-see at the readouts on the display, but she shielded it as she fed in the last bundle.

Nothing changed in her demeanor when a wide smile stretched her lips. The dark flinty look she tossed him sent a chill spider-walking down his spine.

"Magnificent." She picked up one glass of bourbon and handed it to Redland, then cupped the other.

Redland's smugness returned, and Crystal's spine tensed. She clinked her glass to his. "Well done. Drink up."

"Does this mean we have a deal?" Redland asked.

"Papers are ready to go." She spat out the words.

Liam had a tricky time deciphering her escalating emotions. Redland must've tossed a negative or nasty sentiment in his head and she picked up on it. So much emotional baggage circled Liam, not even subtly cracking his knuckles helped diffuse it.

"Well then." Redland touched his glass to hers again and downed his drink in two gulps.

Drink untouched, Crystal set her glass on the table. The clank of glass on glass didn't obscure the thunk of Redland's glass tumbling out of his hand and crashing to the tile floor. Glass shards scattered the room, pinging the walls.

Horror shrouded Liam, and he listed to the right, stumbling to balance against the edge of Crystal's chair.

Redland clamped one hand on his neck, and a scarlet haze crept over his face. "What did you do to me?" he gasped out. Foam bubbled in the corner of his mouth, and he tried to stand up, staggered. Redland collapsed in his chair, drooling more foam out of his mouth. His eyes turned vacant in a blue-tinged complexion and deep convulsions rolled up his abdomen.

Calm and unmoving, Crystal said, "Your product failed the test, imbecile. You dared to pass off shoddy bills on the Estenson org and plan to pay our seventy percent with the same fucking shit. You're too stupid to live."

Unintelligible words gurgled up from Redland's throat. Liam felt the poison burn in his blood. Felt the man's death in every bone of his body, and it took all he had to remain standing. Sweat broke out in his pits. Stars exploded in his mind, and he couldn't block Redland amid the bright lights. "Crystal?" Everything around him went blinding white, and he felt himself falling in slow motion.

"Next time you call me a dumb bimbo, you better make damn certain I can't read your mind." She tapped her chin. "Oh, wait. There won't be a next time. Nice doing business with you, Redland. Have a fantastic trip. Say hello to your predecessor in hell."

Hell gleefully cushioned Liam's fall into its blistering depths.

CHAPTER TWENTY-FOUR

The two sheriffs who'd escorted Eva into the county precinct left her alone in an interrogation room. They'd cuffed her to the table like a common criminal. Worse than a common criminal, she was a judge killer in their eyes.

The search warrant arrived before they'd left her house. If she didn't get out on bail, at least Liam had access to the flash drive in the small closet safe at the safe house. The critical one remained sewn in the seam of her leather jacket, which she still wore after they'd patted her down while reading her Miranda rights.

And Neal never showed up.

Eva drummed her fingers on the standard-issue table that seemed to find its way in every police station, grungy, pitted, and stark. The small, gray room stank of old sweat, fear, and dirty socks.

A burly detective in his late forties entered the room, and the door automatically shut behind him. He reminded her of an elephant, rotund and ashen, matching his more salted than peppered military buzz cut.

"Good morning, Eva Marie Midnight. Or is it Estenson?" He sunk his weight onto a decrepit chair and regarded her coolly from across the table. Then he set a recorder on the center of the table. Did he expect her to cough up a confession?

"It's Midnight." Eva stared at his badge. "Detective Clarkson. When can I get my phone call?"

"We've already called Alex MacKenzie. He's hooking you up with a lawyer."

"Perfect. Guess we're almost on the same page." She leaned back in her chair as far as her shackles allowed. "Can you remove the cuffs?" She canted her head toward her right wrist. "I'm not a flight risk. My record's clean. I'm a cop for God's sake."

"You said it, not me."

"Lovely." She enunciated the word as sarcastically as she could muster. "I still want my phone call."

"If you insist." Clarkson shucked a cell phone out of his front shirt pocket and slid it across the table. "It's unlocked, safe, not tapped. You need privacy?"

"Yes. *Please*. You taking a cuff off or do I need to use my toes? Please. *Sir*." Better not antagonize him or she might find herself cozying up to a real murderer in a jail cell. Popularity didn't extend to cops in jail except as someone's prison bitch or punching bag.

The detective pushed back his chair, and his paunch jiggled as he rose. Pain lanced his face, and he limped around the table. "Did I tell you Martinelli was a good friend?" He unhooked a key ring of a million jingling keys off his belt and unlocked her left cuff.

Oh, hell to the flipping no. A new round of acid agitated Eva's belly. She bet Martinelli was on everyone's payroll around here. The hit could've stemmed from any number of vengeful asswipes.

"I'm sorry for your loss." Eva rubbed her wrist against her middle, staunching the sting of the cuff.

Clarkson snorted and left the room, leaving the stench of his oily musk of disgust behind.

Eva realized she couldn't call Liam, nor anyone in the Guild without jeopardizing them. Neal's and Crystal's phones were incommunicado. She couldn't call her parents without risking them too, not that she wanted them to know what shitstorm she'd blundered into. Humility a small price to pay, she dialed the only other number that made a lick of sense in one small part of her mind.

The phone rang twice before the dreaded voice answered with a curt "hello."

"Hello, Mr. Estenson," Eva replied.

"Who is this? How did you get my private number?" A large degree of annoyance laced his words.

"It's Eva. I need to get hold of Neal."

The uproarious guffaw dashed her humiliation away. "Oh, Eva, my dear. You're an absolute gem. Nice try. By the by, have you thought about my offer?"

Click. Dead silence met her ear.

Growling out her frustration, Eva banged the phone on the side of her head. Before Clarkson returned, she dialed Alex's personal cell.

"Alex! I'm so sorry to involve you in this disaster of my life." The words streamed out in a raging torrent.

"Eva, don't worry about me. I'm on your side."

"Then what the ever-loving hell?"

"I know. I'm on my way." Alex heaved out a sigh. "Jake McAllister's girlfriend, Lily Falbrooke, retained a criminal attorney. He should be on his way now. Just don't provoke the police and keep your mouth shut."

"What do you know?"

"They have the weapon that killed Martinelli. Has your prints all over it. Forensics identified it as a match."

Part of Eva didn't want to believe it. She bent forward, the phone slipping out of her hand. Why had Neal turned her in? Did he suspect she'd drugged him last night? As bile burned the back of her throat, she scoured the dismal room for a trash can.

"Eva!" Alex's voice coasted from the phone as if he were

a million miles away.

"Neal set me up."

"I don't know how the police got their hands on the gun. But I'll find out."

She thudded her forehead on the table to still her rampaging emotions. Her voice dropped to a lower register. "Keep Liam, all of them, away. I can't expose them. It's too great a risk to Connor and the Guild. Liam needs to be there for Connor if I end up in prison."

"I've alerted them. Couldn't get hold of Liam, but I spoke to Niles and Jake. They know the score. They'll contact Liam and keep working the plan from their end."

"I notice you didn't say I wasn't going to prison." Eva tried to instill a light, funny tone.

"It goes without saying, Eva. You didn't do it."

She cupped her hand around the phone. "Have you ever fought the mafia?"

"Can't say I have."

"Then you can't promise me anything." For the first time since the police had cuffed her, tears brimmed her eyes, and she wiped them off on her shoulder.

"I can promise I'll do *everything* possible to make this right." Resignation edged Alex's voice, and Eva felt his compassion practically radiate on the air waves.

"Thank you. That's all I can ask." Butt numb, she slumped back in the hard seat. "I owe you big-time."

"All you owe me is to clear your name and return to the force, clean and ready to work again."

"You have no idea how much I want my life back."

The door slid open, and Clarkson stepped inside, his shoes squeaking on the linoleum floor. "You done?"

"I need to go. See you soon." She punched off the phone and slid it across the table to Clarkson. "I called my boss." He resumed his seat and pocketed the phone.

"Then you also know we have the weapon that fired the

killing shot. Your weapon."

"We're done talking until my lawyer arrives."

He nodded. "I figured you'd clam up."

"Do you blame me?"

Without a grain of mirth, he chuckled. "Your lawyer's checking in now. Arrived a few minutes ago. Interesting choice. He's good though, I'll grant you that."

The lawyer arrived quicker than Eva expected. She wanted to ask Clarkson for his identity but preferred to act as though she had her crap together in the tempest flinging her life asunder. She hadn't been in the Bay Area long enough to get friendly with too many criminal defense attorneys. Some she knew by name, reputation, and others she'd confronted in court. None had left a lasting impression on her. A mistake on her part.

"Will you behave if I uncuff your other wrist?" Keys jangling in hand, Clarkson stood.

A wry smile twisted her lip. "I'm not going anywhere."

Eva didn't have long to wait after Clarkson left her before the door pushed open. Briefcase in hand, dressed to the nines in a coal black custom-tailored suit and pristine white dress shirt, Neal Estenson crossed the threshold.

"No. No. No." Eva thrust off her seat. "Clarkson?" she shouted.

Neal held up a hand to quiet her down. The detective stood behind Neal, his height hidden but not his girth.

"Your lawyer or not?" Clarkson asked.

"Who else did you think would come?" Neal stepped into the room, gave a sniff, his nose crinkling up in distaste.

"Are you fucking kidding me?" Eva battled to stop herself from lunging across the table at Neal. "Get him out of here. He's *not* my lawyer."

"Guess there's some bad blood between you exes." Clarkson winked. "Well, Estenson, shall I lock her up to await another lawyer?"

"Why are you asking him? I'm the suspect. It's my choice who I choose to rep me." Eva slammed her palm on the table at the same time she spotted Alex MacKenzie behind the two men hogging up the space and air in the small room. He brought a peaceful influence to the tempest, and the aching knots in her shoulders loosened.

"Eva," Neal said evenly, "my colleague Jasper Jamison notified me about the arrest. He's a good criminal lawyer. No offense, MacKenzie." He tossed over his shoulder. "He thought I might be better suited to represent Eva." He had the audacity to wink.

"You mean after you blackmailed him?" Eva simmered, hot and flushed, refusing to remove her jacket in case they discovered the flash drive and she lost her one chess piece.

"Midnight?" Clarkson queried.

"Fine. Whatever. I'll let you know." She fanned her face, sat back down. Neal and Alex both entered the room and the door shut Clarkson out.

"You can't be in here, MacKenzie," Neal said.

"Give me a moment with Eva. Alone." Alex flashed his badge, not that he needed to. He had no jurisdiction over a police officer under arrest outside San Jose.

With a scowl, Neal stepped out, and the warring testosterone levels dipped to a more manageable level.

"Why is he here?" Eva demanded.

"I don't know." Alex played with a roll of antacids. "We hired Jamison. Is this another one of Neal's games?"

"Considering he planted the gun"—Eva gripped the edge of the table, her knuckles whitening—"*my* old service revolver with my prints all over it, then the answer's a big fat flipping yes."

"How do you want to play this out? I'll call Jamison, let him know it was a mistake. It's your choice."

Either Neal knew she'd conned him last night, knew

she'd snuck into his laptop, or something else triggered him to plant the gun in the path of the Martinelli detectives. It proved the Estenson involvement. They'd killed Martinelli. She'd stake her life on it. And she may very well have to.

"I'll talk to Neal. I want to drill into his angle." Despite her dire predicament, Eva succumbed to her curiosity.

"Should I call Jamison?"

"Please. Keep him on ice. If Neal set me up, I don't want... can't have him as my attorney. Talk about conflict of interest. I can guarantee you he's using this ploy to his advantage."

Eva pressed the flash drive in the seam of her jacket, making a final, grudging decision. "Alex, can I trust you to hold something for me? I wasn't ready to divulge this until I had more evidence. Swear you won't use it until we have every nail hammered home."

Alex gazed at her quizzically. "Are you withholding evidence?"

She nodded, shook her head. "It's complicated. You can't judge me, and you have to agree this is confidential." The challenge sparkled the silver flecks in his lagoon-blue eyes as if the overhead lights pierced a veil of clouds.

After a long pause, he said, "Agreed."

Eva picked at the seam on her jacket and popped out the flash drive. A long look at what it represented shot home her need to lay all her cards on the table, if only to save her son. She slid the thumb drive across the table. "Self-explanatory once you view the contents."

Alex reached for the tiny drive. "Should I view?"

She bit the inside of her cheek. "Eventually, you'll need to."

"What about the others?"

Eva picked at her fingernails, tapped her shoes on the floor, and studied a cross someone had gouged into the table. Finally, she confronted the question. "If it helps. I'll leave it up to your discretion."

Alex pocketed the flash drive and headed for the door, wheeled around on his heels. "I guess I needn't tell you the PD has suspended you."

Eva groaned. "I may as well be dead right now."

"Don't say that. Connor needs you."

Tears welled again, and she blinked them away to preserve the remainder of her dignity. "I may never see him again. Then it won't matter." She lowered her voice. "Just get him out of Estenson hands and to his rightful place." She didn't want to say Liam's name to avoid exposure.

"You'll see him again. Count on it." Nodding, Alex opened the door.

"Alex, I didn't deserve the luck landing on me when you became my boss."

"You deserve my friendship. I knew from the moment I met you, we'd become friends. I'll go to the ends of the earth for my friends."

"Me too. At least I hope I get the chance to."

"Counting on it." He gave her a reassuring smile and opened the door.

Neal barreled past him in his rush to her defense. *Defense, my ass. More like lynching.*

CHAPTER TWENTY-FIVE

Liam leveraged his eyelids open long enough to check out the vaulted ceiling and sunshine-bright room. A jackhammer went to town in his skull, and every muscle and bone in his body had liquefied him onto a sofa. A bleary glance at his watch proved he'd been conked out for over four hours. He tossed off the damp compress from his forehead, which smelled of camphor and other herbs he didn't recognize. Someone had unbuttoned his shirt and the herbal smell arose from the slick poultice slathered on his chest. *Did the Guild healer doctor me up? Where am I?*

With a silky pillow beneath his head, he lay on an expensive overstuffed sofa long enough for his full length. Gray-and-black-veined white marble floors flowed beneath thick wool rugs. The sparse but opulent furnishing did nothing to hit his familiarity buttons. But Liam remembered dying. Oh, right, Redland died and took him along for the ride. *Shitballs in hell.* He'd never been empathically connected to a dying person. Never wanted to ever again. At the moment, his empathic abilities had taken a hike. He barely sensed his own emotions, other than debilitating exhaustion.

Soft shuffling footsteps sounded on the other side of the sofa.

"Liam! I thought we'd lost you. Georgie, he's awake,"

she yelled.

The voice sounded familiar, but he couldn't identify the owner. He struggled to sit up, collapsed in a heap.

"Don't get up. You've been out for hours." A strong woman's hand pressed his shoulder down, forcing him to stretch out flat again.

Crystal Estenson.

"Where are we?" he croaked, his mouth dryer than a desert in drought central. "Water, please."

"Coming right up." Crystal perched on the sofa next to him. "Our family doctor had no clue when you'd awaken." She waved a dismissive hand in the air as if dying in a man's head was an everyday occurrence.

Liam threw a small pillow across the room. "Do you realize I almost fucking died? Why didn't you tell me what you'd planned?"

Crystal sprang back as if slapped. "I'm sorry. I didn't realize—"

"What kind of telepath are you if *you* escaped his mind when you poisoned him?" Liam's aggravation took another spin at her. He didn't give a rat's ass if she dumped him. She'd almost killed him!

Crystal sputtered. "I didn't know that could happen. I quit reading him before he drank…"

A gaunt woman sporting a gray bob cut and librarian glasses on her lined face entered the room. The doctor— Liam presumed—carried a tray with water, pill cups, and a mug containing a steaming concoction that rivaled pig swine.

"Hello, Liam. Good to see you awake. I'm Dr. Hildebrand." She set the tray on the granite-topped, wrought iron coffee table. "I'd like to run a few tests if you don't mind. I'll just get my bag." She darted away.

"Who is she?" Liam stalled for time. He wanted no one touching him other than Guild healers. "Is she versed in psychics?"

"Dr. Georgina Hildebrand. She's an MD and empath, different from you. Her empathic skills come in the way of hands-on healing, and of course herbs and regular old medicine."

The Guild healer, Elizabeth, was the only other empathic healer he'd ever known, but she still relied more on her herbal remedies and modern medicines. "She heals with her hands? Does she absorb the pain and emotions?"

"In a way, yes," Dr. Hildebrand responded. She set her black leather medical bag on the coffee table and handed Liam the bottle of water and a pill cup.

He frowned at the two pills. "What are these?"

She smiled. "Paranoid, are you? Acetaminophen. I'm assuming you have a headache." Liam took the water and downed the pills with half the bottle. "Answer enough. On a scale of one to ten, how bad?"

"Twelve."

"Will you allow me to examine you? I'll only physically examine, nothing more."

Liam suffered through her peripheral examination, and he kept his answers to her questions curt and tame, without revealing how much he knew about psychic healers. Or without disclosing that his empathic power had taken a hike. He wanted to slap his brain to yesterday to unloose the rope knotting his abilities.

"You should be okay after a good night's rest. I don't see or sense any permanent damage. If your abilities seem off, that's normal for an event like this. Give it twenty-four hours. The poultice will absorb. It works to relax you and alleviate bodily pain."

He didn't know what he'd do if he lost his abilities for good. Currently, he couldn't erect his walls, and it made for an uncomfortable experience trying and failing to sense Crystal and the doc.

"Thanks." He sank onto the sofa, the softness a boon to his aching head.

Crystal escorted Dr. Hildebrand to the front door and returned. "Again, I'm sorry."

"Is Redland dead?"

"Yes. He tricked my father and two of my father's partners, tried to pull a fast one on me. Actually, he cost my father about five million dollars, no telling how much he cost the others. He also had an Estenson guard killed last month. No one returns from that. Eliminate evil is the name of the game."

Brutality was the Estensons' currency, cunning the Cabal's cash of choice. "Does your father condone your actions?"

"My father calls the shots." Crystal leaned against his side as if touching him helped assuage her guilt. It annoyed the crap out of him. "Will you ever forgive me?"

"Forgiven." Unenthusiastically, he linked their fingers in a show of good faith he wanted to run from.

"Do we need to have a come-to-Jesus talk about what happened today?" She danced the fingers of her other hand up his bare arm to where someone had rolled up his shirt sleeve. When she inched across his hidden injury, he stifled a flinch. "Or are you on board?"

"Pay me enough and I might mix the drinks next time."

Crystal's braying evolved into tinkling glee. "Believe me, I plan to pay you in diamonds."

"Cold hard cash is good. The good cash, though." He forced a grin he didn't think he'd ever feel again. He lay back and closed his eyes to block the late afternoon sunlight streaming through the windows. "How did I get here?" Fighting to keep his mind clear in case Crystal was reading him, he suffered renewed throbbing arcing from one temple to the other.

"I had help, obviously. We're at my brother's house,"

she replied. Liam's pulse revved up at the mention of Neal Estenson and help. Had anyone recognized him? "It's safe. He's away on business, so he won't bother us. I think you should stay overnight."

In reality, he needed the quiet interlude to recharge both mentally and physically. And determine if he needed to escape in case Crystal's men were former Guild. Weakness kept him rooted to the sofa, though. He'd prefer his own bedroom, bolted doors and windows, and sound-canceling headphones. Or a quiet stroll in the woods alone. The opportunity for the walk may yet materialize since Neal's house was located in the lower foothills. Yet, his nerves screamed bloody murder at him. What if Neal returned early? What if he'd seen Eva's photos of Liam?

"I don't mind staying." *Let me be a tick on your dog while I scour Neal's house for clues.* The primo opportunity was too good to pass up.

Crystal preened and purred. She brushed her lips over his, depositing a trace of coffee on his mouth. "Neal has the better house between us. It's a great family home. One day, it might be my home." Avarice glittered in her eyes as she swept the room, then rested on him as if she expected him to help fill her dream home with kids.

The only woman he wanted popping out his kids was— he zipped his thoughts before they got him in way deep... in more ways than one.

"I'd love to explore the grounds later, if you don't mind. The outdoors will help me heal," he said.

The pitter-patter of small feet hopped down the curving stairway behind him. A small hand squeaked on the handrail and preceded the small voice, "Auntie Crystal, can I come downstairs now?"

The heavens opened up and the lilting voice of Liam's son flooded his mind with indescribable joy. He nearly brained himself on the table lamp trying to rise to view his son for the first time.

CRSO

Neal plopped down in the popular chair across from Eva at the interrogation room table. After grimacing at the floor, he set his briefcase on the tabletop. "Before you say anything, I didn't plant the gun," Neal interjected in a rush.

"*Really?*" Eva stretched out the word, arms crossed over her chest. "Is this another ploy to get me in your bed? If so, you're up crap creek without a paddle. If I get booted down the river for offing a judge, how will that work out for you? Conjugal visits gonna be enough for you? I can't help you from prison, you know. Cops rarely fare well against other inmates. I'll be lucky to live out a year. What will you tell our son?"

"Are you through?"

"Not by a long shot." Eva slammed her palms on the table. "You can't rep me if *you* turned me in. What ration of bull is this, Neal? I thought last night went well for a new start. When I left, I anticipated a second date, hoping we'd turned a corner. I really believed you'd changed."

Shock hinged Neal's jaw open. *Holy, fake sex.* He believed they'd done the nasty last night, believed her ruse. Maybe he hadn't turned over the gun. Stunned, face a blank slate, Eva contemplated a new tactic.

"Eva, sweetheart. Last night was awesome. I mean, I passed out at one point, but I remember going to bed together. I drank too much. It won't happen again." His face flushed, turning him into a lobster. "Did we do it?"

"We fooled around. It's too soon to go all the way. We had fun. Like old times."

His smug ego staged a roaring comeback in the squaring of his shoulders. "You enjoyed it?"

She squirmed on the hard-bottomed chair. "I'm lonely. It felt right for the first time in a long while." *Let me hurl now, please.*

"It felt right when I woke up. I wished you'd stayed for breakfast."

"I had to work this morning. If it felt so right to you, then why did you plant the gun?"

Neal placed his right palm over his heart. "I swear I didn't do it. The gun was locked in my house safe."

"Really? Then who?"

"I'm sure my father had a hand in it."

Eva knocked her spine against the chair. "What? So, he hired a hitman to kill Martinelli and set me up? You had no part in it? Come on, get real. *You* taunted me with exposure. Don't play me for an idiot."

More red splotches flowered on Neal's cheeks, but he hid his emotions behind the color. "I left the gun in the safe after I took Connor. Someone broke in, stole the gun. My father mocked me about it, told me he had a way to get you out of my life for good. When I checked on the gun, it was gone." Contriteness on him was always a prelude to trouble or pain. He wore it for real in that moment. "I swear I wanted... *want* to work things out with you. I'm still so in love with you, and I want our family reunited. I'll admit I used the photos to sway you. But I never would have turned the gun over."

"Your father wants me gone from your life." And so much more it made Eva's skin crawl, remembering how his touch was as lethal as Neal's. "You can't have it both ways." Eva's voice dropped to a near whisper, and she wrangled a sudden sob. "He's making you choose between him and me. I know where this is headed."

Anger burned the light flecks in Neal's eyes, dying stars winking out. "I won't let it come to that. I'm working to get him to accept you as part of our family."

When hell freezes over. Or over my dead body. No better clichéd metaphors fit her situation. "The dark side has claimed him. Are you willing to make the leap? Is that where you want our son to live?" She shut her mouth before she voiced things she had no business knowing.

"I've never told you this." Neal's hopeful glint stuffed her with loathing. "I want you and me to take over the business together. With Connor—" He stomped the brakes on his train of verbal thought. "My father didn't just want me to return from Florida. He wanted you to come with, become a real Estenson wife."

Eva blinked away her surprise. "That was before the divorce." *And for reasons not even on your radar.*

"It can still happen."

"He destroyed the old you. He murdered *us*. Nope. Not while your father draws breath."

"Exactly." The hope in Neal's voice turned smug. Deadly.

Did Neal intend to kill his father? For me? Eva's stomach flipped upside down and splattered.

CHAPTER TWENTY-SIX

Crystal held out her hand, and Connor's soft footfalls carried closer. "Come here, Connor. I want you to meet a special friend."

Liam's head reeled, and he yielded to the pressure of her touch to keep him prone on the sofa. His heart near burst through skin and muscle when Connor came into view. Just like his photos, he had the McAllister youth blond hair, the same shape and color blue eyes, mirroring the color of Eva's eyes too. His eyes exuded a wisdom far behind his years, the old soul Eva mentioned. He was angelic and so serene that Liam almost wept.

Connor smiled at Liam and held out his hand for a shake. Liam clasped the boy's tiny hand, marveling at the strength in his grip. Connor's emotions slammed into him, shocking in so many ways. His son unlocked the doors to his wayward empathic abilities. Curiosity conquered the familiarity Connor experienced. Liam hungered to sweep him into his arms, to hold his little body tight, and never let go. As his gaze drank in every feature of his son, he battled one of the greatest urges of his life.

Ice balled in his chest. He set his finger to his lips, hoping Connor got the message to keep his identity zipped.

"If you know who I am, say nothing. It's our secret, our game to play. Just you and me. Show me a sign you

understand." Liam voiced the thoughts for Connor to hear mentally, believing Crystal had no ability to ferret out the voices in the tiny door Liam opened to Connor. The boy shyly pressed Liam's hand and acceptance flowed from him to Liam. His Achilles heel just became his newest confidant. Strangely enough, he no longer felt Crystal's emotions, but Connor's emotions flooded every pinprick of the empty crater of his being.

In fragmented words refusing to coalesce, Connor's inner voice zinged in his brain. Shock froze Liam for a few seconds. He wasn't a mind reader. Yet what he mentally heard was totally telepathic. As Connor continued to drop fragments into Liam's mind, Liam tried to read Crystal and hit a dense wall. Still no emotions, let alone thoughts. Again, he wanted to slap around his head to rattle his brain into a semblance of normal. Instead, he shut down his mind to any outside intrusion to enable him to glory in meeting Connor without the babble pervading his aching head.

"I'm honored to meet you, Connor Estenson. I'm Liam Riley, a friend of your aunt. She's told me what a wonderful boy you are and how we might become great psychic friends."

"Hi, Liam, I mean, Mr. Riley." Connor giggled, and they released each other's hands. Liam's reluctance to let go poured a cup of cold water over his joy. He'd fallen in love in two seconds flat, and he didn't want to relinquish another moment with his son to the bowels of time.

Connor rubbed his forehead, turned to Crystal. "Can I call him Liam?"

She slung an arm over Connor's shoulder and hugged him to her side. "Of course. We'll be great friends, the three of us. Liam has a lot to teach you about your psychic abilities."

Face darkening, Connor pushed out of Crystal's arms, hugged his arms across his stomach. "Will it hurt?"

"Absolutely not!" Liam chuckled to put the boy at ease. "I couldn't hurt a fly."

Connor giggled. "Flies are pests. They deserve it."

"Okay, then I couldn't hurt an ant."

"Ants are worse than pests."

"Not if you treat them with respect." Liam wanted to banter with his son all day. "Give them an ant hill to populate, watch them grow a colony and thrive. Have you ever done that?"

Excitement bounced Connor on his toes. "No! Can you show me how?"

"I'll show you anything you want."

"Well, let's start with dinner first." Crystal interjected herself into the conversation and ruffled Connor's mussy hair.

"Auntie Crystal, do I have to go back to Granddad's tonight? Can we stay here? I miss my old room." Connor shuffled his stockinged feet on the marble floor, and his dread leaked into Liam.

"Yes. We'll stay here until Dad and Granddad finish their business meetings this week. They don't want to be disturbed."

"Yay!" Connor hopped up and down. "Can Liam stay too?" Biting his lower lip, he peeked at Liam. Silent curiosity emanated off him.

Liam's happiness knew no bounds. The boy was indeed a McAllister, no doubt about his mannerisms that reminded him of himself and both his brothers growing up. Damn Eva for hiding the secret of a lifetime. Before his walls fractured and allowed Crystal or Connor in, he clamped down tight and reinforced them. Pain sliced across his brain, but he didn't give a hoot about the sacrifices he had to make, not when the moment gave him so much happiness. He wanted to bundle Connor up and spirit him away from all the madness.

"I'm starving. What about you, buddy?" Liam eased into a sitting position, fighting the explosion rocking his head. He waited a moment to ensure his head stayed on his shoulders and the bombs dissipated.

"Yes!" Connor punched the air. When he reached out to take Liam's hand, tears welled in Liam's eyes, and he quickly blinked them away. "Let's go into the kitchen. Auntie already bought take-and-bake pizza. My favorite is salami and cheese. What's yours?"

"What a small world. That's my favorite too." Not such a small world after all. It was also Eva's favorite.

Crystal hugged Liam's sore arm to her side. He exchanged the radiating ache with his momentary joy. He kissed her temple, holding the kiss for a few seconds, giving her thanks. "I'm sorry for snapping at you earlier. It's hazardous to connect in that manner." He was so glad she'd set her sight on only him, otherwise, she might notice the similarities between him and Connor, the way they both rubbed their forehead when thinking.

They entered a gleaming white, black, and stainless steel kitchen that dwarfed his kitchen three times over. "I've not experienced something like that with a psychic. I owe you so much," she said.

"Well, then how about that job?" He nipped a tress of her sleek hair, and her remorse and truths flooded him. The return of his empathic abilities eclipsed her lack of guilt over killing Redland. "Except I draw the line—"

"We'd never expect you to do that. We have others on the payroll. You got the job."

"Starting tonight with Connor? I already sense something special about him."

Preening and purring, she gushed all over him. "I knew you would. If you're up to it, we'll be undisturbed here for a couple days."

"Good. I'll need alone time with him to gauge his

abilities." He propped a hip on the barstool next to Connor at the humongous kitchen island of gray-veined white marble.

"Your phone's been blowing up." Crystal slid out a large pizza from the double-sided refrigerator. "A girlfriend I should worry about?" The angry jealousy rolling off her contradicted her light tone.

"There's only you, Crystal." The lie bumbled off his tongue. "Shoot. Probably my buddy Juan. I was supposed to help him move today." More lies, more deflection.

Ignoring them, Connor began coloring robots in his coloring book. Liam checked his phone. Five missed calls. Three 911 texts. All anonymous. *Level Ten freak-out time.*

Woozy, he hopped off the stool. "Yep. Juan. Bathroom handy? I'll give him a ring."

Crystal pointed out a narrow hallway to the left. "Second door on the right." She slid the pizza in the oven. "Pizza coming up in eighteen minutes."

"Yay!" Connor shouted. "Can I have a soda too? Dad never lets me have one."

Liam wanted to remain in the kitchen forever with his son. He'd give him a case of sodas if he wanted. Well, maybe not all at once. *Man, this fatherhood bit's gonna take time to wrap my head around.*

He locked the bathroom door and turned the overhead fan on to drown out his voice. Like the other rooms, the monotone marbles in the bathroom reeked of custom design and money. After using the facilities, he dialed Ric's anonymous phone. It barely rang once.

"Hey, bro, did you ring?"

"Where've you been?" Ric's agitation devoured Liam's good mood.

"With Crystal," he mumbled. "I'll tell you about it later. What's going on?"

"Eva's been arrested for Martinelli's murder." Ric's

words filtered into the new chaos setting up shop in his brain. "Stay the course. MacKenzie's handling it. We need to keep separation from her."

"How?" Liam demanded, fisting his hand.

"Estenson planted Eva's gun on Martinelli's property and tipped the detectives off."

Liam banged his head against the wall. A new pile of shit just splattered the fan. "Did she lawyer up?"

"You'll never believe this."

"She called Neal." Liam was only half joking. The rumor mill said he was an excellent criminal lawyer, even if he skirted the dark fringes of the law. Or *because* he did.

"No, man. He just showed up to rep her. Gave the lawyer Alex hired the boot."

"Son of a bitch." A thought hit Liam and sweat popped on his neck. "He's supposed to be out of town on business."

"Sure. If you call Santa Clara out of town. What does it matter?"

"Because I'm sitting in his house in the foothills. With my son."

Ric whistled. "No kidding. Far as we know, he's working on getting Eva's arraignment set for tomorrow, negotiating with the DA for a decent bail. He may show up there later. You freaked?"

"Not really. Figured I'd meet him one day. I just have this great opportunity and don't want him spoiling it."

"Don't get cocky, man. You're on a mission."

"Thanks for the vote, bro. I need to jet. Crystal and Connor are waiting for me. Keep me updated on her situation. Keep the texts coded."

"Will do. Later." Ric hung up and Liam stared at his phone. The fleeting plan to steal his son away evaporated. He wanted to hear Eva's voice so bad, he almost called her voicemail. He cooled off his face with a washcloth and left the bathroom, leaving his heart in a blender and tossed in a million directions. Seeing his son hunched over his coloring book fitted some tattered pieces together.

Hands on her hips, Crystal said, "Everything okay?" The icicles she cast him sent chills down his spine. Had she heard his convo?

"No prob. I gave my apologies and promised to help Juan on home remodeling projects next weekend to make up for my no-show."

The scent of melting cheese and Italian sauce permeated the kitchen, instigated hungry rumbling in his gut. Liam sat on the barstool and picked up the bottle of microbrew Crystal opened for him. He took a healthy swig. "Thanks. I needed that after today."

"Are you okay drinking? You took a couple pain pills, but I thought you could use that."

"A few sips won't hurt." Liam set the bottle down, grateful for her reminder about the pain pills. "You're doing an awesome job staying in the lines." Liam tapped the coloring book.

"Can you spell your name?" Connor asked.

"Sure." As Liam pronounced each letter, Connor wrote them above a picture of a caped superhero slaying a decrepit robot. Then he wrote his own name above a smaller caped superhero standing behind the robot. They wore matching blue capes and black tights, holding twin light sabers. The remaining bits of Liam's heart dissolved. Did the boy know?

As Crystal cut and served the pizza, Connor finished his coloring. Tongue between his teeth, he carefully tore the page out of the book and slid it across the counter to Liam.

"That's for you. To remember me."

"Ah, buddy, I don't think I'll ever forget you. I hope we'll have some fun times together."

"Me too." Connor scrounged in his backpack hanging

on a hook beneath the counter, drew out a small piece of paper, and stealthily handed it to Liam.

Keeping the card stock hidden from Crystal, Liam turned it over. Every cell in his body froze as his hungry gaze landed on a crinkled photo of Eva from their college days. He'd held her in front of him, her head flung back against his chest. The joy on her face seized him, and a strange fluttering started in his chest. In the photo, he nuzzled her neck, his face buried in Eva's hair, but the color of his hair, and other physical features gave him away.

Liam never truly believed in fate... or second chances, until now.

CHAPTER TWENTY-SEVEN

Connor pinched his thumb and index finger in a zipping motion over his lips to lock away their secret. Crystal set plates of pizza on the counter. Steam wafted off the slices and prompted a new round of grumbling in Liam's empty stomach.

He hid the old photo in his back pocket to devour it and the implications of Connor's action alone later. He attempted to drill into Connor's mind telepathically and got nothing except a sharp pain across his skull. *What freak sideshow had he tripped into now?*

Liam hopped off the stool to help Crystal with a bowl of salad. "This looks amazing."

Connor crinkled his nose. "Except for the tomatoes."

Liam scooped a small portion of salad onto Connor's plate and spooned the grape tomatoes onto his own plate. "You like everything else?"

"Yes. Can I have extra croutons?" Connor made a grab for the crouton bag as Crystal set it on the counter.

"Pour extras on mine too, kiddo. Croutons are the bomb."

Sitting on the other side of Liam, Crystal beamed, and Liam wondered how long she'd wanted a family. Everything about her brightened, and she seemed in her element with Liam and Connor. Domestic bliss. But she wasn't Eva, and Liam wished Eva sat next to him. The shock of his wish nailed him to the barstool. Kicking aside Eva's duplicity, she still never left his mind.

Eyes misting, Connor patted Liam's leg, his hand comforting.

Liam relocked the door to his thoughts. How much did Connor know about Liam and Eva? He didn't believe his locks were strong enough to keep Connor out.

"They're not strong enough," Connor whispered through a mouthful of pizza.

"Did you say something, sweetie?" Crystal asked. "Need more ranch?"

Connor trained his focus on the pizza slice flopping in his tiny hands. "No, thank you."

Liam's stomach roiled like a ship in a squall, and he tossed his pizza on his plate. Mental walls floundered in his head at Connor's intrusion, and he shut down all thought, except one. *I'll tell you all about me and your mother. It'll be our secret. Later, buddy.*

Dinner flew by as Crystal diverted their attention to the flat screen on the wall across from the kitchen island. Connor's favorite cartoon played, and it thankfully engrossed him.

"After dinner, I'll let you test Connor." Crystal wiped pizza sauce off his mouth and licked her finger like it was a Liam Lollipop. If it'd been Eva, he might have gotten off on the erotic display.

Liam shuddered and locked down his mind tighter than the US Mint. He shot Connor a side-eye, but the boy seemed intent on picking salami off a piece of pizza.

Unfortunately, his shudder only encouraged Crystal's fantasies. "Would you care to spend the night in my bed?" she whispered.

Ants skulked over his scalp. "Not a good idea with the boy here. I thought we were taking this slow."

Her lips puckered. "After tonight, let's speed it up a tad. I get it. You're still recuperating from my major screwup. I'll give you a break. But tomorrow—"

"We'll see." Liam kissed her cheek, her floral marinade clogging his nose.

They finished dinner, and Crystal insisted upon cleaning up alone to give Liam and Connor a chance to test the boy's abilities in the living room.

Once in the room, as far from the open entry as possible, Liam turned to Connor, who was dumping LEGO pieces out of his backpack.

"That's you in the photo." Connor didn't bother asking. "You're Mommy's secret friend."

"Yes. Did you read that in my mind?"

"I heard you say Mommy's name in your head."

"And you pieced it together?"

Connor rubbed his forehead, nodded.

Liam sat stiffly on the sofa next to Connor kneeling on the floor in front of the coffee table separating his LEGOs into piles. The boy's intensity scared him. Liam didn't understand how at six years old Connor had blasted through his blocks.

"Because you have no blocks." Connor didn't even look up. "Why do I scare you?"

A nervous chill whipped down Liam's back, and he cleared his mind. "You have awesome abilities for a boy your age. You should not have been able to get past my blocks." Liam squeezed Connor's shoulder. "Do you have lots of secrets?"

Connor shrugged. "I guess."

"Are you good at keeping them?"

Connor titled his head to the side. "Mommy says I have to keep my secrets, or I might get in trouble because I'm not s'pposed to read minds." Tears teemed in his eyes. "Mommy's in trouble, and Daddy's trying to help her tonight. I hope he brings her home." His bottom lip quivered. "I miss her. Daddy's being mean to me," he whispered.

Liam's heart sundered anew in the wake of his shock over Connor's clairvoyance, hitting the matter square-on. "Did your dad hurt you?"

Fearing his father, Connor's gaze shot from one corner of the room to another, and he lowered his voice, "Can you keep a secret?"

Liam crossed his heart. "Everything you and I talk about stays super private secret."

Connor's lips quirked up in a smile. "Daddy's making me practice my magic with the others. It hurts my head. Mommy doesn't like me doing it. He says when Mommy comes home, we'll be a family again. She'll make him stop."

The most intense craving to kill Neal swamped Liam, but he forced himself to focus on Connor and his words. *The others?* Did Connor mean Crystal and other psychics helping him hone his powers? "If it hurts too much, maybe you and I shouldn't play any psychic games?"

"Games are okay, like the ones I play with Auntie Crystal. I don't like the weird ones I play with the others. They're not like me or Auntie."

Liam scratched his head, plucked tufts of hair into chaos. "Where are these *others?*" Again, he tried to read Connor's mind or emotions, to no avail.

"I can't tell you." Connor pieced together LEGOs to form a platform base.

"One of your secrets?"

"Uh-huh."

"Can you tell me what else you see in the future?" Flabbergasted, Liam sat back on the sofa, a new sledgehammer going to town in his head.

"Barney chewed up one of your boots," Connor said over his shoulder, grinning. "Can I play with him someday?

I've always wanted a dog. Daddy doesn't like dogs."

A steamroller barreled over Liam, flattened his thoughts. "I'd love for you to meet him one day. He loves little boys. Guess I'll have to buy a new pair of boots, huh?"

Before Liam could explore Connor's empathic abilities, shouting emerged from the kitchen, a man's voice followed by Crystal's angry retort.

Connor's back stiffened, and he began stuffing his toys into his backpack. "Daddy doesn't like me playing in here."

Liam helped Connor stash his toys. "Remember, everything we said and everything you read in my mind is our secret. Can I count on you?"

Connor looked him point-blank in the eye. "You can't tell Daddy anything I told you tonight. He'll be mad at me."

Chucking Neal's threat in a shallow hole, Liam said, "I promise, not a word." He held out his pinkie. "Pinkie swear."

Connor's eyes brightened. "Mommy and I do pinkie swears."

The contact of their skin electrified Liam. It wasn't enough. He wanted to wrap his arms around Connor and never let go. The emotions ran so deep they staggered him. He'd never known the love of a child could consume him so instantly and thoroughly.

Wiping her hands on a towel, Crystal hustled into the living room, the storm of Neal Estenson close on her tail. The man's crimson complexion looked ready to blow a gasket or at least a couple blood vessels, obscuring the charm Eva had fallen for. Liam shielded the boy from Neal's wrath.

"Crystal, take Connor to his room and get him ready for bed. I'll come up and tuck you in soon, son." He kicked a couple stray LEGOs under the sofa.

With a single wary glance at Neal, then Liam, Connor followed Crystal up the stairs.

"Liam *Riley*, is it?" Liam took Neal's extended hand in a firm shake. Neal jerked Liam's arm forward and said under his breath, "Try to escape and my men will gun you down."

Liam flung Neal's hand off. "Neal Estenson, I take it. What's this about?"

The man's smug grin drove a nail into Liam's spine. "I think you know. Liam *McAllister*."

Although he'd prepared for this eventuality, the recognition so soon after his eventful day startled him. "Family name. I don't use it much. Too many negative connotations."

"Such as your connection to the Psychic Guild?"

"My family's connected, not me." *Who ratted me out? The doctor? One of Crystal's guards?* He wracked his brain to recall ever meeting the psychic doctor. He didn't recognize her, didn't recognize her name either. But he never saw the guards who'd carted him to Neal's house.

"Your lies to my sister are black marks against the entire Estenson family, and you dare to sit here and play with my son?"

"Wasn't my choice." Anger surfaced and ignited. "Your sister almost killed me today. *She* brought me here. I didn't have a choice in the near coma state *she* caused."

"Well, too bad for you." Neal signaled to someone behind Liam.

Liam flung around. Too late. Three Estenson guards tackled him, yanked his arms behind his back, and secured his wrists with zip ties. Before he could utter a word, they'd gagged and blindfolded him. He kicked out and his heel met the meaty thigh of one man. The guard grunted and slugged him on the back of his head. Not hard enough to knock him out, but the pain on top of his aching skull dropped him like a stone, and his knees met the cold, hard floor.

"Take him to the vault," Neal ordered. "I'll deal with Crystal."

Two guards manhandled Liam into a standing position, and his head spun. They sandwiched him between them, supporting his boneless legs from giving out, and tossed him into the back of a van. Locks thumped into place, killing any chance of escape. The odor of new vehicle plastic tickled Liam's nostrils. The scratch of cloth against cloth, and a loud belch gave away the guard in the cargo hold, forestalling Liam's ability to search for a weapon. Well, he wanted to infiltrate the Estensons, right? What better way than to get inside their mysterious vault.

Close to an hour later, by Liam's reckoning, the van stopped on level ground, and the purring engine shut down.

"Let's go, McAllister. Play nice and we won't knock you to yesterday." The guard in the van grabbed Liam's upper arm, and a hot stabbing pain lanced his injured shoulder.

The van doors swung open, and near silence greeted Liam as the scent of oak trees and dry loam joined the silence. Quiet country replaced the hum of the city, which meant they might have climbed into the rolling foothills in various Bay Area towns. One thing for certain, they had not driven into the Santa Cruz Mountains or he'd recognize the scents of redwoods, cedars, pines, and the ilk.

A guard prodded a beefy hand between his shoulder blades. "Move it." Two men flanked him, steering him on a walkway of brick pavers.

Liam contemplated fighting his way out, but three armed men against one only armed with his teeth slayed his odds of escaping alive. He'd wait it out. They were bound to trip up and reveal their location. For all he knew, he was stumbling into a Cabal stronghold. *Hallelujah. Totally worth the price of admission.* He kinked his neck left, then right, trying to level out his pain.

The guards guided him into a building, down a set of

stairs, and through a couple more doors. Pine cleanser rode the air, reminding Liam of a lab. Otherwise, his walk down the green mile remained silent, until they unlocked a door and nudged him through.

"Sit."

A seat banged Liam's knees, and he twisted around to plop down onto an aluminum chair.

"Wait until I'm gone, then remove his headgear. Stand guard until Estenson's next order," one guard said, preceding the click of the door.

Once the other guard took off his mask and gag, Liam assessed him and his surroundings. He didn't recognize the linebacker guard with the long, rocker-length hair similar to Jake's. Nor did he recognize the empty holding cell, not a window in sight.

"Where am I?"

Standing in front of the door, the remaining guard crossed his arms over his barrel chest. "Ever been waterboarded?" His evil grin hardened Liam's stomach.

CHAPTER TWENTY-EIGHT

The arraignment was over, bail paid, and Eva took her envelope of belongings from the clerk at the sheriff's department. She slipped her step-counter on her wrist and jammed her tiny diamond stud earrings in a pocket. Then she stared at her filigree ring. She loved the ring more than any other piece of jewelry she owned. Liam had wanted to buy her this same ring for her birthday before they split, but she talked him out of spending so much money on her. It became her "push" gift to herself when Connor was born to remind her of him. How had she forgotten? The ring represented love and comfort, and she slipped it on her right ring finger never wanting to remove it.

She doubted she'd ever see her badge or gun again. The idea of never working as a detective, never working period, sank like an anchor in her growling stomach, layering the grief of never seeing Connor, or Liam again. As a walking sideshow freak, she needed to invent a new language to describe how she was feeling.

Neal stood in the foyer by the main reception area yakking on his phone. True to his word, he'd sprung her on bail. Alex had the other lawyer in the courtroom on standby in case things went sideways. Once she booted Neal to the curb, she'd need to lawyer up anyway. According to Alex's cryptic responses within Neal's hearing, the Psychic Guild had paid her bail after she refused to allow Neal to pay it and refused to call her parents. The funds mysteriously wound up in her bank account from a private holding company untraceable to the Guild. Neal had no clue who'd paid and seemed relieved, therefore didn't question her. No way did she plan to be beholden to the Estenson family further.

Pissed at her refusal to ride home with him, Neal squealed out of the parking lot in his latest expensive toy. Alex snickered beside her as he unlocked the door to his tall SUV. She'd told Neal she needed alone time to sort things out. Didn't matter to him, he still thought she owed him her life. Maybe in a way she did. Without the shitstorm he'd landed her in, she'd never have found something— someone—she'd missed for seven years, never would've realized how much she still loved Liam. No life or love was worth losing her son over, though. As much as she wanted Liam in her life and not just for the sake of their son, she'd forego him to get her boy out of Estenson hands. A part of her wanted it all, wanted Connor *and* Liam, the three of them a family. Done making crappy choices, she'd accommodate the Guild for Connor's sake. The larger part of her didn't want to hope for such a future, not when her life now skated toward becoming Big Bertha's prison bitch in an atrocious orange jumpsuit.

Thoughts of Liam had kept her sane in her holding cell overnight. The mental image of him bonding with their son filled her with so much joy, it stayed the nightmares. She wished she'd been with them when Connor met his father for the first time. Liam wouldn't have revealed his true identity, but Connor may have conjured up his own ideas from the bits and pieces he knew about Liam. It scared her for them. Giving in to Liam and trusting him, trusting her choices with men and trusting him with her son remained a teaspoon of hope in her core. She lobbed aside the thoughts to dwell on later and concentrated on her next steps.

"Thank you again, Alex." Stretching out her arm to grip the handhold, she hiked up into the front passenger seat. "Did you ever think I'd be so much trouble when you hired me?"

He clambered into the driver seat with little effort. "When I hire, I hire the whole person, not just the detective. Granted, you're more trouble than most. Whether you'll admit it or not, you're part of the Guild family, which means you're my family too."

She groaned. "You knew I was related to the Estensons." She playfully backhanded his arm.

He sobered, maneuvered into traffic. "Speaking of."

Eva gnawed on a fingernail, trying to avoid her craggy cuticles. "You watched the videos, listened to the audio, saw the photos?"

"Eva." He exhaled her name, his sorrow tailgating.

"Did you think anyone ever escaped the mafia alive?" Her upbeat tone turned the dire question light and fluffy, killed her churning hunger.

"Why did you save that on a flash drive that could end up in anyone's hands?"

A Sahara-dry laugh escaped her. "That's the first question to pop into your head?"

"Let's get it out of the way."

"I have a copy on a secure cloud. I also wanted the capability of handing it over to one or the other when the time rolled around. Any other logistical questions before we get to the meat?"

"Are you okay talking about this? Are we on the record?"

"The recordings are not enough evidence to nail them. It's why I haven't revealed them and why I... we keep digging for more."

"There's enough for a murder investigation and more."

"Still not good enough!" She slammed her fist on the seat. "One murder leads to a dozen more in that family, and once Neal stole my son, it placed him in their crosshairs."

Alex slid his cell phone onto the center console. "Are we on the record?"

"Hell to the yes."

Alex recited the date, time, and their identities into his recorder. Eva refused to fault her superior for protocol.

"Tell me about the first audio recording. Did you record it, if so, when?"

"It's a recording of Neal Estenson"—she used full names for the record—"and his uncle Davide Estenson. I witnessed and recorded the discussion. It occurred on May third of this year."

"How did you obtain the recording?"

"I arrived early at Neal's house to pick Connor up after his weekend visitation. Neal was busy and couldn't drop Connor off and told me if I didn't pick him up, he'd just keep him. Anyway, I heard shouting from the backyard and snuck around the side of the house. Neal was inside with the rear slider open, reaming his uncle a new one over some slight or another. I don't know what it was about."

"What was their relationship like?"

"As far as I knew, they were on good terms. Neal never said a bad thing about him, not that he spoke much about the Estenson family."

"Go on." Alex continued driving toward San Jose, not in any hurry to reach her condo where she'd asked him to take her in case Neal followed.

"I hid in the bushes and recorded their conversation."

"Why? What was your angle?"

Without seeing, Eva stared at the cars whizzing past on the southbound freeway. "Neal returning to his mafia family became my worst nightmare. I didn't want my son mixed up in mafia business. I feared for him."

"Did you think to acquire evidence to take them down on your own?" The sneer didn't quite escape Alex's voice. Did he think her a complete idiot?

"Neal had already threatened to seek full custody of Connor if I *stepped out of line.*" She sank into herself, then cracked her window to let cool air fan her broiling skin. "I wanted leverage to protect my son." She splayed her fingers against her suddenly throbbing head.

Alex shut the recorder off. "What else aren't you telling me?"

She hiked her knees against her chest and buried her face in them. "I wanted *anything* to help me take him down." Alex didn't say a word for the longest moment. "You already knew?" She sounded muffled as she spoke to the seat between her legs.

"I suspected," he said softly. "Juliana knew it."

"She read my mind the day Neal took Connor?"

"Yes. She didn't mean to. You were so anguished, Juliana couldn't erect her walls fast enough."

She raised her hand from her head dismissively. "Liam's pretty much already guessed from what I've confessed."

Alex tapped the recorder on. "What did Neal and Davide discuss?"

Stomach in full-bore revolt, Eva stretched out her legs and settled back into the seat before dry heaves set in. "It's all on the recording. Uncle was pissed at Neal and told Neal if he didn't toe the line, he'd tell Neal's father, Daniel Estenson, that Neal ordered the hit on his older brother, Daniel Jr., well before Daniel appointed Neal as primo mafia boss."

"Why didn't you go to the authorities with this evidence?"

"You know it's not admissible under the two-party

recordings consent law. The Estensons would've destroyed the evidence, or me. Even if we found corroborating evidence of murder, I needed more than an illegally obtained recording. Then Neal took Connor. Liam and the Guild hit the scene, and now they're saying the Estensons may be this mysterious Cabal they've been hunting for a while. The snowball keeps on rolling downhill, growing and gaining speed."

"Why didn't you offer the evidence to Daniel Estenson? It might have helped you escape Neal, pit father against son. Or did Estenson senior want his oldest son dead too?"

"I don't think Daniel wanted to kill his oldest son. But Neal was the second coming in his father's bible. It's why he allowed Neal to move to Florida and pursue his passion outside the family and didn't get in Neal's way in pursuing me. Of course, from the other video, it's also why he didn't mind me in the family, regardless of outward appearances." Angry heat tore at Eva. "If you watched the video clip on the flash drive, you know why. The apple doesn't fall far from the tree."

"They chucked you in the middle."

"Without the other knowing. Now my son's in the middle, and if I pit father against son, it won't end well for him or anyone."

"None of Neal's hatred for his brother arose while you were married?"

"I didn't even know he had a brother. That's how close to the vest he kept his family. Call me an idiot."

"Hardly. You were hoodwinked by the best."

"Hoodwinked is generous."

"Can you explain the events on the video?" Sympathy weighed heavy on Alex's voice. "Only if you feel ready to discuss it."

"I'll blab anything to put these people away, no matter the hit to me." Gnashing her teeth, Eva silently suffered a jolt from a large pothole. "It wasn't long after Neal let the cat out of the bag on the hit that his father accosted me at Neal's house. Neal got stuck in court, and he'd asked Crystal to meet me when I dropped Connor off."

Eva sucked in a deep breath. "Daniel intercepted Crystal and ambushed me. Connor had gone up to his room. Daniel forked over a jeweler's box with a massive diamond engagement ring in it and a prenuptial agreement that gave me millions and a slew of privileges during the marriage but cut me dry if we divorced. All business with him, certainly no romance going on, not that I encouraged or wanted it." She shuddered. "It was then I suspected he knew Neal had killed Junior. Never in a million years would Daniel otherwise seek his son's leftovers. He wants nothing to do with Junior's widow and he *likes* her. But none of her three kids are psychic. That's the kicker."

"You're saying he wanted you to marry him as a business transaction? Or revenge on Neal?" Alex drove into the parking lot at her complex and parked in a guest spot near her unit. They remained seated. Eva didn't want to chance any bugs in her condo, whether Estenson or McAllister bugs.

"I didn't know his motives, until now." Eva laid her head back on the headrest. "He said he admired me, loved Connor. Also said he wanted me to bear more children like Connor. He didn't elaborate on the now obvious. There's our Guild-Cabal involvement."

Alex held up a hand. "Whoa. Connor's not Neal's son, and you have no psychic abilities. What did he think another child would bring to the table other than to expand his family or replace the son he lost? I get that the Estensons have psychic blood, but it seems random with just Crystal's telepathy out of his three kids."

Eva squirmed on the seat, picked at her threadbare cuticles. "When Connor's telepathy first manifested in a big way, I told Neal his psychic abilities stemmed from my family. Skips generations. I did it to keep Liam's identity safe. By that time, Neal was just getting involved with the Estensons after staying incommunicado for so long. My intuition that I needed to lie paid off."

Alex whistled. "Daniel wanted you for your ability to birth another powerful psychic."

"He wants a full football team of psychics."

"Yet, we still don't know why the Cabal's hoarding them."

"A mafia full of psychics can rule the world. Take Martinelli for instance. They had him in their back pocket. How? Did the mafia threaten him or did the Cabal coerce him?"

"The Guild's thinking the same. It's a clusterfuck anyway you pick it apart." Alex grumbled a few curses. "What happened after the video shut off? There was a lot of muffled noise. You laughed at his offer, and it appeared he—"

"Hauled off and slapped me for laughing at him? Yep. My phone dislodged in my pocket, and I grabbed it and hid it before he noticed the recorder on."

"Geez, Eva. I'm sorry. What a piece of work."

"His slap knocked me to the floor. He flew into a tirade, yelling and ranting. No one laughs at the egomaniac and gets away with it." Shaking until her bones creaked, her voice drifted away.

Alex touched her jacket sleeve. "Did he hurt you further?"

Choking up, she wobbled her head. "He had a minister and two guards as witnesses waiting in the kitchen. He told me if I didn't marry him, he'd kill me and take Connor, exploit his powers." She raked her fingernails across her scalp. "Man, I wish I'd gotten that on video."

"Son of a bitch. That family's psychotic. How did you

escape?"

"Kneed him in the balls." Eva's triumphant grin faltered. "Which set him off."

"It's why he's hounding you? He still thinks you might marry him?"

"He's not ready to kill me, and he probably thinks framing me for Martinelli's murder will sway me to his side. Once I give the word, he'll find a way to get the charges dropped. He'll frame someone else who slighted him."

"And Neal taking Connor is just icing on the cake. What happens if you cave to Neal? Won't Daniel go postal since Neal wants you too, or vice versa?"

"Depends on what Daniel really knows about Neal killing Junior. Daniel lied to Neal about wanting me out of the family. Outwardly, I'm dog crap on the bottom of his custom-leather loafers. Privately, I'm the breeder queen."

"All based on the lie you're from a powerful psychic family."

"The lie destined to break them."

"Or bury you six feet under." Alex sobered.

Eva turned toward her boss. "Please promise me that if I'm killed, you and Liam will get Connor out of their hands."

Alex popped an antacid into his mouth, handed the roll to Eva. She shook her head, and he pocketed it. "The Guild and I won't stop until we get Connor and beat the Cabal down. But if Neal adopted Connor and has custody, it'll be a tough battle."

"I had my mother mail a package to Liam, care of the Guild compound. It contains DNA proof that Liam is Connor's father, a certified copy of Connor's birth certificate, and..." Eva paused for emphasis. "The adoption papers Neal thinks I filed and never did."

"Whoa, what?"

"Neal let me handle everything. He pressured me into

the adoption, and since I lied, yep, again with the gut feeling, I forged Liam's signature on the parental relinquishment form and faked a court order. He was too busy dealing with dear old dad to question it."

"So many lies and deceit, Eva."

"I knew my world was sinking." She almost screamed at him, backed off. "I learned who the Estensons were. Neal had just started being abusive. I needed to protect Connor and myself. I knew it wouldn't end well if I sat around and played the good little mafia wife. That's not me. It shocked the crap out of me when Neal allowed the divorce. I had to promise to return with him to California and give him a chance to make it up, give him hope for a future together. To him, the divorce was a temporary separation. In my eyes, it was the beginning of dismantling the Estensons one brick at a time. How was I supposed to know Neal would kidnap Connor or that they're suspected Cabal, or—" Sobs shook through Eva, and she buried her face in her hands.

"Or what, Eva?"

"Or that Daniel would try to rape me after I damaged his family jewels. He tried to strip off my clothes when he'd pinned me to the floor. He'd unbuckled his belt—"

Alex slammed his fist against the steering wheel, his ire palpable in the close interior of the SUV.

"While he screamed bloody murder, I finagled my gun out and coldcocked him. Then I snagged Connor and we got the hell out of Dodge, his two stupid guards chasing us down the driveway on foot."

"On the recording before it shut off, I heard you tell him to stop multiple times. And you called him Neal."

"I did. Apple. Tree." To her, they had been one and the same. Reliving the attempted rape brought back the memories, twisted them in her mind until Neal and Daniel became one again.

CHAPTER TWENTY-NINE

Eva's admission of the attempted rape—Daniel's rape, not to be mistaken with Neal's various abuses—to her boss sent a rivulet of relief down the raging river of her emotions. Not quite a waterfall flowing off her shoulders, but she'd take it. She just hoped she'd get the chance to tell Liam. He needed to understand her later motives where it concerned Connor and his safety. Knowing him, he'd try to kill Neal and Daniel. Not that Eva didn't want them dead, she was more calculated in her revenge. She wanted them to suffer where it counted.

Alex hesitated in leaving her alone while the McAllisters remained undercover. She assured him again the Estensons didn't want to kill her since she was the grand prize. After a genial hug from him—who acted more like a good friend than her superior—and words of sympathy and encouragement, Eva took a long hot shower to scour off the county-lockup grunge. She tugged on a clean pair of skinny jeans, a close-fitting black T-shirt, her sneakers, and leather jacket. Then she inhaled a cup of black coffee and ate a protein bar from her empty cupboards to adrenalize her sleepless body. A few canned soups and an unopened box of cereal, Connor's favorite, remained the sole items in the pantry the Estenson men hadn't ransacked.

With her weapon confiscated, Eva had to rely upon her personal Taser hooked on her belt. She was just strapping her backup knife on her left leg when her old cell phone rang. She almost ignored it, yet figured it wouldn't do to ignore Neal now. The frazzled voice of Liam's brother Ric greeted her.

"Sorry to use this phone, but you left the other behind."

"Can't be helped."

"Check the phone and call me back from outside."

Eva did as he instructed, pecking for recording devices in the guts of her phone. Phone clean, she locked her door, and headed to the lawn in the small courtyard.

Scoping out her surroundings, ensuring she had privacy, she called Ric. "What's up?" She hated that she had to check her back every minute of every day.

"Liam's missing."

Her heart sank into the morass of her battered soul. "What do you mean *missing?*"

"Did Alex tell you Crystal carted Liam to Neal's house yesterday after their meeting?"

"Yeah." The hairs on the back of her neck rose. "She was on babysitting duty, and Liam met Connor."

"Well, he never came home. I think something happened to him before *and* after my call. He said he'd explain later but never called."

Eva's pulse roared like ocean waves pounding her ears. "He's probably still with Crystal."

"I installed a tracker on his phone. It's at Neal's place, and Crystal's car's gone. Liam's vehicle never left the bar."

"Then he's still with her," Eva insisted. "I'm sure once he met Connor, he connived a way to stay. She was totally into him and probably jumped at the chance."

"Something's off. I feel it."

"Brother intuition?"

"Yes." Ric didn't hesitate. "He's missed three check-ins.

It's not like him to leave his phone behind. What if Connor busted him?"

"I'm heading over to Neal's house." Eva jogged to the parking lot.

"I'm coming with you. It's not safe for you on your own."

"You can't be seen there. Just keep searching for him from your end. I'll watch my back. Neal won't be surprised if I show up. I told him after my bail hearing we'd be in touch to discuss my options." Options that numbered zero.

"You might have time. I stuck trackers on Neal's car at the courthouse parking lot. Right now, his car's at a large estate in the Los Altos hills."

"His father's estate."

"From online maps, the property contains several outbuildings. There are also unidentified buildings on two plots of adjacent land. No homes."

"Who owns those plots?"

"An LLC connected to the Estensons."

Eva wound her ponytail in a bunch and groaned. "I want to hit Neal's house before he busts me."

Ric groused his defeat. "FYI, the Guild verified the court records you and Liam dug up. The defendants were former Guild members. Seventy-five percent have psychic powers, the other twenty-five we don't know if they were victims of the false brain scan reports."

"Is it credible evidence to link the Cabal to the Estensons?"

"Enough to instigate a full-blown investigation. With a little more digging, we'll have absolute proof."

"Was there proof of Estenson wrongdoing, or just pointing to the former Guild members?"

"Not enough to take the Estensons down. Good cover-up on their part."

"Or maybe the mafia are just a front for the Cabal."

"It's my best guess."

"Look, Ric. There's a flash drive in the closet safe at the safe house, combo's Liam's birthday. Liam and I couldn't decrypt it." A flush worked up Eva's chest and her breasts tingled. No sense in owning up to their distraction. "If crap goes sideways, get your software guy on it."

"Don't flip your lid thinking about sideways. Why wait?"

"Do it if you have time to kill while hunting Liam."

"I need to run by the safe house, anyway. I'll call you if he checks in."

The undercover work and constantly searching for bugs and tailgating had affected them all. With Liam missing, they didn't need a new wrench thrown onto their path. Eva didn't begrudge Ric's attitude. She'd crawled through the chalk outline on the sidewalk and still lived to drive her car without offing anyone. Yet. If Liam were missing, the fault lay one hundred percent with her. Now, more than ever, she needed to close the gap and stoop to Neal's level of stupidity. Screw Daniel Estenson and the ass he rode in on. As long as she kept her mouth shut and didn't confess Daniel's offer to marry her to Neal, Daniel would back off. That is, if he trusted her one wit. And screw any personal video or audio on the flash drive. Let the freaking world see what abusive pigs the Estensons were, no matter her part in their personal sandboxes.

"Bow down to Neal and get your son back. Give in to Daniel, get your son back, and Neal kills his father. Give the recording of Neal affirming his hit on Junior to Daniel, he'll kill Neal, and I'm at his mercy. Don't give in to either and wind up in an orange jumpsuit behind bars. And Connor?" Eva tossed her hands up and screamed.

"Son of a freaking bitch," she muttered as she started her car. "I'm doomed no matter how you slice and dice it. Who made me the crown prize?" *Empty promises, calculated betrayal, sociopathic greed. Just another weekday.*

Connor and his three powerful psychic abilities were the real treasures. Abilities the Estensons—the Cabal—want to exploit. Why? What world domination plans were they hatching? Surely, they had other psychics onboard and weren't relying on a child or the nebulous idea of Eva popping out more Estenson psychics. Where were all the psychics the Cabal had recruited? Or were the McAllisters off their rockers about the Estensons bankrolling the Cabal, and Eva's crapstorm had zilch to do with the Cabal?

No. It boiled down to the Cabal. Nothing else made sense. The Estenson mafia was probably a front for as well as bankrolling them.

"Holy hell. Talk about serendipity in a small-ass world." Eva turned on her satellite radio, and the lulling nuances of Chopin calmed her senses. Liam had loved classical music. Did he still love it? Or had she ruined music for him too? Did he still love her? Or had she wrecked everything good between them. Did she even want him to love her? Dare she gamble? No-brainer question. She wanted Liam more than ever, more than any man in her life. Nothing had changed about him. All the good in him remained, and he'd be an awesome father to their son. She only wished she'd given him the chance much sooner. Now she had years to make up for whether or not he wanted her. No dodging that bullet.

"Argh!" She honked her horn at a car clipping her lane, easing her frustration on the long and loud blare. "Get out of my way, you piece of garbage!" She let loose a string of curses until she began to laugh hysterically.

Heaving in draughts of air, Eva's heart settled to a steady rhythm, and she shut her brain down until she parked in Neal's empty driveway. A breeze fluttered dry leaves off a sycamore, and they rained down on the lawn in a layer as brown as her mood.

Hand on her stun gun, she rang the doorbell, knocked, and waited. A spooky quiet greeted her. She slunk to the three-car garage, found it empty, and then scurried over the fence into the backyard. Not a soul in sight. Last she knew, Neal hadn't installed any surveillance. Who knew from one day to the next in his power grab for the royal treasures?

Using her multipurpose pocket tool, she jiggered the lock on the patio door and slipped inside the static house.

"Neal?" she called out. "You here? I wanted to continue our conversations." Let any potential cameras pick up that epic bucket of waste. "Neal?" She raised her hands to signify her lack of a weapon.

Eva checked the downstairs rooms and found Liam's cell phone stuck between the cushions of the living room sofa. Holding the phone caused a strange tickling against her hand. An eerie connection between her and Liam played havoc in the sensation, yet she also experienced a flush of unease. Regardless, she pocketed the phone and continued scoping out the house. The only other items of interest were a few LEGOs under the living room coffee table and one of Connor's superhero T-shirts tossed onto his bed. Neal was finicky about order in his house, and the tiny puddle of cloth drove another glacial prickle up her spine. She held the shirt to her nose, sniffing Connor's familiar boy and baby shampoo scent. Stuffing the shirt in her waistband, she finished her upstairs reconnaissance. All the beds were made including the guest room where Crystal slept on babysitting duty.

The moment she set foot on the top rung of the stairs, the front door deadbolt clicked, unlocking another round of ice slithering down her back. Reliving her altercation with Daniel Estenson earlier had plunked her on a steeper edge, and she hurdled out of view of the foyer. Dipping to the side of a slender console table, she hid and waited. Heavy footsteps tromped into the foyer, and the door clicked shut. The deadbolt thunked into place, killing her escape hatch. The footsteps slowly trucked into the living room, and Eva knew from the tread it wasn't Neal's quick and light rolling gate.

"Eva Marie, I know you're here. Can't hide your car out front." Eva cupped her mouth and searched for a way out from upstairs. "It's time we continue our little talk. No guns this time." He chuckled, an evil, insidious sound. "No escape either."

Daniel Estenson's voice strangled Eva's heart, exactly as she recalled it. Tranquil with a charming, sometimes concerned, edge. It stalked her like a predator, nudging her closer to the precarious edge.

CHAPTER THIRTY

Once again, Liam's bleary eyes focused on unfamiliar surroundings, an industrial panel ceiling to replace the vaulted one. The pounding in his head had downgraded to a dull thump. This time, his location impersonated a sterile padded room, versus the modern opulence of Neal's home and without the padding on the white cement block walls. Other than a drain hole in the center of the floor and a locked door, the eight by eight room contained no windows, no other furniture except the cot he lay on. A small shelf opening with a sliding door broke the starkness of the white door in half. A pass-through for food?

Estenson guards had removed his wrist and ankle bindings and the tape across his mouth. Last he remembered, Neal Estenson's goons had trussed him up, and then knocked him out with chloroform. Crystal had prevented Neal from coldcocking him. Small favors. Maybe she wasn't as brutal as the rest of the family. *Mental forehead smack.*

Memories surged and clobbered Liam's stupidity. He scraped his index finger across his brow, hoping to stimulate his sluggish brain cells to life. She'd outright killed a man, which caused his current jam. Her actions had also enabled him to meet his son for the first time. Joy laced the memories until a ball of snow formed in his gut.

What had they done with Connor? Did Neal know Liam's connection to the boy? Had he believed him when he told Neal the Guild had kicked him out?

And the voices... he remembered hearing voices in his head. In his head! And he wasn't telepathic. Yet no denying he'd mentally heard Connor. As he stretched out his legs and flexed his arms, he strained his mind, using his standard empathic skills to gauge nearby transmitted emotions. Nothing. A granite mountain thwarted his attempt. Whatever powers he'd regained after his aborted death had scuttled off, as if someone had peppered psychic wards around the room.

"We're not living in fantasyland. Or are we?" The more he picked apart the idea, the more it mushroomed. He jumped up on boneless legs to inspect his prison walls.

Ear to the cement blocks, he heard nothing except the sound of his own breathing. A small round speaker was embedded in the ceiling in the far corner opposite the door. Liam suspected it contained video watching his every movement. He flipped the screen off and stepped to the door. The odor of bleach covered up a coppery tang, the scent of despair and pain.

He clutched the doorknob to feel the emotions of anyone who'd recently touched it. Nothing. Deader than a doornail... or doorknob. His powers had half-assed returned at the Estenson house. Why were they now gone as if the devil had ripped them from his soul? The feeling reminded him of his emptiness once Eva decided to go back to her asshole ex-husband. Despite their ruse with Neal and Crystal, would he ever see her again? Would they recover from all the subterfuge and enjoy their belated happily ever after? If they lived. He flung off his dire thoughts... he had no business thinking about Eva now.

"Hello! Anyone hear me?" he shouted at the door. Silence greeted him until a slight crackling drifted from the ceiling speaker.

"Mr. McAllister, please refrain from exerting yourself." The monotone voice laughed. It fucking laughed. Had to be speaking into a voice modulator.

"Why are you holding me in this"—he waved his arms to encompass the room—"cell? Where's Crystal Estenson? She'll verify my employment."

"Really?" A sneer taunted Crystal's voice. "Liam Riley works for me, not Liam *McAllister*." No modulator necessary to hide her derision. "Tell me, Liam, why did you sucker me?"

He adopted a blank facade to hide his usual expressive emotions. "I didn't trick you. I just didn't divulge my real name. If I had, you'd have turned me down flat if you know who the McAllisters are."

"Of course, I know who the McAllisters are. The Psychic Guild's pride and joy team of Guardian idiots."

Liam ignored her dig. "The Guild kicked me out. One too many infractions. That's why I'm exploring something new, better. Once you offered, a job with the Estensons seemed like a good deal. I was legit down on my luck when you ran into me at the bar. Trying to drown my sorrows and write a new life plan. I was really into you, Crystal." Liam paused, adopted a sorrowful tone. "I'm sorry. I dead-to-rights lied. You have to believe I was honestly looking for a place to fit in where my last name and former affiliation didn't matter."

Silence for several long minutes gave Liam a chance to chill and rebuild his strongest mental walls. Who knew who might be telepathically listening to him outside the walls?

Crystal's voice boomed through the speaker. "Prove it, or a truth serum sounds hella useful right now. Or we can start with the waterboarding. I won't bother using a telepath to read your mind. We all know how that'll go."

He didn't believe the Estensons-Cabal had a telepath strong enough to pierce his walls. Except Connor. Which might mean they didn't know Connor possessed the rare ability. Liam held one ace up his sleeve. If he played it, and the Estensons snatched it up, it would solidify their link to the Cabal. On the flip side, he'd be committing Guild treason.

Getting Connor and Eva back was so worth it. Maybe Eva might want to reunite with him if he left the Guild, not that he'd ever leave his family. She'd have to cope due to Connor's abilities. *Stupid-ass...* thinking he'd already bagged Eva again. Again? He'd never stopped loving her. Never ceased hoping one day she'd waltz back into his life and they'd pick up where they'd left off. Only he never anticipated her toting along a child born from their last incredible night together. A night of intense sorrow and passion. Their unplanned last hurrah had left an indelible mark on his mind, his heart, and soul. When Liam had left her, he'd believed the intensity of their love would bring her back to him. He didn't think it would take seven years. Eva had much to reconcile to accept him, and Liam planned to work his magic on her until the day he died.

"McAllister, Neal Estenson here. Talk is cheap. I want actionable proof."

"What do you suggest?" Liam finessed his offer in his head. "How interested are you in the Guild?"

"We already know about your altercation in the parking lot with Saldivar. Who ghosted him?" Neal replied. "Any ideas?"

Liam wracked his brain. "He was drunk, accused me of the same thing you're accusing me of and wouldn't take no for an answer. I took him home to sleep it off. Haven't seen him since. It'd be awesome to work with him again under the Estenson umbrella on a level playing field."

Neal continued. "We know you're aware the Estensons

use psychics."

Neal's evasion prickled at Liam, lent an inner excitement to his fear. "What's your angle employing psychics?" He chanced the question.

"Every business or deal benefits from a psychic, don't you think? You experienced a positive aspect firsthand yesterday. You and Crystal saved the Estensons millions of dollars and a ton of strife." A static pause erupted, and Liam recoiled, poked his ears. "I hope you've recovered. We'll give you a better room with access to a medic soon. If you cooperate."

Fuck you, asswipe. Every word Neal spouted off about psychics and the Guild placed the Estensons squarely in Cabal territory.

"What's a guy got to do to prove allegiance to the Estensons? How about we talk face-to-face? I can't read your mind, so you're safe from me. No need for hidden speakers." Liam was dying to test out his new freakish telepathy. Had near death handed him new abilities? Did it only work with Connor? He needed to test it outside the mental-dampening room. First and foremost, he wanted to explore outside the room to determine where they'd taken his son.

"We can arrange a meet and greet," Neal responded. "I have a task that'll solidify your position in our organization. If you succeed."

Curiosity didn't kill him like the proverbial cat. He bet any task Neal gave him would have him committing a half-dozen crimes.

A few minutes later, the three door locks thunked open. Four guards, all armed to the nines, guarded the outside of the door. Liam recognized two former Guild Guardians. They smirked at him, cuffed his wrists behind his back, and then led him down a wide hallway with identical doors on each side every twelve to fourteen feet.

An underground bunker? Not one door contained an electronic lock. Certain telekinetics can kill electronic power with a mere thought. *The Estensons know. No need to dumb it down.*

The guards prodded Liam up a flight of stairs to another bare hallway and into a windowless conference room. A large oval table took up the bulk of real estate with four swivel chairs around it. One lone bottle of water stood on top of a food cart in the far corner. A door at the far side opened to a small bathroom.

A guard untied his wrists, and his meaty hand steered him toward the bathroom. "Use the facilities if you need." They left Liam alone in the room, and he took them up on their offer. By the time he dried his hands, Neal and Crystal had filed into the room. Two guards stood at the door armed with assault rifles strapped across their shoulders. One of the guards tied his hands behind his back again.

Criminy. Did they expect him to multiply and wage war?

Neal waved at a chair opposite from the door. "Take a load off." He set the bottle of water in front of Liam. Liam ignored it and sat.

Eyes flinty, Crystal shot icicles at him. Since he'd conned her, he didn't blame her. The only problem, he didn't feel her emotions, nor did he feel Neal's or the guards. Another dead room. White noise hissed from what appeared to be motion detectors in each corner of the ceiling. The small triangular white boxes resembled no motion detector he'd ever seen though. His emerald isle and grassy fields remained brown and barren.

Neal's gaze chased Liam's glance to the unmarked detectors. The asshole grinned. "Psychic dampeners. Killed your empathic abilities, didn't they?"

Hiding his awe, Liam glowered at Neal. His mind

skipped from one idea to another, speculating how to get his hands on one.

"One of our companies has perfected the technology. Of course"—he gestured to Crystal—"it kills Crystal's telepathy. We haven't worked out how to get around that."

"Maybe I can help." Unable to disguise his awe further, Liam's mouth parted halfway to hanging open. "I own a security company. We've dabbled a few times with deadeners." No lie there.

"Why? Guild members are all about psychic abilities for good. Why would you want to dampen them?"

"They've had paranoid clients request the technology."

"Send them my way. I can hook them up." Neal clasped his hands against his washboard abs encased in a custom suit. Not a hair out of place, his smooth tan face rivaled a Greek god. Eva never went for the rich, suave types. What made her go for Neal Fucking Estenson? Or had she changed so much? Did he even have a chance with her? Did he want one? *No* wasn't a word in his vocabulary where it concerned Eva. He definitely wanted. If he escaped the mafia. Because no one walked away from the mafia. *Son of a mob bitch!*

"Sure," he said through gritted teeth, remembered his tenuous position and loosened up. "If we work out a deal, I can hook the Estensons up to many... things. I tote a lot to the table. It'll be worth your while to hire Liam *McAllister*. As I told you, I'm done with the Guild."

"Such as?" Crystal's dark, slanted eyebrows pinched together into an unflattering unibrow.

"My securities expertise, my empathic abilities. I helped save you a bundle today. I'm ready to start a new venture." He spouted off a mission statement like a man on an interview, or a man trying to save his ass. *Check.*

Neal inclined forward. "You can do better."

What were they trying to drive out of him? Liam wasn't

ready to tip his hand, not until they divulged a provable connection. "What do you want? I'm open to suggestion."

Elbows on the table, Neal steepled his long-fingered hands, touching his nose, a smarmy smile on his G-fucking-Q face. No wonder Eva had fallen for him. He could charm the pants off a lesbian. No wonder he hurt his son, and Connor continued to love him. *Bastard times ten.*

"The Estensons love expensive, irreplaceable art objects, paintings, antique and estate jewelry. We find value in our holdings, beefs up our street cred in certain circles."

"As do most families of means. I work security for many rich clients. I'd be glad to offer my expertise."

"We don't give a crap about your *security* expertise," Crystal spat out.

Neal held up a hand to short-circuit her. "Of course, we want his expertise in security. First, we wish to add to our unique collection."

Oh, hell to the no. "If you're asking me to steal from a client, it's a no-go. I can't jeopardize the business for my brothers, even if I'm out."

The Grinch's evil grin stole across Neal's face, and he slowly shook his head. "Not a McAllister client per se."

"Okay." Liam stretched the word out. "Who? What?"

Neal bestowed a phony benevolence upon Liam in the softening avarice in his eyes. "We hear the Psychic Guild's in possession of a rare collection of jewels as old as dirt."

Wearing a blank mask, he tamped down a flinch rippling down his torso. Seems word had surfaced about the Guild's recent acquisition. "Not sure what jewels you're referring to. I'm not privy to such information, you know, being kicked out and all."

"Seriously, Liam!" Crystal banged her palm on the table. "Your brother Jake and Lily Falbrooke found them. Don't BS me. You know exactly what Neal's talking about."

"The Twilight collection," Liam replied in a monotone. *Son of a bonehead move.* This was far from what he'd anticipated. "Right. Jake mentioned it. Our company beefed up security at the Guild compound. It's impenetrable from what they say." He shrugged nonchalantly. "I wouldn't know. I haven't been on Guild grounds for months, well before Lily handed over her family jewels."

"Are you saying they belong to Falbrooke and not the Guild?" Neal asked, not at all surprised by Liam's admission.

"They belong to the Falbrooke family."

"Why are they at the Guild compound?" Crystal swept a stray strand of hair off her reddening face.

The zip strips around his wrists dug into his skin, tightening with his increased horror. "For safekeeping."

"How safe?" Neal asked.

"NORAD safe. Not even my brothers can bypass the security they set up."

"Well, you'll just need to figure out a way to get them, won't you?" Crystal's sneer rolled into a snarl. "Prove your loyalty to the Estensons. We want the collection."

Sweat wet the back of his neck. Collectors had been literally and figuratively dying to acquire the Twilight collection. Lily Falbrooke had recently discovered they belonged to her family and hunted them down. Belief among the Guild was that the Cabal had killed Lily's father to get their grubby paws on the collection.

No need to ask why the Estensons wanted the necklace, earrings, and ring containing huge sapphires, precious gems, and icy diamonds. And the chalice. The chalice was worth a mint alone. Artifact collectors believed the chalice and the collection together were triple the value of the Twilight jewels. The Twilight sapphires are the rarest and strongest, conferring loads of psychic powers on the beholder. *Bingo on a bitch's ass.*

Sweat now trickled down Liam's spine. "The vault is impenetrable."

"Find a way." Neal's smarmy, suave voice edged up a tad.

The collection in the Estenson or Cabal's hands was a game changer. They could rule the world. One reason the Guild had stowed the collection, never to see the light of day.

Left with no choice, Liam forked over his ace. "What if I had a better, more accessible offer?"

Crystal and Neal traded a look. "We're listening." Wetting her lips, she clicked her nails on the table.

"The Guild obtained a book stolen from a member by a man named Kenneth Delaney." The barest flicker of Neal's right eye triggered interest. "It contains detailed information on every known psychic family across the globe." Neal's flicker twisted to a greedy gleam. Crystal's eyes shone like a beacon as she licked the lipstick off her bottom lip. "Are you interested in it? *Instead* of the Twilight collection."

Neal lost his calm with his uttered exclamation. "Yes." He smiled, showing the barest hint of straight, white teeth.

Crystal squealed. "You can get *the* ledger?" Neal shot her a warning glare.

Their reactions spelled Cabal with a capital *C*. He didn't need his empathic abilities to mine for their emotions written all over their twitchy bodies.

"This ledger"—Neal swished his hand—"what is the Guild doing with it?"

Liam played dumb, tapped the chair back to diffuse his excited energy. "Like I said, it belongs to a Guild member who recently stumbled upon it."

"Not what I meant." Neal pushed away from the table and strode around it. "What are they using it for?"

"No clue. Remember, I'm out of the Guild."

"Then how do you know about this book and its authenticity?" Neal glared down at Liam.

"My brothers talk. They still trust me."

"They won't if you get caught stealing it."

"No. They won't." True that.

"Then don't get caught," Crystal blurted out. "You get this book without blowing your cover and you're in."

Neal shot Crystal another withering glare. "Well, you'll be on your way to acceptance. We need to put you on probation as we do with all our employees."

Liam cracked his knuckles behind his back, the motion reverberating up his spine. "You place a lot of emphasis on psychics in your business. Do you employ many?"

"They have their uses." Neal deflected. "Just stick to the plan and keep your nose out of Estenson business for now."

"What's up with the holding cell your men left me in? Did it also contain psychic deadeners?"

"What do you think, love?" Crystal smiled her saucy smile. "We can't let your mind wander and learn our secrets, can we?"

"Guess not." Liam cringed at the word "love." Only Eva had the right to call him that, not this horny mafia princess. "Are we square now? I get you the ledger and you leave the Twilight collection alone?"

Neal turned toward the table again. "It won't matter. I hear the Guild's imploding. The Twilight collection will soon be up for grabs."

"Awesomesauce. And you plan on making a first grab." Excitement trembled inside Liam. Along with Saldivar's admissions, he'd pretty much nailed the Estensons' connection to the Cabal. Why else would they want the ledger other than to hire or capture and exploit the best in the psychic universe. Few outside Guild circles even knew about the ledger.

The four guards entered the room and escorted Liam back to the cells. This time, they dumped him in a larger furnished room, housing a double bed, table and chair, a dresser containing new generic men's clothing in his size, and a small but serviceable bathroom. Again, no window cut a wall, and the pressure in the room, in his skull, led him to believe he was in a basement. If not for the white noise hissing from a vent in the ceiling, the silence might kill a little something in him. A tray with two covered plates and a bottle of water sat on the table.

After they shut the door, he tested the deadeners and knocked on mental walls of steel. Fruitlessly, he knocked again and again, searching for a fissure.

He swiped the doomed covers off the plates to discover an appetizing garden salad, steak, baked potato with all the trimmings, and garlic bread. A large slice of chocolate cake rounded out the restaurant fare. He dug into the salad, wincing at the ranch dressing, not his favorite, and wolfed down a few bits. He was just about to slice into the rib eye when a buzz echoed in his head, like a bee trying to fly out of his skull.

The fork dropped from Liam's hand, clanged onto the tray. The buzzing grew louder and splintered the shroud on his empathic abilities. Fear seeped into him. Not his fear.

Whispers clouded his head, created a swarm of the buzzing bees.

His knife clanked onto the plate, and he gripped his head to steady his sudden trembling. As he tried to make out words or sentences, his heart pulsed in his ear, blocking the white noise hiss.

"Liam?" A tiny voice rose among the others.

"Connor?" Liam mentally shouted.

"It's me," Connor replied, his tremulous voice growing

louder, more confident.

"Where are you?"

"They locked me in a room near the others." A sob chased Connor's response.

CHAPTER THIRTY-ONE

Eva expected Daniel to seek her out, eventually. But his voice smacked of rusty nails on a chalkboard. A chill wrapped her in a barbed blanket. No sense in dodging him and his goons surrounding every exit point.

Squinting, she stepped into the light streaking through the skylights above the second-floor landing. Light dazzled her, placed her in a perfect spotlight. *Halo on my head, anyone?*

"Hello, Daniel." He wore his age well, reminding her that Neal would follow in his hereditary-genes footsteps, except Daniel had an aura of age-old expertise Neal lacked. Daniel's thinner head of hair painted with distinguished gray highlights, gray-stubbled and chiseled face celebrating his age lines, accented a well-toned body softened a tad by age. Although a silver fox, he did nothing for Eva. Too many nasty connotations.

"Ah, my dear. You're absolutely stunning standing in the light. Despite my initial misgivings, I've always known why Neal was drawn to you."

"Oh, so it wasn't my witty conversation or my psychic genes?"

Daniel chuckled wryly, his impatience making an appearance. "Why don't you come down here and have a seat?"

"No, thanks. I prefer the distance."

"Have it your way."

Eva sat on the top step of the circular staircase, sighted Daniel between wrought iron slats in the first curve.

"Do you see what happens when you don't play the Estenson game?"

"I'm tired of dodging your minions and their bullets all over town. You do know they shot at me last Friday, right?"

"Only trying to scare you."

The fact that he didn't mention her "mystery friend" meant his men had no clue about Liam. "They could have hit me." She gnashed her lips in a firm line, forced her hand away from her next-to-useless stun gun. "What do you want?"

"You know what I want."

"I have no interest in marrying you or beefing up your psychic ranks. End of story."

Daniel reclined on the sofa, and Eva shifted to narrow her sights on him. A lock of his impeccable hair slid across his forehead, lending him a much younger appearance. "It's Neal or me. Since you've already made yourself clear about Neal, I only see one choice."

"Is that a threat?"

"Take it however you want." He flashed his right hand, and the waning light glinted off the large ruby ring on his right ring finger, his Estenson status symbol. Neal wore its twin. "You'll always be connected to us because of Connor. However, if you don't play your cards right, you may never see him again. Neal owns the boy lock, stock, and barrel. You're merely his breeder. Unless you return *home* and be a mother to Connor."

Nothing new in his long-winded proposal. "Is that all you want from me? To pop out more kids who may *or may not* possess psychic powers."

"You know what I want."

"What do you think Neal will do if he finds out you propositioned me, or if he finds out you... touched me?" Refusing to voice what he'd done to her, she swallowed the lump of cool words down. "He'll kill you." She almost said, "Just like he killed your other son," but chomped down on her teeth in time.

"Don't fret about Neal. I can handle him."

Pitting father against son remained an option. She only had to utter the words "Neal killed Junior" to set off a tsunami of suspicion in Daniel since Junior's death remained suspect.

The light bulb in Eva's mind brightened her dark cavern of thoughts. Since Connor wasn't at Neal's house, she bet he was at Daniel's estate. Yet if she ended up at the estate, she might never leave it single. Or alive. *Ding, dong, this cop might be dead.* She changed her tactic.

"Did you plant the gun that framed me for Martinelli's murder?"

Another swish of his hand. "Is that what you think?"

She pressed forward, drew her knees up. "It's what Neal *said*."

A frown eclipsed his smarmy smile. Although she'd only suspected, Daniel's response convinced her Neal had planted the gun.

"How well do you know your son, Daniel?"

He stood, and all pretenses of his calm disintegrated in his taut movements. "Cut the crap, Eva. You're not leaving here alone tonight."

She shot her arrow home. "He set you up so he could ride in and play the hero, get on my good side." She paused for emphasis. "It may have worked." Pitting father against son may work in her favor or may get her killed. Either way, she'd see her son before the sun rose again.

Daniel's dark Italian complexion adopted a pink

veneer. "Do I need to come up and escort you down?"

"Where are your ape men?" Eva held her ground. She didn't intend to display her eagerness by handing herself over to him all tied up in a pink bow. "If I go with you tonight, I may not be able to keep from blabbing, oh, certain things to Neal."

A darker stroke of scarlet painted Daniel's neck. He flicked a hand, and two burly guards streamed behind her. They each grabbed an arm and hauled her to her feet. Another minion patted her down and stripped her of her knife and stun gun. Trying to jerk free of the ironclad hold, she kicked backward and hit one guard in his redwood trunk thigh.

"Jordie, take her car back to her condo."

"Sure thing, boss."

"Bring her downstairs."

Kicking and screaming, Eva fought the two guards who carried her to the lower level. Her feet never touched the steps. Without letting go, they dumped her in front of Daniel, and she spit in his face.

With a slow hand, he wiped the spittle off and slicked his hand down his suit jacket. "Ever the uncouth heathen."

"Yet you still want to marry me. Pot meet kettle."

"Name your price."

"For?" Eva stalled, knowing it'd piss him off.

"Your game playing is tiresome."

She baited him. "I thought I had a choice. Neal or you."

"I've changed my mind." The right side of his upper lip curled up.

"So, it's you or nothing?" The guards' hold stretched, and pain raced the length of both arms. They tugged her between them, pulling at her as if to wrench her arms out of their sockets. "Stop it," she growled out, but they only yanked again.

Daniel held up a hand, signifying them to stop. "I'm a

generous man. Name your price."

Ideas collided in Eva's head. She had an opportunity to see Connor, to get onto Daniel's estate and possibly find Liam there, to gather more evidence against the Estensons, to help the Guild ruin the Cabal, if the Estensons were indeed the Cabal. So, what if she had to endure a temporary sham marriage to an egomaniacal master manipulator and all-round evildoer?

Liam's beloved face revolved in her mind, and she almost crumpled into a ball of despair and desolation. The only one to touch her tenderly and lovingly since the brutality of Neal and Daniel. The idea of losing him over this mess, even if she gained Connor back, broke her already fracturing heart. After everything they'd experienced in the last few days, she'd come to rely upon him, his help to solve the puzzles, assuring her, holding her. He'd picked up pieces of her shattered soul the other night and fused them together. She loved him again. No. Not again. She'd never stopped loving him, but she'd come to love the man he'd become, the father he'd be to their son. The only man she'd ever allow to make love to her and feel the joyful and tender passion she'd experienced with only him. Maybe someday, they'd have that passion again, once she escaped her current jam. She just hoped he'd want her and they didn't lose another seven years.

By the end of the night, the broken pieces of her being may scatter asunder never to be spotted again.

She lowered her head, studied her scuffed sneakers, fought the pain rippling down her body. "I'm willing to discuss my price." Lifting her head, she witnessed the sun rising on Daniel's face. The man appeared to have won the frigging lottery, godhood, and immortality from her words.

"Let her go," he commanded. His minions released her, and her aching arms hung at her sides. She stretched out the pain and rubbed her right shoulder before sitting stiffly in a comfortable armchair. The distance from the couch became her momentary respite from Daniel's larger-than-life presence. He sat at the end of the couch as far from her as possible, his best viewing position. Flanking her chair, the guards took up their stations.

"I want custody returned to me."

"Done."

"Get the murder charges against me dropped."

Daniel flicked a hand. "That's a given. I can't have a murderer for a wife."

Talk about calling the kettle black. "How will you do it?"

"Leave it to me. The gun will disappear."

"But I can't get involved in ghosting it from evidence."

He stroked his goatee. "Don't be absurd. You aren't our only insider."

How many insiders did the Estensons employ, or *own*? "Freedom to come and go as I please."

"Agreed, after an acceptable trial period. I may not allow you to remove Connor from my estate quite yet."

She nodded a grudging assent. "I want to keep my job."

Daniel steepled his hands in the same manner as Neal, touching his manicured fingertips to his chin. "I'd rather you didn't work as a cop when you are pregnant."

The word "pregnant" set off churning acid in her belly, spurring her next want. "*If* I get pregnant, I'll take the requisite time off work, however, I will not be a stay-at-home mother. I need to work. It's in my blood, it fulfills me, gives me separation from mother and individual."

"Acceptable, however, if I were to offer you a job at one of my companies, would you consider it?"

A minion job with a gun! "Sure, I'll consider something in security. Nothing illegal."

"Agreed. Next."

Her next want hovered in the air before she uttered

the words. "We have a proper engagement period." She reddened, unable to hide her words from big ears. "No sex until our wedding night."

Daniel smiled. "You may change your mind."

Her strained smile turned into a grimace she failed to hide. "You never know."

"Next."

"Prenuptial agreement."

"Seriously, Eva? I wasn't planning to force you to sign one this time. What do you have to protect?"

"If we divorce, I want designated full custodial parent of any children *we* have. With proper visitation to you, of course. I only want reasonable child support for our children. Unnecessary for Connor since Neal pays." Neal paid her a pittance she didn't even want.

A frown creased the loose skin between his eyebrows. "Whatever you think is best, Eva. I'll have my attorneys draw up the agreement tomorrow."

It didn't take Einstein half a brain to know he played her as much as she played him. He'd never grant her full custody of any children they had. He'd see her dead first. She'd see herself dead before she ever slept with him.

"Anything else?"

"I'm good." She stood, and the guards closed in. "May I see my son tonight?"

Grinning, in his fluid grace, Daniel strode to her and held out his arm for her to link hers around. The gesture, gentlemanly on any other man, became controlling with Daniel. "I knew we'd reach an understanding." He steered her toward the foyer. "By all means, you will see Connor tonight."

The fresh woodsy air of the foothills surrendered to her exhaustion as they exited the stifling house. She inhaled the pine-scented breeze and wallowed in the last moments of freedom she'd experience in who knew how long. Silence reigned as they settled across from each other on the black leather seats of Daniel's limo.

"That wasn't so bad." His fatherly smile gobbled her smidge of excitement over seeing Connor.

"Why did you kill Martinelli after the fake custody order was a done deal? Am I worth that much to you?"

"You and your son are worth the moon to my organization." He settled into his seat, grimacing and bouncing as the back tire skimmed the curb. "Neal called the hit on the judge. I had nothing to do with it. He wanted to please me and put you in your place. Two birds."

Shock jerked her spine taut. "What?"

"Notwithstanding the emergency custody order, the judge wasn't ruling the way Neal wanted. He'd caved on the Estensons. Martinelli became a liability. We had to stop him from gaining too much power, balance him, eliminate any threat to us." Red anger flared across Daniel's face.

"You do recall I'm a cop, right?"

"I hold the cards, Eva dear. I hold your son and so much more." A smirk replaced the angry slant of his lips.

"What will Neal think? You're poaching his ex-wife."

"Neal couldn't win you over, so we're doing it my way. Leave my son to me."

"He'll go apeshit once he learns you've stolen something he covets." The idea adrenalized her, merged with her anticipation in holding Connor again and never letting go.

"The same way he took something precious from me." Steel framed the deadly words spilling from his mouth. "Neal has set me up and blamed me for the last time."

Eva's bowels churned. Daniel knew Neal had killed Junior.

CHAPTER THIRTY-TWO

Endorphins pumped through Liam's sluggish veins. He didn't care how he heard his son in his head as long as Connor never left him. *"Where are you locked up? Who are the others?"*

"I have a bedroom in the vault. I don't know which room you're in." Connor's mental voice quaked.

"Are you locked in your bedroom?"

Connor giggled, hiccupped. *"Yes. Don't tell anyone I can open the lock."*

"Your secret's safe with me, buddy. Just like all your secrets." Are you freaking kidding me? They lock Connor up at night? *"Who are the others?"*

"The other psychics."

Although the evidence was stacking up for the Estensons ruling the Cabal, hearing another affirmation sent his heart flapping like an eagle trying to escape a cage. *"Are the other psychics locked up?"*

"Yes. Granddad puts the strongest ones down here with us. He says it's safer and no one can hurt us."

Safe, my ass. *"Did he tell you out loud, or did you read his mind?"*

"He told me we need to stay safe 'cause we're special. I got two bedrooms and two video consoles." Excitement swamped Connor's voice. *"One down here and one in*

Granddad's house. But I'd rather be in the house. I can't see outside here."

"Can you read the thoughts of the others in the vault?"

"Sometimes. I'm not s'pposed to."

"Have you told anyone you can?"

Connor adopted a stage-whisper. *"It's a secret."*

"Okay. I won't tell anyone. It'll be one of our special secrets." A million questions reeled in Liam's mind. *"Have you ever heard your dad, grandfather, or anyone else talk about the Cabal?"*

A long pause ensued. *"It's their secret. No one knows I know it."*

Bingo. *"If you tell me, we can make it another special secret."* Connor's quiet sob stuttered his heartbeat. *"Buddy, what's wrong? Are you hurt?"*

"My head hurts. But Auntie Crystal gave me medicine."

"Is the medicine working?" Liam wanted to kill Neal and his fucking training regime. Thank God for Crystal's voice of reason.

"Starting to."

"That's good. Maybe you should go to sleep. You'll feel better in the morning."

"No!" Connor shouted. *"I mean, I like talking to you. I'll tell you another secret if you let me stay up and talk more."*

Before Liam uttered a word, Connor continued, *"That name, the Cabal, Granddad runs that company. Granddad and Dad talk about it a lot when they don't know I'm listening. Please don't tell them. I'll get in trouble."*

"Don't worry. Anything you and I talk about is just between us. Always. We got the special powers. Okay?"

"Okay. Cool." Connor's voice lightened. *"All the psychic people work for the Cabal. Granddad has lots of money to pay them. He's always talking about his money. He said one day he'll pay me to be a psychic, and I'll get to run the Cabal. That's why Daddy is training me so much. He says I can't*

run the company if I don't know how to run myself."

And there you have it! Corroborating it beyond the hearsay of a six-year-old boy might prove difficult, but at least he'd exposed the truth. That is, if he lived to tell the Guild about it. *"Thank you for telling me your secret. Do you want to hear one of mine?"*

"Sure."

"I still love your mother. How would you feel if I spent more time with her?"

"And me too?" Hesitation wobbled Connor's voice again.

"Only if you want."

No hesitation. *"I do. And Barney too? I've always wanted a dog."*

Connor's enthusiasm flattened Liam, and he vowed once again to deliver his boy from the Cabal's evil overlord. *"You can play with Barney anytime you want. Maybe your mom will let me get you a dog."*

Liam felt Connor's excitement so vividly it quaked through his entire body. Had his empathic abilities staged a comeback through the deadeners in the room?

"Mom says I can get a dog when we move into the house Nana and Papa are buying. Daddy won't let me have a dog."

"Then it's all settled. You can visit Barney anytime."

A tense hush hovered so long Liam wondered if Connor left his room. *"Buddy? You still awake?"* More silence. An eerie sensation tickled his brain receptors, as if his power was trying to return to the roost. Different. Something unusual had happened to him when Redland had taken him for a spin into his death. He may have dangled on the edge of his own demise, but he felt more alive than ever, his mind a willing and waiting sponge, regenerating itself. *"Connor, you still there?"*

"Liam." Connor sounded like he spoke from a hole in the ground. *"They're talking to me."*

Liam's spine arrowed. *"Who's talking to you?"*

"The Six."

"Who are the Six?"

"The others. There are six who can move things like me and read minds."

Six telekinetic telepaths? He'd hit the motherlode. Telekinetic powers alone were less common, but the ability became the rarest psychic gem when mixed with other psychic powers.

"Are they locked in the vault?"

"Yes. We aren't s'pposed to hear each other. The deadeners are not working."

"You know about the room deadeners."

"Sure, don't you?" Connor faded to almost nothing, and it took all of Liam's concentration to hear him. He covered his ears to block out the white noise hiss.

"They want to know who you are. They want to talk to you." Connor's voice cracked, and he hiccupped again.

Liam tried the lock on the door for the umpteenth time, searched the walls and floor for a trap door, any way out. *"Connor, are they hurting you?"*

His son sobbed steadily now. *"It's okay. They hurt too. They say the deadeners are hurting us. Mikaela says we're being smothered. Aidan says we're drowning."*

Desperation hissed out between Liam's teeth and joined the mildew air of despair in the room. He feared doing too much more than his stealthy survey of the room in case of big brother video. *"Does it hurt talking to me?"*

"No."

"Good. I'll open my mind and see if I can connect to them. Hold on."

"Don't leave me!"

"I won't, buddy." Mentally stepping onto the top of his Ireland mountain landscape, Liam surrendered his walls. They crumbled, and a meadow breeze carried the dust out

to the nearby sea. Lush lawns replaced the brown desolation. Clean spring air swept away the morass of the last few days. Every thought, feeling, emotion drifted out on a misty cloud until nothing remained, not even his own thoughts. Connor disappeared, carried into a safe chasm on the mountainside. Dust from the last wall blew into the valley deep below his feet. His mind became an open cavern of pure, blissful sunlight warming the coolness of early spring.

One word sifted in on a breeze. *"Hello,"* she said. Her elation zinged into Liam and collided with his own.

"Can you hear me?" He pressed onward to connect, to coerce answers out of her. He didn't know if it would work the same with his newfound telepathy.

"Yes! Oh my lord. I don't know how this is happening! Who are you?"

"Where are you?"

"In the vault. Different room."

Even though he knew she couldn't be far, relief danced in his bloodstream. *"I'm Liam McAllister. Who are you?"*

"Liam McAllister?" A wispy Spanish accent touched her voice. *"I know you. You were in the Psychic Guild. Did you defect to the Cabal?"*

"Is that what you did?"

"I can't discuss it. Sorry I brought it up. We're not allowed to speak about the Cabal with new people. Didn't you sign a nondisclosure agreement?"

"Can you tell me your name?"

"Carina Saldivar. Do you remember me? My brother Lucas worked as a Guardian."

Stunned, Liam froze and cracked his knuckles. *"I remember you. You're a powerful telekinetic. I don't remember you being able to read minds."*

"It came later," she said. *"It's why I had such difficulties in the Guild."*

"*Are you better? Does the Cabal treat you well?*"

"*I'm much improved. As for the Cabal, well, they pay well. I'm not sure what purpose they have for the six of us down here, well, eight with you and Connor. Are you telekinetic too?*"

"*No. Empathic.*"

"*That's strange.*"

Several other voices slammed into Liam's head and talked over one another, halting Liam's response. He grasped his head and groaned, tried to force them to stop talking. The voices pinged his brain, and their tangled excitement inundated his valley floor in a flurry of snowflakes. Liam staggered to the bed and sank down.

The indistinguishable voices shouted over one another until a distinct chant steamrolled the other voices. "*Connect us, Connor. You can do it.*"

"*No!*" Liam yelled. All the mental talk stomped across Liam's skull, and he paid the cost for his powers in the price of a sword slicing and dicing his brain.

The voices ignored him. "*Concentrate. Connor must connect us in his mind.*"

"*Liam. They're hurting me.*"

"*Stop talking to Connor. Release him, now!*" Liam screamed bloody murder. His words went unheeded, but his mind quieted, stilled, even Connor quieted.

The lock on his door clicked, opened. Liam heard other locks down the corridor click. Legs rocky, he lunged for the door.

"*I can't stop it,*" Connor cried, his clear voice quivering among the stasis in Liam's mind.

The building rumbled and swayed, the earth quaking, knocking Liam against the doorjamb.

"*Connor! Get out of the building. Run, now!*" Liam used every ounce of telepathy and coercion ability he had left to wield.

The ceiling creaked as if a crane snagged it off the support beams. An explosive roar inundated Liam's ears, obliterated the voices, even his own.

CHAPTER THIRTY-THREE

For the first time, Eva entered Daniel's mansion in the rolling Los Altos hills. Neal's description hadn't done the estate justice. It dripped gold from the lush acreage in the prestigious California community of millionaires. The massive mansion sprouted Grecian columns in the front, double-sided palatial staircases, and dripped gilt and marbles. The foyer was bigger than her entire condo. *Welcome to your nightmare since you're expected to live in the palace of mafia kings.*

"Come this way." Daniel took her elbow in his thin-fingered paw and guided her behind the staircases to his ostentatious office/mancave overlooking a rival to the world's top botanical gardens. A parade of lights lit up the dark space. *When had the clock ticked to nighttime?* A conservatory and several gazebos prompted liberal amounts of envy inside Eva. Her mother had a gardening thumb and would kill to own a fraction of the space to call her own. God, she missed her parents. What would they think of everything happening to her, Connor, and not least of all Liam? They had accepted her original decision to keep her distance from Liam. Neal's charm became the currency to their parental happiness for their daughter and her so-called perfect life. A good husband, a darling son, and a sound career. What a crock of bull. Mortification spun the dial on Eva's heat.

The scent of tropical flowers wafted from the ventilation, veiling the stench of money, greed, and power.

"Would you like a drink?" Daniel handed her a glass of tawny liquid. Like she'd ever accept a drink from him, probably laced with poison or date-rape drugs.

She skirted around him to the bar between bookcases of journals and books and snatched an unopened bottle of water. "Just water, thanks."

"Have it your way." He set her glass on the colossal black desk as wide as the picture windows behind it. Several monitors and stacks of files and history books littered it.

"I want to see my son."

"In due time."

Anger grounded her, fueled her determination. "Am I expected to stay the night?"

"Of course." Daniel smiled that crazy-ass smile that dinged warning bells inside her.

Before she could question him further, the double doors opened and emitted three of Daniel's minions, men she didn't recognize.

"Ah, there you are." Daniel strode over to shake the hand of the front man, an attractive darker-skinned man in a suit, flanked by two guards from the looks of their linebacker physiques. "Eva, dear, come meet Pastor Anton."

The warning bells clanged into full-fledged tornado sirens. The bottle of water slipped from her hand, bounced onto the rug, and rolled toward the bar. "You lied," she gritted out between clenched teeth.

"No. You misunderstood me."

Eva realized her mistake during their "negotiations." He played people, a con man toting a smidge of integrity, per Neal's drunken lapses. He'd never agreed to her terms for an acceptable engagement period. *Fan-friggin-tastic.* She'd just bumbled into the viper's pit.

"Not tonight. *Please.* You promised I'd see my son."

"And you will. Afterward. I'll even let you spend the night with him. Although I'm not a patient man, in this case, I'll make an exception. We'll have a lifetime together."

Stalling, Eva wracked her brain until another dim bulb illuminated an idea. "I want to see Neal first. He needs to know our plans. It's only fair to him... to you, and my son. I don't want us hiding anything from him."

Daniel's nostrils flared, and his eyes grew stony, dark as death. "He can't help you, Eva."

"I don't want his help. He deserves to know you're taking what he covets. Let's do it now. I want to see the look on his smarmy face when you tell him. I want to provide the proverbial punch to the gut as he absorbs that he's lost me forever."

"He's indisposed. My revenge will be just as sweet later."

Eva's ears perked up. "You admit this is revenge. What did he do to you?"

"He's thwarted my every step where it comes to you, many other things. I know he has his plans to destroy me." An evil grin concealed his wrath. "He missed his chance."

Before Eva could retort, a rumble shook the floor beneath them. The house swayed, and an ear-thundering explosion rent the air as if they stood in the middle of a detonating minefield, or at the epicenter of an earthquake. Several piercing snaps joined the explosion, the gates to another hell opening. Eva darted to the window, Daniel on her heels. The shadowy gardens conjured up more creepy crawlies. Then she noticed an amber spark on a distant outbuilding. A plume of smoke or dust mushroomed over the roof. She squinted to make out the scene in the darkness. More undulating amber flames appeared, illuminating the side of a large one-story building.

Someone knocked on the door and opened it without waiting for a reply. "Mr. Estenson, the vault has exploded."

Eva's gaze swept from the man in the doorway to Daniel's white-as-a-ghost visage. "The Six are housed there." He raced to the door, stopped. "Was my grandson in his vault room?"

"Yes, sir."

"What?" Eva screamed and chased after Daniel. "Connor's in the building that blew up?" Ice sheathed her legs, and sheer adrenaline kept her mobile. "Answer me! What are you doing to my son?"

Daniel didn't stop running. "Neal's locked in the vault too." Without breaking his long-legged stride, they passed through a French door leading to a garden patio. "Who else was in the building?"

"Another psychic. Liam McAllister."

Eva toppled, would've fallen if not for the pastor clutching her arm, stopping her from face-planting into a thorny rosebush, the season's last bloodred roses dying on their stems, dying to feed upon the unwary.

⋘⋙

The building shuddered and swayed. Walls splintered and creaked as they fractured off their support beams. Heedless of his own safety, Liam sprinted from the protective doorframe down the hall, stopping at the next door, searching for his son. Other people emerged from the rooms, like zombies arising from the dead. Ignoring them, he checked each door until he stood in the open doorway of a small room identical to his first one. Stunned, his gaze landed on Neal Estenson, hog-tied to a chair, his head lolling on his neck to the side, conked out. Naked from the waist up, purpling bruises painted his flesh.

A series of small explosions rocked the building again. After an indecisive few seconds, Liam raced onward to find Connor, maintaining his coercion chant in his head to urge Connor out of the building. He convinced himself he'd return for Neal or send someone else to rescue him.

In a trance, the six zombie psychics formed a circle in a gathering room near the stairs rising toward ground level. Dust and debris dripped from the ceiling on everyone. Liam shook shards of glass out of his hair. Frantic, he opened the last door to the left, saw the video game console and a few other toys. Empty. Where was his son? Had he escaped? He spun in a circle to see if he'd missed a room. Nope. *Screw me.*

The voices infused his mind with undecipherable words and deluged his body in their intensity, almost crippling him. They blocked his ability to think, command his body, or feel. Unable to prevent the Six from cramming him full of their emotions, he slogged through the brain morass and forced his legs to set one foot in front of the other.

The ceiling cracked and rained more drywall and dust upon him. A wood beam crashed near the room he'd just vacated, thumped to the floor, and dispersed fissures across the cement.

"Get out!" he yelled at the psychics, but they remained in a group immune to him. As if praying, they held hands with their heads bent together. Their chant invaded his mind, and their exaltation, relief at their freedom, and pride in their accomplishment shrouded him. He rammed his shoulder into one of the larger men. "Get out. The building's imploding." He shouldered the man toward the stairs before he ran up three steps at a time. As he stepped onto the landing, another booming explosion rent the ensuing chaos. The upper floor ceiling began to crash down. He ducked near a table. The back of his head hit hard and he fell. Before he winked out, a beam settled across his legs.

"Come on, man." Within seconds, a man tugged at Liam and the beam's weight became a feather. Another hauled him out from the stack of debris that blocked the beam from landing on him. "We need to get off this floor before it collapses."

Through gritty, blurry eyes, he recognized the psychic he'd tried to motivate moments ago. Was it only moments ago? Groggy, Liam sat up, massaging his gunshot shoulder. Pain crawled up his leg, but he didn't think he'd broken anything.

Rubble covered every inch of the upper floor, and the night sky blanketed the room with a moonlit ceiling. The knockout tempered his empathic abilities. Not one word crowded his mind. Cool, fresh air rushed in amid the dust whirls and smoke clouding the building. It refused to blow away the cobwebs knitting in his brain.

"Did the others get out?"

"We're safe." The man held out his hand to help Liam stand, bracing Liam against him until he gained his balance.

"What about Neal Estenson? He's tied up in a room down there." Liam glanced toward the stairway and the wreckage now blocking the path to the lower level.

The man's eyes bugged out. "No fricking way. I wondered who they were pounding on. Thought it might be you. Not sure we can get to his room. Leave the asswipe. He deserves to die."

Liam sucked in a shocked breath. Neal may be an asswipe, but Liam wasn't into blatant homicide. His role of Guardian taught him to help others, similar to a doctor's Hippocratic Oath. "You were all linked to Connor. Where is he?" An icy panic surged like tears and ashes through Liam, and he swiveled around, peering into every nook and cranny for his son.

"We're looking for him. It appears he left his room before the roof caved in. It was the room closest to the stairs." The man clapped a hand on Liam's shoulder. "I felt your coercion, and I'm certain Connor did too. Let's go before we're trapped for good. My name's Aidan. You're Liam, right?"

"Yeah. Connor tell you?" Frantic, Liam smashed through furniture, pieces of drywall, and wood chunks.

"What do you think? That boy's a rare gem. He cracked the code on the room deadeners."

"How long have they caged you down here?"

"Me? About three years. The others between a few months and three years."

"You join the Cabal or did they abduct you?"

Aidan hauled on Liam's arm. "I hear something to my left. Help me lift that bookcase." Together, they worked to free the area around a behemoth bookcase, tossing books, two-by-fours, and other construction detritus aside. "The Cabal recruited me. I was leaning toward joining the Guild as a Guardian. I remember you, McAllister, and your brothers. You were part of my interview committee."

"Sorry, my mind's a bit rattled."

"Glad you were here. You kept Connor focused. You helped open his mind. Got us out of here."

Liam's stomach sank. "And he caused this." He found a handgun, wiped the dust off and jammed it in the back waistband of his jeans. He took a mouthful of cloying air riddled with drywall dust and hacked it up.

Aidan's large hand on Liam's arm halted him from slinging a broken chair aside. "You got us out, man. They planned to exploit the Six with Connor at the helm. They may have recruited me in the beginning, but it didn't take long to understand the magnitude of what I'd signed up for, what they'd planned. You saw our power. They've forced us to connect, kept us locked up like zoo animals. We've had only monitored contact with our families." He slung aside a coffee table, and they managed to move the bookcase. "Guess I made the wrong choice."

"Was it the money?" Liam spotted a jean-clad leg crushed under the weight of the bookcase. They freed the man, and the bookcase crash-landed against a standing wall with another small explosion.

"Money, fame, you name it. The Cabal, or I should say, the Estensons, promised it in spades. They deposited the money into a bank account for my family's access. At least I got money out of them, if nothing else."

They pulled the downed man to a relatively clear spot on the floor. "Thought it might be Lucas Saldivar. I owe that fucker a slug or two." Aidan checked the man's neck pulse. "He's dead. No great loss. Another Estenson murdering asshole. He beat the shit out of me a half-dozen times my first year. Let's go. Connor can't have gotten far."

"The Guild has Lucas. He tried to kill me a couple nights ago."

"Serves him right. He exploited his sister, lied to his parents about her needing psychic mental health and training. Forced her into this program and accepted the Estenson money on her behalf."

"Aidan!" Liam recognized Carina Saldivar's voice from moments ago. "Hold up. We're coming with you. No one else in here far as we can tell."

Carina and another young woman led two other men supporting a limping blonde woman between them. They slogged through the nebulous path Liam and Aidan had carved in the rubble. All three men had the build, the demeanor, to belong to the Guild as Guardians.

Carina caught up to them and flung her arms around Liam. "Thank you. Your son is the most precious gift. Without him these last few days, we'd never have reached our full potential. He gave us hope of escape if we put our heads together." She laughed. "Literally! It's been an honor to know him under the circumstances." A chorus of agreement went up among the group, and the brunette woman standing next to Carina hugged his arm.

Shocked and shaken, Liam hugged her back, taking in the ragtag group of psychics who set his world on fire. "How'd you know he was my son?"

"We all know," Aidan replied. "Even Connor. Dude, we're all telepaths." His quick flash of teeth faltered. "Let's find your boy before *they* find him first."

CHAPTER THIRTY-FOUR

They seemed to run for miles to reach the large outbuilding connected to the expansive estate gardens. Horror forced Eva's lungs to work overtime to maintain airflow as she exhausted her energy reserves. When the one-story building hit her sight, her right leg buckled, and she teetered into a low-slung rock wall.

The building's roof had caved in, the walls imploded inward, exposing the interior in a jumbled heap. Plumes of dust and smoke soared into the sky. Flames shot off the right side of the building, crimson and amber waves dancing toward the stars, fanned by the night air and freedom.

Daniel stopped several feet away. The men trailing them cautiously entered the front door of the nearly demolished building, followed by several others who'd arrived from various directions.

"Where's my son, Neal, and the others?" And Liam McAllister, she wanted to add. The space in her rib cage where her heart should sit had caved in with the building. If Connor and Liam died in this travesty, she didn't expect the hole to ever fill again, didn't expect to ever recover.

"They're in the vault."

"What's the vault?" She slugged Daniel's arm, who just stood there like an idiot. Without waiting for a response, she jetted toward the building.

"Don't go in. It's not safe." Daniel lunged forward and tackled her lower legs. Eva hit the ground hard, the wind gusting out of her lungs. She kicked back at Daniel, but he strengthened his grip on her ankles. Two of his guards picked her off the ground and another helped Daniel up.

Pain shot up her legs from her knees hitting the lawn, and she swiped grass off her face. She swung on Daniel. "Where's the vault?"

"The basement. If the first-floor roof caved in, they're probably okay," he replied.

"Probably!" she screamed. "They could be dead, and you're sitting here making fucking suppositions. Let me go." She twisted and kicked to free herself from his goons. Eva didn't feel death in her crumbling heart, didn't feel a complete darkness in her core, which offered her hope that Connor and Liam lived.

Fire popped and hissed, and men shouted. The building shifted and imploded in tiny explosions, filling the night with the sounds of destruction and death. The tragedy exposed the world to the Estensons' avarice and their underground business.

A stream of men began to douse the fire from an onsite fire hydrant. Smoke billowed as ashes rained down, gritty on her face. A trio exited the gaping maw in the building's front where a door once hung, two dark-haired men bolstering a blonde woman between them. As one body, they collapsed to the ground, clear of the spreading fire. They wore jeans and sweatshirts, not the typical Estenson guard uniforms. Did they escape the vault? Hope lightened the fringes of terror trying to submerge her in a black hole.

"Connor!" she called in her mind. *"Can you hear me?"* If he did or didn't, she wouldn't know, but she wanted him to know she was near. "Connor! It's Mommy. I'm here," she shouted at the top of her lungs.

Distant sirens joined the chaos. The guards holding Eva stiffened.

"Who called the fire department?" Daniel railed to his nearest guard, flicked his hand at her sandwiched between the other two cavemen. "Take her to the helicopter pad." He shouted orders into his phone for his pilot to ready the chopper.

Eva shook her head. "You can't escape this mess. Don't take me away from my son."

Daniel coiled his arm back and slammed his fist into her face. By sheer proximity of his chest, one of the guards holding her prevented her head from careening off her neck from the force of the hit. Blood spurted out her nose and embers twinkled in her vision. A guard gathered her in his arms and oblivion captured her.

⋙⋘

Keeping out of sight to the outside world, Liam and Aidan guided the three psychics through a hole in the front of the building to sidetrack the rescuers from finding them. The three didn't need to ask him to rescue them from the Estensons when the night ended. They sacrificed their lives for Liam and Connor. The fourth psychic, a woman named Mikaela, followed Liam, Aidan, and Carina through the ruins to the rear of the demolished building. They forged a rocky path from one end of the building to the other, checking every nook and cranny, calling for Connor in their minds and aloud.

Spreading flames at the far end of the building stopped them. A door to a large laboratory hung off its hinges, the lock blown out. Glass and liquids smeared the floor, flames licked at the outer wall of the lab.

"Do you think he went inside?" Liam turned to Aidan.

"The door is always locked. Connor knows the lab's

dangerous. He may have left the building in a trance. His father... I mean Neal Estenson used to find him wandering in the dark after a long training day."

In dismay, Liam surveyed the wreckage to his left and an open doorway to the outside. "You keep searching or get out if it becomes too hazardous. I'll search outside."

"Connor loved the gardens. Look for him in the conservatory to our left. It's hidden from the main house. There's a butterfly garden and a bird sanctuary there. Meet you on the flipside." Aidan clasped Liam's hand. "Were you joining the Cabal or had they kidnapped you?"

"Joining in a ruse to get my son. They discovered my identity." Liam trusted Aidan, felt an instant kinship from the moment they'd met, no empathic skills needed. He envisioned Aidan as a Guardian. Something about him set off all the floaty, airy flags in his chest. "I'm Guild through and through. That'll never change."

"Then go find your boy." Aidan barked orders to Mikaela and Carina to keep searching. Carina flipped him off. Aidan hooted, reminding Liam of his brother Ric, always willing to find the fun or good in the bad.

Liam bounded over a crumpled wooden table and rushed to the door.

"Hey, Liam," Aidan called.

He turned, impatience bouncing him on his toes.

"Will the Guild accept the Six, after all this Cabal madness?"

Liam smiled. "If they're all like you, definitely."

Aidan shook a lank of dark hair off his forehead. "Good to know. I'm sure they'll have a few hundred questions to vet us." He waved Liam off.

Cool night air struck Liam in the face, and he breathed in deeply of smoke-tinged freedom as he loped down the length of the building. Pinpricks of yellow lit a path, the landscape lights providing enough illumination for him to wind his way amid the dark and shadows. Tall and dense oleander bushes provided a privacy hedge, hiding Liam from the mansion. "Connor," he called out in a loud whisper every few steps, scanned the bushes, moved on to the next spot.

The large conservatory loomed ahead, its frosted glass walls containing the murky interior shadows of various sizes and shapes. Liam slipped through a rear door and entered the muggy atmosphere. Sirens pierced the outside air, joining the soft hiss of manufactured ventilation inside the greenhouse. A bubbling creek and a cascading waterfall joined the litany of sound. Afraid to turn on any lights even if he found a switch, he waited a few moments for his sight to adjust to the ethereal dark. The shadows of trees, bushes, and flowers of all shapes and sizes, were indistinguishable in the murk.

"Connor." He elevated his voice to normal levels, marched the gravel pathways around flora and fauna, fountains, and a manufactured creek fed from a mini waterfall. *"Connor, are you in the greenhouse?"* he mentally voiced. A feather brushing his mind accompanied a faint indecipherable whisper. *"It's Liam. You're safe, buddy. Can you show yourself to me? I'll take you to your mom."* A gentle breeze carried an invigorating fruity, floral scent, replacing the smoke and fear in Liam's nostrils.

The thought of Eva in that moment nearly unhinged him. He'd craved her so bad all night until confronted with Connor and hadn't spared a moment of thought for the woman he loved beyond reason. Hell yes, he could admit he loved her and needed her back in his life, firmly planted in his heart and soul. As bad as he wanted her by his side, he hoped she remained safe in a jail cell, of all the crapass places. Not the place he wanted her, but it was better than in a collapsing building on the Estenson estate, or in Neal Estenson's arms.

Rustling and the squeak of a sneaker yanked Liam's attention ahead to his left. The outdoor landscape lights turned the conservatory into a parade of shadows, and Liam followed each one, calling Connor's name. Moments later he reached the bird sanctuary. A few chitters and ruffling feathers joined the eerie silence. Then Liam saw Connor's hunched shape, sitting on a bench near the birdhouse, gaping at the birds.

He raced around the small screened room and slowed as he rounded the final bend. "Connor. It's Liam," he said softly.

Connor swiveled toward Liam, then launched off the bench and into Liam's arms. He scooped his son up in his steely grip and hugged him, kissing Connor's damp hair. The floral scent sifted within the panic and boy sweat, carried it away as the boy collapsed into Liam's arm.

"When did we come to the greenhouse?" The darkness cushioned Connor's voice.

"You don't remember coming here?" Liam pushed back to peer into his sleepy son's face. Connor shook his head. "What was the last thing you remember?"

"I was in my second bedroom, the locked one, until I unlocked the doors in the vault." He giggled. "I've never done that before."

"You did good." Liam hugged him tighter. Connor gasped, and Liam relinquished his hold. "What else do you remember?"

"I joined minds with the others. It didn't hurt this time like it did before. Something inside me told me to get out of the building, made me move my feet. It wasn't a voice." The knots in his shoulders softened as Liam realized his coercion had worked on Connor. "I dunno," Connor continued. "I woke up on the bench watching the birds sleep." His eyes shone bright, grew wider. "Liam! I hear Mommy!"

Liam's heart raced into overdrive, and he spun,

drilling into the dark for Eva. "I don't see her."

"Not in here. Outside."

Holding Connor to him, weightless as a feather, he ran out of the greenhouse, following the path he'd taken. "Are you reading her mind?"

Connor smiled. "I'm not s'pposed to."

"I won't tell." He jogged down the path behind the oleander hedge.

Sirens wailed and overshadowed the chaos. The crunch of wheels on the driveway led to the burning building. Red lights glimmered drops of blood on the trees and bushes, granting an unearthly hell that scraped along Liam's consciousness. Shouts rang out. A melody of emotions sang to Liam until he bolted the gates to the unhinging song and concentrated on his son and tracking Eva.

"Where do you hear her?" What if Eva was in a room near Neal and the others, and he'd missed her? "Is she okay?"

"She's with Granddad." His dejection and dislike filtered into Liam. "I don't feel well. My head hurts." Connor laid his head on Liam's chest, an action worthy of his trust in Liam.

He braced Connor's head to protect him from additional pain. "I'm sorry, buddy. I'll get you to safety, and you'll feel better soon. First, can you tell me where you hear Mommy? Is she in the house?"

"She's by the chopper."

Chopper? *Son of a bitch*. As if on cue, the whirl of helicopter blades filled the northern area of the estate between the conservatory and the vault. Jouncing his son in his arms, holding Connor as steady as possible, he raced toward the hum of the helicopter.

"Do you still hear her?"

"Yes." The word burst out of Connor as Liam's feet hit

the tarmac leading toward a hangar. None of the emergency personnel had infiltrated the isolated helicopter pad, concentrating their efforts on the fire, and probably saving Neal Estenson's one life too many. Liam rounded the hangar and sprang out of sight as the bird hit his vision. Panting, he set Connor on the ground, and allowed his breathing to stabilize and his heart to stop jackhammering a door in his chest.

"Do you still hear her?"

"She's inside the building with Granddad. Granddad's mad at her. He's taking her up in the helicopter. She's mad at him because he won't let her find me." He took a step away from the building. "I want to ride in the helicopter." Liam stopped him with a hand on his fragile shoulder.

"Hold on, Connor." He peeked around the building just as three people emerged from the hangar service door. A caveman and what appeared to be the older Daniel Estenson, rocking the same body shape and height as his son, sandwiched Eva. "Can you stay here and not move until I get back? I'll go get her."

"Granddad won't let her leave him. He's making her get on the helicopter." Connor made a break for it and escaped Liam, running around the side of the building. "Mommy! Mommy." His voice barely penetrated above the whirling helicopter.

Simultaneously, Eva and Daniel swung around. Liam dashed after Connor, waving the gun he'd found in the vault. He didn't want to shoot Estenson in front of his grandson, but if push came to shove, screw propriety. No way on God's green Earth would he let Eva or Connor get on that helicopter with any Estenson.

He tackled Connor and scooped him into his arms, angling the wavering gun at Estenson. The chopper blades whipped up dirt, and he dipped his head to avoid it. It was bad enough Connor's hair was flying into his face, but he refused to release his son. Not now, not ever. And he'd never give Eva up again. The first time broke him. A second time would cremate him.

Her footsteps stuttered, rooted to the tarmac as Estenson and his minion clamped on to her, detaining her between them. Both men trained their weapons on Liam.

"Get in the bird," Estenson yelled at Eva.

"Not without my son!" She beat her fist into his arm. In the overhead lights, Liam recognized the entreaty in her eyes and in the cock of her head. He understood by the gesture that she'd maintained the ruse and hadn't exposed their relationship. Still, he wanted her to say, "and not without the love of my life."

"McAllister, give up the boy. He's Eva's son and coming with us," Estenson yelled. "Come, Connor." Despite Liam's hold on Connor, Estenson waved the boy forward. "Let him go, or Eva bites it."

"Why threaten her life now if you'd plan to take her without her son?"

Estenson guffawed, an evil sound scoring streaks down Liam's spine.

"A bird in the hand is worth two in the bush and all. Connor's a proven machine. Eva"—he shrugged—"may not produce squat again."

Eva stomped her foot down on top of Estenson's custom loafers, and he back armed her across the face. Connor sobbed, shaking his tiny body against Liam.

"Cut the crap and just get in. I'll get Connor."

"Leave McAllister out of this. He's just another pawn in your power play. Let him take my son to Neal and let's go." Eva wiped her bloody nose on her jacket sleeve.

More police cars descended upon the estate. Estenson's head swiveled around. "We don't have time to waste. Have it your way, Eva. Try anything, McAllister, and she's dead. You'll not see tomorrow either." He motioned to the guard on her other side, and they backstepped toward the whirling helicopter. "We'll retrieve Connor later."

Eva motioned to Liam with her eyes, cast her loving gaze on Connor. "Let him take you to Daddy, Connor. Stay with your father until I come back. Okay?"

"That Daddy's not here anymore." The wind whipped the words out of Connor's mouth. In his mind, he said to Liam, *"I know you're my real daddy. But I don't understand."*

"Your mom and I will tell you later," Liam replied. *"Let's get you to safety first."* Torn in two, he wanted to protect his son on one hand and the heart of his soul on the other.

Savage eyes bright and blazing under the cockpit lights, Estenson wavered on the threshold of the helicopter doorway, released his grip on Eva inside the chopper. The guard thrust her all the way inside and signaled for the pilot to lift off.

Estenson's empty threats spurred Liam into action. He set Connor down and told him to hide in the building. "Go!" He nudged the boy in his butt until Connor took steps toward the hangar.

As the bird ascended into the air, Liam lunged for it and grabbed the rail below the door. The helicopter's takeoff trajectory jerked the rail out of his grip, and he felt himself free-falling. He hit the tarmac, rolled, and leaped to his feet.

Dismayed, he watched the chopper ascend higher and higher, the door still open. The bird rocked as if caught in a strong gale. Eva stood on the threshold, hanging on to the handgrips inside. Estenson appeared beside her, embraced her, and they scuffled, rocking from side to side locked in each other's arms. The bird climbed higher, and Liam had a tricky time discerning what was happening. Night devoured the bird, leaving its flashing lights the only beacon to prove it existed.

"Eva!" he yelled, his inner turmoil refusing to give up. A wintry fist squeezed his heart, and he felt tiny arms wrap around his legs from behind. He turned and lifted up his son.

He buried Connor's face in his chest and watched the helicopter steal the woman he loved to only God knew where. Who knew when he'd see her again, if ever? The final pieces of his heart shattered, and he wasn't sure he had enough left to even love the boy in his arms.

The chopper dipped and rocked again, plunged lower, appearing to suffer from mechanical problems. Two silhouettes crammed the hatch opening, battling one another or struggling to maintain balance inside. The bird banked hard right over the back lawn of the estate grounds, knocking someone from the doorway out into the night air. The body hovered, a black silhouette in a star-studded backdrop. Silent, the body dove in a free fall and hurtled toward the backyard.

With Connor still in his arms, shielded from the nightmare, Liam raced to the gardens, praying with everything in him that Estenson had fallen from the bird. Not the mother of the boy in his arms who didn't deserve a minute of the crap handed to him since the day he'd been born into the Estenson family.

Before he reached the garden grounds, an explosive crash radiated off the mansion's roof, and a ball of fire mushroomed into the air, swaddling the helicopter in amber and red flames. "No! Oh, God, no!" Liam floundered into a low rock wall, almost dropped Connor. A helicopter blade whirled in the air and chopped off the top of a palm tree, taking Liam's heart with it.

"Mommy!" Connor screamed and struggled to get free from Liam's arms.

The sound sliced Liam's splintering soul, his imploding life.

CHAPTER THIRTY-FIVE

Imagining the worst and hoping Eva hadn't just blown up, Liam rushed toward the garden plot where the first body had fallen.

"Liam!" a familiar voice shouted. Slowing but not stopping, Liam looked over his shoulder and saw Alex MacKenzie sprinting toward him.

"What are you doing here?" Liam yelled.

"Came behind the FBI. Ric and I unlocked the flash drive. It implicates the Estensons in the Cabal, illegal crime, and so much more."

Without breaking stride, Liam shoved Connor into Alex's arms. The boy whimpered and tried to cling to Liam's neck. "Take him somewhere safe. Don't let him out of your sight." Liam kept on heading toward a long row of close-knit hedges. He refused to allow Connor to see Eva or his grandfather broken on the ground or in the falling debris from the helicopter.

"Where's Eva?" Alex shouted after Liam.

Liam almost lost it in that moment, but brute strength held his terror at bay. "I'm about to find out." Outdoor lights flickered on, granting needed illumination to the dark threatening to obliterate him.

His gaze bounced from spot to spot as he searched among trees, bushes, planters, and garden decorations.

Emergency personnel, FBI, and Estenson employees milled about, some in a daze, others jetting around willy-nilly. They all blurred in Liam's tunnel vision. Emergency personnel combed the grounds with large flashlights. Firefighters sprayed water on the roof and the burning helicopter dangling down the side of the mansion.

"Eva!" Liam shouted over and over.

"I need help over here!" someone yelled to his right.

Liam sprinted toward a tall and wide hedge where a female firefighter stood, waving her flashlight around.

"I see someone not too far from the top." The firefighter shined a flashlight up into the innards of the hedge. The shrubbery was too thick to discern more than branches and leaves until the light landed on the black silhouette of what appeared to be the side of a body.

"Someone tumbled from the chopper before it crashed," Liam explained as he began scaling the sturdiest branches of the hedge. "Eva?" *Please let it be her. Please let her be alive.*

No response. Liam reached the body, and the firefighter came abreast of him on his right. He swiped his fingers down the side of the still form, recognized the softness of her face, his hand tangling in her long ponytail. A tiny piece of his heart began to remake itself. "It's her. Can we get some help here?" he shouted to anyone listening on the ground. Who fell from a helicopter into a hedge? Fate. Luck. The love of his life had eight more lives to live with him, and no stinking row of shrubs would kill her.

Several more emergency personnel joined them, and they leveraged her out of the bushes and laid her flat on a gurney. Scratches spider-webbed her face and the backs of her hand, a nasty purple bruise expanded around her right eye and the side of her nose, and dried blood caked her upper lip. A thinly veiled icy calm rooted Liam as he waited for a pronouncement from the paramedic checking her vitals.

"She's alive," the male paramedic said. "We won't know the extent of her injuries until we get her to the hospital."

Liam offered up a prayer for her life. A seed of hope blossomed, invigorated his exhausted body and strained mind. They strapped her down and wheeled her off toward a parking lot of vehicles lighting up the estate.

A police officer detained Liam. "I understand from Detective MacKenzie that you were here during this mess. I'll need a statement."

Embers blistered a hole in Liam's chest, and he elbowed past the cop into the golden pool of a landscape light. "I'm going with the ambulance." Compassion washed off the cop's determination, and Liam fought to reestablish blocks, thought better of it and coerced the cop to back off. His coercion failed in the wake of his exhaustion, and the cop remained waiting.

Alex joined them, shoving a sleeping Connor back into Liam's arms. "Hold on to Connor. She'll want you to stay with him. It's best he doesn't see her like that yet."

Although something slowly burned Liam to ash, he knew Alex was right. The police officer led them to the expansive patio, covered by a wide pergola dripping with fairy lights and hanging plants. Enough people to populate an estate party milled about in various states of disbelief and sorrow. Liam had to block the emotions from submerging him. They found an unoccupied corner with several empty patio chairs. Another medic tried to take Connor from Liam to set him on a lounge chair, but Liam refused to let go. Instead, they draped a blanket over Connor, and his son slept, using Liam as his body pillow. The slight weight of the boy lying against him gave Liam the impetus to slog through the interrogation without going mad crazy to follow Eva.

With Alex behind him, a hand on his shoulder, Liam

gave his statement of the night's events, holding back the identity and details regarding the Cabal. They'd divulge those details to the Guild and FBI, but not to the local police investigating the night's tragedies. Liam didn't care. He wanted the world to know what the Estensons and the Cabal had done to the woman he loved and his son. But he didn't want to muddy the evidence, and when Alex's hand on his shoulder cautioned, he held his tongue.

The police would never understand what Connor and the Six had accomplished, so Liam hid it in his mental vault for Alex and the Guild's ears. He sure as hell didn't want his son or the Six to become freaks for the media to hound.

As far as the local police knew, an explosion in the lab started the nightmare. Liam hugged his sleeping son closer, dying to follow Eva to the hospital to reunite her with her son... with her true family.

Smoke had cleared and stars sprinkled the vast, empty sky. No longer a void, it infused him as endless as his love for Eva. Midnight tempted every fiber of his being.

CR&SO

Eva flitted in and out of consciousness. The sweet relief of drugs dripping into her thrashed body kept the nightmares and the insidious darkness at bay. A sprouting seed inside her told her goodness and joy waited for her when she awakened. The overwhelming urge to embrace the reality on the fringes of consciousness, as well as the sunlight slanting through the angled blinds, impelled her over the edge.

Her eyelids fluttered, and her bleary gaze opened to one of the two people she wanted to see beyond reason. She dredged up moisture in her dry throat as tears slipped into her hair. Liam anticipated her need and brought the water cup and straw to her mouth.

"Few sips only," he said, the love in his eyes enveloping her entire being.

"Connor?" she croaked out.

"He's safe. At my house running Barney ragged. My brothers are watching him." He placed the scraggly stuffed lion in the crook of her arm. "He wanted you to have Lion King to keep you company and make you feel better."

Eva hugged the stuffed animal. Sobs rocked her, and she couldn't stop them. Tubes stuck in her arms and wrists, and a cast encased her left arm, but Liam maneuvered around them and gathered her in his arms, stretching his body around hers. The blips and beeps of the machines joined her sobbing until she'd burned to a crisp the remnants of the past week. "I don't want him to see me in the hospital. It'll scare him. How bad do I look?"

"Scratches and bruises that'll fade." Liam caressed her face, and she bit down the stinging pain as his fingers skirted a bandage. She didn't care and took his hand in hers, holding his touch to her skin.

The hospital's antiseptic smell filled her with a strange peace. She was alive to hate the smell. It told her she'd survived the worst life could ever throw at her.

"Fucking Daniel punched me twice." She refrained from touching her aching and puffy face. "I thought you and Connor were both dead. When he said you were in the building that blew up..." Another gut-wrenching sob shook her.

"Shhh." Liam placed a finger over her lips, and she kissed it, gestured for him to release her. He did, so gently, so lovingly, she dissolved for him.

"I thought I'd lost you again."

"Impossible." The most brilliant smile lit up his face, reminding her of all she'd missed, all the denials she'd buried deep.

A nurse entered the room, lifted her chart off the wall hook, and punched in keys on the monitor keyboard. "Glad to see you awake, Ms. Midnight. I'll get the doctor to go over your chart." Liam unraveled from her and perched on the side of the bed, holding her hand tight as if afraid she'd evaporate if he let go.

Dreading the news, Eva studied the cast on her arm, felt the pain traveling up her back, strapping her to the bed.

"What happened?" she asked Liam after the nurse left.

His forehead scrunched. "You don't remember?"

Eva combed her drowsy memories. "Oh. The helicopter. Thought I was a goner."

"You would've been if you hadn't landed in a freaking hedge. Thing saved your life."

"Daniel escaped?"

A cloud passed over Liam's eyes. "No. The helicopter didn't recover from your fight and crashed into the house. Blew up. He's gone, Eva. I'm sorry."

Eva sputtered, took another sip of water. "Sorry? The bastard tried to marry me, had a pastor ready and waiting. He abandoned my son, you, Neal, everyone for his own altruistic purposes. He deserves to rot in hell."

Relief relaxed Liam's face. "Okay. Good, then."

"I guess I needed to suffer through the darkest days to find my sun."

Liam leaned in, kissed her for eons, and she soaked him into her being. "Your sun is here to stay."

"Is it? What about Neal? Tell me everything," she implored, squeezing his hand, refusing to let him go. "What day is it, anyway?"

"It all happened last night. You lost no time." Liam raked a hand through his tousled hair. "Eva, Neal's... dead." She drew in a tiny breath of sorrow and let him tell the story that nearly wrecked them for good. "Alex and Ric unlocked the flash drive in the nick of time. It implicates the Estensons in a boatload of illegal activity, bribing multiple judges and law enforcement, explicitly tying them to the Cabal. You did good gathering up that evidence."

"Wow." The only word she felt confident saying amid the turmoil stirring in her body. "Our son, what's this going to do to him?"

"He doesn't remember a thing. He knows he connected to the Six, but that's it."

"I hope he never remembers. Are the Six and other Cabal psychics safe?"

"The Guild's taking them in, working with them. Some psychics are blinded by the Cabal and won't have anything to do with the Guild, others have scattered. They may resurface. The Cabal had incarcerated the Six with little privileges for far too long. The three women and three men are happy for the Guild's help. They were being trained to destroy or infiltrate buildings as part of Estenson's plans for world domination or whatever he had up his sleeve. Alex only saw the tip of the iceberg on that flash drive."

A soft and warm lull accompanied Liam's kiss on her forehead. "Tell me what happened with you and Daniel."

Fearing his reaction and her ability to tell everything she wanted him to know, she related the content of the recordings on the other flash drive. She hungered to get it on the table before she chickened out. If she even had a chance with Liam, he deserved all the facts. No more lies, no more withholding. When she recounted Daniel's previous assaults, Liam's hand turned frigid and inflexible in hers.

"I'd kill that motherfucker if he wasn't already skating through the subterranean ashes. What a fucking pair of psychos. They deserved everything they got."

Tears welled in Eva's eyes, and Liam brushed them off her cheek, his fingers lingering on her unbruised temple. "I wasn't sure how you'd react. I've hidden that from you."

"No, you didn't. You don't owe me every secret. I understand your reasoning for keeping it buried."

"No more. There are no more secrets now. I want a clean slate between us."

Liam's hand stiffened again, then flexed as if to fling her off. But she refused to release him and continued recounting her day from hell until the moment her body hit the hedge. "You know the rest. What happened to Crystal and Daniel's brother, the others?"

"Crystal and Davide are in jail pending arraignment. Word is that bail will be denied due to their connection to Martinelli and other judges. Davide Estenson had targeted Marisa, Ric's girlfriend, when we outed Delaney last month. We knew him as the 'fat Italian.' Other family members and employees are being questioned. The Guild has the Cabal records and is shutting it down. You're safe. Connor's safe."

"Have you uncovered more evidence of what the Cabal had planned?" she asked.

"We have it all. They wanted power and money, to form a network of psychics around the world to work for their various businesses, hiring out psychics to wealthy clients. They recruit with the lure of money to those who're in trouble like gamblers in high debt, addicts, criminals, or those searching for the golden ticket." Liam paused, cracked his knuckles. "They researched anyone identified in the Guild as a potential candidate, found their worst vulnerabilities, and exploited them to onboard the Guild member. The Cabal imprisoned powerful psychics like the Six. Coerced others with software to do their dirtiest deeds with their wealthiest clients. They targeted Marisa in one such coercion scheme."

"What about you?"

"The Guild has reinstated my Guardian status. I'll

help clean up the Guild, getting rid of potential Cabal sympathizers, working with the Six. Since I've developed a second psychic ability, we're all planning to work together to finesse our abilities. The Protectorate's thinking of turning them into an elite team of Guardians."

"The women too?"

"Hey, we believe in equal opportunity?" He laughed.

"Then maybe I'll join the Guardians." She winked, and he groaned. She'd clawed her way out of the darkness, and joining Liam and the Guild seemed a small price to pay to keep the lights burning.

"How will you work with the Six if you don't have telekinetic ability?"

Liam flushed. "Guess the slight coercion ability I already had and this newfound telepathy is a weird form of telekinetics. They'll be training *me*."

Eva mock groaned and grinned. "Guess you'll need to build me a room with those deadeners."

The door opened, forestalling further talk, and the doctor gave Eva the rundown on her injuries. Other than internal and external bruising and cuts and scrapes, her broken arm was a cakewalk concession for tumbling out of a helicopter.

"We'll release you tomorrow. Now it's time for you to eat and then sleep," the doctor warned, his glare evicting Liam on the spot.

CRSO

True to the doctor's word, the hospital sprung Eva the next day. The anticipation of holding and touching her son buried the pain of her broken arm and bruised body. Freedom never smelled so good through the vents of Liam's SUV, the wind blowing in the open passenger window, swirling the heady scent of Liam around her. A whiff of exhaust fumes didn't even mar her independence. During the entire drive to the Guild compound, they finished recounting their last few days. She wanted all the negative stuff in the open before she reunited with Connor.

Liam held her hand, and she loved the strength of his fingers twined around hers, the imprint of her gold ring digging into his finger. He parked in the Guild parking lot next to Ric's SUV. "Why are we here instead of your house? Not that I'm complaining. I'm so freaking glad to get out of that safe house, the hospital, my condo, anywhere that reminds me of Neal and Daniel."

"Your jail cell too?" His bright gaze slurped her up.

"Haha. Funny."

Liam rubbed his finger over her ring. "This ring... it looks exactly like the one I wanted to buy you, but you didn't want me spending the money."

Eva blushed. "It's the same ring." And she told him how she'd acquired it, how it was meant to solidify him as Connor's father, how it helped her see light at the end of every tunnel she got sucked into. Liam kissed the gold filigree, vowing to put another one on her other ring finger... one day.

She towed her badge out of her back pocket and laid it on her thigh. "Alex came by earlier. Returned my badge. Internal Affairs still needs to clear me and I need to mend." She patted her encased arm. "But I've got my job back."

Liam nodded. "Just a formality now. They'll clear you, and you might even receive a commendation for taking down a mafia family."

She grimaced. "Ugh. Don't remind me. I'd rather just slink under a rock."

"How about slink into a room upstairs with me? Or better yet, a bed." He winked and jogged to the passenger side to help her out.

"We need to talk." Eva dreaded this talk, feared the

outcome. Did Liam want what she realized she never stopped wanting? "About *us*." She refused to allow another day to drag by without forgiving herself for her past choices. First, she needed Liam's forgiveness. She needed a new sunrise, to draw a breath of new air, and a second chance at finding a forever happiness.

Liam thrust back his head and groaned. "Now, Eva?"

"I want a clean slate before we open the door to reality."

"Is there really an *us*?" A wariness pinched at Liam's face. "Because, damn it, Eva, I want there to be an us. I've never stopped wanting it, never stopped loving you. There's nothing to forgive, but if you need me to say it, I forgive you."

Sunshine poured golden rays of warmth and joy through her bloodstream. She slanted forward and fell into his outstretched arms. "Shut up and kiss me, love of my life, heart of my soul."

And he did. The most passionate kiss she'd ever experienced, flashing a million rays of sunshine inside her. Liam cupped her face and kissed her until she grew breathless and drew away, her grin stretching her mouth into painful territory.

"I take it there is an us?" She arched an eyebrow. "Because damn it, Liam, I want there to be an us. I never stopped wanting it, never stopped loving you."

"Mommy! Mommy." Connor's voice broke apart their moment. The clap, clap of his footsteps running down the sidewalk eclipsed every other sound in Eva's ears and every thought in her head. The final ray of sunshine missing from her life bloomed and meshed with Liam's light already erasing her darkness.

Liam held Connor back from throwing himself at Eva. "Careful, buddy." He'd already prepared Connor for Eva's battered appearance, and their son thought it was "cool" his mom wore a cast.

Eva cried as she savored the feel of her boy's slender body in her arms. He held a slobbery tennis ball in one hand against her back. "Seeing you two together is like the first sunrise of spring after a long, dark winter." A large black Labrador retriever loped over to them, tail wagging a mile a minute. "What's with the ball, little man?"

"I'm playing fetch with Barney." Connor took her hand and slung his thin arm around her waist, and they helped her down from the vehicle. "We have a surprise for you."

Liam winked at Connor, and the boy giggled.

"What are you two up to?"

"Mom, you're going to flipping flip out."

"I'm going to *what*?" She turned on Liam under the gate mantle leading into the compound's parklike backyard. Connor flew off to the patio. "What are you teaching my son?" *Our son*, she mouthed.

Liam held up his hands in defeat. "Blame it on Uncle Ric."

Eva rolled her eyes. Familiar laughter joined the fray of a barking dog and Connor laughing at Barney, fueling Eva's recovery. Without letting go of Liam's hand once again laced within hers, they strode toward the patio. The back door opened, and her mother's and father's grinning faces met hers.

"Surprise!" Connor yelled. "Nana and Papa are here! They came early for Thanksgiving next week."

Her mother and father embraced her, smothering her with relief. The soothing childhood scent of Old Spice aftershave engulfed her in fond memories. Happiness burst in Eva's resurrected heart as she pulled Connor into the group hug. All the bad of the last couple years dissolved into the purple twilight air, promising a new beginning for Eva and Connor. Through bleary eyes, her gaze locked on to Liam's behind her father and she mouthed, "Thank you.

I love you."

Fairy lights sparkled and winked on the trees, dripped off a gazebo, and encircled the perimeter fence around the yard. Ric and Marisa served drinks and snacks while Eva caught up with her parents on the patio. They kept the conversation light with Connor in the vicinity. She wasn't sure how much to tell her parents. Another time. For now, having her son and Liam back made all she'd been through so worth it.

"Mommy, Liam says I can get a dog." Connor tossed the ball, and the dog raced down a stone walkway toward the woods fringing the backyard.

"He did, did he?" She hugged her son, never wanting to let him go.

"I said when you get a bigger house, I could help you find the perfect pup," Liam replied, tousling Connor's hair.

"Another reason we're here," her mother interjected. "Your father and I have found the perfect house for you two with a big backyard for a dog."

Eva refused to stop hugging Connor, even when Barney barked at him and nosed the ball closer to Connor's feet.

"Mommy!" Connor squealed as he struggled in her arms. "Barney's waiting for me."

Reluctantly, she released him. "Don't go into the woods."

His chin quivered. "You're not going anywhere, are you?"

"You can't ever get rid of me!" She kissed his forehead, ruffled his hair. "Love you to the space stations."

"And back to Earth," he yelled over his shoulder as he chased after the happy pooch.

A short while later, everyone but Liam went inside to prepare a barbeque dinner. She spied the familiar large envelope on the patio table. The cheerful rough and tumble play of Connor and Barney filled her heart to capacity, and the peace she'd first felt upon awakening in the hospital overflowed her. No more constantly looking over her shoulder for an Estenson prick. No more hunting and hiding evidence. No more secrets.

"That's the envelope I had my mother send you." She picked up the rumpled envelope that had seen better days. "You didn't open it?"

She returned to the padded bench, and Liam slung his arm across her shoulder and tugged her closer. "I was afraid to."

"It's proof you're Connor's father. Proof I never filed the adoption papers."

Standing again, she moved to a pergola under the budding stars winking a goodnight to twilight. Liam followed, taking her in his arms, then loosened his hold when she winced at the pain slicing her bruised side. "Guess we don't need the evidence now."

She shivered. "Connor might be in Neal's will."

Liam's lips landed on hers, forcing her to zip it. He kissed her hard, soft, and every firmness in between, leaving her breathless. "Let's take a break from this nightmare before we drill back into it." He punctuated each word with a kiss.

"Okay, okay!" She planted another one on him, unable to stop touching and kissing him too.

"I need to get you by myself before I burst." He nuzzled her neck, and goosebumps chased his touch.

She tipped her head back and tittered. "When you have a kid, you're never alone." His lips traveled to her ear and she gasped. "You have a lot to learn about alone time."

"I'm absolutely willing to learn." His thumb flicked her nipple, driving a rush of heat southward.

"I'm absolutely willing to teach you."

"Um." He drew back a fraction. "This house your

parents are buying..."

"It's been the plan all along, I told you. Besides, I'm not moving in with you and *Ric*." Liam pouted. "We need time, all of us. You know, go on a few dates, get to know one another." Eva felt safe and loved in Liam's arms, like she had conquered the darkness enshrouding her for so long. But she didn't want to rush their life or rush Connor into another new life. He needed to heal, and he was her number one priority.

"Are you insane?" Liam laughed so hard he almost offended her. "We have a kid together. I'm ready to be a father and a husband. We don't need to date. I love you more than ever. Almost losing you for good made me realize there's no future without you. The last seven years were just a prelude to the rest of our lives. We needed to live it to find what we had again. I'm all in. Now!"

"Don't freak. I'll let you build me that deadener room." Eva winked and stilled his hand on her left breast. "In due time. In the interim, we'll make it work. Speaking of fatherhood, how about we hold off telling Connor that Neal's dead for a day or two?"

"What? I'm ready to father him now." Exasperation stiffened him against her. "You said once that Florida ruined us. It's not true. It strengthened us to confront life together. I've never been readier to be a father."

"I know you're ready, and I love that about you. Connor loved him and needs time to grieve Neal." Sucking up the body aches no longer tempered by pain drugs, she pressed against him, felt his heart rumbling. "I already told Connor on the phone earlier that you're not going anywhere and you'll always be in our lives."

"He already knows I'm his father."

Her lips twisted in a half grimace, half smile. "I know. He told me. He's baffled about what it means."

"The Guild has assigned me as his Guardian." Liam

said the words tentatively, gauging her reaction. "And yours," he blurted out.

She had more faith in Liam and his abilities than she did in the rising sun. She'd be a fool to disallow his protection of their son. "I'm his guardian." She fake pouted. "I own a gun and I know how to use it." Liam growled into her neck. "Teasing." She snickered. "He needs you as his father, his Guardian, always in his life."

Love and passion blazed from his every pore. He twisted a lock of her hair around his index finger, binding her to him in more than physical ways. Heat swarmed her, shivered down to her southern hemisphere.

"What about you? Will I always be in your life? I can't have you back in my life and not *have* you."

Wincing, she pressed her breasts against his chest, needing to feel the hardness of his body. Her lips met his for a quick, possessive kiss. "You're not going anywhere, over my dead body." The familiar scent of his shampoo, his cologne, all of him boosted her happiness. All was right in the world. She could overcome the shitshow of her life and finally have a future to believe in. Even if that future included the Guild and psychics around every bend.

"You got that right. Never again." Love more than anything radiated from Liam's kiss. An unfulfilled love she was hell-bent on fulfilling for the rest of her life. "I love you more than yesterday, but not as much as tomorrow."

"Did you say husband a few minutes ago?" Eva grinned against his mouth. "You're the only one in the world I want to call husband... someday. For now, you're my Guardian, and I'll let you guard my body all day and all night. Now kiss me, already." Not even the joyful sounds of Connor giggling and Barney barking tempered the blistering, hungry kiss that fused her resurrected soul with Liam's forever.

DID YOU ENJOY
TEMPTING MIDNIGHT?

If you have a few moments, I'd love for you to leave a review for *TEMPTING MIDNIGHT* at your favorite online retailer or review site. Your review is greatly appreciated!

To stay up to date on Erin Richards' latest happenings, including new releases, sales, special announcements, exclusive excerpts, and giveaways, subscribe to her newsletter at: **www.erinrichards.com/connect.htm**

Catch the Psychic Justice Series from the beginning with *CHASING SHADOWS*.

ABOUT THE AUTHOR

After lamenting the lack of young adult books to read, award-winning and *USA Today* best-selling author, Erin Richards, wrote her first novel at the age of eighteen hoping to shift the tide. But the only tide she shifted was moving from high school to college. Then everyday life took its toll on her writerly dreams until she couldn't ignore the writing bug any longer. By then, she had immersed herself in reading adult fantasy and romance novels. Writing suspenseful paranormal and fantasy romance was a no brainer and she went on to publish two adult romance novels and hasn't stopped since. But her muse wanted to give that YA writing gig another chance, and Erin finally realized her lifelong dream of publishing a YA novel with the debut of *Vigilante Nights*.

Erin lives in California. In her spare time, she enjoys reading (of course!) and re-landscaping her backyard, even though she hates digging holes...unless she's burying fictional bodies! She also confesses to a fascination with American muscle cars...and reality TV shows!

Please visit Erin Richards online at:
www.erinrichards.com

www.ingramcontent.com/pod-product-compliance
Lightning Source LLC
Chambersburg PA
CBHW051331250626
47155CB00007B/2545